SHARKS IN THE CITY

GARRY J. PETERSON

CAPTIVATING ··· AMUSING ··· CREATIVE ··· AUDACIOUS ROMP

Robert D. Reed Publishers

Robert D. Reed Publishers   *   Bandon, OR

Robert D. Reed Publishers
P.O. Box 1992
Bandon, OR 97411
Phone: 541-347-9882; Fax: -9883
E-mail: 4bobreed@msn.com
Website: www.rdrpublishers.com

Editor: Cleone Reed
Designer: Amy Cole
Cover: Pam Cresswell
Soft Cover ISBN: 978-1-63821-502-8
EBook ISBN: 978-1-63821-503-5

Library of Congress Control Number: 2021940428

Designed and Formatted in the United States of America

DEDICATION

This book is dedicated to young women who find themselves struggling in a social climate where harassment, exploitation, abuse, or simply misunderstandings, have become the world they live in. With a young daughter myself, I feel her pain and your pain, as much as any man could.

I also feel the tremendous resolve and determination to take their attributes and improve on them ... and to take their weaknesses and learn from them. This is a story of hope, mixed in with the trappings of reality; work, family, relationships and, in the age of exploding social media information, *fact-checking* almost becoming a go-to app on your smart phone.

These stories focus on the development of several romantic relationships and with explicit sex. The sex is not an integral part of the story, but it does drive character growth and relationship development, as our cast of fabulous women strive for the *happily ever after* end game.

Real, pure, intense sexual encounters as well as thrilling plot twists will, hopefully, gain and hold your attention, as sometimes life just isn't a squeaky-clean nirvana that we all hoped to grow into as adults. Maybe there will be a nugget or two in the "lessons learned" here that will enable you to *live the life you imagined!*

ACKNOWLEDGMENTS

I would like to thank the lovely ladies appearing on the cover of
"Sharks in the City."

Their contacts are:

Vaune @ Instagram.com/jonathangarrett24
Sarah @ Instagram.com/sarahbaker_la
Peyton @ Instagram.com/Peyton.nnicole
Summer @ Instagram.com/_curly_headed_ice_dancer_

Front Cover Photographer:
Instagram.com/m.a.w.a.d

Back Cover Photographers:
Instagram.com/marinas_photography
Instagram.com/littlehippiemamaphotos

Book cover:
www.littlehippiemama.com

I would also like to express my sincere thanks to my wonderful publishing team of Cleone and Robert D. Reed, for continuing to have faith in me and my stories, and for believing that my writing range even extends to the adult romance novel genre.

Their website:
www.rdrpublishers.com

CONTENTS

PRELUDE

Sharks in the City is a rousing fictional tale of sexy romance and intense relationships, made remarkably entertaining and totally relevant in today's dating scene. Although the story itself is fictional, each person, each incident, and each scene have been drawn from either actual situations or from credible witnesses. *Some "creative license" may have been taken.*

Most of the stories and events in this tale are absolutely true. They happened! Whether it happened to the author, his family, associates, or close friends … it did occur. Some stories were the result of interesting leads that proved to have merit. Again, the names and locations have been changed, mostly to protect the *embarrassed.*

The plot of **Sharks in the City** is enhanced by several dramatic twists, adding suspense and thrilling action to the eventful lives of the characters in our saga. And there is some steamy, erotic sex. Keep in mind that this is a tale of young people's relationships.

The narrator is **Jonathan Garrett**, considered one of San Francisco's elite businessmen, with ties to several key people and important goings-on in the City. A multi-genre, multi-volume published author of business books, romance novels, and a science fiction fantasy epic series, Jonathon enjoys the spotlight.

The *sharks* are basically the *men behaving badly*, which has been a hot topic for women for centuries, and evidence to the same will be vividly detailed. Unfortunately, female exploitation is evident throughout the story, but hang in there, as fairness will ultimately prevail.

Sharks is an erotic tale involving the lifestyles and careers of several successful women, but told primarily from a man's point of view. I won't say that Jonathan Garrett is self-absorbed, but he does believe he is a *legend in his own mind.* You can draw your own conclusion as to whether Jonathan would be considered a man behaving badly.

From time to time, as is so apropos, and so fun, the shark DNA of men behaving badly will transfer over to a female shark or two, as they are not perfect, just human.

Hopefully, you will be *hooked* by the irony!

Sharks will make a good *beach read* or a perfect companion for a lazy rainy day or chilly, snowy evening. This audacious tale is perfect for a bathtub read to relax following a busy day, or as a go-to nighttime read for a specific chapter or two of your choice.

INTRODUCTION

Sharks in the City is about five very different women, and their characters cover all stereotypes of female behavior. They are single, career women living and working in the San Francisco area in 2021, and the writing topics in this novel will be honest, funny, sexy, glamorous, and relevant in today's world. It will describe both their work and personal lives, with a heavy emphasis on their relationship issues with men of all types, behaving as men do, in the vibrant cosmopolitan city of San Francisco.

Through serendipity of fate, these women meet and become friends, helping each other live lives in a demanding and male-oriented Silicon Valley. The novel will include stories about each woman's individual life experience, as well as some stories that they all shared. It will jump from office to bars to restaurants to parties to wherever young people meet and socialize. And, the huge impact of social media on daily living, is undeniable.

When it comes to sex, an old adage applies. *The more you know … the more you don't know.* And there are lessons to be learned throughout the adventures of these young women, and the men and women that enter their lives. Some lessons will be humbling; some will be self-fulfilling; some will be just plain steamy!

CAST OF CHARACTERS

Nikki Wallace is a 38-year-old African American woman who is an assistant district attorney in San Francisco with two business degrees, both summa cum laude, and a law degree from UC Berkeley. She is our *main character* and has a no-nonsense demeanor, and is considered an ambitious woman with political aspirations. Her aggressive behavior polarized many in her community, but she has a mostly positive rating from her constituents. Nikki is 5' 7" tall, who prefers her dark chestnut hair straightened, spending countless hours and considerable money to do so. Nikki favors pencil skirts and four-inch heels, and bright red lips and nails are her signature.

Back story – Nikki was always a career woman, never married, and considered too intimidating to even date by many professional men in her life. Complicating her psyche, Nikki has had two sustained lesbian relationships with women she still considers friends. She has had male lovers in her life, one in particular, which brought levels of stress to her tightly wound world. In addition to her law degree, her advanced economics degree has provided her with financial savvy that has her hanging with venture capitalists throughout California.

Quirks – Nikki is a believer in all things extraterrestrial. She is convinced of alien presence here on Earth, and at the last two AlienCon conventions in Southern California and Dallas, Nikki has dressed the part of ancient alien researcher to get closer to the professionals. She is friends with Jonathan Garrett, who writes young adult science fiction fantasy. She believes that climate change is real, and her hard image is betrayed by her commitment to work with various agencies that help the poor and abused, as well as with the ASPCA, the American Society for the Prevention of Cruelty to Animals, in San Francisco.

Sara Sullivan is a 31-year-old woman, the EVP of an Indie production company based in Southern California, but with several studios in San Francisco and Hollywood. She was a Midwest girl who went West to seek her fortune in both career and, hopefully, married life. As of now, she has yet to marry. A trained singer and part-time model, she is the lead singer in a pop-rock band based in San Francisco, and does modeling for an agency, also in the City. Sara is a blonde, with flowing locks, 5' 6" tall with steel blue eyes.

Back story – For several years, Sara has been in and out of relationships with a variety of male types, but setting such a high standard for her men has made long-standing relationships difficult. She excels at her job but gets much more satisfaction from her part-time singing and modeling work. She tends to sometimes go out on the town in various makeup and hairstyle looks, where her alterego resides, and can be seen in outfits from trendy to outlandish. She has a multitude of female friends and is never bored or lacking company or things to do.

Quirks – Sara's fondness for musical lyrics has been an enjoyment since very young. Even though her favorite music is pop-rock, electro-dance, and trance, she just loves music. She has such a photographic memory for song lyrics, that she often answers questions by using a favorite lyric answer. Friends think she is nuts to do this … she thinks that is cool!

Lina Chang is a 27-year-old Asian American woman who is a senior editor for the local newspaper, and is a well-known journalist. Lately, her passion for writing has resulted in her becoming a published author of four books, with several more in the works. Originally from Los Angeles, she moved north to San Francisco to get a fresh start following several personal and career problems. As a volunteer for several charitable causes, she is highly respected in the community. Lina is 5' 2" tall, perfectly petite with minimal makeup, a conservative dresser, and favors her hair in a precise blunt cut.

Back story – Lina was raised by wonderful parents, but was physically abused by a family member, and at her early workplaces. A somewhat timid person, she allowed too many people to take advantage of her sincerity, Asian morals, and life choices. Never encouraged to write as a child, Lina found a mentor at her first newspaper gig in San Francisco, and she absolutely blossomed into a fine newspaper editor and much respected columnist, being added to their editorial board.

Quirks – Lina is a very conservative person who still clips coupons at the grocery store or local big-box stores. She also has trust issues with philandering men, who consequently cause problems when she is with a truly trustworthy gentleman. Lina suffers from occasional depression, mostly from her uncle's double life, but hides it well with her coworkers. Lina is a moderate drinker with very few character flaws.

Jacqui Johnson is a 40-year-old woman who has rode her education, skills, and experience in cloud computing and A.I. innovation, to become the top *hired gun* in the city for many of the elite Silicon Valley big caps. Educated at Stanford and having lived abroad for several years, Jacqui has business savvy and reeks of self-confidence. Following the death of her philanthropist husband, she has continued to live in their multimillion-dollar estate in Sausalito. Jacqui is 5' 9" tall, with jet black hair and a statuesque figure in her Christian Louboutin high-end stilettos with shiny, red-lacquered soles, and showing off her legs that *go to her rib cage.*

Back story – Following years of single living in Europe and South America, Jacqui returned to the U.S. to apply her consultative skills in the fast-paced Silicon Valley business climate. Quickly gaining a reputation for out-of-the-box business solutions, she moved around in the circles of movers and shakers, where she met and married James Johnson, a billionaire and very well-known celebrity. They seemed to be a match made in heaven, as far as life in the "fast lane" was concerned. A liberated couple who shunned monogamy, they constantly experimented with slashing the norm. They threw outrageous parties and made the headlines nearly every single weekend. About three years after they were married, Mr. Johnson was indicted on sex-trafficking and money laundering charges, and was murdered before his trial began.

Quirks – Jacqui has one primary character trait that defines her and most of her decision-making. If you look up the term risk-taker in the dictionary, Jacqui's name will appear. One of her tag lines is: *only those who risk, are free.* This trait has caused many problems in Jacqui's life, especially when key decisions needed to be made. With a bubbly and outgoing personality, this social butterfly is a woman who most women want to be friends with, and not have as an enemy!

Dr. Samantha Vandenberg is a 46-year-old woman, who has become very famous in a somewhat niche portion of the health-care industry. She is a life coach exclusively for men, and her mission is to make men more responsible for their own happiness, improve their relationships with women, and become a better version of themselves. She received her psychology degree from Princeton University, and is an adjunct professor at UCLA where she teaches in their graduate programs. Samantha is 5' 7" tall with a porcelain complexion and with rich, soulful hair in shades of chestnut, and rarely seen green eyes. She is curious about nature, very passionate, and she possesses a positive and creative outlook on life. Samantha is seen as mature, sophisticated, and extremely smart. With her sultry voice, she delivers a popular weekly podcast and always makes her business suits look sexy.

Back story – Following her graduation from Princeton, Samantha began her practice in a small town in New Jersey, so she could be close to her family. Shortly after she began her practice, she met a New York City broker when they both attended a fund raiser for Manhattan charities. They dated for nearly two years, and when he moved to San Francisco, she closed her New Jersey practice and joined him. Their relationship was a mix of highs and lows, and after five turbulent years, they split up, both staying in San Francisco. She also had a short and painful marriage to a professional baseball player. Her desire to become a *man coach* stemmed from those failed relationships, and a self-induced challenge to become a "relationship expert."

Quirks – Compared to the other young ladies in the tale, Samantha's quirks are more like behavioral traits and make her more of an empathetic and soulful person. Being born an Aquarian, she is a giver and one who will go out of her way to help those in need. Even though she is only 46 years old, she has a passion for classic films, like *Gone with the Wind* and *Casablanca*. She loves Greta Garbo movies, often seeing herself as the cool and distant ingénue preferring solitude to the professional limelight. Samantha has a strong heterosexual sex drive, which at times makes her career of man-coaching awkward and stressful.

Supporting Cast

Brad Edwards is the CEO of a dynamic cloud computing start-up that plans to go public late in 2021. He is a bit of a dichotomy. His good side is caring, giving, and a joy to be with. He is what men call a "man's man." But his dark side is unabashed flirting, and blatant infidelity.

Logan Tannehill is a distinguished attorney from San Francisco, who has a career path similar to Nikki, but being a man in a man's business world, his opportunities outweigh anything Nikki can do purely on her talent and abilities. As with Brad, Logan has commitment issues.

Ramon Gilbert is a professional businessman in San Francisco whose reputation to provide exceptional sexual service to women is highly understood and well-earned. Women value respect and honesty in a man. Ramon has that quality, in addition to his bedroom skill set.

Gabe Suarez is a struggling reporter who is juggling work, education, and a social life, all proving to be challenging. Inexperienced with women, he blurs the fine line between social and business needs.

Brandi Bohannon is a young woman who has bouts of depression, working primarily as a waitress and bartender, looking for love but often disappointed. She values impulsiveness over long-term prioritization.

Cherri Berry is a young woman with a dull and boring career in government service, constantly harassed by a male supervisor, who seeks a social and emotional release as a part-time "B" actress. She loves risk-taking, which nearly always has its downsides.

Portia de Angelis is a very wealthy "kept woman" who has a dual life. In addition to being in a loveless marriage with a powerful, military retiree in the Valley, who is twice her age, she is the EVP for a millionaire lesbian finance group.

Christian Windsor is a drop-dead gorgeous man, straight out of "central casting," who provides the story's sexual relief as a sex therapist who practices what he preaches. He understands women, too, but often uses that knowledge in a superior manner.

Mimi Rainey has a cameo appearance as a previous, dear love of the narrator, Jonathan Garrett. With little specific info on this character, the reader is free to draw his or her own conclusions from the limited detail provided.

There will be three Acts and a Finale to the novel, with poems relating to life's passages:

Act I – The Set Up
Background details on the main characters

Act II – The Confrontations
Conflicts and stories

Act III – The Resolution
Climax or lessons learned

Finale – The Last Word
Walking the Talk

"When you look for things in life like love, meaning, and motivation, it implies that they are behind a tree or under a rock. The most successful people in life recognize that they create their own love, manufacture their own meaning, and generate their own motivation."

—Neil deGrasse Tyson

"Nothing is as real as a dream. Responsibilities need not erase it. Duties need not obscure it. Because the dream is within you, no one can take it away."

—Tom Clancy

"Be forever curious. Focus your vision and your soul forward on what you can do, not backward on what you cannot change. Don't trip over your past. Live the life you imagined!"

—Jonathan Garrett

OPENING CURTAIN

Rather than spend intimate time making love,
Using a wonderful gift sent from heaven above.
I selfishly spent my precious love-making time,
Thinking, oh what the hell, this life is mine!
When I was young, physical attraction prevailed,
When to stay in port ... or when to sail.
Sometimes when two of us would touch,
Feelings of love or lust were simply too much,
Whether it was the smiling moon or rising sun,
We'd be together soon; another love story just begun.
I've run from my truth finding somewhere to hide,
Until the fear of closeness and commitment subsides.
At times we act like strangers,
Searching for an understanding friend.
Someone to talk, to hold and to be with,
Till the damn passion flairs again.
Passion shaped my sexual being
All those great, young, romances.
But they never kept me from thinking,
What I offered in return gave us those chances.
Some thought themselves to be a loved attraction,
Some thought themselves missing other great action.
Some lessons learned had one of us lying,
Some lessons learned had one of us crying.
It often felt like one of us simply had to go,
To prepare one's self to be part of the next show.
Today I'm bulletproof with nothing to lose
So, take your aim and fire away.
But do be wary of which path you choose
Your hurtful bullets may ricochet.

Then we parted ...

ACT **I**

THE SET-UP

BACKGROUND ON THE
MAIN CHARACTERS

1

PARTY PARANOIA

W*e're going to start this story with Nikki Wallace, as impressive a young professional as you would ever find. A tall, beautiful, and highly educated attorney living and working in San Francisco, she was rapidly gaining a reputation as a hard-hitting prosecutor with plenty of notches on her gun.*

As a young African American, Nikki had a difficult childhood, and those experiences drove her to become, as her parents proclaimed, a trusted and respected leader.

Fasten your seat belts … this ride will be wild!   .

♥   ♥   ♥

It was 2018, pre-COVID-19, when Nikki was fully engaged in the later portions of a criminal trial in Oakland. She was putting together the final arguments on a trial having all of the Bay Area buzzing.

James Johnson was a filthy-rich businessman, with ties to drugs, sex trafficking, money laundering, and tax evasion. Before he could go to trial, he was brutally murdered in Jamaica, slashed with a Samurai Sword in an unresolved crime.

Across from Nikki was Attorney Thomas Shaughnessy, a savvy attorney representing the Johnson estate, trying to get some restitution awards waved by declaring Johnson's widow, Jacqui Johnson, a co-conspirator and deeply liable for damages from her existing inheritance.

Nikki was returning a text message from her friend, Sara.

> "Who won? You or God's Gift?"
> "Neither. Off til Mon."
> "He hit on you yet?"
> "No and no f'ing way he will."

"No smash?"

"No. Talk later."

Wrapping up this Friday afternoon session at 3:00, and being adjourned until Monday morning, Attorney Shaughnessy, a tall, handsome man with exquisite tailor-made suits, approached Nikki, an associate who he knew, and a woman who always fascinated him.

"Hey, Nikki, nice job today. I really liked your last two arguments and those first two witnesses were strong."

"Please," Nikki thought, annoyingly. "Thanks, Thomas. I'm afraid I'm no match yet for your presentation."

Thomas chuckled and then asked crisply, "Say, would you be interested in a party Saturday night at a friend's rather lovely estate in the country?"

"No thanks, Thomas. I have too much work to do." Her immediate thought was, *"Keep asking, big boy."*

"Come on Nikki, this one will be cool. It's a masquerade party with dozens of the Bay Area movers and shakers. You'd be hard pressed to find a more fun event ever!"

"So, it's an invitation-only party with big names and big titles?"

"Damn straight. You won't attend any public event ever … to match this one."

Thinking for a moment to not seem too anxious, she quipped, "Sure, what the hell. Text me the plan."

Thomas thought nonchalantly, *"Wonder what that black beauty looks like naked?"*

♥　　♥　　♥

As Nikki and Thomas gathered their docs and notes and filled their brief-cases, Thomas felt an opportunity to move a little closer to his rival, assuming he just gained some points with the party invite. As the last pair to leave the court-room, he placed his arm softly on her shoulder as they walked.

"You know I admire you and find you extremely attractive."

"Thank you, Thomas. I can honestly say, likewise. Even though you have this nasty reputation as a 'player,' I think you are one special man." Nikki flinched and thought, *"Why the hell did I just say that?"*

Thomas remained silent as the two walked by an empty vestibule of the courthouse, somewhat off the main hallway.

He turned to face Nikki, placing one arm around her waist as they stopped. "You got somewhere to go right now?"

Nikki thought for a moment and replied, "No, I don't. Want to get coffee or a drink?"

"Nah, maybe later," Thomas said cagily.

Thomas smiled and then gently grasped Nikki around the waist and guided the pair into the nearby small, empty office and closed the door. This was a seldom-used room with tables, books, and computers sometimes used for small meetings or training.

"Thomas, what the hell!"

Dropping his briefcase on the floor, Thomas gave Nikki a long, wet and warm kiss on her mouth. Not immediately rejecting his advances, she also dropped her case and placed her hands around his neck and shoulders.

"I've been wanting to do this for quite some time, you incredibly sexy and beautiful lawyer."

Taking a deep breath, Nikki responded, "I'm glad you did. You're a good kisser."

Sensing they were still close to the door Thomas offered a suggestion. "Let's move to the back of the room so we can continue our marvelous kiss."

With no pushback from Nikki, they picked up their briefcases and he led them past a row of books and tables, to a spot in the corner of the room with a large drawing table.

Once they were there, Thomas picked her up and set her on the table. He leaned forward and began kissing her neck, cheeks and lips. Not as much of a risk-taker, Nikki was getting aroused by both the spontaneity and the physical attention.

"Thomas, you are a fricking player, as we both know. I'm not even a girl who kisses on the first date."

Thomas responded by placing his hands firmly on Nikki's neck and giving her an irresistible long, luscious, wet kiss.

"I'll keep that in mind when we have our first date!"

She spread her legs slowly, allowing Thomas to get even closer and to press his torso against the sitting Nikki's inviting body.

She gave an impatient sigh and thought bewilderedly, *"I can't do this ... I want to do this!"*

Thomas slowly removed Nikki's blazer, stroked her hair, cupped her face, gave her another warm kiss, and removed his suit coat.

Nikki reached forward to grasp his growing erection, and as she unbuckled his belt, he was reaching behind her blouse to undo her bra. She murmured to herself, *"This is good. I feel good. I do want his sex!"*

As he slowly unbuttoned and removed her blouse, Nikki again leaned forward and unzipped his fly and gave a quick pull to get his pants to drop to the floor. They were hot for each other and the small room was heating up, big time.

Thomas placed his hands on her hips and spread her legs further, as Nikki got a strong hold on his throbbing penis, thinking, *"Oh yes, he is as big and hard as I imagined."*

Thomas placed his hand under her now wet panties, and with his long middle finger, probed her core hoping to find and stimulate her feminine bud to bring her arousal to a peak. She gasped as Thomas's probe hit its mark.

"Thomas, that feels so good. Use your thumb. Rub it up and down."

"Oh God, Nikki, you're so wet and warm."

She took his probing finger, brought it to her mouth, and raised her legs to where they laid on his shoulders. She was aroused.

Thomas, getting all the signals needed, kicked his pants off and put one arm around Nikki, and the other hand grabbed his throbbing erection, about to find the perfect penetration angle.

"Go slowly. I'm not gonna last long."

Thomas wasn't thinking about what Nikki had just said. He wanted inside her now and was getting his erection fully engorged by stroking it himself.

As Nikki firmly secured herself by placing her interlocking hands around his neck, she turned her head quickly and blurted, "What's that?"

A stunned Thomas, manhood in hand, replied, "Nikki … what?"

"I heard a noise. Quiet!"

As the pair momentarily let their arousals pause, another sound was heard; this time voices.

"Okay, girls, find yourselves a computer cubicle, keep your voices down, and we can get you registered for the courthouse intern program."

"Shit!" Nikki had been so close to climax. Thomas's erection ran and hid.

Yep, today's sexual escapade was a frustrating failure, following a heart-pounding buildup. Being as quiet as possible, they wiped off their sweat with a handkerchief that Thomas provided, got quickly dressed, took their briefcases in hand, and slowly emerged to the startled group of young women in Miss Morgan's high school civics class.

As they awkwardly exited the room, not really making eye contact, they both attempted some small talk to disguise their foray into exasperating sex. Nikki grabbed a book from a shelf to enhance their "studious intentions."

As they reentered the main hallway, Thomas said calmly, "That was truly incredible. You are incredible. I will look forward to finishing our ride next time."

Thinking to herself, *"Now I know he is the risk-taker I thought he was."*

Glancing directly into his eyes, she replied, "Yes, we will. I enjoyed every moment."

"Good." As they walked toward the down staircase, Thomas uttered, "We still on for Saturday?"

"Absolutely. By all means, we're on."

Smiling, Thomas responded, "I'll have a limo pick you up at 10:00."

"Ten is pretty fricking late."

"Well, most of these people live busy lives, so late on a Saturday works fine." Winking at Nikki, he continued. "There will be about sixty people there, so plenty of networking, for sure."

"Okay. I'll be ready at 10. Let me give you, my address."

"No need, Nikki. Our driver knows where all the important people live."

She thought, *"Should I be flattered or worried?"*

"Oh, one more thing."

"Yes, Thomas?"

"The driver will have assorted masks in his limo, in various styles and colors. So, you can pick your favorite as you are driven to the party."

"Oh my God!"

2

MIND WIDE SHUT

At exactly 10:00 on Saturday night, a large limousine arrived outside and Nikki got a text to come down for her ride. She returned the text, indicating she would need a few more minutes. Looking into the mirror, she liked what she saw and thought, "*Tall, dark, and stunning, if I do say so myself.*"

This would be the first time she would be wearing this dark blue, plush velvet evening gown with gold embroidered accents. A flattering V-neckline focused any admirer's eyes to catch a peek at cleavage that screamed, "Heads up." Bishop sleeves with shirred cuff and embellished slit made her silhouette both distinctive and glamorous.

Her dark chestnut hair was straight and flowing, and she had her signature four-inch heels. Rather than go with her usual red lips and nails, tonight she used hues of blue for both … light on the lips.

Nikki walked down to the waiting limo. The driver exited and opened her door. "Evening, Ma'am."

Stepping into the car, "Good evening … thank you."

Shortly after pulling onto a freeway, Nikki began to peruse the fancy box of masks on the seat. Incredibly, a small light came on and lit up the box, making for an easier selection.

She picked a turquoise and blue mask, trimmed in black with tasteful sparkles glittering in the cabin light. "*This is gonna be a fun party,*" she whispered to herself. "*So glad I'm going.*"

After nearly an hour's drive, and according to her phone GPS, they were now deep into the rural area of Marin County, on the Tiburon Peninsula. They arrived at an enormous mansion, similar in style to the famous Hearst Castle in San Simeon.

The limo slowly came to a stop, and a valet opened the door and gently took the now masked Nikki's hand as they walked up to the massive front door. He did not speak but allowed her to enter the double door where she was greeted by a huge doorman with a small black mask against a chiseled face, who welcomed her inside with his hand. He did not speak.

Waiting inside was a scantily-clad young woman who approached Nikki and said, "You must leave your purse and cell phone here with me. I will keep it safe, Miss Wallace." She did not make eye contact and Nikki complied.

The doorman gestured for Nikki to follow a long passageway, which she did, and soon she saw the perfect sight ... a bar, and headed straight for it.

At the bar, she leaned over to the bartender and uttered, "Scotch please. I'll just have the house; neat."

"Yes, ma'am." Moments later, Nikki grabbed her drink and took an extra-large guzzle. "My, this is a good scotch. May I ask the label?"

The bartender replied, "It is a Macallan Sherry Oak 25."

"Wow. They're around $2,000 per bottle."

"Yes, that's right, ma'am."

"What's the venue here?"

"Ma'am, I can't talk with you. We rotate in here for these events and only get called back if we don't screw up. I will make more money tonight than I will in a couple months of my regular job."

As that remark was sinking in, Thomas approached Nikki dressed in what appeared to be the uniform of the day for the male attendees: black suit, white shirt with cuff links, and a dark tie. Nikki was tall, but Thomas was a big hunk of man, about six-three or six-four and with massive shoulders. Nikki knew he had been married and divorced three times, and he was barely forty.

Giving her a slight embrace and kiss on the cheek, he asked, "Are you enjoying yourself?"

"I just got here. I see mostly men and some women, but this place is remarkable."

"Yeah, Nikki, it was built over a hundred years ago, and now is owned by a group of men who use it strictly for entertainment. And, you look amazing. Love that gown, and if I told you who had worn that mask before, you'd freak out!"

At that moment, a clock struck midnight and most of the attendees began moving from one person to another, like a bizarre speed dating at the local men's castle.

"Got to mingle. See you later." As Thomas walked away, he whispered to himself, *"I need to get a picture of that brown beauty totally naked!"*

Nikki had sensed she was being observed since she arrived, but blew it off to nervousness. She was approached by a handsome man and his pretty female companion. They introduced themselves, chatted for a while, and then moved on. This went on for about an hour.

While observing, Nikki recognized a major bank CEO, the young guy that owned the California rights to commercial solar energy, and a retired senator and his wife, appearing to be half his age.

This went on until a clock struck 1:00. The same ritual began. Nikki was getting good at avoidance, but she finally headed to the ladies' room to get away and collect her thoughts. So far, this party was boring, and extremely strange.

That was about to change …

Leaving a restroom stall, Nikki walked over to the sinks and was surprised. There was soap and sanitizer, of course, but laying out across the back of the sinks were a variety of sexual lubes in assorted colors, flavors, and purposes. *Damn!*

"The *Relax* desensitizing anal lube is nice because it has a nozzle tip, and the *Astroglide X* is good everywhere. I recommend it."

Nikki thanked the helpful lady for her advice, and then washed her hands for the second time.

As she left the restroom and headed to the bar to get drink number three, a clock struck 2:00. Almost immediately, everyone started to move, virtually on cue, from the spacious lounge toward a large meeting room with a stage. She followed and once inside, she could see the room had no chairs, but it had a well-lit stage with footlights for specific illumination.

Then, with no audio warning at all, a lovely young masked woman walked onto the stage from the left, and paused in the center facing the crowd. She was wearing a shirt collar oversize trench coat, which she promptly opened to expose a totally naked body with pubic hair shaved. Many hands in the audience were raised, and the young woman closed her coat and proceeded to exit to the right.

"*Oh my God. WTF. This is fricking disturbing,*" Nikki anxiously thought. Without a moment to be wasted, another young woman followed the same route, did the same thing with the open trench coat revealing she also had her pubic area shaved. Hands again went up, signally some form of acceptance. Nikki counted nine women in all.

What happened next was chilling. Curtains on both sides of the stage opened, and the nearly sixty people assembled walked through the curtains, to a viewing area the same level as the stage on the previous side. Near naked women brought drinks, and, sure enough, a pretty young girl brought Nikki her usual Macallan 25 scotch.

"Everything tonight was highly choreographed," she grimaced. At that moment, Thomas appeared and moved quickly over to Nikki.

"Something quite different, don't you think? This is where the rich and famous hang out."

"Different? You call is different … I call it appalling."

Thomas just smiled as another curtain opened, but the sight before Nikki was horrifying. The nine women were now victims or participants in an arena with 10 stations, from beds to chairs to slings for mild bondage, or whatever the men leaning over them intended. One station, a leather cross with padded arms, was still without a young woman.

"Where is the poor thing who is number 10 for that cross?"

"Well, Nikki, that is reserved for who we call 'member's choice.' This club is seventy years old and most of us are second generation members. The masks are part of the ritual to place the attendees' attention solely on those beautiful women."

"Listen, Thomas, this is selling their bodies and having depraved men crush their souls."

"Not so fast. These women, if selected, get anywhere from $5,000 to $10,000 for just one night. They make the decision."

"What the hell kind of decision. They obviously need the money and have little choice."

"To the contrary, Nikki." Pointing, "Four of those nine women are professionals making six figure incomes. It's their alter-ego. Watch what happens … no one gets injured. This is just entertainment."

Smiling at Nikki, Thomas added, "Listen, all this stuff you see can be purchased at Amazon. And with Prime, the shipping is free!"

"I got to get out of here," she thought anxiously.

"You said number 10 was member's choice. The harsh-looking leather cross doesn't look like fun for the woman who is impaled on it … who is the lucky lady who is member's choice?"

Thomas responded excitedly, "Why YOU ARE. It was nearly unanimous!"

"You fricking bastard. You can go screw yourself … I'm out of here."

"Hey wait, we can even cover your pubic area with a nice thong. I asked!"

Nikki turned and headed back the way she came, struggling to find her way to the hallway leading to the front door. It took nearly five minutes to reach the hallway, and then another two minutes to quickly navigate to the front door.

Upon arriving there, stressed and sweating from running with heels in hand, the young woman who took her purse and phone was waiting to return them. The doorman had his back to the door, facing Nikki with his left hand behind him, and his right hand at his side.

As Nikki turned and faced him, he motioned with his right hand. He pointed to her and then to the door. Then, he put one finger of his huge hand to his lips in a "shushing" manner, meaning no one is to hear about this place from you.

Nikki put her heels back on and moved through the door to a waiting limo. Her pulse went from racing to elevated to oddly normal, as she knew she was now safe, and headed home.

Trying to disconnect from a terrifying experience, she whispered exhaustedly, *"It's four o'clock in the morning and it's starting to get light."*

When she got back to her place, she undressed quickly and tossed her pretty blue dress on the floor. With a deep sigh and happy to be home, Nikki opened her purse to see if anything was missing. Everything was there, but so was a note with a phone number:

Please help me
Portia 415-XXX-XXXX

3

WAITING FOR
A STAR TO FALL

*L*et's change the pace from the wild sex adventure with Nikki and continue with Sara Sullivan, as she and I, Jonathan Garrett, have had numerous encounters over the years. We first met about five years ago when my agent was pitching a streaming of my science fiction series with her production company, "Star Gaze Ventures."

Sara once told me, "I was born to be famous." I never thought that to mean, "at any cost." She is a good person and has a strong work ethic. To begin our story and from my vivid recollection ...

The scene was a warm and lovely twenty-fifth floor condo at the Watermark on Beale Street in downtown San Francisco. On a cool and moonlit Friday evening, as romantic a setting as it was peaceful, an enthusiastic Sara Sullivan was frantic, but in a good way.

Sara was preparing a lavish birthday dinner for her current boyfriend, Brad Edwards, the CEO of a dynamic cloud computing start-up with a mission to go public. They had been dating off and on for nearly three years, a kind of record for Sara, and, apparently for Brad as well.

A ring from the doorman downstairs indicated a visitor was about to take the elevator up to the twenty-fifth floor. Sara acknowledged the doorman and returned to the kitchen.

Minutes later, there was a knock on her door, breaking Sara's train of thought. A stunning blonde beauty, about five feet seven in height and with the bluest eyes, Sara was wearing a cherry red flowing dress with a silver necklace and matching heels.

As she opened the door, the visitor said, "Hi, I'm from '*Monde de la Cuisine*.' I have your Chateaubriand for two with Béarnaise Sauce. Shall I bring it in?"

"Yes, please." Sara was so happy with her choice. Not at all the cooking type, this exclusive restaurant, although pricey, has been reviewed as five-star in nearly every survey.

As the food was unpacked, the delivery person uttered, "Is there anything more I can do?"

"No. Thank you. That will be all."

Giving the man a forty-dollar tip, he left the condo smiling and Sara glanced at the time.

Brad would be here in about twenty minutes, and Sara had a few things to do to complement the dinner, and had a bottle of Napa's finest wine, a 2017 Caymus Vineyard Cabernet Sauvignon, ready to open.

She had put together a check list so everything would be done on time. Not one to plan too far ahead for any social gatherings, this one was special, as Brad was marking his fortieth birthday tonight.

She glanced again at her watch and had about ten minutes to go.

Sara went into the bathroom to freshen up, along with her three-year-old Siamese cat Eja walking briskly to keep up with Sara. She lightly sprayed onto her skin, another mist of her Bandit Perfume, a Chypre floral exotic and sultry fragrance, of flowing jasmine and musk scents.

Sara went into the bedroom where a black lace plunging camisole top, garter panty and stocking set lay for the grand finale of the evening. She also put a tube of a *Piña Colada Aloe* lubricant and moisturizer on the night stand, as Brad really enjoyed using it. Not only did it enhance Sara's pleasure and comfort, but Brad liked the gel because it was 100% edible and vegan.

Having successfully completed her portion of the dinner prep, Sara had her Three Olives Grape Vodka and Seven-Up in hand, getting a good buzz on prior to dinner. The excitement of the awesome surprise dinner and romance being planned for the two of them gave her goosebumps of anticipation.

She sat down with her kitty and waited … and waited … and waited.

After nearly thirty minutes of waiting, she got a text message from Brad. She took a deep breath and looked nervously at her phone before pulling up Brad's text message.

"Sorry Babe, something came up.
Can't make tonight.
Talk tomorrow. Love, Brad."

Sara sat stunned for several minutes, with a tear running down her cheek. Even Eja knew something was wrong and curled up at Sara's side.

"Again, Eja," Sara said sadly. She stroked her kitty for several minutes and then reluctantly sent a text to her friend, Lina, who lived a few blocks from Sara.

"Hey GF. Whatcha doin?"

Moments later. Her text message was returned.

"BBB. Why?"
"Wanna come for dinner?"
"Stood up?"
"Yep."
"Be there soon."

"Well, kitty, no reason to let a three-hundred-dollar dinner get wasted." Sara thought dejectedly, *"Is Brad the best mistake I ever made?"*

"Eja, I do keep making the same mistake ... waiting for a star to fall."

REBOUND OR
FREEFALL

*S*ara's friend Lina had become one of her closest and dearest friends, having met when Lina was covering a documentary film on peaceful protests produced by Sara's Indie Company.

The documentary was a couple of years ago, and they became much closer as they helped each other through the worst of the COVID-19 Pandemic in San Francisco. Lina firmly believed she was put on this earth to help mankind. Yep, there is a downside to that thinking …

Having been buzzed up, Lina knocked on the door of Sara's condo.

"Come on in, girlfriend. Can I get you a drink?"

"I'll have what you're having. Grape Vodka and Seven-Up will work fine."

Pouring Lina her drink and refreshing her own, Sara stated the obvious.

"Why do I continue to do this to myself? This wasn't the first time," Sara said despondently.

"But, Sara, this was a big deal. You know it. He knows it. And he knows you know it."

"Yep. Same old … same old. So, what's up with Lina these days?"

"Oh, same old … same old," Lina responded smiling.

Both girls laughed as Sara headed to the kitchen and began to serve the Chateaubriand with Béarnaise Sauce.

"Did he give you a reason this time?"

"Nope. Said something came up. Wasn't the first time and likely not the last time."

"And yet, you press on, right Sara?" Lina replied sternly.

Plating out her rather expensive two dishes, Sara didn't answer. They talked a bit more regarding Brad, and Sara inquired as to anything new with Lina.

"Not really. I'm juggling that piece on social unrest here in San Francisco, with another young adult romance novel I've been writing. This book will be a bit unusual, inasmuch as romance novels are concerned. Good stuff, though."

"How's your dinner?"

"You kidding? Best darn meal that I've had in years."

Both girls laughed as Sara brought the topic back to Brad. "You know I think I can change him, Lina; you know, make him more responsible."

"Yeah, which hasn't worked so far, Sara. You know the definition of insanity, right?"

Pausing, Sara hissed. "Yes, I do. Truth hurts."

"You've been there, and we've seen that" Lina replied looking directly into Sara's eyes.

Sara got up and walked over to the kitchen counter to open the bottle of Cabernet.

Lina gave some thought to tonight's disappointment for her friend, knowing the pattern was becoming clear. She understood that Sara would never accept, "*love with little lies,*" so her chances at true love were uncertain. *"Hope I'm wrong,"* she thought, reflectively.

Turning to respond to Lina, Sara added softly, **"It hurts to be in love … "**

5

SEEKING BALANCE

Following an awkward discussion, but having a wonderful meal, Lina returned to her warm and cozy apartment on Fremont Street. As she entered her place, she wondered which of the two girls were in a better, or worse, situation now.

She thought conclusively, *"I guess it doesn't matter … either way we are here for each other."*

Tossing her jean jacket on a chair, she looked at her pending priorities.

"Do I work on the social unrest story that is taking over my mind and body, or do I go back to writing my novel, which will lift my spirit?"

Her upcoming novel, an entirely new genre for her, *"Charade in the City,"* was going to be about "men behaving badly," and she actually had more material than she needed, given her friends were delighted to help, and had contributed tons of relevant info.

"Gosh," she thought with a smile, *"I may have enough material here for two books!"*

Lina turned on the TV and got her answer. There were peaceful protests at the downtown Federal Building that had been going on for days, and she knew one of the reporters covering the story. She sent the reporter, Gabe Suarez, a brief text message.

"Hey, Gabe, it's me. You okay there?
Hit me back."

She didn't get an immediate response, so she opened her laptop to do some research. As she waited for her computer to boot up, she walked into the kitchen to get a glass of cold water with lemon. She hated the taste of plain water and always needed to boost it with some lemon tang.

Returning to her living room, her laptop was ready to go. As she browsed the timeline of the unrest on a government site, Gabe returned the text.

> "Hi, Lina, all good here.
> Just a peaceful protest re: the decision to limit minority rep in the voting council."
> "Ok Gabe. Ur thoughts?"
> "I see both sides of the issue. Just taking it all in."
> "K. Let me know if you need anything."
> "Will do. Thnx."

As Lina continued navigating sites having various sides of the issue Gabe mentioned, she got two posts on her Instagram page. The second one was from a good friend. However, the first one was from a guy, whose name she couldn't even remember, who had sex with her a few months ago, and Lina just assumed that she would never hear from him again.

Bringing up that crappy night in her mind, she could recall many of the yucky details:

After a brief and sloppy kiss, he moved directly in front of me, grabbed my crotch and announced, rather oddly, "Let me undress you."

He slowly undressed me as I tried to relax. His manner was so arrogant that I soon became distracted by his approach. Once I was naked, he laid me on my back.

"Are you okay?"

I recall thinking, "Just get it over with."

He removed his clothes, except for his white, non-descript underwear, and then straddled me.

I remember all I could feel was his "sweaty junk" on my belly.

He took my left hand and placed my palm around his junk, and then he had me lick my palm, now covered lightly with the sweat of his manhood. Yuk!

"Open your mouth and spread your legs," he said rather casually.

With my open mouth, he massaged my tongue and then inserted his tongue into my mouth and slowly rotated it while I groaned slightly and he moaned loudly.

He then firmly swiped my nipples and they became erect.

It was a bit painful as he squeezed my nipples. "Can you just roll your fingers over them?"

He did back off, and the sensation was less painful.

He then moved up my body to kiss my lips and he ringed my mouth with his tongue. He took his tongue from my lips to my nipples to my tummy to my inner thighs to my vaginal opening. Then he began a deep probe of my core with his rather long tongue. I do remember that I enjoyed that attention.

Then he said, "Wrap your hand around my penis." I did.

"Squeeze it ... harder."

I did and it began to get more rigid.

"Now, remove your hand." I did so reluctantly. "Why?" I asked.

"When it is your time, and I will know when it is your time, your touch can make me hard. I want to be able to thrust deep inside you. But for now, I am not done touching you."

"Roll over." He began to massage me from top to bottom. That part was good. He then brought both hands to my butt cheeks and then further separated my legs, allowing himself to massage my inner thighs. He kissed my butt, which I liked, and then ran his tongue around my butt cheeks.

He then grabbed a pillow and put it roughly under me, so he could elevate my entry point for his penetration. "We're gonna do lazy dog, because I don't think I can last very long."

I knew what position lazy dog was. With my face down, prone position, and my buttocks slightly elevated, he could control the thrusting. Prone rear entry is a twist on doggy style. It was like missionary, but with me flipped over.

I asked, "Tell me what you want me to do."

"Just be still. I want you, and I'm close, but I'll try to go slow."

I was locked into "his" sex, not mine, and my panting was a combination of mild arousal and minor contempt. I knew in a moment he would climax, which he did, and then had the audacity to ask the question of the day.

"Was it good for you?"

"Yes," I said. "It was good for me."

"Unfortunately, I recalled the miserable incident clearly and can't get it out of my mind. It was despicable. Definitely filed under the category of *worst sex ever.*"

Back to her Instagram posts. The second one was from Joyce, a very good friend from back in her LA days. Joyce had been her sounding board for venting through many difficult times. Lina had been the victim of sexual abuse from a family member, with Joyce her pillar of strength, who helped her get through those trying times.

Joyce had posted a short, but extremely flattering, article on Lina's social media page indicating that Lina Chang was a young "mover and shaker" who was making an impact on journalism in San Francisco.

Smiling and sitting back on her couch, Lina knew immediately who had written the article that was posted. It was her good friend, Joyce, and she thought lovingly …

"A true friend."

REAL WORLD

With the uplifting moment of Joyce's comment fresh in her mind, I recall Lina mentioned that she texted Nikki, her one solid sounding board for all things real world based. Nikki not only thought she was a born leader; her actions reinforced that persona, 24/7.

Cascading through her list of contacts, Lina found Nikki and realized that she needed to delete a ton of text messages, as they were heavy users between them.

"Hey, Nikki, what r u doin?"

Moments later, Nikki responded.

"Laundry."

Nikki was washing everything she could from the orgy the night before and was thinking, "*this dress is probably ruined!*

"K. So, not interrupting anything."
"Nope. Wanna talk?"

Lina immediately called Nikki. "Just wanted to get your opinion on something."

"Shoot."

Still thirsty, Lina grabbed a cold Dasani, sat back on her couch, and gazed over the nearest high-rise on the Embarcadero.

"Just texted Gabe Suarez down at the latest protest. Ya know him, Nikki?"

"Yes. Yes, I do. He has a habit of putting himself in harm's way a lot. What's up with Gabe, Lina?"

"Well, he gets more than his share of bad pub, wouldn't you say, Nikki?"

"Dunno. Don't really get into those kinds of details. Sorry."

"No. I understand. I mean, I feel bad for people like him. They just seem to get the short end," Lina said caringly.

"Hey, Lina, we could go on here for hours. The reason for your call?"

"Good old Nikki, straight to the point."

"Guilty!"

Both girls laughed.

"Yeah, Nikki, I have a favor."

"Go ahead," Nikki replied affirmatively.

"Could you do some digging down at the Courthouse, or wherever, to see what or who is behind this relentless slamming of Gabe in the press?"

Pausing a moment to drop a note, Nikki replied. "Sure. I'll see what I can do."

"Great. I don't know what, or who, is behind this, but I know Gabe and he is not the kind of person that does anything but try to help people, sometimes to a fault."

"Again, I'll do my best. One thing for sure, any friend of Lina is a good person."

"Thanks, Nikki."

Then, a social media chat was opened by Sara for both Nikki and Lina, who read the message and both smiled.

"Barhopping tomorrow night at 9. Will start at the Mission District's Valencia Street and go from there."

THREEPEAT

S *ara, Lina, and Nikki got together more often than they did laundry … literally. Whether it was at a bar, a club, or a party, these three lacked only the swords to make a legit case as the Three Sexy Musketeers.*

It's Saturday night around nine o'clock, and Nikki and Lina are meeting at their usual place on Valencia Street to kick off a night of barhopping and boyfriend bashing. Lina has her usual, a Cosmo, and Nikki is toasting her friend with a glass of one of her favorite Napa reds, Silver Oak 2015, Cabernet Sauvignon.

"Cheers, Lina. Good to be with you," Nikki said with an upbeat tone.

"Likewise, Nikki. Sara is late, as usual."

"Yep, with Sara, late is on-time; on-time is early!"

Both girls laughed and enjoyed the scenery, including several good-looking guys. "Hey, Nikki, check out those two guys next to the ATM."

"Why?"

Lina grins and says, "They're carrying purses."

"Oh shit, you're right. Just 'cause GQ is hawking 'em, doesn't mean guys should buy 'em."

Pausing, Nikki adds agreeably, "There is a fine line between trendy and ridiculous."

Clinking glasses, Lina nods her approval.

Running from an Uber and stowing her ear buds, realizing she is once again late, a bubbly Sara arrives at the girl's table with a loud, "Howdy ladies."

"Howdy?" Nikki replies with an amused expression.

"I'm working on my old slang, Nikki."

Lina chimes in, "Slang from the seventies?"

"I was out with a 'cowboy' the other night," Sara adds with a grin. "Don't ask."

Nikki smirked, "Does Brad know, Sara?"

Sara winced and then sat down and waved to a waitress. "Can I have a Macallan Double Cask Twelve Scotch?"

The waitress nodded that she heard Sara and asked her, "Neat?"

"Yep," Sara replied, settling into her seat.

"You are avoiding the question," added Lina pointedly.

Nikki added, cynically, "Sara, you are into song lyrics, and a Stevie Nicks phrase comes to mind, *'There's no need to dance around the subject.'* We're waiting."

"Okay guys. The 'cowboy' is in one of our streaming videos with Amazon Prime, so it was all business."

Lina thought, smiling, *"Monkey business."*

"And Brad, the shit, stood me up last night. As Lina knows, I 'cooked' a wonderful birthday dinner for him and he stood me up."

"Hey," Nikki offered sarcastically, "you've only been dating him for, what, three years now? We girls all know it takes at least five years to change a guy's behavior."

Sara had to laugh, thinking *"I resemble that remark."*

As the waitress brought Sara's Macallan Scotch, Lina then suggested moving inside, closer to the bar and the guy action.

"Are you okay?" a serious Nikki asked a much more somber Sara.

"Hell yeah. Big girls don't cry."

8

FOUR SURE

Thistance random encounter was the icing on the proverbial cake, as the fourth
and final puzzle piece was added that enabled me to tell this adventure in
its entirety.

Finding a table within close range of the bar, the ladies took their seats,
drinks in hand. Sara gave Nikki a detailed explanation of her disappointing
Friday night. Nikki was getting a little angry with the consistency of Brad's
inconsistencies.

Nikki hissed, "Why the hell don't you just tell that obnoxious ladies' man
where to go? It's not like this hasn't happened before."

"And before, and before, and … " Lina added firmly.

"Guys, I appreciate your input, but I do love the shit. Nikki, you like Brad,
don't you?"

"Well, yeah, but not as a guy friend. He's one of those men who other men
like to be around. It's hard for you to compete with that kind of male adulation."

"Nikki makes a good therapist, eh Sara?"

"Yep, Lina, as usual, arguing with this broad isn't gonna get you anywhere,"
a resolute Sara replied.

By then, another waitress approached them with their drink orders. They
continued with the same drinks, and Lina spotted someone at the bar being
harassed, and her radar kicked in.

"Hey, guys. Look at that luckless, beautiful woman over there," as she
pointed. "A stunning lady who has been getting 'hit on' for the last twenty minutes or so."

Sara and Nikki looked over in the direction of Lina's remark, and noticed the high level of male interest in the tall, dark-haired beauty with the Blue Manolo Blahnik Satin Pumps.

"Geez, I wish I could get that kind of attention," Lina scowled. "Just once!"

As the three ladies made small talk for the next ten to fifteen minutes, it was apparent that one current harasser of the long-legged beauty wasn't going to take no for an answer.

Sara was busy on her phone with a client when Nikki asked her excitedly, "Sara, I think I know who that woman is."

"Really? Who?"

"Google 'Jacqui Johnson,' Sara."

"Okay. Hold on," muttered Sara as she shifted her priorities.

Once Sara had the woman's info on her phone, she confirmed Nikki's observation.

"Yep, Nikki, that is the wealthy high-end financial consultant, and ex-wife of the sexual deviant, James Johnson. That is Jacqui Johnson."

Sara jumped up and winked, "I'll be right back."

Nikki blurted, "Oh shit. This ought to be good."

Sara moved quickly from the table, ran over in the direction of Jacqui Johnson, and then slowed a bit to not draw too much attention. As she got close to the "damsel-in-distress," she shoved her way between Jacqui and the intolerable gentleman with the smug grin on his face.

"Hey, Jacqui, sorry I'm late. Excuse me, sir," Sara said emphatically.

Sara pushed the man aside, took a somewhat surprised but thankful Jacqui Johnson by the hand, and announced. "Our friends are over there at the table waiting for us."

Sara waved to Lina and Nikki and those two half-heartedly waved back. *Act One ... Scene One ... of WTF!*

Sara gave the man, still refusing to leave, a stern gaze and once again, "Excuse us, please!"

As Jacqui got up to leave with Sara, she uttered bewilderedly, "So, who the hell are you?"

"Sara Sullivan. Pleased to meet you, Jacqui," responded Sara glowingly.

"Thanks for stepping in." A curious Jacqui murmured, "How did you know it was me?"

"Well," Sara replied, "You are kind of famous, and I'm kind of pushy."

Sara led Jacqui back to the table where her two friends' thoughts were somewhere between embarrassed and impressed. They introduced themselves by name, as Sara winked.

Jacqui queried Sara, "What did you see that caused you to jump in?"

Sara just smiled, shrugged, and replied confidently.

"A bad romance ... for sure."

GOOD KNIGHTS

*S*o now these four women have met, either coincidentally or fatefully. As you will see as we continue this story, I will have had the privilege of meeting and knowing all four of these wonderful people. These lady "knights of the beverage table" will frequent a plethora of San Francisco establishments. That will be part of the fun!

Jacqui inquired, "It is great to meet you guys, and I'd love to get further acquainted. Can we go somewhere else and have a drink and talk?"

Nikki replied eagerly, "Great idea. Sara, what's your recommendation?"

"Well, likewise Jacqui, I'm so glad we met. Why don't we head over to a friend's private club? Let me see if I can reach him."

As Sara texted her friend and work colleague, Troy, the ladies finished their drinks and paid their bill. Jacqui threw in the tip, smiling at the wonderful turn of events.

Sara announced, "We are all set at the notorious *Power Pit* on Jones Street. Is that okay?"

Jacqui thought worriedly, *"Oh shit. Power Pit was one of my husband's hangouts. Hope I don't run into anyone."*

They directed their Uber driver to take them all to the *Power Pit*, and once at the door, their friend Troy had already arranged for their arrival.

A very sexy doorman, sporting a shadowy beard, greeted them, "Good evening, ladies. Please proceed upstairs."

"Thanks, ya hunk," Sara uttered admiringly. "Maybe we'll see you later."

They headed up to the top floor lounge where several scantily-clad waitresses were poised to take their drink orders.

"Do you fricking believe this place. Exploitation in rare form."

"Yep, Nikki," Jacqui agreed. "But this is the ultimate man cave. I think it's somewhere between funny and sad."

Jacqui asked her new friend Sara, "Why here?"

"Oh, sorry. It's kind of business. Member Troy is an Executive Producer at our Indie, *Star Gaze Ventures*, and we have many contacts and resource needs firmly planted right here in this shithole. Kind of a networking opportunity."

Lina offered a brief explanation to Jacqui. "Sara Sullivan doesn't do anything that isn't going somewhere, or providing some kind of value. You'll get used to it. She's special."

"Yep," Nikki replied smiling, "We follow her lead and even when we get into trouble … it's good trouble!"

Sitting down, they were asked for their drink order by a waitress wearing the number 17. Names of the servers were not allowed.

Jacqui ordered a Caymus Red Cab, and Sara ordered a Macallan Scotch, neat. Nikki was in a serious drinking mood and ordered a Long Island iced tea. Lina just stuck to her Cosmos.

As their young, sexy waitress left with their drink orders, Nikki winked admiringly at their server, who had glanced back at their table, and she murmured an instantaneous sexual thought.

"Seventeen has a nice ass … very pert and very shapely!"

10

AGE OF DEVOLUTION

After their drinks arrived, a bubbly Sara began a round of personal details. The gleam in her eyes reflected her joyful mood, and hyperaware of a possible new friendship.

"Jacqui, we are happy to meet you. I'm Sara Sullivan and I live in the city." Sara paused as Jacqui nodded. "I am the EVP of an Indie production company, and I do some part-time singing and modeling. I'm from the Midwest and have been in San Francisco for about six years."

Jacqui smiled as Sara continued.

"My real passion is acting and singing, so I hope one day to leverage my work at *Star Gaze* into a new and exciting career."

"Well, Sara, it is indeed a pleasure to meet you and thanks for saving me earlier."

Sara returned a smile and gave Jacqui a thumbs up.

"Okay," Nikki replied, "I'll go next. I'm Nikki Wallace and I am currently the assistant district attorney here in San Francisco. I have two business degrees and a law degree. You gotta keep up with the men, if you want a chance, don't you think?"

"I hear ya," responded Jacqui approvingly. She was thinking, *I know Nikki Wallace by reputation. Tough as nails lawyer.*"

"In my real-world flip side, Jacqui, I strongly believe in extraterrestrials, and am a frequent attendee of alien and paranormal conventions. I love watching the Ancient Aliens series on the History Channel."

"Cool, Nikki. A renaissance woman," Jacqui offered encouragingly.

"Guess so. Thanks."

Sara interjected, "Lina, you're up."

"Sure. I'm Lina Chang and I am a senior editor for the local paper, and the author of four books to date. I do a lot of volunteer work, and I get so much support and love from these two ladies. I'd be lost without them. I am originally from LA and have been here for a couple of years."

"Thanks, all," Jacqui responded. "I guess it's my turn. I'm Jacqui Johnson and I'm surprised that you didn't recognize me. Not that I'm famous ... just kind of infamous."

The other girls didn't let on that she was a bit of a celebrity, and that was what lead to the saving encounter.

"Following my graduation from Stanford with an Electrical Engineering degree, I got into the wild world of cloud computing, and AI and Advanced AI."

The girls were paying close attention to Jacqui's dialogue and demeanor and were impressed.

"Some family conflicts here in California kind of forced me to go to Europe, where I hooked up with some big caps and had many huge successes, and that brought me back here to the States."

All three ladies were seeing someone far more professional and successful than the society glam magazines and press reports depicted.

"While in Europe I met an entrepreneur, James Johnson, and found we had a lot in common. We were both Type A's who loved living in the fast lane. We got married, built a gorgeous home in Sausalito, and should have lived happy ever after."

Jacqui paused with a tearful sigh.

"I think y'all know what came next."

"Yes," Nikki added politely. "I was actually involved in his pending prosecution for sex crimes and money laundering. Both the Feds and the state of California had practically air-tight cases against him for crimes here, and in a couple of Caribbean islands."

Jacqui offered a brief update. "He was murdered in Jamaica before we even went to trail. The killer was thought to be the father of one of his victims. He drove a large tribal sword right through him, and is still at large."

Nikki had the headlines of the article on her phone:

Wealthy American Playboy Murdered
James Johnson, 54, of Sausalito, California ...

"Hey guys, chill out," Sara advised sternly. "Let's just enjoy this evening and agree that today is the first day of a new beginning for the four of us."

Raising her glass in a toast, Nikki added agreeably, "This is to a new and everlasting friendship. Cheers." Clinking glasses were heard all around.

"May I add something?"

Lina replied, "Of course, Jacqui."

"In my experience with men, and I've had more than my share … although humanity is in evolution and progression; men are in devolution and degeneration!"

So, from my perspective as narrator Jonathan Garrett, a good time was being had by all.

11

SARA'S SERENDIPITY

I'm going to pause from the ladies' enjoyment of the Power Pit, and get back on point following some premature elaboration on our main characters, and some of the weird encounters of this fab four. Returning to the characters' backgrounds, I'll continue with Sara and a nice blast-from-the-past event.

A successful Silicon Valley businesswoman, Sara Sullivan's real passions were singing, dancing, and modeling. Those were interests that never became career prospects, but they didn't stop her from enjoying those opportunities as often as possible.

There were many boyfriends that came in and out of Sara's life, with mostly bitter endings given she had such high expectations for the "man of her dreams."

Robb was a guy Sara believed had great potential. A strikingly handsome 35-year-old who enjoyed surfing, when not running his dad's real estate business, his blond hair and outgoing personality became a magnet for the opposite sex. Dealing with nothing but upscale clientele, he always dressed as if he walked off the current issue of GQ.

Robb accompanied Sara to many of her social events. One was a red-carpet modelling show at the Moscone Center, where Sara was one of several models from the exclusive Donna Daly De Beauté Model Agency. She would be wearing several sets of Monet and chainmail clothing from *Designs by Kate*, and was excited as Robb reached her condo.

As Sara opened her condo door, there was Robb in an elegant ivory tuxedo jacket with contrasting black pants. He looked amazing.

Stepping into the condo, Robb gave Sara a warm and loving kiss. Sara held Robb tight as they enjoyed the moment.

"Bring your hot manly self in and I'll fix you a drink," Sara said crisply.

"Look at who's the hottie," Robb responded, looking at the sexy Sara dressed in a long sleeve heavily embellished gold and black see-through mini-dress with a plunging neckline. Ankle-tie block-heeled sandals in beige gave off the aura of a movie star about to hit the red carpet.

"Thanks, Robb. Your usual Dewar's Signature Scotch?"

"Yes. That'll be great."

Sara prepared a couple scotches for Robb and herself, when he presented her with a gift for the evening.

Opening the gift box, Sara was delighted to find a lovely rhinestone lariat necklace. Robb helped put it on for her, and she gave him a strong hug and a long kiss.

"Thank you so much. You are such a sweet man."

"A special gift for a special lady," Robb added happily.

As they drank their Dewar's and discussed the evening agenda, Robb had sex on his mind and Sara could see his manly arousal showing as he caressed her thighs and buttocks, having not been given any reason to halt his minor advances.

"Hon, we will have time for that later. Got to go right now."

A somewhat dejected Robb agreed, "Of course. You're just so damn sexy!"

With that comment, Sara grabbed a light wrap for the evening chill and they were off.

♥   ♥   ♥

As they reached the Moscone Center and Robb left his BMW M440i with the valet, the event was quickly filling up with beautiful and well-known people from both the San Francisco entertainment and fashion industries.

Fashion designer Kate Knuvelder met them as they reached the backstage, and Kate gave Sara a hug and simply said, "Sara, you look ravishing, and will be heavenly in the designs that I have picked out for you. I am so happy to have you headlining tonight."

"Thanks, Kate, for giving me this opportunity." Looking at Robb, Sara said, "This is my date, Robb Quinn."

"Hi, Robb, good to meet you."

"Likewise, Kate. I am pleased to be able to see the show from this unique perspective."

"It is unique, Robb, but also about to get crazy busy."

At that moment, a young model was approaching them in a silver chainmail outfit that caught Robb's eye. "Oh my God, is that hot or what?"

Kate, seeing the rise in Robb's temperature, motioned the model over. "This is Peyton, daughter of Donna Daly, whose modeling agency is supplying these beautiful ladies, and Peyton is wearing a powerful warrior design from my collection, *Metal and Monet.*"

Kate handed Robb her business card with her website: *www.kateknuvelder. weebly.com.*

"What's up with those long nails?" Robb asked.

"In the trade, we call them 'claws' and they definitely complete the warrior look."

"Damn straight," Robb offered. "I wouldn't mess with them."

"Robb, will you please excuse us?"

"Certainly. I'll try to stay out of the way."

Sara gave Robb a quick kiss and took Kate's hand, and they quickly were off to the series of dressing rooms.

Once the show began, Robb was overwhelmed at the beauty and professionalism of the models and the remarkable outfits that several designers were promoting. Trance and techno music kept the mood and pace fast and furious. Armin Van Buuren's music was contributed virtually.

Following a 45-minute show and a brief time with several members of the local media, it was off to the after-show parties, which lasted until about 2:00 in the morning.

♥　　♥　　♥

Arriving back at Sara's condo, Sara tossed her wrap on a chair and fixed them a nightcap. She looked over at her man and thought, *"He really can be such a great guy."*

"Sara, your modeling tonight was fantastic. You were the whole show, my Dear," Robb spoke as he gave Sara a warm and loving kiss.

"Why, thank you, Robb. I appreciate the compliment, and I am so glad you were able to attend. We made a nice-looking couple."

With that, the tired but still sex starved couple moved immediately to Sara's bedroom, drinks in hand, where their batteries would soon get recharged.

Robb undressed down to his gray European Sheath boxers, as Sara appeared from her bathroom with a black lace open front teddy. She pushed Robb back onto her bed and straddled him with her warm and wet anticipation. The two lovers embraced in a long and loving kiss.

As the two nearly naked bodies got even more excited with the hugs and long kisses, Robb pulled Sara closer with his long arms, and together, the two lovers rolled onto the middle of Sara's large bed. She took a deep breath as his lips met hers, and soon a voracious kiss brought out the pent-up frustration in his sexual needs, and a rapidly growing hunger in her libido.

"This is what I want and need," Sara thought impatiently.

Sara was visibly swept away by his passion, and got even more excited as she felt his weight pressing her deeper onto the bed. His skin was warm and his scent was so captivating. Sara sighed, with caring thoughts of this man.

"I missed you, and I remember our last wonderful night together," Sara reassured him as she wrapped her arms and legs around him. He noticed her slight moan and countered by nipping gently on her earlobe.

Robb then straddled her heated body, facing her and leaning into yet another long kiss and with his hands running through her hair, she could see that his manhood was fully erect, and he needed only a slight signal of her eagerness to get his mojo moving.

Sara flipped off her teddy, parted her legs, and as they broke their kiss, said, "I'm ready." He swept his tongue from her breasts and abdomen to her inner thighs, reaching her vibrant core, which was rapidly pulsing. "Open wide," he blurted.

Robb didn't need any help getting penetration, as her canal was already wet and puffy. He rocked against her and rolled his hips in a not-so-subtle movement, giving Sara various pleasing sensations, and a noticeable arousal shook Sara's entire body.

"Robb, wait."

"Wait for what, Sara?"

"It's the rotation. Stop rotating. I just want to slowly feel all of you as you enter. Let me control our sex right now. Let me make the moves with you inside."

"Of course. You feel so warm and so good. Can you relax and let me work into you gradually?"

"Gradually?"

"I don't get my pleasure from thrusting hard." He paused. "Feel this."

His gentle hands lifted her hips and thighs as he got himself into a better position. Sara responded quickly, as even that movement was arousing.

"Yes, Robb. Yes."

He then took control of her noticeable stimulation in a caring manner that Sara just loved. He used slow rotation, skin-to-skin friction, changing angles and depth of penetration to get Sara's anticipation to build.

"Oh, you feel good," Sara exclaimed crisply.

The variations in technique of this talented lover were impressive, as she was writhing beneath him and absorbing the many sensations he stoked in her warm and sensuous body.

"It seems so easy for you to get me high. Now, Robb. I want you now."

With a deep moan, as her hips thrust upward and her channel was tightening around Robb's rod with a need to come, she began to gasp with utter satisfaction. Sensing the timing of his sexual aggressiveness and her response, he plunged one more time with full and deep penetration. They both came hard and fast together; him with a loud shout and her with a wordless cry on her lips.

With a smoldering gaze, Robb stated, "Sara, that was great. You are great."

"Oh my God, Robb. I missed that ... I missed you!"

12

SARA'S ZEMBLANITY

*O*kay, fair enough. Let me define zemblanity. It is a real word. William Boyd coined the term zemblanity in the late 20th Century to mean the opposite of serendipity; unhappy, unlucky, and unexpected discoveries. This part brings pain into the previous relationship. Damn!

The Robb you just met was the CFO of a very successful high-end real estate business in San Francisco, built by his late father and with a client list reflecting the city's *Who's Who*. He had plenty of wealth, but to his credit, he didn't spend it all on himself. He was known in the city as a frequent financial resource for many needy charities … a responsible guy.

Robb had a tumultuous relationship with an indie actress years ago, which I got wind of through my experiences with Sara's movie contacts, and that relationship resulted in a drug habit which he was able to hide from Sara. *That story is for another chapter.*

Regrettably, Robb had the keys to many San Francisco mansions contracted through the listing and sale of hundreds of multi-million-dollar homes. He frequently used his house showings for sex, *which will be a story for this chapter.*

Sara had a friend named Brittany, who Sara liked a lot, except for certain elements of Brittany's daily covert life. Brittany is what was called an *influencer* on social media. She had well over 25,000 followers on several sites, and made a nice living promoting and representing clients and products.

Sara got a call from Brittany one sunny San Francisco Saturday.

"Hey there Sara, it's Britt. What ya doing?"

"Some project management stuff. What's up?"

"You're dating Robb Quinn, right Sara? The hottie with mucho dinero and the fab body?"

"Well, sort of. We are dating a lot these days, but we're not exactly exclusive."

"Bullshit," Brittany thought intuitively.

"Well, girl, I have it on good authority, and from more than one source, that your guy is banging broads at several of his 'open houses,' and I would guess none of those babes are you."

"What the hell are you talking about?" Sara snapped, angrily.

"I'm just trying to help, Sara, to give you an honest perspective of what the A-hole dude is doing behind your back."

"I appreciate your concern, but I find those allegations hard to believe, and Robb and I aren't OTP right now." Truth was, Sara probably would consider Robb Quinn for a "one true pairing."

"Tell you what, Sara … if I find out any specific info, I'll let you know."

"Sure. Please do." Sara hung up on Brittany and was annoyed, firmly believing that Robb would not be involved in such despicable behavior. Pissed, Sara did some digging, to no avail.

♥　♥　♥

About two weeks later, Sara got a call from Brittany describing in vivid detail a sex party going down that afternoon in one of Robb's open houses.

Brittany arranged to replace one of the young women invited to the sex party, and instructed Sara to don an exotic disguise, as Brittany knew she had done before, and come to the front door to allow Brittany to let her in, if the door was locked.

At exactly 5:00 p.m., Brittany joined Robb and an unnamed young woman at the home holding an open house earlier in the afternoon. Brittany, using the name Diane, could play the sex scene if need be … and it needed to be.

"So," Robb asked, "you must be Diane. I'm Robb and this is Susan."

"Nice to meet you. I have my friend, Linda, coming soon. Where's the booze?"

Susan, who already had a light buzz on, showed "Diane" to the massive liquor and wine cabinets. Robb was likely drinking all day, or possibly a little high on drugs, which Brittany assumed would make the afternoon unforgettable. *"He's gonna get his today,"* Brittany assured herself.

About thirty minutes later, Robb had the ladies dress down to their sexy undies, and he got himself buck naked, showing off his fully operational manliness.

"Where is Linda, Diane? I want to get started."

"I'll get us started," Susan replied excitedly. "I have two hands wanting to exercise your disco-stick."

A smiling Robb quickly moved over to Susan and let her wrap her well lubricated hands around his throbbing manhood, as Brittany could see Sara walking through the unlocked front door in a pitch-black wig, dark horned-rim glasses, a daring cage bustier set, and matching black heels. It was a perfect disguise, and didn't look at all like Sara.

"Sorry I'm late. I'm Linda," Sara spoke with a rather husky voice. Noticing Robb was lying flat on his back, getting seriously aroused by Susan, Sara said, "I'll just wait my turn."

Robb was reaching a point of pending climax, not seeing who just spoke, and began to moan. Diane was rubbing and stroking his throbbing erection, and getting aroused as well.

Robb then responded irritably to Sara's initial comment on "waiting her turn," still having no idea it was Sara. "That's fine." He panted. "Diane is next and then the three of us. That's the plan. Squirts everywhere!"

"I don't think I can wait to squirt," Sara snapped, in her normal voice. "Look up, you bastard."

Robb hurriedly grabbed himself, and his now diminishing asset, and quickly turned to face that voice. "Sara? Is that you?"

"Damn straight, you shit. We're done." Sara glanced at Brittany and headed quickly for the door.

Sara thought she could change him until that ugly and disgusting sex thing. She was devastated.

"I can't make you love me …"

13

LINA LAMENTS

ina Chang was a very good person who was too naïve for her more righteous self. As a young adult, she trusted a boy she was dating, with terrible effects. Her uncle's double life and his manipulation of her and unlawful and unethical behavior had a profound and disastrous effect on her at a very young age. More on that in a moment.

A 2016 graduate of the University of California at Santa Barbara, Lina looked forward to a career in journalism. Not knowing that UCSB was a top party school in California, with the slogan among students as "*U Can Study Buzzed,*" she was often out of her comfort zone attending parties and school related gatherings.

During her senior year, she met a liberal arts major named Mike, who seemed to have a lot in common with Lina, or it simply appeared to be the case. After going out on several dates, Mike invited Lina over to his apartment, as they had done before, and they drank and talked for about an hour. It was early evening.

After twice having had safe sex, Lina was trying to remain open-minded about this relationship. As is often the case, there were pluses and minuses with Mike. Unfortunately for Lina, this time a determined Mike took his impatience and horniness to the next level.

"Mike obviously wants sex tonight," Lina thought pensively. *"Maybe I should have declined coming over, this time."*

Finishing their drinks, Lina was having second thoughts about sex with Mike, who was getting a little impatient with just foreplay. She tried to look at the upside, given the fact they were trying to build some chemistry, and no red flags had appeared. Having enjoyed some heavy kissing and petting, they moved to his bedroom.

Mike quickly disrobed and began stripping Lina of her clothes as he guided her, somewhat roughly, onto his bed. Mike was naked and Lina still had her bra and panties on. Being a typical male with visual stimuli, this time Mike had turned on the bedroom lighting to dim so he could see all of Lina's physical sexuality.

"Come on, girl, get naked. I want to make love to you."

Lina was very self-conscious about being flat chested, and sex in the dark before was much more manageable. She thought somberly, *"I really don't want him to see my small boobs."*

As they embraced on the bed, stimulation became quick and selfish for Mike, as he had his hands in every orifice of his date's trembling body. He roughly pulled her bra off as her panties had already been removed. Lina was tense and uncomfortable. Cupping her small breasts in his hands, he ran his wet tongue around her nipples and moved quickly to her waiting vagina.

"Damn girl, you're a hot little thing."

"Thing," she thought disgustedly. *"I hate this."*

With little or no concern for his partner's desires or objections, he spread her legs and, with her slight resistance, had to push inside her thighs to get her to open wide for him.

"Easy, Mike. Please. I'm dry."

Mike was horny and not in the mood to do "easy." He thrust his still growing erection into the tight core of Lina's channel, not yet wet enough to keep Lina from giving off a painful groan. He gasped loudly, with strong gratifying moans as he reached the climax he needed and wanted, as his weary partner wept with emptiness over a sexual encounter, truly unlike the one that she had expected.

When she gathered her composure, she asked him a simple question. "Mike, where was your condom? I didn't feel a condom."

"Didn't have time, Babe. Just let it rip!"

About two weeks later, complaining to her doctor of vaginal itching, a rash in the genital area and some vaginal discharge, test results indicated that Lina had apparently contracted an STD from Mike. Not only did she have a bad romance with someone she trusted, her womanliness was now scarred.

Lina presumed, sadly, *"Everyone seems to have their own personal agenda,"*

♥   ♥   ♥

Lina had an uncle, Chin, who was fairly wealthy and had several businesses in Hong Kong as well as in Southern California. Lina's parents looked up to Chin as the most successful member of Lina's family. Little did they know that he led a despicable double life, and his sexual manipulation of Lina described an unlawful predator with immoral and unethical behavior.

After being asked several times to accompany him to Hong Kong for business meetings, Lina was instructed by her parents, against her vehement disapproval, to go on this trip with Chin as an opportunity to "expand your horizons."

Without going into the sordid details, once at their Hong Kong hotel, Chin's treatment of his niece went from usual to decidedly horrible. Lina knew things were about to change during this trip, as her uncle had been very vague about what she would be doing during her uncle's business dealings.

Chin had Lina fitted for a prostitute's sexy clothing and had trashy photos taken of Lina for distribution to his wealthy friends. A now devastated Lina, was sold as a sex worker for nearly a week. She had to perform as his sex slave on command, often several times each day, for the entire stay, never once being able to leave the awful hotel room and all of its terrible sexual horrors.

As they were checking out of their hotel, his disturbing words to Lina were etched in her mind forever. "If you tell anyone about this, I will kill you. You know I can!"

Lina's only devastating thought was, "*I have been to Hell and this experience will only make me stronger. I can't tell my parents the truth, as they have such respect for my uncle.*"

Months later, as soon as she graduated from college, she moved to San Francisco.

Her mission was to become a guide for the needy and the downtrodden and to begin volunteering efforts as soon as she found employment. After such a truly bitter and hurtful lesson, she was determined this horrible experience would not define her as a person.

As she became deeply involved in meditation and constant soul-searching, she decided that she needed to find a mentor for both her career and personal life.

"God help me find someone that I can trust!"

14

NIKKI'S NEBULOUS
NORMAL

A truly complicated person, Nikki Wallace hid her intricate life choices well. She was passionate about everything she did, and her glass wasn't just half-full; it was over flowing with optimism. As mentioned before, she thought herself to be a natural-born leader and exuded those qualities in every endeavor and for any challenge.

Nikki had a strong belief in extraterrestrial existence and found comfort among the fans and believers of alien presence. Later, she would plan to meet Jonathan Garrett at an AlienCon event, and they would begin a subject matter sharing relationship.

She had a great business reputation in San Francisco, and her legal accomplishments were well documented. Before her rise to prominence, she formed and managed a free legal aid service for the underprivileged and found time to give one-on-one help when she could. Good person.

A bi-sexual, Nikki had several gay and straight relationships and seemed to juggle them well. One of her favorite sexual positions with men was dependent entirely on the man's height and his penis size and form.

As a rather tall girl, Nikki liked stand-up sex. It equalized the control thing and allowed her to play with her man's junk and squeeze it in and out of position. As she rose and fell, her arousal tempo was under her control, not necessarily the man's. It got her hot!

A couple years ago, while at a pool party in San Jose, Nikki came across the pool attendant masturbating to an old *Penthouse Magazine* in the storage room.

Nikki had been looking for some sort of pool floatie and surprised the young and well-endowed pool boy. Pool toy?

"Hey, big guy, whatcha doing?"

A startled and embarrassed young man turned and said something inaudible. As he tucked his curvy penis back in his swim trunks, Nikki was getting a sexual high on her radar screen. She had noticed that this young man's penis was shaped like a banana, when fully erect.

"Stop. Let me see what you are holding in your hand."

"Lady, I'm sorry. Please don't tell anyone."

Walking over to see for herself, she blurted out, "Damn, that is one special tool you have in your toolbox."

The boy was puzzled. *Was she complimenting my curved penis?*

"Let's take advantage of this moment, shall we?"

The pool boy was surprised, yet still interested in what this MILF had in mind. Nikki gave the boy a wet kiss, smiled teasingly, and then dropped her bathing suit bottoms. She turned her back against the wall, spread her legs, and pulled his body and erection up and into her. Firm contact.

"Oh, young stud, that's good. Don't lose your hardness. Stroke it if you need to. Let me rock you."

His demeanor went from scared shitless, to "Hell yes!"

After several minutes of up-and-down pulsations, she let out a quiet moan as she came, and his ejaculation left a trail of semen everywhere. He wasn't able to aim his exploding cannon, given her lively gyrations. She found a towel to swab both of them, taking her time to wipe off his limp biscuit, looking hungrily at his muscled frame.

With a contented smile, she kissed him on the cheek and turned to leave.

"What's your name?"

"Dick."

"You gotta be kidding."

"No, ma'am, my name is Dick."

She smiled as she exited the shed. "Thanks Dick. You now have a story to tell your friends."

Pool boy Dick waved sheepishly.

♥   ♥   ♥

As she walked back toward the pool, her phone rang. The caller I.D. displayed Portia, from the note placed in her purse at the infamous sex orgy. Nikki had called her a couple days ago, but didn't receive a call back.

"Hello, this is Nikki."

"Hi, Nikki. This is Portia. Thank you for calling me. Is now a good time to talk?"

Nikki waved to the people around the pool, and then motioned that she was going inside the house. "Yes, Portia, it is a good time for me. Please tell me why you contacted me."

"My name is Portia de Angelis and I am the wife of retired Air Force General Bradley de Angelis, and I saw you at the party Saturday night."

"Portia, I need to explain."

"Please don't. I knew you were there under false pretenses, and our member Thomas Shaughnessy invited you."

"But I …"

"Nikki, I don't have much time. Please let me finish."

"Yes. Of course."

"The members were irate at Tom for bringing you. Apparently, your reputation as a prosecutor in the city is stellar. And, they won't let you return. Nikki, if you think my call concerned the women objectified, you are mistaken."

Nikki thought inquisitively, *"That is precisely what I took from, 'please help me.' Oh boy!"*

"Nikki, most of the women there are happy to attend. Many of these women are type A's who control men all day and need to feel submission occasionally. The ones needing money are fine with the debasement, when they receive tens of thousands of dollars in cash."

Nikki did recall Thomas's words at the sex orgy, when he told her they often received $5K to $10K, which Portia now confirmed. Nikki was getting an education on a topic that she didn't even know existed. *"Damn,"* she thought, confused.

"And the sex workers, Nikki, are happiest of all. They make a ton of money, have no 'Johns' to support, and the men penetrating their orifices are clean, professional, and healthy."

"Excuse me, Portia, if that is the case, why call me?"

"Because central to the wealth of several of these members is a Ponzi scheme, which is now growing in size and beginning to involve innocent men and women."

"Portia, you sure?"

"Nikki, why would I take this chance if I wasn't 100% sure. You need to help us … them."

"Portia, I can't drop everything and take on such a monumental project. But I will meet with you, and we can discuss the facts as you have them."

"Oh God, that would be great."

"Okay. Treat this with all the utmost of confidentiality, and we will find a time to meet. Portia, is your husband one of the criminals? I have to ask."

"No, he is not. At least I don't think he is. We don't go to these very often. He has a bad heart."

"When is the next orgy?"

"Dunno. They are never planned out, but rather spontaneous. It's their best way to keep out undesirables. Got to go."

With her last comment, Portia hung up and Nikki concluded, ***"Another day in the jungle!"***

15

NIKKI'S NOTORIOUS NIGHTLIFE

Nikki's alter ego drove an alternate personality, which she often used to change her Type A business focus to almost the exact opposite. She had a well-hidden diversion, given her incredible mental release, which actually aligned well with me, Jonathan Garrett. That interest was all things alien, and a part of her brain was definitely wired to the galaxy … and beyond!

Her favorite alien departure tract involved the annual AlienCon events. She could mingle with many similarly wired alien conspiracy theorists and never worry about being recognized in this rather weird society of extraterrestrial believers.

Their event in Pasadena in 2018 was a *triple blessing* for Nikki. This three-day event was packed with famous entertainment celebrities, cast members of the History Channel's Ancient Alien series, and a plethora of books, posters, and assorted outer-space paraphernalia.

Nikki booked the sparkling Sheraton Pasadena Hotel and had stayed there before, as it was close to eclectic Old Town Pasadena, which housed the vibrant business district and had its share of lively nightlife.

Blessing number one was simply the ability to meet and have conversations with the legendary science fiction writers and explorers who she followed religiously on TV. Connecting with actors from the *Star Trek* series was a wonderful experience, and Nikki's vast knowledge of hard science fiction and her 155 IQ fit right in. She was certainly in her "element" here far away from reality.

Nikki got photos with David Childress, Giorgio Tsoukalos, and Caroline Cory, all famous celebrities from the History Channel.

Blessing number two was, as you might guess, a sexual encounter. Nikki got cozy with a young lady at the hotel bar on her first night there. This woman, Kim, in no way attending AlienCon for its subject matter, made Nikki's pursuit of sex that much easier.

A high-level sex worker, Kim was looking for action, male or female, and she found Nikki to be irresistible from many perspectives. Nikki's main concern was discretion; she needed to be as careful with this stranger as possible.

With Nikki being Nikki, Kim needed to produce hard evidence showing her female stuff was clean and healthy. Nope, not making this up. Once the check sheet was completed, it was on to a "quid-pro-quo" that Nikki could only dream about.

In exchange for two nights of steamy lesbian sex and top-of-the-mountain joint pleasure and satisfaction, Nikki agreed to provide a certain level of legal support down the road.

As Nikki was about to lead Kim up to her room, Kim excused herself to grab something from her car. Five minutes later, Kim returned carrying a beautiful Gucci traveling bag with KK monograms.

As they approached the door to the room, Kim uttered a surprising WTF, "Room number 69 … you reserved room number 69?"

"Yep. I usually set very high expectations. And, look what has happened. You know what they say about luck?"

"Yes, I do," answered Kim amusingly. "When planning meets opportunity."

"You got it, Kim. Come on inside." As Nikki unpacked her computer and travel bag for the weekend, she curiously inquired, "That is a lovely Gucci bag. May I ask what is in it?"

A smiling Kim opened her bag and revealed a small store of everything two females might need for red-hot sex.

She began the tutorial. "We have a mighty tool here. It's my favorite; a thrusting, stroking rabbit vibrator that gets the job done in ten speeds."

"Oh my," Nikki uttered, thinking "*This is gonna be good.*"

"Next we have a dual-purpose pearl white clit stimulator and G-spot vibe. I love the color and it hums."

"I'm getting hot. Damn, that is the coolest. What's in the zippered bag?"

Opening a silver rhinestone bag, Kim laid out several nice accessories. "We have flavored arousal gel and nipple gel, and a spearmint clit sensitizer for solo use anytime."

"Yeah, I do self-sex a lot, Kim, so I'm interested."

Kim then got to the layer of large devices at the flat bottom of the bag. "Here are several glass and silicon dildos for rear entry, if we need them, plus two of my favorite strap-on."

"Not my favorites, Kim."

"Understand. But keep an open mind. I'm pretty good with these. You know the sensation with two guys in a ménage a trois?"

"I do. I definitely do. Well, I think I do. The perineum area between the anus and the vagina, I'm told, can be very pleasurable."

Kim winked, tilting her head, "You're told?"

"Yep. Never had any luck with that."

"I can get you close, Nikki."

"Damn!"

"Yep. This weekend, if you'd like."

"Let's wait and see, Kim. For now, let's get some dinner."

"Sounds good, Nikki," and they headed for the hotel's fairly decent restaurant.

♥   ♥   ♥

Nikki was thinking, erotically, "*Sitting in this restaurant next to a sexy woman who you want to have sex with has its ups and downs. You know, if God gives you lemons, you make lemonade, right? I'm gonna crush those fricking lemons!*"

Following a very nice dinner, but now in the mood for dessert and some brandy, Nikki gazed at her newly found lover, Kim, and her thoughts were overpowering; she could hardly wait.

The first thing Nikki noticed was the slit in her dress was perfect for her to access her leg and see what, if any, response she'd get from this sexy woman right away. She was quite optimistic as she had looked at her with a devilish grin. Nikki clenched her teeth to keep from crying out immediately, as Kim grabbed her hand and directed it between her legs, to the soft skin of her inner thighs. She gazed fondly into her eyes, and way past temptation.

Kim was powerfully striking, and nothing she could have done would turn Nikki on more. Nikki had touched women intimately on many occasions, but she was usually the initiator. To have Kim show her exactly where she wanted her to go was a sensation that she realized had been missing most of her life. She was good. No surprise ... so far.

Kim, it appeared, shared Nikki's willingness to explore, and when Nikki let her fingers graze the lace between Kim's legs, it was her turn to squirm. She loved it! Nikki applied pressure where she knew her hard clit nestled behind some inconvenient fabric.

"Yum," she said with a pleasing smirk.

Her wetness soaked through, and she wanted nothing more than to have more access to what Nikki knew would be her swollen, slippery slit.

"Good brandy?' Nikki asked, amusingly, while at the same time rotating her fingers in a small circle.

"Oh, yes." She gasped, and a mischievous smile formed at the corner of Kim's mouth. "Sweeter than I expected." As they were getting away with this and Nikki got more excited, she was amazed with how readily she had accepted this risky behavior. She was getting aroused in anticipation of her arousal.

Nikki slid the lace of Kim's panties to the side, feeling her folds and giving her complete access to her hot and wet core. She was now dripping wet, hot with desire and so alive, as her walls clamped down on the warm, probing fingers. A slight moan of pleasure came from her throat, as perspiration appeared on her forehead with a wary facial expression.

Nikki leaned in to wickedly whisper in her ear. "How quietly can you come?"

Kim turned to Nikki, and she saw her pent-up sexual release reflected in her steely eyes. "I think you know the answer to that," she murmured in response. Nikki chuckled, moving her fingers lower until they slipped deeper inside her. Kim moaned, ever so quietly. Nikki smiled.

Nikki watched her face and saw her bite her lip gently. The urge to plant a wet, sloppy kiss on her inviting mouth was strong, but they couldn't have that type of attention.

"Do you want me to stop?" Nikki teased, pulsing her hand back and forth, working her with two moist fingers just enough so she knew she could make her come at any time. She shook her head, "No, no," as her breathing turned noticeably heavy.

As Nikki started to move her hand again, she quickly closed her legs, trapping Nikki's hand in her love nest. Seconds later, she smiled and opened her legs slowly, and her fingers found her tiny bud. She let out a very light sigh, and they could both feel her climax building.

Twisting her wrist, Nikki plunged deeper into her core, and it was precisely what she needed. She opened herself fully as she struck clit gold. Her mouth opened slightly in a small cry of release as she orgasmed, and now her body twitched with a hunger for her that had grown even more lustful.

The only thing on the horizon for them now was a couple nights in bed where they could get down and dirty and enjoy each other immensely. Several thoughts went through Nikki's mind, but one intoxicating theme for bi-sexual lovemaking hit her radar screen.

Nikki thought impulsively, ***"Oh yes, I want to be her submissive!"***

16

NIKKI'S NOSTALGIA

Blessing number three occurred during an afternoon group session at Sunday's AlienCon involving the famous certified "past life regression" therapist, Dr. Dawn Baker. Past life regression is a method using hypnosis to recover what practitioners believe are memories of past lives or incarnations.

Following the Q&A from the session, Nikki waited for several curious people to finish asking Doctor Baker their questions. As the doctor gathered her things, Nikki approached her and introduced herself.

"Hello, Doctor Baker, my name is Nikki Wallace and I'm pleased to meet you."

Extending her hand, Dr. Baker replied, "Hello, Miss Wallace. It's nice to meet you as well."

"Please call me Nikki."

"Of course. I'm Dawn. What can I do for you?"

"I enjoyed your session immensely. I missed your opening narrative, as I was on my cell with my office."

Tilting her head, Dr. Baker asked, "Are you *the* Attorney Wallace that is handling the Johnson case in San Francisco?"

"Why, yes I am."

"Then it's my privilege to meet you. Your reputation is pretty solid."

"Thank you very much." Nikki paused. "Back to your opening?"

"Sorry. Yes. Past life regression therapy supports the theories presuming, as a person moves through life, they collect memories which are stored in the mind. Even though the subconscious memories are not able to be accessed, regression therapy believes those memories can still have a significant impact on a person's development and ability to function in daily life."

"Thanks for explaining it so clearly."

"Do you have a reason to believe you might be a candidate, Nikki?"

"I do, Dawn. I have progressive dreams and recurring dreams, which I'm trying to understand. Maybe there is a past life memory hidden in my mind."

"How long are you in town?"

"Leaving later today. I already checked out of my hotel."

"Give me a moment while I check my itinerary and next week's schedule."

Nikki thought, *"Could I get a session with her now?"*

Dr. Baker was perusing her tablet as Nikki was getting excited.

"Tell you what. I can give you two hours first thing tomorrow morning. I have a 2:00 appointment and was just going to review client records in the morning."

Nikki had already looked at Monday, in anticipation of this happening.

"Nikki, can you see if you can make it tomorrow morning?"

"Scheduling it as we speak, Dawn."

"So, you are who you are reported to be. A well organized and a highly functional Type A."

"Guilty!"

Both ladies laughed as a new journey path was being established.

"I'll get a hotel for the night and meet you in the morning at your home or office."

"Nonsense. You will spend the night with me. We can get further acquainted and be fresh for tomorrow morning. Plus, I live in Palm Springs, which is about a two-hour drive. My assistant can book you a return flight from Palm Springs to SFO for tomorrow afternoon."

♥   ♥   ♥

Nikki was very impressed with everything about Dr. Baker, and her invitation was unreal. They drove the two hours to her Palm Springs home, and she introduced Nikki to her two adopted greyhounds, Max and Bella. Apparently, they were rescue dogs from a local racetrack, and Dr. Baker had them out running on her large grounds as soon as they arrived.

"This is a wonderful woman with a big heart," Nikki thought positively, *"So cool and so nice."*

They grilled salmon and shared a 2018 Sonoma Coast Pinot Noir, which matched the salmon perfectly. Following dinner, they adjourned to her conservatory where there were books galore and a nice, soothing fireplace.

"So, Doctor Baker, how long have you been involved in past life regressions? I'm sure you didn't begin your professional career as a regression therapist."

"No, you are correct. I have a psychology degree from UCLA, and then graduated from the Stanford School of Medicine. I did a two-year residency at Stanford, and after that went on to become Head of Psychiatry at Cedars-Sinai Medical Center. And, again, please call me Dawn."

"Well, Dawn, that was an impressive start. How did you transition into your current profession?"

"You know, Nikki, you have a bit of a reputation for being direct."

"I do?"

"Yes. I have read about how a determined Nikki Wallace has been working hard to clean up the City by the Bay. It's nice to be able to put a lovely face with the name."

"Thank you. I'm humbled."

"Nikki, one should never need to apologize for being successful."

"Appreciate the compliment, Dawn."

"How about a nightcap before I send you to your room? Tomorrow, we can discuss my transition to past life regression."

Nikki nodded as Dawn went over to the well-stocked bar and brought a bottle of Grand Marnier Liquor. "This is a blend of refined Cognacs, aged up to 25 years, and is special."

The ladies toasted and enjoyed some "wind down" conversation before Dawn showed Nikki her guest bedroom.

"Good night, Nikki, see you in the morning."

"Good night and thank you for the lovely evening."

"It's been my pleasure. My rooster will wake you in the morning and we will have breakfast and begin your journey."

"*Gosh,*" Nikki thought. "*I remember waking up to roosters the last time I was in Key West!*"

♥   ♥   ♥

Over breakfast, Dr. Baker explained how she got started in the past life regression therapy.

"One of my patients began discussing past life experiences under hypnosis for a totally unrelated issue. Then, she began bringing up events from the past ... many years in the past, and I was quite surprised. When I confirmed elements of her story through public records, I became a believer."

"How long ago was that?"

"Nikki, it happened nearly twenty years ago, and after significant research and additional education, I am very comfortable providing this therapy."

Dr. Baker paused. "Are you ready to begin, my Dear?"

"Absolutely!" Dawn led Nikki to her dedicated area for meditation, massage, and hypnosis.

Getting Nikki comfortable, Dawn began by hypnotizing her, and mentally leading her through a door and into the light. After some relaxed dialogue between Nikki and Dawn, Nikki said she "found" her grandmother, who had passed away nearly fifteen years ago.

"Let your grandmother become your spiritual guide, Nikki."

For nearly two hours Nikki described the "conversation" that she had with her grandmother, who wished she hadn't died so soon.

Dawn had her relay to the grandmother that her memories are strong and shared by family constantly, which reassured the grandmother.

This went on for nearly two hours before Dawn brought Nikki back to consciousness.

"How are you feeling, Nikki?"

"Actually, quite relaxed. The entire experience was so real."

"We can do this again, if you'd like."

"Of course, I would. Dawn, I have a question ... one of many questions," as they both laughed.

"Is reincarnation a part of this hypnotic process?"

"Why do you ask?"

"Because I felt strange visions from a future life that seemed to be my life."

"Oh my, Nikki, that's odd!"

17

JACQUI JUGGLES JET-SETTING

J acqui Johnson has always had a very large ego, once actually telling me she was born beautiful. She thought the laid-back California scene was beneath her. This next segment is quite detailed, but truly important to appreciate this woman's fateful journey.

Jacqui had been married before. She dated a wealthy Silicon Valley banker, and after a short engagement, they were married. Their sex life during their engagement was decent, reaching a level of two or three times a week, which pleased Jacqui.

Her husband, Charles, was well endowed, and even with his preference for mostly missionary sex, the sex was good. However, oral sex was one way with Charles. Fellatio was "permitted," but cunnilingus was a "no-no" for him, much to her disappointment. So, Jacqui's sex glass was only half-full, but their bedroom intercourse was usually enough to keep her satisfied.

Once they were married, everything in the bedroom changed. Charles was a workaholic and sex became an obligation to him. After two years of sex only when she would beg him for it, and becoming totally bored with their "arrangement," she simply sought a divorce, which he gladly provided.

Miserable with an unsatisfying marriage and bored with the California lifestyle, she moved to Europe and quickly was introduced to a high-energy think tank in Brussels, where she thrived. The simple combination of brains and beauty was impossible to ignore. She knew it ... she knew they all knew it ... and she thrived.

She traveled extensively throughout Europe, and managed technical projects that got her fame and recognition. Intertwined with her career work, Jacqui had many sexual encounters which she categorized simply as "romantic trysts."

She ran several high-tech start-ups in Europe and South America from her office in Brussels, and she gained a reputation for AI implementation and cloud computing that made her a big "catch" back in the States when she later returned.

A very wealthy international businessman, James Johnson, came into her life after nearly four years of Jacqui's stint in Europe. He had been trying to establish a business presence in Moscow, with little or no success.

Jacqui was recommended to James by a mutual friend, and the long and short was that she managed to get James set up for his business needs in a relatively short period of time. She was very good at this. James was blown away with her beauty and capability.

♥   ♥   ♥

I'm going to pause the story with a sidebar that is very interesting, and may or not be true. It's titillating, for sure, and that's why I'm including it.

Jacqui had done some work in Serbia to enhance the EC's international data sharing, primarily with Russia, which brought her under the attention of Vladimir Putin. Although that project began rather innocently, Jacqui soon discovered other priorities from Serbia in what is called in business, scope creep.

Putin was informed of Jacqui's skills and beauty, and it is alleged that she spent two or three weekends in Moscow as a guest of Vladimir Putin. An underground Serbian newspaper referred to Jacqui, who had used the fake name of Josephine, the first wife of Napoleon Bonaparte, as Putin's Princess.

What was verified regarding Jacqui's stay in Russia, was her being seen and photographed by paparazzi for two non-concurrent weekends in the famous Petroff Palace Boutique Hotel in Moscow, built in 1796, and the pinnacle of Russian architecture and style. One can only draw their own conclusion, but the entire situation made sense to anyone following Jacqui back then.

♥   ♥   ♥

James and Jacqui immediately established themselves as a couple moving and living in the fast lane. However, the downside to all of this exuberance and success took on a steamy and dark sexual side. Were they seduced by a burning chemistry, or, to Jacqui's needs, by pain as a stimulant?

One night, as the two were working on a project in James' high-end office conference room, they had consumed nearly the entire bottle of The Balvenie Single Barrel 15 Year Malt Whiskey. After some heavy kissing and fondling on both sides, they reached a point in the evening where sexual tension needed to be released.

This couple had another thing in common. They were a well-matched sexual couple in bed, compatible, and willing to experiment whenever the opportunity came about. A strong physical attraction resulted in a unique ability to enjoy multiple and simultaneous orgasms.

Even though they were a vigorous sexual couple, Jacqui was being introduced into an entirely different sexual practice.

James' thought to himself, rather excitedly, ***"She is going to feel an out-of-body experience, or subspace, which is the ultimate goal of a submissive."***

18

JACQUI'S JOYFUL JITTERS

"It's been a productive night. How 'bout we take a break?"

As James gave Jacqui a tight squeeze, she replied, "Sounds good to me, James. Let me put these files away."

"Great." As Jacqui cleared the conference table, James quipped, "You have a great body, but your long legs make me nuts." Jacqui smiled, but James wasn't quite finished, grabbing his crotch. "These nuts need a workout tonight, my lovely lady."

"James, what do you have in mind?"

Reaching for a box in the corner of the room, he tossed it over to Jacqui and replied. "Here is something special for you … to get us both in the mood."

Catching the small box and opening it, Jacqui was a bit surprised and totally blown away with the timing and prospects for the evening. Their sex life had been good and getting better, so it was with mixed emotion that she gazed at the revealing attire.

Inside the box was a black strappy caged open cup bralette and caged panty set, featuring a slender G-string and lace top fishnet thigh-high black stockings, trimmed in pink. There was also a black blindfold with pink trim and four satin easy-tie restraints.

It was obviously James' desire to explore erotic submissive fantasies with his sexy partner.

"You game, sugar?"

"Hell yes. Let me change and I'll be right back."

As Jacqui left to slip into her newly designated sub costume, James cleared the desk and secured a soft silver-padded covering, apparently for his lady to lay on, and a couple cushions. Moments later, the gorgeous, sexy, and scantily clad lady of the evening made her appearance.

"Damn," James exclaimed excitedly. "You are one hot sub."

Thinking about the term submissive, she immediately knew that this was the beginning of a whole new sexual experience for her. She was being introduced to a mild form of bondage, but tonight, it was not by her choice. Believing that even the slightest of bondage pain would make her body hypersensitive, Jacqui was willing to put herself out there.

"This is about trust. You trust me, right?"

With a deep breath, Jacqui simply said, "Of course."

"Oh my God, what have I gotten myself into?" she thought apprehensively. *"I know my past married life was boring, but ... "*

James was a middle-aged man, in decent shape, with a slightly receding hairline. He was only slightly taller than Jacqui, but he was built well and looked like a guy who worked out at the gym. His voice was commanding, which often put Jacqui into a surrendering mode, which helped to feed James' sub fantasy.

While Jacqui had been in the bathroom changing into her sexy outfit, James was feeling quite good. He had removed his shirt, pants, socks, and shoes. He had oversized boxers on that didn't give away their contents. He had placed a small men's bag on a nearby chair.

"James, just tell me what you are going to do," she asked as she returned, somewhat nervously.

The light air in the room went a bit stale. He gave her a reassuring kiss and answered. "I'm going to open you up to a side of sex; a side only trusting lovers can experience. Enough said?"

"Yes. I'm ready to be opened to anything new."

James gave her a warm and reassuring hug and a cute nibble on the ear, which was enough to break the ice with what he had in mind. He gently slid his hand so his entire palm was pressing against the tiny fabric of her panties.

"Oh my," Jacqui flinched. "As always, I like your touch."

"You're already warm, my love ... and wet. Please, get on the desk and lay back for me."

Jacqui did so. She was now lying prone on the desk, and James raised her arms and hands above her head and gently spread her long legs. Jacqui was feeling some anxiety but took a deep breath and waited for his next steps.

He moved to a position behind her head and gently took her left wrist with one hand and wrapped the satin tie around it and secured it to where the desk leg met the desk top. He did the same with her right wrist and secured them both, leaving Jacqui's arms immobile.

"Does that hurt?"

"No. I'm fine. Please put a cushion under my head."

An annoyed James did that, but was not happy getting any direction from his soon-to-be sub.

"There, how's that?"

"Fine. Thank you."

"Now, close your eyes." She did, as James put a black, ringed choker and blindfold on her.

"Is that okay? Not to tight?"

"James, why the blindfold?"

"Please, relax. I know you trust me and I will not disappoint you. With a blindfold, you will focus on what you feel, not what you see. Tonight, is all about your pleasure."

Once the blindfold was secured, darkness flooded her vision.

James moved to the other end of the desk, which at five-feet in length was perfect for what he had planned.

He gently pulled Jacqui towards him so her legs were dangling over the edge. "You have lovely legs, Jacqui, and a body that men must lust over."

Jacqui smiled as the timing of the compliment was much needed.

"Thank you, James."

As he pulled her feet together, he used them to massage his crotch, up and down and side to side, getting an erection that Jacqui could feel, but not see.

"*WTF?*" she thought irritably. "*This part is more for his pleasure.*"

Moments later he separated her feet and tied her ankles to the desk legs with two of the satin ties so her legs were spread and bound securely. Jacqui sighed.

He stepped back and with a remote from his bag, activated several video cameras that would record the helpless Jacqui from many disgusting angles. One camera was pointed directly at the opening between her spread legs. James smiled.

He then took another cushion from a chair, placed it under her butt cheeks, exposing her core to his full-frontal view. Jacqui was securely bound and at the mercy of James, and she knew it. She didn't know that this entire depravity would be recorded.

"What are you going to do now?"

With that whimpering request ignored, James reached back into his small bag and pulled out a red gag, which he had planned to use on the blindfolded Jacqui. At the last second, he threw it on the floor and gave a soft *hush* verbal request to her and then inserted his fingers into Jacqui's gaping mouth.

Stepping back again, he gazed up at the video cameras, confirming that his bound beauty would be photographed from several vulgar angles, and with close-up shots of her private parts that were no longer private.

"Relax, my lady. Now is when I give you pleasure."

Twisting her head in the direction of his voice, she replied, "James, I can't see but I can feel. I need you to turn it up, James. I am ready. I don't want to wait. Make me come!"

He placed his two fingers in her wide and inviting vagina, and probed clumsily for her clit, her ultimate pleasure point. As he rubbed and caressed that spot patiently, he asked, "Does that feel good?"

"Hmmm, yes" she nodded, while thinking, *"He is doing this for his own selfish pleasure."*

He then sucked one of her taut nipples into his mouth and gave it a gentle tug. This sensation was pleasing, but not earth-shattering, for the now horny Jacqui. Sensing her enjoyment from his slight biting, he took the other nipple into his mouth, sucking, licking, flicking, and biting until both peaks were erect.

Detecting her heightened level of passion, he reached over to pull her power bullet from her purse, turned it on, and waited for her reaction.

"Is that vibrating sound what I think it is?"

"It is." He slipped the bullet into her waiting vagina, while still probing her lips and parting her folds, eliciting soft gasps from her trembling body. Once his finger finally began rubbing her clit, she jerked and whimpered.

"Oh, that's good, but I want you to fill me up with your erection and with my bullet on my clit."

His fingers continued to play inside her; finally, a full fist thrust deep into her channel and he assumed that this forceful sensation would help her reach the top of her sex. Her arousal climbed another notch, but only due to the size of his fist in her core.

"Am I wet?" she inquired passively, thinking past the pain she felt from his large fist.

"Yes."

"What part of me?" she asked timidly, wishing he would just penetrate. With a low rumble of a voice that held all the sexuality of a mild bondage tryst, he answered, "Shhh. Don't spoil it." With the addition of the higher vibration from her power bullet, she was close.

"Come now, sweet thing." He withdrew the bullet and thrust his fist as far as it would go, and she released a shimmering, tension-relieving moan, not a burst of rush or an explosion. It was a soft cresting, as her orgasm rolled through her, a smooth dissolving of the maxi-buildup. As far as a climax was concerned, it felt anticlimactic.

Her immediate thought was, *"Why in the hell didn't he do me himself?"*

With the cameras now turned off, James had completed the video photos of Jacqui. The slightly trembling lady on the sex table, still blindfolded, tried to process the events of the evening. It was somewhat disappointing for her, but he had accomplished his well-planned salacious mission.

She was having some serious bittersweet thoughts, having no idea James's only desire tonight was to observe and measure his control over her pleasure. This was a sign of things to come!

He had jotted down notes for his future entertainment: *Playroom, Yield, Surrender, Subspace, Pinwheel, Shibari Ropes, Spreaders.*

James eagerly concluded, *"Her complete submission won't take long at all."*

Jacqui's powerful thought was, *"**I'm bulletproof, nothing to lose ... fire away, fire away!**"*

19

SAMANTHA SEEKS
STABILITY

D r. Samantha Vandenberg had literally created the man-coach sub-section of male versus female relationship building, and became a leading authority on the subject. Although not a member of the fab four just introduced, her character will become clearly important as I move on. So, let's give the lady a little background, okay?

Her looks, sultry voice, and magnetic personality resulted in a vast clientele of customers from the everyday guy to the well-connected in the Silicon Valley community. Her parents reinforced at an early age that Samantha could be successful in any career or lifestyle she chose. Her self-esteem was never lacking for positive feedback. For the most part, she was a pretty lucky girl.

At an early age, on an entirely different track, she developed a huge attraction to anything concerning the legendary actress, Greta Garbo, seeing herself as a similar ingénue, needing privacy and solitude frequently. Garbo's screen phrase, "*I want to be alone,*" rang true with Samantha most of the time. She chose when to navigate outside that "bubble" and had developed a regiment of socially selfish behavior that pushed all of her buttons.

She experimented sexually with men and women and was often disappointed. She perceived herself to understand men and what drove their libidos, resulting in her gratification with the career of man coach. That work became her clear focus and subject-matter authenticity, and as she dove into the intricacies of man coaching, she found significant satisfaction and reward, both personal and monetary.

Understanding her insecurity outside of her comfort zone enabled her to become the best in her profession with accolades and credibility that raised her self-esteem to a very high level.

Since she had been married twice and divorced twice, Samantha used those relationships as a baseline for how "not to" approach a disappointing married life. She began volunteering at a local suicide prevention center, giving supportive talks while finishing her education. It was during that timeframe a significant emotional event confronted her.

One of the men in the suicide prevention sessions, Rich Osbourne, was drifting away from the support group, and one night he climbed up to the top of the office building and threatened suicide. As soon as Samantha was informed of what was taking place with a member of that session, she dropped everything and headed immediately to the scary scene involving Rich.

After a few harrowing minutes of persuading police to let Rich's "therapist" through to talk to him, she took the stairs to the roof, where Rich was standing close to the edge, and began her critically important support work.

After about an hour with Rich listening and interacting with Samantha, she was able to get him to step back from the building's edge.

"Rich, from this moment on, I will always be here for you … night or day. Don't ever hesitate to call me."

"Thank you, Doctor, I will. And I'm sorry for doing this. Sorry to worry you."

"Don't be sorry, Rich. We just need to have better choices for our day-to-day problems. Does that make sense?"

"Yes. Yes, it does."

They embraced and this event reinforced her commitment to be the best man coach she could be.

It was this story told the next day in the press that spiked my interest in meeting this woman and eventually becoming one of her clients. She was truly a very special person.

Yes, Jonathan Garrett needed to meet the interesting Dr. Samantha Vandenberg.

SAMANTHA AND JONATHAN

W hen I met Dr. Samantha Vandenberg, it followed several years of separa-
tion from my ex-wife, Amanda. Meeting Samantha was the beginning
of a life-changing experience, and one I didn't recognize at the time.

Waiting in her office, I was impressed by both her solid educational cre-
dentials hanging on the wall, as I was with the reading material that covered the
gambit of all the things guys would like. So, I already liked Dr. Vandenberg.

"Can I get you something, Mr. Garrett?" the receptionist said for the
second time.

For the second time I replied, "No thanks. I'm fine."

About five minutes later, a stunning woman in a gray business suit and
upswept hair walked over and introduced herself.

"Hello, I'm Doctor Samantha Vandenberg. You must be Jonathan Garrett?'

"Yes. Yes, I am. Pleased to meet you Doctor Vandenberg."

"The pleasure is all mine. Come. Let's go into my office."

As I got up, and followed her into her office, my only thought was, "*Damn,
she's hot. I want to have sex with her; right here and right now.*"

I entered her office and was just blown away. It looked like what was called a
while back, a "man cave." I would love to have an office like hers!

"Come. Please sit down wherever you'd like," she gestured with an open
hand and with an eye-to-eye glance at me.

There was a silky leather black L-shaped couch and a pair of armed chairs. I
choose the couch, sat down, and relaxed.

"Can I get you something, Mr. Garrett?"

"No, I'm fine. Please call me Jon."

"In that case, Jon, please call me Sam."

And it began. From unknown strangers to first-name basis; maybe bedding this babe isn't that far out!

Let me tell you a little about myself, Jon, and then we can get into you.

I'd like to get into her!

"Fine. That would be great, Sam."

"As you know, I am a California-licensed psychologist specializing in men and their relationships with women. Was that your expectation, Jon?"

"Well yes, yes it was … is."

I was fumbling with words. WTF!

"And you have been to my website?"

"Of course, Sam. Figured it was a good way to get some background info. It's an impressive site and your endorsements are impressive as well."

Shit, I used the word "impressive" twice!

"And do you have any questions regarding any of the topics or with my advertised sessions?"

"No," I responded distractedly, "But I will want to discuss them later, I'm sure."

"Great, Jon, let's do that."

Pausing to look at her notes, Sam sexily re-crossed her legs giving me the opportunity to see a little more of the good doctor's legs. She tossed her heels to the floor. I smiled, without making eye contact.

"According to your chart, you are a Scorpio, Jon."

"Yep. Guilty."

"May I ask your age?"

Without hesitation, I replied, "Forty-eight."

Sam smiled, as if she knew that I was actually fifty-four.

"Well, you look great and I'm sure you take care of yourself."

"I do work out a lot, Sam, and I am also an avid diver and kayaker."

That'll impress her!

"What kind of diving, Jon?"

"I'm a PADI-certified scuba diver," I proudly announced. "Do you dive?"

I didn't expect a "yes," but didn't expect her answer.

"Not scuba." She paused. "I do sky diving, though."

"Shit!"

21

HOT AND HORNY

F ollowing a forty-five minute "get-to-know" session and some brief digging into
my life in general, Doctor Vandenberg and I planned to meet again in a more
structured session, the first of many to come.

*Damn, she made an impact on me. Sam is one fine-looking man coach. It was
probably after three or four sessions that I realized she was a friend to me when I
really needed one, and if not for her, I don't know where I would have ended up. Yep,
she had that effect on me.*

I left the doctor's office, jumped into my Lunar Blue Mercedes Benz C63,
and headed off, horny as hell. I called my friend, Jacqui Johnson, from my car.

"Hey girl, it's me. How ya doing?"

"Hi Jon. Fine. What's up?"

Laughing, I replied, "Nothing 'up' at the moment."

"And, Mister Garrett, you need some help in the sex department, eh?"

"Well, you busy?" I asked impatiently.

"Love to see you too, Jon?" responded a somewhat irritated Jacqui.

"Sorry. I mean, are you busy? Is hubby still out of town? Can we catch up?"

"If ya wanna come over, we'll do more than catch up. And yes, James is still
in Jamaica hosting some banker bullshit meeting on the island."

Pausing a moment, Jacqui responded with a chuckle.

"First, I gotta Zoom Daryl, my dipshit lawyer, who is handling that damn
lawsuit with the SEC."

"Whoa, that's a big deal. Maybe later is better, Jacqui."

"Oh no way. Some mindless sex is just what this lady needs. Give me about
an hour ... make it an hour and a half, okay?"

"You got it. See you then. Bye."

My next call was to my bar buddy, Steve, a well-known and well-connected photographer.

"Hey Steve, it's Jon. How ya doing?"

"Yeah, I see your name. We're not cruising till next weekend," a puzzled Steve replied. "Is there a problem, Jon?"

"Oh no. Just need a little info. Thought maybe you could help."

"Go ahead, Jon." Steve was thinking, "*Here we go again.*"

"Steve, you know Jacqui Johnson; right?"

"Hell yeah, everyone knows JJ."

"I'm headed over to her place now."

"Lucky you. Need a wing man?"

"You know all the stuff she's doing now … advising the Young Entrepreneurs Club or high-level VC crap?"

"Of course. She is active in a bunch of shit because she's smart and sexy as hell. Every org with old, white guys is competing with the YEC for her time. So, what?" a puzzled Steve asked.

"Has she gotten any awards lately, Steve? You know, the kind of award that I should know about before I go over there? I want her to think I'm really interested in her stuff, although today … not so much."

"Are you shitting me? Mister shallow."

"Hey," I was getting impatient. "Do you, or don't you?"

"Let me check. I'll text you if I find anything."

"Thanks, Steve. Did you score with that hottie from last Friday?"

"Scored a date, that's all."

"Well, good luck and thanks again."

After hanging up with Steve, I phoned my combination agent, PR guru and trusted assistant, Amy.

"Whatcha need, Jon?"

"I have a meeting with Jacqui Johnson in about an hour, and I want to take her something. You know Jacqui."

"Yes. Sure, Jon. I'm listening."

"Can you find out what month she was born?"

"May I ask why, Jon?"

"Sure. I want to get her something personal with her birthstone. I'm headed over to Taylor's Jewelry on Fifth Street. Text me the info, okay?"

"Will do. Give me five minutes," said Amy firmly.

As I was parking my Benz, Amy's long text arrived.

Birthstone for Leo is the peridot. Their zodiac sign also responds to onyx, diamond, and ruby. Get it in a pendant. Amy.

Well, the jeweler did not have anything in the peridot birthstone. What they did have, and I was happy to buy, was an oval rhodonite solitaire pendant with a 3.0 carat weight diamond.

As the gift was lavishly being wrapped, I muttered to myself, "Hell, that was easy."

QUID PRO QUO

Arriving in Sausalito at Jacqui's sprawling mansion, I buzzed the gate and it opened. I checked my phone for any text messages from Steve, and there were none.

"Hi handsome." The tall, dark, and striking beauty, Jacqui, gave me a hug as I reached the front door.

"Hi sugar." Handing her his gift, "This is for you."

Jacqui was startled. "For me? Why?"

"Just to congratulate you on all your many accomplishments. I haven't been in touch for a while and you deserve something nice."

Jacqui gave me another big hug, grabbed my crotch with her free hand and said, "Thanks. Let's go get naked."

We stopped in the kitchen to get a couple glasses of one of Napa Valley's most iconic wines, Pahlmeyer 2012 Proprietary Red. Jacqui already had the bottle opened and chilled.

"Damn girl, you got a lot done since we talked."

"Not really. I blew Daryl the *dipshit* off, to better prepare for Jon the *dragon slayer!*"

"You're putting pressure on me girl. Gonna make it hard for me to get it up."

"Oh, I'll get it hard." Jacqui again grabbed my crotch.

With that comment, Jacqui led me into her massive master bedroom, a place I had seen often, and always with a younger man's anticipation.

She pushed me onto the bed and went into her sitting room to get into something skimpy.

As I disrobed down to my sexy, mesh G-string underwear, still sipping that awesome wine, Jacqui appeared in a black silk nighty, with her large breasts exposed through cut-outs, and the target of my gaze. She wore a matching G-string nearly too small to see.

Her not-so-subtle Paris perfume, Fracas, left a trail of intoxicating scent as she floated into bed. It was dizzying, one of her signature touches to put a guy in the mood, which was totally unnecessary tonight.

I wrapped my arms around her in a genuine embrace. This was pure pleasure, and making love to Jacqui's celestial body would be heavenly. As we kissed and relaxed, the mood was already set.

She immediately slipped her hand down my boxers probing my genitals, and placed her other hand warmly on my face and cheek.

"You're warm, my Dear. And your 'Johnson' is ready for this Johnson."

"Clever. I love when you talk dirty like that to me while we're making out, Jacqui."

"Bet you like the moaning better, right?" Jacqui said with a twist of her head.

"Damn right I do."

"So," tilting her head back slightly, "Captain Garrett, what's your pleasure tonight? In addition to the moaning?"

Pausing briefly, I replied. "Reverse cowgirl."

"Reverse cowgirl, it is."

"Can you get your big, black Texas hat, Jacqui?"

"Sure thing, Babe. Be right back."

"And," I added with a tone of expectation, "Can you bring one of your double-dong-dildos?"

"You're not going to hurt me, Jon," Jacqui said amusingly.

Jon, smiling, replied, "Of course not. Just want to add to your pleasure, Babe. Just get the curved, purple one … the one where one end is small and the other end is large."

"*Her pleasure, hell,*" I thought selfishly. "*My eyes are gonna be popping.*"

"Will do. Ya want anything restrictive for your family jewels? You know I have a nice selection of rings."

"Not this time. And next time it'll be ladies' call … promise."

Minutes later, a completely naked Jacqui returned, still wearing her big Texas hat, sipping the last drops of her wine. She gave me a "thumbs up" and then straddled me in reverse, massaged my balls attentively, and caressed my penis with long, unhurried strokes, to near-full erection. Her touch … her damn hot touch.

I lubed the small end of the curved dildo and slowly eased it into position for Jacqui to ride it slowly into her rear end opening, slowly twisting as she moaned.

"Oh yeah," she groaned, apparently enjoying the rear insertion more than I had expected, and this made me happy that I suggested it.

By then, I had the purple pleasure plug pulsing to the rhythm of my two fingers in her vagina. As I methodically probed her core, running my fingers up and down her folds, my thumb worked its way up to her stiff bud, rubbing against it with each thrust of my magic fingers.

"There you go, Mister ambidextrous."

"Hey, watch out what you call me."

We both laughed at my comeback. Jacqui liked my sense of humor; as I did hers.

Fully content, Jacqui grimaced, then sighed, then moaned noticeably again. While the plug was well-lubed and glided smoothly in and out of Jacqui's backside, her love nest was getting warm and very wet. Her gasping told me that I had reached a high point on her hypersensitivity scale. "Yes, master," she muttered forcefully, "let's get it going!"

As she began to rock up and down, I placed my hands on her shoulder, brought her up to vertical, and gently massaged her warm back and strong shoulders.

"Jon, I love your touch." She caught her breath. "Anywhere and anytime."

With this lady enjoying my touch, I continued, but with additional lube that I got from Jacqui's nightstand drawer. I greased the purple plug even more, knowing this would please the lady when it was the right time. We had done this before.

As Jacqui leaned forward moaning more loudly, I reinserted the plug, but with the additional lube. I then took the larger end of the dildo and inserted it into her wet channel. "Oh, Jon."

For the next few minutes, I just played with her using an in-and-out technique with the curved dildo. She had guided me before, and had shown me what it took to give her pleasure. She was in control of this hot action, and my eyes were bulging and enjoying the sight.

"Now, Jon. I want you now."

I removed the sex toy and softly lifted her vertical to allow for a penetration position where I could get maximum leverage and she could rock up and down.

I entered her slowly and then began to thrust myself into Jacqui's welcoming channel as she turned slightly and rocked. She grabbed my thighs for leverage.

I grasped her hips and moved her thighs, as I got myself into a better position. She responded as the movement provided more clit stimulation and was pushing her arousal to the point where sweet moans could be heard. As her walls clamped down on my penis, filling her fully, and heat rose up in her trembling body, she cried out compellingly …

"I want it hard, Jon. Real hard. Make me squeal."

With that cue, I worked her as fervently as I could, like we did many times before, using our collective friction, again changing angles and depth, and pure force of my penetration. The less-than-subtle changes of my love-making technique were not lost on Jacqui, whose moans got louder as the sensations being stoked in her warm and sumptuous body got me excited.

She turned her head toward me and said appreciably, "I could never fight against such arousal, Jon. You hit my sexual highpoint. You make me as hot as any man ever has."

I smiled as my grasp of her hips pumped her body upward and her core was tightening with a need to come. I twisted gently a couple more times with full penetration, as her body bucked and thrashed and she squealed … loudly.

The aching in her sexual core soon turned to pleasure and moments later, Jacqui let out a powerful scream as she reached her climax, while I squeezed her warm and ample butt cheeks. "Oh God! Oh my God! Oh Jon."

Over the next hour, she would have two more orgasms in both a leaning forward cowgirl position and my preference, doggie style, where I finally had an orgasm that was nearly as loud and exuberant as hers was.

I thought, it wasn't just, *"Been there, done that. It was more like, been there … enjoyed that, again."*

We often lost track of how many times we came, when fully committed to each other's sexual needs and physical wants. At that time, I honestly didn't know if I could take credit for her pleasure, or was it simply the fact that she had compulsive sexual behavior inclinations?

"She may not be the marrying kind … but that girl can scream!"

23

SOMETHING CAME "UP"

Remember the night that the prick Brad cancelled Sara's wonderful fortieth birthday party dinner? Well, a mutual friend of Brad and mine gave me the details, which I promised to keep secret.

So, here it goes …

Brad had a female friend, Erica, who was an exotic dancer at one of San Francisco's finest gentleman's clubs. He had gone with her to buy some new outfits, as she wanted his opinion and preferred to be with a man when buying erotic apparel.

Arriving back at her apartment around six o'clock, Erica opened a couple cold Molson's and thanked Brad for his help.

"Let me put these on and get your opinion, Brad." Erica said excitedly.

"Sure. Be glad to," as Brad thought, "*Eye candy' for sure.*"

Walking into her bedroom, she changed into one of her new outfits in the bathroom and came out to model the red shorty for Brad, who was sitting on the edge of the bed.

"Damn, girl, they are hot. You really have the perfect body, ya know?"

"Thanks, Brad. I really like red," as she fingered herself sensuously, allowing Brad to take it all in and knowing he was enjoying the brief show.

"Yeah, red is your color," Brad responded glancing up and down at Erica's lovely body, paying attention to her masterful fingering.

Brad was getting aroused, as Erica was one, hot, erotic woman, and they had plenty of sexual encounters over the last couple of years. Luckily for Brad, she didn't "talk."

Brad had a category he called "Penetration Pinnacle," and Erica was a ten on that list.

"Yes, I am horny, Brad, and my fingers are getting tired. You need to take over in my wet panties. You 'up' for it?" she asked devilishly. "I'm wet from just you being here and remembering our last lustful encounter. I am not embarrassed to pleasure myself under your watchful and jealous eyes, if that's all I get tonight."

Brad was getting hot under her wicked gaze.

"Make me come alive." She paused, "Turn me on, Brad. Feed it to me. Now."

The somewhat contrived words just burst from Erica, and Brad sensed her growing desire and absolute impatience. She moaned slightly as Brad pulled Erica to him and took her hand from its warm and wet place and replaced it with two fingers of one hand, reaching for her breast with the other.

"You can squeeze my boobs, Brad,"

She didn't mind the direct approach, as raw sex was the only thing on her mind, not technique. He swept his hands up her chest to her large, soft, breasts, teasing her pebbled nipples with his fingertips until her areolas were a rosy pink. As her tips peaked, he moved elsewhere.

Brad then followed a path with his dripping hand from between her well-spread legs to just in front of her mouth, smiling at Erica as she knew the next steps he had in mind. Brad was following his "Erica 'been there, done that' script," and she was fine with a repeat.

He touched her lips until she parted them, and he pressed two fingers inside her mouth, feeling her moist and sensitive tongue. Her tongue curled around his fingers in an anxious way, soaking up every drop of her juices that Brad's fingers had brought to her waiting mouth. She groaned.

"I want to feel your thrusting rod where your hand was just giving me pleasure."

Brad knew it, but he was happy to torture this impatient babe a bit longer. He really enjoyed this control. Instead, he held Erica firmly by the wrists so she couldn't pull away as he sucked her fingertips, licking it like he was at her core, teasing her until her entire body ached with desire.

"Brad, I can't remember the last time I've wanted sex so badly." She began panting, which Brad really enjoyed. "I am even more soaked, Babe."

He guided his fingers back and forth, in tandem with his thumb searching for her clit, in a slow, methodical manner, long enough that he could feel her orgasm building. With her body trembling, he knew just how much her body wanted to let go.

"If you are going to touch me everywhere, let me put my hand on your stiff rod so I can feel it pulsing."

"Be still," he replied, as he kissed the delicate skin along her inner thighs.

"Touch me," she begged. "I want your mouth on me everywhere."

He brought his wet fingers up to her mouth, tilted her head to contact his open mouth, and they sucked Erica's juices together. Brad could see and feel that she was as wet as she could be with her on the brink of an incredible orgasm. She murmured excitedly, "*This is good … so good. I want more!*"

As her pulse quickened to a crescendo, and he sensed her heightened state of arousal, he finally repositioned his body into a cowgirl position that would allow Erica to grasp his mighty rod.

Within a few seconds, she was on top of him and felt his large penis now engorged beneath her. Excited at the prospects of finally getting some hot sex from her boy-toy, suddenly everything came to a halt.

Brad stopped for a moment, then caught his breath. "*Shit,*" he thought annoyingly. Although he did expect to be laying Erica, he realized that he had a problem … a huge timing problem … a 40th birthday, *Oh shit problem.*

"Wait, Erica. I'm sorry, something just came up! I gotta text someone."

"You gotta do what? Now?"

As an extremely frustrated Erica eased back from her sex play, fingering herself in climax-limbo, Brad grabbed his cell phone and texted an apology message.

> "Sorry babe, something came up.
> Can't make tonight.
> Talk tomorrow.
> Love, Brad."

Erica was beyond annoyed, assuming it was a "chick text," which really pissed her off. But she certainly needed to "get herself off," so she tried to ignore the interruption.

Once back to "business," and allowing a few minutes of recovery time, the sex-starved Erica and the A-hole Brad came together, and Brad totally forgot about Sara, the 40th birthday dinner, and even the apology text.

"Damn, you were good tonight, Brad … even with the bullshit text."

"Hell, that was great," a now very content Brad thought uncaringly.

24

KARAOKE KILLERS

*S*ara was usually in charge of setting up the "'girls' night out" *and no one objected, as she always had a new slant of fun stuff, making the evenings enjoyable, informational and, mostly, unbelievable. Tonight, it was singer Sara's favorite entertainment. They would meet at the highly enjoyable and never boring, Karibbean Karaoke, in downtown Oakland. Yeah, the name … we assumed the owner just liked alliteration. Had to be the only explanation for the best karaoke club in the Bay Area.*

Also, par for the course with these types of informal events was some high-spirited venting, complaining, or simply, guy-bashing. A great time to clear the air and point the blame for something, squarely where it should be pointed – the obnoxious men!

Nikki, Lina, and Jacqui all arrived at 9:00, with Sara already there, this time, so she could secure the large table in front of the stage. Sara was dressed in an ultra-sexy, black with rhinestone, deep-V sequin mini dress. She was looking hot!

Nikki was in a striking burgundy crisscross neck bodycon dress showing the dark beauty's cleavage from across the club. She was looking like the huntress, a literal sex magnet.

Lina had a floral print halter ruffle-hem maxi dress and looked enchanting. Sara gave her a "thumbs up" as soon as she saw Lina.

Jacqui wore a white lace trim cutout puff sleeve plunge dress leaving nothing to the imagination. Two images could be drawn from the looks of our beauties tonight. Either they were hunting men, big time, or they owned the place. Unfortunately, neither image nor supposition was true.

Sara was all set for the evening. She was so well organized; several of the songs were selected by Sara, to reflect each girl's personality or alter ego. Tonight, the four lovely singers just shared a pitcher, or two, or three of some good Irish Brew.

"Okay, ladies, I'm gonna lead off with *Black Velvet* by Alannah Myles." The girls all smiled, as Sara always opened with the same song. She was magnificent and brought a standing ovation at 9:15. Not bad. Sara gave the girls the details of the bad 40th birthday of Brad's and her encounter with Rob at the "open house" sex party.

"Yep, ladies, when we say 'private open house,' there were at a lot of women opening their own privates!"

"Boo. Bad joke, Sara."

"Sorry, Lina. Why don't you go next?"

Lina preferred to go last, but it was too late to pass. She picked *I Will Survive* by Gloria Gaynor and did a nice job. Upon returning, filling her beer glass, she gave sketchy details regarding Mike and the STD, and when she started to describe some of the hurt from her uncle's abuse, Nikki stepped in to change the subject by grabbing the mic for her first song.

Ladies, I'm going to do *Billie Jean* by Michael Jackson. The girls applauded as Nikki just killed the song. The men in the karaoke ballroom were impressed by a very sexy African American beauty belting out Michael Jackson and with a "moon walk" to beat!

When she finished, she gave the girls the update on her romancing getaway with Kim, and her most exciting encounter with Dr. Dawn Baker.

"Past life regression is so cool, Nikki."

"Yeah, Sara, I am very excited to continue this journey with the good doctor."

With the process of elimination, Jacqui knew she was up next. "How's this, guys? I'm gonna do *Bad Romance* by Lady Gaga. That brings back memories of the night we all met."

Sara whistled her approval. "You go, girl."

Following a spirited performance, Jacqui felt it was a good time to give her friends the lowdown on her early sexual encounter with James Johnson, so she picked the European incident with the light bondage on the office desk and even some exclusive details regarding the alleged "soiree" with Putin.

"So, it really happened, Jacqui?"

"Let me say this about that. We met a couple times. They called me *Putin's Princess,* but nothing could be proven, as I was using the alias, Anastasia Ivanov."

"Cool," Lina uttered. "Tell us more."

"Not tonight. It's worth a long conversation. Maybe next time, okay?"

"Sure," Sara chimed in. "Lina has *Wannabe* by Spice Girls. Lina, you're up."

Lina did very well with the upbeat song, and when she was done, she gave the girls the update on her main squeeze, Gabe. All the girls had their fingers crossed that this would eventually work out.

Nikki then took the stage and belted out *Born this Way* by Lady Gaga. She got another standing 'O' from the guys, and wasn't the least bit bashful to throw out a few "thumbs up" to the guys in the front row.

"The tall guy with the neat beard is quite a hunk," Nikki uttered.

"Damn right," Sara added enthusiastically. Nikki went on to describe her "stand-up" sex with the pool boy, Dick. It got a few laughs, but Sara thought specifically, "*Hey, gotta keep that in mind. I have a hottie pool boy back at my condo that is worth a look and feel.*"

Jacqui then announced, "I'm next with *My Own Worst Enemy* by Pink." It was super and Jacqui was pumped. Nikki had bridged the topic of the sex orgy to all the girls already, so Jacqui thought it fitting to put a little more info onto the sexy mess that Nikki had experienced.

Once all the girls' glasses were filled, Jacqui began to explain a few details, some of which involved her.

"Regarding the men's sex club and the orgy that Nikki was deceived into attending," Jacqui blurted, "I had been there before, both as an observer and as a stage victim. By then, James entire moral compass was defunct. I was a piece of meat and he enjoyed showing me off."

The girls all were quiet. "Our first two years of marriage were actually quite good. Our personal life, our social life, and our sex life were all terrific. Then, something happened with him … I don't know what, but, from then on, I was his sexual possession."

"Did you get paid at the orgy?"

"Sara!" Nikki was blunt.

"Just asking."

"Probably, Sara, but the money just went into some obscure account. Current membership is some very old, wealthy, white guys, with teeny weenies that have gone inert." The girls laughed. "Just a sad vehicle for these old farts to get off while tramping on poor young women's souls."

Nikki was awash with emotions. From her actual experience, to her talk with Portia, this was an event in her life that would not go away. She was forming a plan, or two.

The night flew by and the girls were tired but thoroughly enjoyed the collaborative banter coming with these get-togethers. Several guys tried to get to know the fab four, but that wasn't part of the plan for this night, for sure.

As the ladies gathered their things, Sara concluded the eight-song set with "*Dancing Queen*" by Abba.

It was a very special night and Sara was pleased at how it worked out. She thought to herself as they left the club, "***Girls just wanna have fun.***"

25

LINA LOUNGES

I t was spring of 2021 and San Francisco was slowly coming out of COVID-19 restrictions. While many people were in some degree of lockdown and the fortunate could work from home, Lina was doing both in her lonely apartment.

Twice each week, she would volunteer, either at the food bank in Oakland, or in one of many of the city's COVID-19 testing facilities. When time permitted, she also helped out at the local shelter for abused women.

Arriving home one afternoon and booting up her laptop, she kicked off her shoes and sat back on the couch. There were no important emails and she had already returned several text messages, mostly with Sara or Nikki.

She had been sweating all afternoon; it had been an unusually warm day in the City. She pulled off her soaked blouse and threw it on the floor. She reached between her legs and felt her warm, wet sex core.

"Pussycat, you need a bath."

With that self-evident mention, Lina walked into her bathroom and drew a hot bath. As she disrobed, she added a generous scoop of coconut oil to the bath for its moisturizing benefit with some Epson salts to soothe the muscles.

Slowly entering her bath, she was getting relaxed and comfortable. While many women preferred showers, she assumed, Lina just loved the warm, sensual bath.

She tied up her hair to keep it dry and gently washed her face and neck. While she spread her tired legs in the tub, she began to wash and slowly massage her small, but perky, pale breasts. Taking a deep breath, she fingered her now relaxed vagina and slightly pulsing clitoris.

Picking up her small, waterproof rechargeable power wand and warming it in the water, she slowly inserted it into her vagina and set the power level at low, just to help to relax her body. *"Every woman should have a bullet or wand,"* she murmured.

Her mind was finally free of the sorrow and grief from these weekly encounters, draining Lina of all things safe and normal.

She worried about the hundreds, if not thousands, of impacted men, women, and children she saw regularly, but Lina also got some satisfaction from knowing she was one of the care workers helping those needy people.

Her thoughts then flicked to a Latino guy she had worked with at several of these events and who had indicated an interest in a date with her.

"Damn," she thought angrily, *"the bastard turned out to be married!"*

With the thought still lingering, she tried to get her mind back on the inviting bath and to caressing her lovely body. She added more hot water to the bath, closed her eyes, and thought nothing but good thoughts.

After nearly forty-five minutes of bathing, Lina stood up, grabbed a towel, and dried off, leaving the bathroom draped in her towel.

She slowly walked over to the computer ... nothing new. Cell phone ... nothing new.

She walked into the kitchen, poured a glass of whatever red wine was left over from last night, and proceeded to her bedroom with her cell phone in hand.

Lina was now in the mood for sex. Solo sex would have to do, but self-pleasuring was now becoming an art form for Lina.

She placed her wine on the nightstand, secured an aloe oil for lubrication, and checked to see if her trusty and often-used *She-Wand* rechargeable vibrating massager was fully charged. With ten speeds and fifteen different vibrating patterns, this was God's gift to self-sex.

Lina also had a newly acquired chic necklace that had a long, thin pendant that doubled as a USB recharging vibrator. Even her friend Nikki was impressed with the big performance in such a small, sexy package.

Her twice-weekly routine was about to begin. She chose her favorite smooth jazz playlist and began the set with her Wi-Fi speaker next to the bed. She preferred smooth jazz for solo sex for two reasons.

First, the heart-rending melody was soothing for Lina and allowed her to disconnect from the stress rather easily.

Second, Lina could prepare herself with each tract to take the driving force of the rhythmic pulse to an explosive crescendo, usually eighteen to twenty minutes into the stimulation.

As the music flowed, Lina would lay back on her pillow, softly pinching her hardening nipples with a dab and scent of the aloe lube, and spread her legs, slightly hiking them so she could see the reflection of her genitalia in the standing mirror.

Next to her was her jelly double dildo, which she could bend for multiple uses. She spent a few minutes getting the moist dildo inserted to her liking, and then began her pulsating vibrator properly addressing her G-spot.

As she slowly circled her folds with finger and thumb, her body heat was rising and her mindset was focusing on only pleasurable thoughts … a fantasy lover.

"I can see you. I just cannot touch you."

With a beautiful fantasy man in her mind, one often recurring in her thoughts and dreams, she spoke with eyes closed.

"Please go all the way … take me!"

At the eighteen-minute mark, she came hard and fast. The highly expected and pulse-charging crescendo was worth the time and effort.

She screamed, "**YES!**"

26

NIKKI NOCTURNAL

Nikki got a text message from Lina at midnight, following Lina's solo love making.

"Hey, GF, you up?"

Moments later …

"Hi, L. Me up? U kno I'm a night owl."
"Yep. Figured. Call?"
"Sure."

Lina called Nikki.

"Just needed to talk. Sorry to bother you."

"Sweetie, you can never bother me. You are a very special person and a dear friend. What's going on this late?"

"Nikki, all this volunteer stuff is getting to me. Between the virus and the racial unrest, gotta say my tank is about empty," Lina said with resolve.

"Hear ya, girl. I'm here to listen."

"And tonight, I had another date with myself, and you know how those go."

"Sure do, Lina. Good self-sex and then you want the real thing."

"I guess."

"Any guys in Lina's life these days?"

"Well, Gabe Suarez is the only decent guy I'm seeing right now, but intimacy, so far, has not been in the cards."

"Is Gabe good in bed? Is he affectionate?"

103

"It's a hard question to answer, as we only had one night together. I did sense he was uncomfortable, but I couldn't tell if it was because of me or if he was just inexperienced. And I don't have a lot of experience myself, which is a problem."

"Lina, you have been with other men. Details, please?"

"Fine. His kisses were kind of sloppy. He tried to French kiss, which sucks. Pardon the pun. His penis is kind of normal size, I guess, because I haven't seen that many." Pausing, "And he came quickly, almost before I got my clothes off."

"Shit. Not good."

"Nope. But, Nikki, my dad always says that good is the enemy of better."

"Can't argue with that logic, Lina."

"So, my orgasm wasn't even on the night's menu. He was nothing like the men in those erotic romance novels I've read. But I know they are fiction. Men like Rhett Butler, Count Vronsky and Christian Grey don't exist in real life."

"Who the hell is Count Vronsky?"

"Oh, the leading man in Tolstoy's *Anna Karenina*. I read a lot."

Laughing, Nikki said crisply, "That may be one of your problems, young lady. You need to get out more and get some good sexual experience." Nikki paused. "And, I think I know who we need to fix you up with."

"No way. No blind dates."

"Believe me, Lina, what I have in mind is no blind date. Blind fate, maybe!"

"Hey I'm good, Nikki," Lina offered.

"No Lina, I have an idea," Nikki announced excitedly.

"Shoot."

"Have you heard about Ramon?"

"Nope." Pausing, "Who is Ramon?"

"Sweetie, Ramon Gilbert is a guy, a really nice guy, who thinks that making love to a woman is an art form."

"Confused, I am, Nikki."

"Okay. First, would you be willing to have sex with a stranger, say Ramon, with only my recommendation?"

"Hell yeah, Nikki. Of course, you live and work with 'high end' people, both men and women. I trust you and your judgement. Sure."

"Let me contact Ramon. Girl, a night with him will make all your sex problems disappear, at least for a little while," responded Nikki assuredly. "And, it will give you a new and special 'baseline' for future sexual experiences."

"Nikki, thanks. I will look forward to a night with Ramon."

"I'll set it up, Lina. We good?"

"Yep, Nikki. Goodnight … and thanks."

"Night."

Nikki knew she would be able to arrange an unforgettable sex night for her friend. But on this night, what Nikki was working on when Lina texted was quite different.

Nikki, as the assistant D.A. in San Francisco, had been working on a criminal case that started with the grand jury case of billionaire James Johnson, but it was now involving several high-ranking politicians, bankers, and well-known San Francisco businessmen and women. Domino effect!

The data and files Nikki perused were as incriminating as anything she had ever worked on. Yeah, the old saying about not being able to put the toothpaste back in the tube was in play.

It was now well past midnight and Nikki would have liked to do some solo sex, too. She was just too damn tired.

"Tomorrow, I will contact Ramon and call a guy for a date for myself."

Thinking out loud, "Maybe I should go to some busy guy bar and get picked up."

Looking at her strikingly beautiful body in her bedroom mirror, and touching herself in all the right places …

"Why the hell not!"

27

NIKKI KNOWS BETTER

E arly in Nikki's career, she had a torrid affair with a fellow attorney who was working in San Francisco at the time they met. This is the relevant background story of the incident that started a tempestuous and reckless love/hate relationship.

This chance meeting followed a stressful courtroom encounter where Nikki and Logan were at opposite sides of a battle between the state of California's CARB environmental issues versus the federal government's mandates. There was some common ground for Logan and her to pursue, and they discussed this over coffee at a nearby Starbucks kiosk inside the office building.

"Nikki, you always do your research."

"Thank you, Logan, and you are always prepared."

As they left the coffee shop, Logan stopped in front of a small library, seldom used, and unexpectedly took Nikki by her arm, drew her close to him, and planted a wet, sloppy kiss on the surprised attorney.

"Logan!"

"I'm sorry … no I'm not. Damn, girl, I find you so sexy and so attractive. Let's sneak into this room so we can talk, okay?"

Nikki, smiling but confused, said, "Fine. Let's talk about this."

They walked into the library, both glancing to assure themselves of solitude. Logan again kissed Nikki, and this time she didn't hesitate to wrap both arms around Logan and brought him even closer to her warming body.

"God, Nikki, you're beautiful!"

Nikki thought cautiously, *"A smart girl … a well-known attorney, would walk away from this temptation. She would say she had clients waiting and head right back out the door."*

But no. "Thank you, handsome man."

As she stared directly into the beautiful blue eyes of Logan, the dragoness slayer, she lamented, "*I shouldn't be standing in a public room with a man I barely know, but I'm still liking the way he has taken charge of this moment.*"

"I can hear you thinking," he softly whispers, tightening his hold on Nikki's waist. "Let's just go for it. Play along with me for now."

That was exactly what Nikki needed to hear, as she relaxed her shoulders and let her head clear. The initial tension melted from her body as she leaned into him. Even though she was in heels and he was inches above her, Nikki lifted her chin and he was there, with the tips of their noses touching.

"I don't usually do this," she said, lost in an impression of a one-night-stand.

"Do what?" Logan asked carefully.

"Letting a sexy stranger think he can do whatever he wants with me. I hardly even kiss on the first date."

She closed her eyes and swallowed, opening them to find him smiling down at the alluring attorney in his lovely grasp.

"I believe you, but I am not really a stranger. Sexy, maybe, but stranger … no way."

He pressed his thigh between her legs and Nikki could feel how hard he was already! She enjoyed the small shifts of his hips as he rocked gently against her body.

"I want you, Nikki," he mumbled while kissing her in a wonderfully delicate manner, like nothing a big and strong man might do. He pulled back, licked his lips, and then moved forward again, moaning softly into Nikki's open mouth, "Can I have you?"

"Now? Here?" Nikki's heart pounded, sending sexy vibes throughout her body.

He nods into another soft kiss. "Here, yes, while we are alone and before anyone comes in. We may have to be quick."

At that moment, it felt like someone lit a match inside Nikki's chest and she wrapped her fingers into the fabric of his shirt. He followed without a word, kissing Nikki while removing her blazer. She could feel every inch of clothing that separated them. Frantic hands removed all bothersome clothing that was in the way of sexual reeling.

As they were both naked from the waist down, and both could see that she was wet and willing and he was rock hard, Nikki asked, "Here, on this table?"

"Yes, one of my favs, the 'Standing O' position."

With that, he cupped her face and gave her a warm and wet kiss. She was all in. He then laid her on the small conference table, reached for a seat cushion and placed the cushion near the bottom of her back, slipping it under her buttocks.

"Thank you. Soft is good."

The cushion lifted her pelvis slightly and, facing Nikki, he grasped her ankles tenderly and placed her legs gently on his massive shoulders.

Nikki was panting and more than ready for his entrance. He slowly glided his fully engorged erection into her waiting core, and with this position, he could achieve deeper penetration and the opportunity to target her G-spot more effectively.

Clamping her channel walls on his manliness, Nikki uttered, "Oh yes, slowly, Logan. You are so close. I can feel your tip."

"You feel so good, Nikki" as he slowed his thrusts and took a short breath before going deep again. She convulsed against his body, totally immersed in his movements and close to peaking.

"Oh God," she says, on the edge of something sensuous tingling at her core and her legs trembling. She put her hands in his hair as his hips slowly rocked to the beat of her heart. With a slight groan, she looked down to watch, nearly losing it at the sight of his mighty manhood consuming her feminine jewels.

"Look at me now," she says breathless. "I am so close … so close. I want us to come together."

"God yes, Nikki," he mutters as he lifts her slightly for a better angle. His hair is a mess and color blooms across his cheekbones and down his neck. She is so wet that any additional stimulation could ignite her to sexual peak. She dug her nails into his shoulders.

With a gasp, he lifted his head taking a couple deep and steadying breaths. "I need a second," and held her hips still. She moaned and whimpered in total sexual bliss.

When he straightened up, he placed his hands around Nikki's neck and with one last thrust, they both felt the tempest together, in a mutual climax shaking the table, and even with slightly muffled sounds, responses surely were heard close by.

They embraced and enjoyed the next few minutes of cool, calm serenity.

This was a spontaneous fantasy come true for both grateful sexual partners!

RAMON REIGNS

veryone knew Ramon. The ladies loved him and the guys, kind of didn't. You see, he was every girl's bedtime fantasy. If you ever wanted to put yourself in the hands of a man whose sole purpose was to give you pleasure, Ramon was your one-stop man.

He had a particular skill, which I'm told goes back to when he was a frat guy and lived in an upper garage apartment behind the fraternity house.

His old friend and fraternity brother David described this college guy's sexcapades to me.

"Ramon's real name was Ralph. Enough said. He was about 5' 10" tall, good looking, and he had a nice, athletic body. His love for the ladies was all that mattered."

"Love as in sex?" I asked.

"Well, yes and no, Jon. Whether his performance ended in sex was immaterial. To Ramon, the journey with his 'woman of the day' was far more important than the sex destination."

"Well, David, you got me interested."

"His mission was to make the woman as happy sexually as he could. Period! Whether it was fulfilling her immediate sexual needs or helping her to live an erotic fantasy, Ramon was locked and loaded."

David paused. "Let me give you a typical example in a second."

"Fine. That would be great."

"First, he was a Sig Tau and his frat was made up almost entirely of jocks. They always won in interfraternity sports and always lost the annual Greek Sing."

"And that is relevant … why?"

"Well, Ramon was also a thespian. He loved acting and was in many plays at the university. Because his frat looked at men who did acting stuff as homos or sissies, Ramon used his real name of Ralph so no one at his fraternity ever found out!"

"The guy had a plan, right David?"

"A plan, a purpose, a mission, Jon. Now the example."

"Say Ramon had a date with Sue tonight. He would check with me, his apartment roommate, to see if I would give him the place for the night."

"So, you and he shared the above-garage apartment?" Jon was getting into this exposé.

"Yes. That's why I am the guy with the story. And Ramon was a super great guy. Just different, but in a good sort of way."

"Go on."

"Ramon has a date with Sue, probably a concert or dinner or both, and then back to our place. Ramon drove an Amazon Green Porsche 911 that was easily recognizable around campus."

"I can relate to that car, for sure," Jon replied emphatically.

"Ramon has already written a fairly special poem for Sue, just for her with her name and rhyming and all those specific details. And a really good poem. He was into that stuff."

"I like him even more, being a writer."

"Got it. So, he would fix her a drink of her choice … one he had already planned to make, and then would go into his bedroom to prepare for the lovemaking."

"Hell. I'm getting aroused."

"He had this technique so well planned that it only took about ten minutes to set the stage."

"Maybe I should be taking notes, David," Jon said impatiently.

"Damn, it couldn't hurt."

"He walks out of his bedroom holding a beautiful black silk robe with an aroma of a burning candle. If Sue takes the robe, it's game on for Ramon."

"So, David, they usually take the robe?"

"Usually? Shit, no. Always!"

Smiling, David continues. "He has her change in the bathroom, which also gives his date some time to 'freshen up.' This guy is a fricking genius."

"Okay, David, so you can't tell me about the sex; can you describe the bedroom?"

"Of course. I have "Sexual Healing 101" embedded in my brain. The date enters the bedroom, gets the poem as Ramon recites the poem, and she is hypnotized by his deep voice as she sits mesmerized on the edge of the bed. Ramon is now wearing only the finest Italian pure silk boxers that would likely cost about $150 a pair today."

"Damn, David, even I don't spend that on boxers."

"Well, Ramon would say that you don't wrap something special in anything other than something special," getting a laugh from both guys.

"Now, Jon, remember the scent of the robe?" I nodded.

"Well, the scent on the robe is from the dozen or so scented candles surrounding the bed. They were three-wick candles that had a burn time of forty-five minutes and just filled the room. Not too strong ... not too light ... just right."

"Holy shit."

"Jon, you wanted the details."

"Anything else, David?" as Jon took a grasp of his penis.

"Oh yeah, the *piece de resistance.*"

Ramon would have two choices of soft, sensual music playing.

"He had music, too?"

"Damn straight. This guy just thought of everything."

David continued with his own style of crescendo. "Either the soothing sounds of rain on the classic album, *The Sea*, or highly intoxicating music of *The Mystic Moods Orchestra.*"

Jon was fascinated by David's description. This guy was truly special.

"You know, David, this approach is really 'old school' and not like any of today's trends."

David responded, "I totally agree, but ..."

"But what?"

"I agree that this technique, or whatever you want to call it, is old school or old fashioned, but I don't know of one modern-day woman who would object or otherwise refuse such personal attention. And, he's providing such female pleasure from a guy whose end-game is to make the lady feel like she is the most appealing woman in the universe and not someone's sex toy."

"Well put, David."

"I think that's part of the magic, Jon, and you want to know the best part?"

"Sure. This is amazing!"

"I never recall any woman leaving our apartment until after breakfast the next day, and Ramon never had the same girl over twice!"

"Was he fairly well-off? Had to be to have that kind of green and time to spend."

"Jon, you would think so, but no. Ramon had a double major, raced his Porsche on the local tracks, and held down two part-time jobs. He put himself through college with no financial help from his family!"

"What a guy, Dave. Thanks for sharing this with me. I now have a much better impression of this guy and I want to meet him."

"Here's an old dog that ... that needs some new tricks!"

29

LUNCH, LAUGHTER,
LESSONS LEARNED

Abbout a week or two after the Power Pit evening, Sara arranged for the five girls to get together for lunch and talk a little more about themselves and their plans. As I recall, Sara was doing a video shoot downtown and met the girls at a popular sushi bar on Washington Street.

"Hi ladies, it's good to see you. Glad sushi works for us. This place is busy for a reason."

Nikki commented first, "Yeah, Sara, I have friends that have told me about this place. Great to finally get over here."

Lina was on her phone as she walked up to the other two girls. As she finished her call, Sara asked if anyone had heard from Jacqui.

At that moment they all got a group text confirming Jacqui to be about ten minutes away.

Nikki glanced at the door and then spoke.

"Hey, I've done a little digging and Jacqui Johnson has gone through some hell with that bastard husband of hers. Even though she hides it well, I'm sure she is struggling big time."

"I agree," responded Sara affirmatively. "I've heard similar accounts."

"Let's just let her talk and we listen for now."

"Good idea, Lina," Nikki nodded, with a smile. "We're here for her whenever."

As they were perusing the menu, Jacqui walked quickly to their table. "Sorry I'm late. Had another damn lawyer call to take."

"Hey, we're in no hurry," replied Sara softly. "Except for Nikki, who likely has someone to prosecute."

"Damn, I'm sorry." Sara said without thinking. "Bad choice of words."

"Sara, it's okay," Jacqui replied. "It is what it is. Let's eat!"

Once their orders were in, Sara chimed in with their basic lunch agenda.

"Jacqui, we usually just bullshit for an hour or so, but do some 'venting' in the meantime … totally voluntary."

Jacqui nodded as Sara continued.

"I've got an author friend who I'm working with on a streaming or series TV project. He is convinced that his work is good enough and maybe it is. And I sing lead for an acoustic band that plays often in the valley."

"What's the name of the band?" Jacqui asked.

"*Tempest*. It used to be *Shock the Monkey*, from the Peter Gabriel song, but we couldn't use it without his permission and he said, no, of course."

"Cool name, Sara."

"Thanks, Jacqui."

Nikki piped in with her usual drama, "I have a tremendous criminal case. It's so exciting, but I can't tell you guys about."

"Nothing new there," Lina offered nonchalantly.

"But," Nikki continued, "I do have something for Lina."

Lina glanced at Nikki with an appreciative smile.

"Sara, I think you know Ramon, right?"

"Shit yeah, Nikki, the Prince of Darkness, in a really good way. He rocks!"

"Have you ever spent a night with him, Sara?"

"No, unfortunately. I'm told he can get inside you both physically and into your fantasies and make your sexual pleasure a reality and make your deepest and most secret fantasies come true."

"Hey, I know Ramon," Jacqui advised. "Gotta admit, though, I didn't know his skill set at the time we met."

"Then," Lina said hesitantly, "I guess I'm the only one who doesn't know this Prince."

"Well, you will, Lina. He has your number and will be calling you."

"Lucky girl," replied Sara.

"Thanks, I guess, Nikki. When?"

"Lina, that will be entirely up to you and your schedule."

Lina thought appreciatively, *"I'm glad I mentioned my solo sex to Nikki. Now I have a real guy to replace the one in my head."*

As the sushi was being served, Jacqui was thinking of Jon; Sara was thinking of bad boy Brad; and Nikki still had number seventeen's sweet ass on her mind.

"Guys," Lina uttered, "I do have a writing project starting soon, and you might be interested in hearing about it."

"All ears," Sara advised.

"I'm writing a mature adult romance novel."

"Wait a minute," Nikki said crisply. "That's way outside your sweet spot."

"It is Nikki … most definitely."

"What's it about?' Jacqui inquired, looking directly at Lina.

"It's about men behaving badly, and even though it will be a fictional piece, it will be based on actual events and stories, which I plan to research from friends and associates. I'll call it *Charade in the City!*"

"Kind of like men's bullshit on parade," Jacqui offered.

"Yep," Lina replied, enjoyably.

Sara glanced over to both Nikki and Jacqui and muttered to Lina, "You can sign me up!"

"Us, too, right Jacqui?"

"For sure." The ladies toasted each other to another typical night together.

Thinking about her own experiences with men, Sara thought about her latest disappointments.

"It's just their jive talking."

30

PORTIA'S
PREDICAMENT

That night, Portia phoned Nikki while Nikki was with the girls and left a voice message for her to return the call. Nikki did, and they set a time on the upcoming Friday to meet at Nikki's office. Nikki was apprehensive, not knowing what the hell was coming.

Friday afternoon came and Nikki's secretary welcomed Portia to their office and announced, "Nikki, your 2:00 is here."

"Thanks, Barb; send her in."

Portia is a striking beauty, likely 30 to 35 years old, roughly 5' 6" with dark hair, nice cleavage, long legs, and dressed expensively in a dark gray pencil skirt suit set.

She approaches Nikki slowly, smiles, and extends her hand.

"Hello, Miss Wallace. Thanks for seeing me."

"Hi Portia, please just call me Nikki.

The young lady is wearing tons of bling. Nikki thinks amusingly, *"Crap, the diamonds could be weighed in pounds, not carats."*

"Please have a seat. Can I get you anything?"

"No, thanks. Your secretary Barb already offered. She's very pleasant."

"Yes, she is."

After Portia took a seat, Nikki got right to the point. "We talked briefly during our first chat, Portia; now let's get into some detail, shall we?"

"Of course. First, I am what you would call a gold digger, I suppose. I married this guy for the money and social opportunities. He put me through Cal State Fullerton for my undergraduate degree and UCLA for my Masters.

Nikki was taking notes, and her opinion of Portia was swinging wildly.

"I have a computer science degree and a master's in economics, and the econ degree wasn't cheap, Nikki."

"I hear you and congratulations. And, Portia, mine is not to judge. So, why are you here?"

"Thank you. Nikki, I have three issues to discuss, and the first one concerns the women at the sex party. These women are not abused; far from it. As I think you know, girls get paid at least $5K to $10K for five hours of work."

"I remember you mentioned that before and I was shocked."

"And then there is *Queens Night.*"

Nikki took a deep sigh, tilted her head and looked up at Portia.

"Queens Night involves celebrities. Movie stars, wealthy foreign women, female business owners, etcetera. A famous Mexican actress received $100K three months ago for her appearance."

Nikki was stunned.

"They use masks, partial clothing, thongs to hide their tattoos, and piercing so they are unrecognizable."

"They still could get recognized, Portia?"

"Yes, but without photos, nothing the paparazzi can do."

"Cell phone photos are easy."

"You don't understand, Nikki. No cellphones, no cameras, and no recording devices are allowed. Period. Surveillance is incredible. If any photos were taken, that person would likely disappear."

"Seriously?"

"Just saying."

"Second is a Ponzi scheme alert regarding one of the members. This is the main reason I am here, and we need to be super cautious. I already told you a little when we first talked."

"Why see me now?"

"The red flag just went up for me because my husband is getting involved, and I don't want to be considered compliant. Co-conspirator doesn't go with my MBA and my other mission. Make sense?"

"Totally. Your other mission?"

"I'll get in to that shortly. My third need is for sex. I know you are bisexual."

Nikki reeled and scowled, "What? How?"

"Club members have a data base for every woman, guest, or performer, which basically includes sex toys and sexual tendencies."

Nikki put down her pen and looked up incredulously, thinking, "*WTF!*"

"Thomas provided your info under the alias of Michelle Marx, so you really don't need to worry about this database. By the way, the members were very unhappy that Thomas invited you, learning who you were. You won't be invited back."

"That's fine with me."

"People stared at me all night, why?"

"Didn't notice?"

"Notice what."

"You were the only African American there, and, as I said, you will not be invited back. The old white guy members don't want Blacks, Asians, or Hispanics, except for *Queen's Night.*

Pausing, and taking a deep sigh, Nikki had to get back to door number three, "Back to the sex issue?"

"My husband and I don't have sex. He buys me sex toys and mechanical stuff. Solo got old after the first year. I'm bi-sexual and he caught me having an affair, so now I get tailed. This meeting today at the courthouse is for me to get a 'ticket fixed.' Do you understand?"

"Understand."

"Back to you, Attorney Wallace. I'm gonna be upfront. I prefer sex with a woman and I would like to have sex with you. I am extremely attracted to you. Your power, your grace and your incredible beauty are most alluring, and I find you absolutely seductive."

Nikki's face got flushed, and heat rose up in her body. It was hard not to touch herself.

"If you were not interested, we could at least have pretended sex, if that would be better, as it would be a good time for me to pass along the Ponzi scheme info."

Nikki thought, approvingly, "*At least she's upfront and honest.*"

Many things came to her mind, but the idea of having exciting sex with this wealthy, intelligent, and sexy creature was a good thought, for now. Portia was hot!

"Nikki, please just think about it, okay?"

"I will. Now, your other mission, Portia?"

"I am a partner in a business dealing with hedge fund investments, and cryptocurrency transactions. The company is run by multi-millionaire lesbian women, and I am the Executive Vice President, handling crypto."

"Surely didn't see that coming. I'm impressed."

Portia reached into her purse for a black, monogramed case.

"Here's my business card."

On the front was:

Lesbian Economic Growth Society – LEGS.
Portia de Angelis, EVP – cryptocurrency
Portia@EVPLEGS.org

On the back was:

Focus your Vision Forward on what you Can Do ...
Not Back on what you cannot change.
Live the life you imagined!

"Nikki, LEGS is actually a lesbian millionaires' investment club."

Nikki just smiled. This was so far from what she had expected.

"So, we good for now, Nikki?"

"We are very good and I am looking forward to seeing you, and exploring a relationship."

"That's great. Thank you."

Nikki took Portia's hand, as Portia then moved purposely in front of Nikki, wrapped one arm around her neck and gently kissed Nikki on the lips and held it for a few moments.

"You taste good, Nikki."

Seconds later, Nikki smiled, thanked her, and then escorted her to the door. She closed the door, turned, took a deep breath, and gave a slight moan.

Walking back to her desk, she thought devilishly and determinedly ...

"So, Domme or sub with this beautifully real, erotic woman? Let's bring it on!"

31

PORTIA'S PORTAL

Nikki and Portia arranged a sex date, which Portia calls her *afternooner*, and Portia arrived to pick Nikki up at 4:00 p.m. at Nikki's downtown office. They had arranged that she would text Nikki when she was curbside and, per the text, she would be driving a white sports car.

She texted Nikki who arrived at Portia's waiting car in a few minutes.

"Oh my God, this car is incredible. What is it? Oh, and 'hi' Portia."

"Hi Nikki. It's a Ferrari Roma … referred to as the 'gentlewoman's Ferrari.' It's fun."

"I love the lipstick-red interior. You have a great car!"

"Sorry, but it's not mine. I'm a Bimmer girl. This awesome ride belongs to a good friend of mine."

"Some friend, who would let you borrow this ride."

As they drove off, "Well, this lady friend does some contract work for our firm, so we do spend some time together."

"What kind of contract work?"

"Can't really get into her work, Nikki. Sorry."

"No problem. Must be interesting. Why not drive your car?"

"I told you my husband has a tail on me."

"Yes, I remember you mentioned it."

"So, by switching cars, my BMW is still at home in the garage, and my handy-dandy detective is likely eating donuts in his black four-door domestic car."

Both girls laughed as they continued to Portia's office.

"I would have preferred dinner with you, Nikki, but I can't really jeopardize our meeting or meetings. Believe me, I would love to do dinner and have my evening free with you."

"Thank you and I totally understand, Portia."

Several minutes later, the girls drive up to Salesforce Tower on Mission Street, where a valet greets the girls.

"Your office is here at Salesforce Tower?"

"Yes, we have two floors here, 57 and 58. The building has 61 floors."

"Holy crap," Nikki thought puzzled by what she was seeing. *"This is gonna be some experience!"*

The ladies went up to the 57th floor, and when they walked in, the receptionist greeted Portia. "Hello, Miss de Angelis."

"Hello, Mandy."

"My, you are looking radiant."

"Thank you, Mandy."

Portia led Nikki to her office, and a breathtaking view that made Nikki's public servant office look like an outhouse. *Sorry. Outhouse might be a poor description, but you get the idea.*

As they entered her office, Portia advised, pointing to matching leather wing-back chairs, "Please make yourself comfortable."

As Nikki sat down, another woman walked into the office. She appeared to be in her fifties, about 5' 10" tall, ash blonde hair, and wearing a dark gray long-sleeve peplum sheath dress.

Extending her hand, she introduced herself, "Hello, I'm Cherise Shandell, and I'm pleased to meet you, Miss Wallace."

Extending her hand, Nikki simply replied, "It is an honor to meet the former U.S. ambassador to Italy. Your work there was well-known, and our relationship with Rome and the Vatican was never better than while you were there."

"Why, thank you. That was years ago, Miss Wallace. Now I am the *face of LEGS.*"

Portia was amused and chuckled slightly.

"Please call me Nikki."

"Fine. Nikki, I am the head of admin here and primarily tend to the PR and international needs."

"You can also call Cherise our 'den mother,'" Portia adds. "She keeps us girls in line."

"Complete with whistle and striped shirt?" Nikki asked amusingly.

"Some truth to that," Cherise added with a smile. "The lounge is ready, Portia, whenever you two are done here."

Giving the irresistibly attractive Nikki a penetrating once-over, Cherise added coolly, "Again, Nikki, it was nice meeting you and I hope to see you again. I'll leave you ladies for now."

"Thank you," responded a somewhat overwhelmed Nikki Wallace, thinking, *"Cherise is one intimidating woman. I'd would love to see her in action."*

♥   ♥   ♥

As Nikki and Portia headed over to the company lounge, Nikki saw a busy, professional, and all-female staff, all dressed to the nines and all young to middle-age. No men and no social mingling. Portia showed Nikki inside and then stepped out for a minute.

"Make yourself comfortable. I'll only be a minute."

Nikki was shocked at what she saw. If there was such a thing as a "man cave," this was the "woman's cave." Beautiful artwork, sculptures, luscious leather furniture, a massive bar, and even a media center with audio and visual equipment – everything quite impressive. Portraits of a *Women's Who's Who* in many fields of endeavor adorned an entire wall.

As Nikki looked down to turn off her cell phone, she was getting excited and wondered, *"I can easily feel the sexual magnetism for Portia, but what else here is worth studying?"*

From just outside the office, Cherise met with Portia. "We have the room all set up. Let us know if you need anything. She is a gorgeous woman, Portia. I am exceedingly jealous."

"Yes, she is. But today is about building some trust."

"I know."

"I have my agenda and the sex is just what I need, I think, to break the ice. She is a pretty incredible person in her own right."

"Of course. Is there more here than just the sex, Portia?"

Not wanting to tip her hand regarding the Ponzi scheme, "Not sure, Cherise."

"Fine. I have your drinks coming. Your usual white wine and her fav, as we were told, a 2015 Napa red Silver Oak Cabernet Sauvignon. We also laid out two vibrators that we know she likes."

"Thank you, Cher. You did great and I appreciate your help and trust."

"What about the cameras?"

"All cameras off, Cherise. This isn't why we have them."

"Thought so. They are already off."

"Cherise ... the recording devices?"

"Also, off."

"Thanks, Cher. I'll let you know how things go."

With that, Portia went back into the ladies' lounge to find a puzzled and perplexed Nikki.

"This is the tip of one huge fricking iceberg," Nikki thought unexpectedly.

32

PORTIA'S PASSION

"Do you come here often?" Nikki asked with a wink?

"Only to relax and get away. This is actually the first time this lounge has been used for my personal needs. Maybe not the last."

As she spoke, a knock on the door indicated that the wine had arrived.

With full glasses of wine, both girls toasted and began to get better acquainted. Within 45 minutes, it was apparent that both women were ready to take their discussion to the next level – physical appreciation.

Portia led Nikki to another room, this one a private bedroom area meant for one thing and one thing alone – sex!

"Oh my, this is incredible," Nikki exclaimed. "I may never go home."

"Yes, this is where relaxation and enjoyment are the only thing on one's mind," Portia nodded as soft mood music played in the background.

A surprised Nikki looked at a nightstand displaying a variety of sex toys, lubes, and gels.

"I recognize a few of these; even the strap-on. I use this clitoral massaging gel," pointing to the Ultimate Passion brand.

"Nikki, I really can't wait another minute to feel you next to me, close to me."

Portia approached Nikki, put both arms around her neck, gave her a long-awaited kiss, and then gently stroked her hair. Nikki responded with a slight moan and placed one hand on Portia's butt and one hand on her hip.

As their lips were firmly enjoying the sweet, new tastes, their tongues explored playfully. Portia moved her hand from her hip to slide down to the hem of Nikki's skirt, and as Portia slipped her hand under the skirt, her palm grazed the soft skin of Nikki's bare thigh.

"Oh," Nikki gasped in utter enjoyment, breaking their long, wet and passionate kiss. Nikki let Portia's hand continue to roam, traveling over Nikki's noticeably warming body, feeling her shiver. One touch on Nikki's lace panties with Portia's gentle fingertips sent Nikki into a delightfully sensuous high.

"Wait," Nikki said abruptly. "Wait a moment, Portia."

"Why? What's wrong?"

"Nothing is wrong, Portia. Everything is right. I want to stop to undress you and have you undress me."

They stepped briefly apart. Portia thought fondly, *"She's in charge and I'm good with that."*

"Strip me naked, Portia. Slowly. I want to feel your touch on my body as you open my sex to you. Your fingertips are so soft and so sweet."

Portia unbuttoned Nikki's blouse unhurriedly and removed it, revealing a sexy bra bursting with two voluptuous breasts waiting to be touched. She groaned and unsnapped the lace bra and gently removed it, exposing perfect breasts, spilling out of the cups, with dark brown nipples that had already gotten firm.

"Touch my nipples. Caress them."

Portia did, and gently rolled her thumb and fore finger around her nipples, squeezing each nub so tantalizingly that Nikki pushed her breasts harder into Portis's hold.

"Suck my nipples, Portia. Suck them with your soft tongue." Portia placed her warm and wet mouth on Nikki's peaking buds and sucked softly, swirling her tongue, and giving Nikki an early sensation of what was yet to come.

She then unzipped Nikki's skirt and lowered it to the floor. Nikki kicked her shoes off so her skirt could be tossed away. What was left was a black thong, becoming wet from initial arousal. Nikki spread her legs slightly, took Portia's hand, and placed it on her pulsing groin. Taking Portia's other hand, she slid it down the back of the thong so Portia could easily remove it.

Nikki touched Portia's lips with her hand, gently swiped around their softness, and then delicately pressed her fingers into Portia's wide-open mouth, which Portia began sucking hungrily.

Nikki gave her another deep, heartfelt and persistent kiss that had Portia tingling. The kiss lasted a full minute, and Nikki smiled when they broke it off.

As Portia gazed at the stunningly beautiful African American goddess, she shed a slight tear. Noticing that, Nikki simply said in a soft and loving tone, "Please turn around."

Portia turned slowly, as Nikki began to undress her new lover from behind. Taking her time to piece by piece remove Portia's clothes, shoes, bra, and panties, she could hear a slight whimper from Portia. As Nikki cupped Portia's firm breasts, Portia let out a sharp moan.

"Are you okay?"

"Oh God, yes. Your touch is way beyond anything I expected. I love to have you touch me."

Nikki smiled, knowing that this journey would be special. "Now, dear Portia, spread your legs, bend over, and place your hands on the bed." She did and Nikki's blood began to boil. She began at Portia's shoulders, and then gently massaged her neck, back, getting to her luscious buttocks. When she kissed Portia's butt cheeks and ran her tongue between them, Portia gasped, "Oh yes."

"She has a perfect ass," Nikki thought noticeably. *"I love a women's sexy butt."*

Nikki then took her tongue on the same journey, licking, biting, and gently sucking Portia's naked body from her neck to her buttocks. Nikki crouched down, and once her tongue was near Portia's genitals, Portia gave out a loud gasp and Nikki continued on her possessive journey, feeling the heat radiating from Portia's warm body. She pulled Portia up and had her turn and lay prone on her back.

"Spread your legs, your beautiful long legs." With what was now a command, Nikki inserted two fingers into Portia's now dripping core. Moving her thumb and finger in a slow circle around her clit, she was so wet that Nikki pulled her fingers from Porta's vagina and placed them in her mouth first, and then into Portia's wide-open mouth.

Nikki spoke with a smile, "You taste so good."

"Do it again ... please, Nikki. Oh God, yes, Nikki. Do it again."

Nikki reinserted her fingers, swirled them around, and then placed them deeply into Portia's waiting mouth.

"Thank you for sharing my juices," as a little cry of surprise and excitement came gushing out from a very content Portia. "Please. Now, I want to feel your tongue deep inside me."

Nikki moved above Portia and straddled her in a purely cunnilingual position, with Nikki's open mouth and tongue just inches from Portia's waiting vagina. Nikki placed both arms under Portia's thighs and lifted them slightly, allowing her mouth to get close to Portia's core so she could insert her long tongue. Nikki raised her pelvis so Portia would need to wait to return the favor. Portia's view was as wicked as it was audacious. She wanted inside Nikki's love nest.

With Portia now aroused and on the verge of exploding, Nikki inserted her fingers deeply, to probe her sexual cavity to its fullest, seeking the tiny nugget meant to release her sexual essence. Once firmly with her finger and thumb on Portia's hard clit, Nikki lifted her head up, sensing a pre-climax feeling.

"Yes," Portia said suddenly. "Yes, you are right there. Roll it slowly … yes, now more quickly. Nikki knew that Portia was now very close.

"Faster. Roll it faster." Within seconds, Portia began to shake and erupted in an orgasm that surprised her. "Oh. Oh. God, yes," she screamed. "Keep your fingers there. Suck my crème. Suck, suck, suck!"

Nikki took her dripping fingers into her mouth, then gave Portia a taste of the still-wet digits. Once Portia had relaxed, Nikki turned and moved her body directly above Portia, spreading her legs with her core now only inches away from Portia's sex-soaked tongue.

"Yes, Nikki. Now I want you."

"Portia, I have never wanted a woman's mouth in my sex as much as I want you in mine – right now."

Portia wrapped her arms around Nikki's hips as her tongue searched for Nikki's wet jewels. The sound of Portia sucking the folds and lips of her lover was unmistakable; genuine lust from the now sexually relieved Portia.

As her tongue was rolling and licking and pulsing … Portia was overcome with sexual delight, thinking, "*This is a feeling of lust that I have ever felt before.*"

Within minutes, Nikki had reached a point that was clearly a summit for her, and Portia could sense her extreme arousal. Portia was getting even more aroused, thinking another orgasm was coming.

"You make me feel alive," Nikki said with a wavering voice. "You are a talented and giving lover." Portia continued sucking her passionately, then inserted her fingers into the pulsing love nest of the shimmering Nikki.

Nikki moaned at the feel of the purposely placed fingers on her hard clit, and she could sense that it would take almost nothing to send her off. She sighed as Portia built up the contact with more pressure on her bud and rapidly rotated her fingers.

"I can feel what you are feeling, dear Nikki. One more gentle squeeze on your nugget and I want to feel you come."

One more squeeze was all it took, plus the sexy encouragement from a satisfied Portia. Nikki exploded in screams that may have been heard outside the bedroom, but that didn't matter to either woman, as sexual paradise was reached.

"Portia ... dear Portia, yes!"

Portia had one thought: ***"I need more of this sexy woman. I want more, now!"***

33

NIKKI'S NUANCE

"I don't want you to leave yet, Nikki. Can we please continue to enjoy each other?"

Thinking out loud, "Well, Portia, our rather filthy sucking of each other, should not be what we both recall, eh?"

Portia smiled, "I was fine with old-school 69. So satisfied."

Nikki grinned and offered, "I do have an appointment." Nikki paused, and smiled. "But wait a minute." Nikki walked over to her bag, pulled out her phone, turned it on, and sent a text message:

> "Got my nose buried in some new biz.
> Move the meeting out 2 hrs."

"Okay, dear Portia, I'm here now and I want you again, too." Portia smiled.

Nikki just can't leave Portia after one heated sexual explosion. She took both of her hands, leaned in and gave her a warm kiss, sealing them together for another sensual moment. Nikki got excited, hearing her moan slightly, even with their lips locked. As their lips part, Portia moved her head back slowly and Nikki could see the contour of her neck and can feel her beating pulse.

Nikki gently ran her fingers over Portia's hard nipples, and she leaned into Nikki's soft touch. "Oh, Nikki, you are so soft and so gentle."

Nikki then teased her pebbled nipples, lightly squeezed the taut tips, and a contented and grateful Portia gave off a loving gasp, and dug her nails into Nikki's shoulders. Nikki responded to Portia's loving pant by trailing her mouth up Portia's neck until she nibbled lightly on her ear.

"I want you, Portia," she whispered softly. As Portia's hands slipped around Nikki's waist and pulled her close, she moaned, "Then take me, Nikki," as her sputtering voice made Nikki's quickening pulse rise.

Nikki felt a sweet ache between her legs, and the heating of her core flared. While wanting to enjoy the moment, the sexual anticipation was rapidly growing. Nikki sensed that she was losing control and commanded, "Lean forward and put your hands on the wall."

Portia immediately did what was asked, in wild readiness of their next sexual peak to be reached, on a journey that was growing in anticipation. As Portia spread her fingers on the wall, Nikki could feel how extremely turned on her partner was becoming, which excited Nikki even more to move her thighs between hers to spread Portia's legs wide apart.

"Yes," Nikki calls out. "Perfect." Not knowing what to expect excited Portia even more. Nikki smiled widely and told her, "I'm going to take you right now from behind." Portia's cry of wicked eagerness was all Nikki needed to slip between her legs and find her swollen lips, spread wide.

"Nikki, I want you inside. I want to feel you inside me again."

"Portia, my fingers are here for your beautiful core."

Nikki filled Portia with her two long fingers while holding her firmly in place by grasping her hair and twisting it in her hand. Portia's movement was restricted in Nikki's grasp, and by her moaning, Nikki knew she loved it.

"Oh God," she cried, as Nikki pulled out and slid back in, each thrust harder and faster. "You feel so good, Nikki." As Nikki thrust inside her again, she asked, "What do you want, my dear Portia?"

"You," she moans loudly, "I want you." Nikki responded with another strong and rhythmic thrust, and feeling the Domme in her, she asked determinedly, "And how do you want me?"

A low moan came shamelessly from her throat, "I want you harder … much harder." She cried. "God, Nikki, you are so desirable and so powerful. I love it."

Nikki needed to hear her confirmation, hoping that Portia would build her satisfaction on Nikki's single-minded tact, and at the same time, surprised herself with exercising control over Portia that felt so damn good to Nikki.

Nikki snapped, "Move your body with me."

Portia then started bucking her hips to match Nikki's hard and fast thrusts, as Nikki's probing fingers rubbed around Portia's folds, rolling over her lovely jewels constantly.

"Tell me when you come, Portia. I want to hear you scream it."

Nikki continued to slide in and out as Portia's orgasm began to rock through her. "I'm coming," she cried out. "Oh my God! What are you doing to me? Oh God, Oh God."

When Nikki heard Portia's zealous cries, it was all she needed to push her own hypersensitive clit, and Nikki slipped out of her core. She immediately pressed her fingers into Portia's channel firmly, and her throbbing, wet slit responded. With Nikki's own well-traveled fingers, she brought herself to climax while the whimpering waves of pleasure were still washing over a drained Portia.

Before the intensity and sexual pinnacle subsided, Nikki turned her around and took her in her arms, both trembling on unsteady legs. A comforting Nikki nuzzled Portia's face in her neck as her heavy breathing began to slow.

"How do you know just how to touch me?" Portia asked curiously. "I could never suitably describe what your touch does to me. It is a sexual well-being that I have never known."

"My body seems to know exactly what you need, Portia, without my even thinking about it. I don't know, I confess. But I wouldn't change a thing."

"No," Portia offers, "don't ever change what you do for me."

Nikki thought lovingly, *"We must do this again, and soon."*

Portia thought excitedly, **"I have found my sexual soulmate. She is everything I imagined she would be."**

Parting was not to be of "sweet sorrow" – maybe only a pause in a special journey.

34

ALL ABOUT ME

O kay, since I've laid out the foundation for our main characters, it's time for you to get a sense of who **Jonathan Garrett** is and why he is important to the story. I am the narrator because my life, for whatever reason, became intertwined with these professional and highly entertaining women of San Francisco. I have encountered many women in my travels, but none who compare to these fascinating five.

Again, these aren't simply a cross section of working women in the Bay Area. These are special people, who just happen to be female and exceedingly interesting. Their measure of success sets them far apart from the mainstream.

Before I became imbedded in the San Francisco business and civic climate, I was just another writer trapped within my truth; a confident ladies-man still trapped within my youth. Although I did have a writing skill, I struggled to find a genre or niche which suited me and one I enjoyed pursuing. Incredibly, a series of recurring and progressive dreams about the universe and aliens from the future focused my mind on hard science fiction with a touch of fantasy.

Having been married to a wonderful woman named Amanda, my occupation was a business consultant, specializing in taking start-up companies to the next level. I gave lectures, wrote a couple business books, and held workshops, all geared toward business improvement. I did not become a published author of science fiction until a couple years after my divorce. We had no children.

My wife was a great woman, a truly outstanding Taurus. To this day, I have not met a finer person than Amanda. However, my Scorpio and her Taurus just didn't match well. We were total opposites trying for twelve years to make it work … finally divorcing. We still remain friends and she is now living with a singer/song writer in Denver.

Unfortunately, for her, I began investing soon after the split, buying into Apple, Amazon, Facebook, Tesla, etc., and made a fortune, enabling me to write at my leisure. Amanda always said she thought I would one day amount to something, and happy to say, she was right!

Now my current writing project is a science fiction epic series titled, **Galactic Disruption,** and I have already published the first three novels in the series. I'm working with Sara Sullivan at **Star Gaze Ventures** to see if we can create a movie or TV series out of the books. This has been a vision of mine for a very long time. Go big or go home!

I am a huge car buff and collector. While I don't have Jay Leno's Garage, mine isn't too shabby. I drive a Lunar Blue 2020 Mercedes Benz C63 Coupe and have a 2018 Porsche Macan Turbo for long trips.

My *garage* houses Ferrari, Maserati, Lamborghini, Bentley, and several of my dad's classic muscle cars; a 1967 GTO, 1972 Chevelle SS454, and a steel blue 1967 Corvette Split Window Coupe, currently valued at over $200,000.

When I'm not writing, or cruising the Embarcadero, I spend my time hiking, climbing, and kayaking when and where possible. And as do several of the ladies in this piece, I am at the finest gym in the city, **Exclusive Fitness**, several times a week. Many stories are intertwined with the people and situations at this club.

At the top of my "favorite things" list is my sex life. At age forty-eight ... I mean fifty-four, I am in very good shape, mostly due to genes, money, and my workout regiment, which is very important to me. I like to have sex, or at least have an orgasm, about three to four times a week, with a partner or solo – either is fine.

If I have a young lady over for an evening at my sprawling home, our lovemaking is usually to the enticing melodies of Ravel's "Bolero!" And, if I don't have a *live-in* for a long weekend, masturbation is fine. In fact, with what is available online, I have no idea why a guy would want to get married. That would involve a truly special relationship. More on that topic later.

Let me ramp this up with someone who is very important in my life, Doctor Samantha Vandenberg, man coach. I found her several years ago when I was in freefall from divorce, having a mid-life crisis, and generally being a *bad shit.* Fate jumped in and my purpose in life and my happiness was changed forever.

She is remarkable. A gifted psychologist whose specialty is working with men and their relationship problems, her best skill is listening. After only four sessions, she had me admit to my greatest character flaw; I cannot tolerate negative people.

Really. I only want to be around positive and upbeat people, and, as she so boldly pointed out, I become mean and nasty around *Debbie Downers*. Sadly, Amanda was a bit of a negativist, and I didn't realize at the time it was driving us apart. That adage, *"If I knew then what I know now."*

Doctor Vandenberg and I discussed trust, respect, and shame and what it takes to be a man in today's micro-behavior society, and to love yourself as well. Being honest with yourself as to who you really are and being an authentic person requires a strong commitment to making yourself a better person.

Following a series of in-depth interviews with Samantha, covering many incidents between Amanda and me, she concluded that we were just two decent people who, unfortunately, brought out the worst in each other. It bears repeating: *"If I only knew then what I know now."*

One point about lovemaking. I was a very selfish sexual partner while married, and it wasn't until after our divorce that I learned how to listen and care for a woman sexually. I met and dated another Scorpio, Mimi, for nearly a year. Being a *control freak*, I usually dictated bedroom activities. For me, relationships with women weren't necessarily about intimacy or sex, but rather me controlling the relationship. That changed with Mimi. It was her use of BDSM techniques to get me to realize how difficult it was to *not be in control*. Today, I would advise women, especially the shy or timid, to take control as best you can.

Mimi had an amazing talent, in addition to her sexual prowess, which was her touch, both physical and mental. She was also a terrific listener, a characteristic lost with most people who I knew. Mimi knew me better than I knew myself, and being a little older and more experienced, I learned a lot from her. I still think of her often and have no idea where she is now.

What comes to mind, is one of the best quotes I ever read, from the book *Chicken Soup for the Soul*. "People come into your life for a reason, a season, or a lifetime." That statement always reminds me of Mimi.

So, there is the big picture of your narrator. I'm just your average guy with a fairy tale life. You should probably know that the many escapades with the lovely women in my life had a delicious endgame for me. It was never about reaching intimacy or having sex; it was only about me being in complete control.

In the chapters that follow, I will either set up the scene, or have the characters' point of view noted, so you are aware of who is doing the talking and running the highlight reel.

Oh, before I forget, ask me later about a young woman by the name of Brandi. I'm not sure that was her real name, but she was in some serious depression and I stepped in to help, I think. So, it was, I sincerely hope ... a man behaving better.

Enjoy!

ACT I
ECHO THE BEGINNING

We began at St. Mary's of Carmel parish,
The two of us standing young and alone.
A life together we would expect to cherish,
So very far from families and home.
Happy and naïve would describe the two of us,
As we began a life together with promise and dreams.
Never expecting that over years of life's reality as such,
There would be battles; there would be screams.
My arms were your castle; your heart was my sky.
I was the only one who could wipe away tears when you'd cry.
The good times and bad times, we've been through them all,
Yet it was always my intention to help you rise when you fall.
I once said I wanted you; I don't remember why.
I often wonder if it's true … and that makes me cry.
I see night after lonely night drifting away,
On the waves of dreams for yet another day.
You struggle with the road not taken,
Your value in life truly shaken.
So many qualities and attributes, so many skills,
But in your mind, a life still unfulfilled.
I have learned to reap what I sow,
Changed for the better; I want you to know.
Long ago you said I love you; I said love you too,
Now we have a choice to make; do we start anew?

INTERMISSION

Y ou may be at a point in this story where you could rightfully ask, "So Jon, how come all these San Francisco girls like sex and spend, what seems like, every waking moment thinking about doing it or having it done to them?"

Good question. First, I have a lot of friends, both men and women. Truth be told, I have more women friends than men. But before you judge, here is the reason:

Men mostly like to talk about sports, sex, and tell jokes. I'm the kind of person who just doesn't like to simply talk about sports, sex, and tell jokes. Although I have female friends that do talk about sports and sex, it isn't usually at the top of their list. They are much more inclined to discuss personal relationships, feelings, and current news and stories.

Many of the fine women I know just don't "buy into" the behavior of the young women who have been a part of this sexy saga of lifestyles and like stories. Or, as you might expect, the vast majority are married with kids and gave up the "club scene" many years ago. So, they remain my friends, just not participants in this frolicking fun!

So there, I simply find women to be much more interesting than men, and, as anyone will tell you, I am a good listener. I learn a lot more, and can contribute a lot more, with women than with men.

II

THE CONFRONTATIONS

CONFLUENCE, CONFLICTS, AND COMMONALITY

35

JACQUI

*S*o as the ladies left the sushi restaurant, they indicated to Lina their desire to either share their most relevant stories at subsequent get-togethers, or detail them in files sent to Lina for her book, **Charade in the City**. Lina assumed she would have a remarkably long list of story material. Jacqui looked at Lina's request as bittersweet ... honesty would be tough!

At the gym the next day, Jacqui signed in with Courtney, the receptionist.

"Hi Jacqui, good to see you."

"You too, Courtney. You guys busy this morning?"

"Not too busy. Whatcha doing today?"

"Gonna do Lisa's Step Class. Need to get my blood pumping."

"She'll do that for ya. Have a good class."

"Thanks." Jacqui moved on to the large studio at **Exclusive Fitness**. She was one of about twenty-five in the class, which was good; not too crowded. She noticed the mindless chatter and had to remind herself that this was what *balance* was all about.

While she was warming up, she got a text from me.

> "Hey, thanks for fab nite.
> You were GR8!"
> "Hi, JG. Yep, enjoyed it"
> "Got a suggestion, JJ."
> "Shoot."
> "Thinking ahead, find a way to get James
> to admit that you had no knowledge of his
> deviant sex life – the criminal stuff."

"Why?"

"Just thinking ahead."

"You always do, JG."

"You'll do a recording?"

"Yes, I'll figure out a way."

"Thnx."

"Thnx to you. Owe you one."

"Can HARDly wait!"

Jacqui looked up from her phone, saw the class was filling up, and then she spotted a regular member walking in.

"Hey Ross."

"Hi Jacqui."

Ross was an extrovert, one of only three guys in the class, and always polite, interesting, and humorous. Although he was married, Ross was very comfortable around women and what he assumed was harmless banter with females at the club; most women looked at him as a flirt.

One irritating member even called him a *social butterfly* when his wife was present. Ross absolutely loved the attention, as most guys would. He would complain, but with a smile.

A graphic designer, he was very impressed with Jacqui's looks, physique, and long legs, and she was referred to by many professionals as the *queen of cloud computing*.

The outgoing Ross had always enjoyed talking to Jacqui, as it stroked his male ego to be in her company. Ross was physically attracted to Jacqui, but even more mesmerized by her social standing. To Ross, social standing mattered. He would measure people by what they had accomplished, not by their looks. Their good looks just opened the door. Shallow, yes.

Jacqui and the class enjoyed an intense 45-minute class, followed by a ten-minute cooldown. Following class, Jacqui exchanged some small talk with Ross, while flirting with him as well. She really enjoyed getting Ross excited over her "forbidden fruit." Jacqui would often tease a guy after having a bad experience herself. This was one of those days ...

"Great class, eh Jacqui?"

"Definitely. Lisa can easily fulfill your cardio requirements for the day."

"Love your outfit. Bright and sexy!"

"Thanks, Ross. A girl likes to look nice, especially in these settings."

"Jacqui, any chance we could do coffee or lunch today?"

Jacqui thought, devilishly, *"I have a better idea."*

"No can't today. But, come with me." Jacqui had always sensed his interest in her, but more of an ego thing than a sexual attraction. She took his hand and led him to the unisex rest room behind the large workout studio. She was feeling particularly nasty, and he was clueless.

Ross was thinking, *"Whatever she wants to do is fine with me."*

When no one was looking, Jacqui took Ross into the small rest room, closed and locked the door and led him into a stall. She had Ross sit down on the toilet facing her.

"Ross, this is your chance to get a glimpse of two of the prettiest boobs you have ever seen."

"Hey girl, I'm not complaining, but why?"

"This way, you'll never need to wonder what Jacqui Johnson's boobs look like … you'll know!"

Jacqui slowly pulled her top up over her head, licked her lips temptingly, and with one skillful motion, unhooked her sports bra. Once Ross saw her magnificent breasts spill from her massive bra, he did what any normal guy would do. He stared. She stroked her nipples, one palmed hand to each, until her areolas were a rosy pink against her milky-white breasts. Jacqui then began to spread her mostly bare legs.

Jacqui watched as he unzipped his fly, pulled out his slowly growing penis, and in a matter of seconds, he was masturbating. Ross began slowly, but soon was stroking himself as heatedly as she had expected … and groaning.

Jacqui allowed him to continue to masturbate, while spreading her long legs farther apart; and even with her gym shorts still on, she massaged her now damp groin area with an open palm, while continuing to circle and squeeze her breasts deliberately with the other hand.

As Jacqui picked up on Ross's heightened moaning, she slid her hand into her shorts and began to pleasure herself, also then moaning, much for his benefit.

Ross went from curious to excited to a purposely muffled orgasm, with his juices nearly landing on Jacqui's leg.

"Why?" he starts to say …

"Hey, big guy. I enjoyed your show as much as you enjoyed seeing mine. No touchy … no feely."

"You're sexy, Jacqui."

"I know I am."

Jacqui smiled and asked herself as she left the stall, "***Who just took advantage of whom?***"

36

NIKKI

Nikki was surprised to see Logan, her former boyfriend and now the district attorney in Seattle. They had a torrid sexual relationship, beginning with that library incident from a previous chapter, that looked promising to Nikki, before he moved away.

They tried a long-distance romance, but when Logan ended up with an American Indian named Song, who he met on a cross-country Canadian train trip from Vancouver to Toronto, it ended.

Song took Nikki's phone number from Logan's cell and gave Nikki the blow-by-blow (literally) of oral sex, steamy intercourse, and lavish gifts and meals over a three-day journey.

As Nikki was walking down the courthouse steps, Logan was below walking by with his cell in his ear. This was a guy that nailed the tall, dark, and handsome vibe like no one else could. One of Nikki's friends, Maggie, said that one look at Logan and women wanted to drop their panties.

"Hey Logan," she uttered, inquiringly. "Hi there."

"Hi Nikki," he said as he finished his phone conversation. He waited for Nikki to reach the bottom of the steps and gave her a warm hug.

"You look great, Nikki."

"Thanks. You too."

"Still working on the Johnson case?"

"Yep, Logan. This one is so complicated and so fascinating. What brings you to the city?"

"Subpoena work relating to that Taylor Ponzi scheme. You familiar with it?"

"No, not really. Only what I read, Logan."

Without hesitation, Nikki blurts out her most annoying recollection. "So, how is Song? Haven't heard from her since that early harassment after you screwed her on the train."

Looking away from Nikki, Logan managed a bit of a smile and responded. "That Song has sung blue. It was an unfortunate tryst that I regret ... very much regret. I never meant to hurt you."

"You never see that phrase in a fortune cookie," Nikki mused.

A pensive Logan continued, "It's good to see you. Any way we could do dinner tonight?"

Nikki paused a moment, thinking *"What the hell ... why not."*

"Sure. Text me the time and place, later."

"Will do." They hugged again and were off to their respective business meetings.

♥   ♥   ♥

Logan met Nikki for dinner at ONE65 on O'Farrell Street, the center of San Francisco's French dining revolution. From this delightful *Pâtisserie* Boutique to the ultimate in French bistro fare, the steak tartare, onion tart and almond croissants were incredible, and Nikki went with Steak Croix. Logan went upscale with the Classic French Chateaubriand.

Dinner was tame, given the thoughts of possible after-dinner sex that were oddly going through Nikki's mind. The more she heard his husky voice, the more warm and wet sensations riveted through her body. *"Damn it,"* she thought shamelessly, *"that shit still is a babe magnet."*

Logan never gave her an indication of any sexual intentions throughout the evening, but Nikki did believe that he would like to reconnect both socially and sexually. She tried to hide her obvious continued attraction to this bad boy.

Following a delightful and satisfying dinner, Nikki and Logan waited for the valet to bring Logan's car around. "That was an incredible dining experience, Logan. Thank you so much."

"You are quite welcome, and I felt honored to be with the most beautiful and successful women in the city, if only for one night."

"He still has the charm," Nikki admitted to herself.

At that time, a gorgeous jet-black McLaren GT approached them with a most notable exhaust sound attracting every ear in the area. The magnificent exotic car stopped in front of Logan, and the valet exited the car via the trademark gullwing doors and handed Logan his keys.

"This is one beautiful car, sir."

Logan smiled and responded, "Thank you. I do love it."

As Logan helped Nikki into the car, she inquired, "So, big boy, how long have you had this?"

Walking over to the driver's side, entering the car and closing the door, he replied, "About six months now. Had that amazing Mercedes AMG prior to this."

"I do remember the AMG. Thought it was as sexy as me. I should have owned it."

"Hell, Nikki, you could easily afford the Benz."

"Yeah, but, not a good image for a public servant in the city."

As they drove off, Nikki wrestled with her more intimate thoughts. "You got time for a drink at my place before you head for home?"

"Sure." Logan thought eagerly, *"I have time for more than a drink."*

Nikki had a small, but elegant, two-level condo near the Financial District; and Logan knew it well from many visits, mostly from sexual encounters lasting for several hours and often resulting in multiple orgasms for this pair of lovers.

Once inside, Nikki immediately blurted out, "Why don't you pour us a couple Cognacs while I slip into something more comfortable? I have some Hennessy and Courvoisier that you can pick from. You know where the bar and glasses are."

"Can do."

Moments later, Nikki appeared in a sexy cold shoulder bodycon dress with lace that showed off her figure in stunning fashion, and her signature four-inch heels were replaced with a pair of stylish sandals.

"My you look lovely for just getting comfortable." Logan gave her a long and warm hug which Nikki did not object to.

"Well thanks, I'm relaxed. Got our drinks?"

As Logan turned to get the two drinks, he murmured, "It's good to be here. Thanks for having me in."

Nikki thought disconcertingly, *"Damn it ... I want him, the shit!"*

♥   ♥   ♥

Nikki whimpered, looking sensual and dazed under this recurring spell and the spontaneity of this encounter. Goose bumps broke out all over her warm and eager body, and the moment triggered an unexpected emotional delight. Was this her real true feelings for Logan, or just a lustful, risky venture meant to rekindle or revisit old memories?

As they looked into each other's eyes, both found the view irresistible and neither was much for small talk. It was the right time for Logan to grasp Nikki's neck with his two large hands, and gently kiss her cheeks, her neck, and her waiting lips. She felt his closeness and warmth, looking hopelessly into his eyes. She was aroused and utterly transfixed.

"Your lips still feel good on mine, Logan."

Logan recognized his opportunity and moved on it. He gently lifted her tight, sexy dress above her waist, exposing the soft skin of her inner thighs. Her torso was beautifully bare except for her teeny high-rise thong exposing her bare, brown cheeks. She tilted side to side allowing Logan to remove the thong. They were already wet.

"You are ready for me."

Nikki smiled, "Yes, Logan. I want to feel your tongue ... your long tongue."

A flushed and panting Nikki opened her mouth and red lips further for Logan to explore with his wet and hungry tongue. He skimmed a finger down her warm body, beginning between her collarbones and working down, circling her breasts and nipples slowly as Nikki sucked in a dazed sigh and felt her pulse begin to race.

"Your touch gets my blood pumping, you shit."

He then fingered his way from her lips down her abdomen, slowing down as he reached the sensitive place where her thighs met. With a slight jerk, Nikki caught her breath and exhaled slowly. Every inch he descended, she breathed in deeply, until her sigh went from a quiver to a quiet moan to a noticeable whine.

"Oh yes, taste me."

Smiling, he slid his full hand into her waiting channel and over her warm and wet folds, swirling two fingers around her nub with enough tenderness to make her cry out his name. She pulled her dress off and wrapped her legs around his hips. So primed and ready to go, Nikki uttered, "Touch me." She sighed. "Touch me there again."

As Nikki reached for his belt, Logan simply unhooked it and let his trousers fall to the floor. While she repositioned herself, he dropped his shorts and she could see he was noticeably aroused.

"I want him inside me ... I need him to fill me up," she whispered to herself anxiously.

Taking no time to spread herself wide for Logan, Nikki groaned with anticipation and a smoldering gaze. Logan placed one hand around her neck and with the other pulled her amazing body firmly against him. The warmth and mixing of scents had never been more enticing.

She moaned, "Yes ... yes."

In an almost teasing manner, he ran his throbbing shaft up and down her wet and wide-open slit, reducing her to a brief cry. "Aah, yes. Big and as hot as ever."

Once fully inside, she pulled his torso even closer, allowing his penetration to go deep and strong. "That's what we need, Nikki ... the contact, the closeness."

She responded quickly, "Don't talk. Go deeper, faster."

Seconds later, as he cupped her breast with one hand and stroked her hair with the other, they came together in overwhelming ecstasy. She was satisfied sexually, but not emotionally.

"Oh God, that was good. Damn, Logan, you're good."

But she wasn't done with Logan the lover yet.

37

NIKKI

Once fully dressed and composed, Nikki took a deep breath and went straight to the issue of the day. "Come on, Logan, out with it. Who is she? Who is Song?"

Logan was surprised by how quickly the sexy moment turned to "truth or dare." He thought nervously, *"This isn't good."*

"Again, Logan, who is fricking Song?"

"Just some girl I met on the train." With a shrug, he tried to sound nonchalant while Nikki's face filled with anger and was beginning to reach the dead space between Logan's ears.

"I can see you're getting another boner from her, just thinking about her. Your lips on hers ... her lips on yours ... yada yada yada."

Logan was silent, trying to find the words to minimize the perceived damage.

"I'm waiting."

"Okay. Those fiery green eyes, cute little butt, pert breasts, and those long legs that seemed to stem from her rib cage ... she reminded me of you."

"You total shit."

"I was just wanting to meet and talk. I swear, that was it."

"So, you met, where?"

"We met in the dining car."

"You had dinner with her?"

"Well, yes, that's what happened. We met and both needed to eat, ya know."

"What was she like?"

"She seemed nice."

"Nice! You don't do nice. Shit, nice isn't even in your fricking vocabulary. Nice. Give me a break, you damn idiot."

150

Logan was in shock, after the best make-up sex of his life.

As Nikki burst into a fit of laughter from her anger, she simply said, "You hook up with starlets, models, wealthy widows. Again, what was it about her?"

Logan had to think, but only the truth came out. "She mentioned that she was into light bondage and relished the role of sub."

"Oh my God."

"Hey, just trying to be honest."

"Go ahead, Mister Honesty."

"I had a double scotch and that sexual message just got me pumped. It is certainly not something you and I would ever do, so I figured just once, what the hell. It was just sex, nothing more."

"So, you tied her up and screwed her?"

"It wasn't like that. Actually, it was very light. Used a couple towels from the bathroom. I think she just wanted sex, and the bondage idea was just a way to get me interested."

"She got my cell number, numb nuts."

"Yeah, I didn't know that. Must have taken it from my phone after we showered."

"So, you and Song still seeing each other? I need to know if this is going any further."

"Understand. No, I haven't seen Song since before I got the McLaren. It was just a damn fling and I regret it."

Nikki was searching for the right words, while trying to calm down and give her man the benefit of the doubt. "Sorry to have to ask. You know I was totally pissed and thought we were good."

"Nikki, it's okay. I messed up and I'm sorry. Please believe me."

After a couple minutes to cool down, they hugged as Logan headed out the door for his car. Nikki was torn between her anger and her desire to patch things up and move on.

Logan had gotten a text message while he and Nikki were deep into their lustful bliss and waited to get in his car to respond.

> "Hey there Stud, you coming over?
> Horny and tired of solo. Need your rod."

Taking a moment to respond to the short but predictable text, Logan answered.

"Can't make tonight. With a client.
Save that precious body 'til morrow at 8.
Stud wants to feel the Song!"

As Logan left her condo, Nikki recalled a comment made by a friend of hers, and cringed.

"Where there is love, there is pain."

38

LINA

L ina and Gabe exchanged text messages several times since he was reporting on the social unrest in the city. He really liked Lina but felt a little intimidated in her presence. She knew he had feelings for her but didn't realize that his shyness was due to his fondness for her.

Feeling a desire to catch up on his perspective of the unrest, she texted him.

"Hey. How ya doing?"
"Hi. Ok. How you?"
"Fine. Where u b?"
"Office. Doin my daily fact sheet."
"Wanna come over?"
"Sure. GR8. Give me an hour."
"Sure. C ya then."

Lina was looking forward to seeing Gabe and catching up, believing he needed a sounding board to discuss and analyze the protest and repercussions from both sides of the issue.

Lina also was aware that Gabe had bi-polar disorder, although this info came from a friend of his. He struggled with the bi-polar illness from a social stigma and worked hard to control the ebb and flow with drugs and exercises. He was too self-conscious to tell Lina.

Almost an hour later, Gabe buzzed her apartment and Lina greeted him with an open door. He gave her a gentle kiss on the cheek and they both turned to walk into the apartment.

"Can I take your coat?"
"Sure. Thanks."

As they walked toward Lina's kitchen, she asked, "Would you like something to drink?"

"Sure. What do you have?"

"Beer, soft drinks, and some wine. What's your pleasure?"

"How about a Coke or Pepsi?"

"Coming right up." Lina grabs a couple glasses and tells Gabe to take a seat in her living room as she gets some ice for their drinks.

Gabe explains the issues on both sides of the protest and how many of the peaceful protesters have been infiltrated with terror organizations, making defense difficult and covering the stories somewhat dangerous.

"So, Gabe, what is your current thinking? What is your strategy going forward?"

"Gonna try to hear from as many people on both sides and report my findings as accurately and honestly as is possible."

"Good luck, Gabe," Lina said reassuringly.

Gabe put his drink down and turned to face Lina and to give her a strong hug as he kissed her lips. Lina didn't push back but tried to get Gabe to ease up on the hug.

"Sorry, Lina," Gabe said sheepishly.

Lina just smiled as Gabe placed one hand on her thigh and ran his other hand through her hair. Lina gently wrapped her arms around Gabe's back and shoulders, and he then placed one hand on her breast and the other between her legs.

This was the first time that anything sexual has taken place between these two, and things got a little heated for Gabe; not so much for Lina. It was all a little too direct.

"I think we should take this slowly for a while, Gabe. Hugs are good for now, okay?"

Drawing his hands back from Lina, Gabe responded somewhat embarrassed. "Of course, Lina. You know I like you and just thought we might get to know each other."

"Gabe, I agree. You are a wonderful person and I do want to get to know you. Intimacy can certainly grow from getting to know each other, don't ya think?"

"Sure. I agree."

Lina hugs Gabe and gives him a warm kiss. He responded and placed his arms around her waist and squeezed her fanny.

"Ouch!"

"Sorry, Lina."

Lina thinks, *"Gosh, he's kind of clumsy."* She was frustrated with his inexperience.

For the next ten minutes, there was some basic foreplay 101, but no sex.

Following an unremarkable encounter, Gabe thanked Lina for having him over and he left thinking, *"I really screwed things up!"*

After closing the door, Lina turned and thought reflectively, ***"I think it's time to have a physical relationship that I've always imagined. I deserve it!"***

39

SARA

*I*t's Friday night in the city, and Nikki, Lina, and Jacqui are having drinks at another downtown bar, waiting, as they often do, for Sara to show up. These Friday nights are becoming the ultimate ladies' night out for the girls, as any boyfriend stuff usually happens on Saturday or Sunday.

The three ladies were chatting as a stunning redhead with green eyes glided over to the girls' table. As Lina just smiled, the gorgeous redhead in tight silver leather pants with matching halter top, strode over and planted a long and luscious kiss on Nikki's waiting mouth.

Jacqui was startled, assuming that Nikki knew this person, but a display like this in public was not generally acceptable. "Damn, that's ballsy," she blurted.

The woman straddled Nikki, moaned lightly, and caressed her breasts as if oblivious to the three women. Both women tilted their heads to begin some serious French kissing. The redhead was quickly messing up Nikki's hair as Nikki was giving the stranger a nice squeeze of her cleavage-exposed breast. Both women began panting noticeably to the rhythm they were generating.

Nikki then said anxiously, "We better go someplace where we can be alone."

"Nah, let's just stay here. I can do you right here and right now," replied the redhead.

"Maybe we should get a room, Sugar."

As Lina gave a light laugh, Jacqui was absolutely petrified … little did Jacqui know that the redhead was Sara and this was a somewhat typical entertaining gig.

Pulling away from the calm and cool Nikki, Sara simply says, "Hi guys. What's up?"

"Looking good, girl," Lina responds. "Is that a new wig?"

"Yeah, Lina, got it from studio casting last night. They are filming a series of ASMR Shorts, and the 'redhead' does the nails on hair brushing."

Jacqui chimed in immediately with a tone of utter astonishment. "Let me start with that wonderful kiss. I'm jealous."

"Sara is a great kisser," Nikki added with a smile. "And, she isn't the shy and bashful type, as we all know." She glanced directly at Jacqui and further explained, "I am very comfortable in the presence of a sexy lady."

Lina remarked, "And those two make a striking couple."

Sara laughed and winked at Nikki.

"Okay. Cool. Understand." Nikki was curious. "Now, what the hell is an ASMR?"

Sara smiled, laughed lightly, and pointed to her head. *"Autonomous Sensory Meridian Response* is a sedative sensation that has immense sexual connotation. Leading edge stuff."

"Say what?" Jacqui replied curiously.

Sara continued. "ASMR induces a sexual response from some people due to sexual stimuli felt through relaxation, or a tingling sensation often called a 'head orgasm.' Just go on YouTube and you'll be swamped with videos describing the many ways one can get off on whispering, crisp sounds, slow movements of contacts with objects, etcetera."

"Thanks, but I'll get off the old-fashioned way," Jacqui announced with a grin.

"So, Sara," Nikki uttered, "You ever get an explanation from Brad on that shitty night when he blew you off?"

"Let it go, Nikki," Lina advised.

"No, it's okay, Lina. He told me some crap that I can't really believe. Yes, I was disappointed, but we aren't exclusive in his mind, and I need to accept it."

Jacqui blurted, "It doesn't sound like you guys have a fifty-fifty relationship." She paused, "You, Sara, seem to give him the benefit of the doubt, from what I hear."

"Yeah, it's a damn work in progress, I guess," Sara quipped. "When he's good, he is very good, and when he's bad, it really hurts."

Sara thought, sadly, *"I take some blame for expecting too much."*

"Hey, it's your business and we should just sit back and support you when you need it."

"Thanks, Jacqui. Appreciate it."

Sara took a deep breath and recalled for the girls some good times with Brad, realizing the girls weren't sold on Brad and his past behavior.

"You guys know I like trance, right?"

The girls either nodded or smiled.

"A while back, Brad got us tickets to a concert by Armin Van Buuren, a Dutch DJ and producer of the radio show, *A State of Trance.*"

"Is *A State of Trance* referred to by fans as ASOT?"

"That's right, Jacqui," Sara said smiling. "Brad took us to Amsterdam in the Netherlands for the epic two-day celebration, *State of Trance Festival,* headed by the Trance Legend himself in February, 2020, pre-COVID-19." She paused. "It was the best time."

Lina uttered, "I remember how excited you were and the pics from that trip were amazing."

Nikki added, "In the immortal words of Stevie Nicks, 'players only love you when they're playing,' and that's a fact, girl."

Jacqui noticed a tear running down the cheek of her newest friend and gave Sara a warm hug.

Lina chimed in, "Hey let's lighten up the mood, okay?"

Sara smiled at Lina while thinking, "***Only a fool will trip on what's behind her.***"

40

SAMANTHA AND JONATHAN

I had many sessions with Doctor Samantha Vandenberg, but one in particular rang sad, but true. It started out with a deep soul-searching discussion into my motives and my value system. Porn and shame come out in this session, as well as an honest initial evaluation of my relationship with both my beautiful wife and my domineering mother.

Having waited only a few minutes for the fine doctor to summon me into her office, there she was as sexy and magnetic as all get out.

"Good afternoon, Jon," a smiling Samantha said with a wink and slight head toss." Good to see you."

"Likewise, Sam. Good to see you again as well."

Stepping into her office, Sam motioned for me to take a seat. "Would you like something to drink, Jon?"

"No thanks. I'm good."

"So, Jon, we decided last session to discuss issues you've had with both your ex-wife and your mother today. You still okay with that?"

"Yes. The big picture stuff, right?"

"That's right. Are you comfortable now?"

I thought, "No," but said, "Yes."

"Good. Let's begin with the statements you made at our last session. As I recall, you insisted that there was a big disconnect between certain events during your marriage, which were interpreted quite differently between you two."

"Yes, damn it. There was what happened ... and what really happened."

"Okay, Jon. Please explain these situations that were interpreted differently. You know this is fairly typical."

"Yes, I know. Just want you to be open-minded."

"Jon, it is in the best interest of us both that I am a good listener for you, impartial and non-judgmental. Now, please, go ahead."

"Fine. I set up a second PO Box that she discovered." Jon paused.

"I'm listening."

"She was pissed … thinking I was hiding something from her."

"And you didn't think having a second, personal PO Box was wrong?"

"No. It was separate from our personal one so I could have business mail set up on a different PO Box than our regular mail."

Thinking about a response for a moment, Sam asked, "And, Jon, was there any other reason to have this second PO Box?"

"Maybe."

"Maybe?"

"Well, I did have my adult DVDs sent to that new box, but that was my business, right … my personal business?"

"I'm just listening right now, Jon. What's next?"

"I bought some sexy silk underwear, and she was pissed when she found them."

"I see. I can understand why you would wear comfortable silk underwear, but why hide them?"

"I wanted to wait and surprise her when we did some frisky role playing on sex night?"

Samantha thought plausibly, *"Frisky … role-playing … sex night!"*

Sensing the doctor's confusion, Jon responded to clarify. "Bad choice of words. Our sex life had become kind of boring. So, we both agreed to spice it up, and wearing something new and sexy was what we both agreed to do. And we didn't have an actual sex night … I meant the next night we had sex."

"I see. Understand. Go on."

"I bought several sex toys for my own personal gratification and that pissed her off."

"The fact that you bought them secretly or the fact that you didn't tell her what they were to be used for?"

"Yes, and yes."

"Okay. Go on, Jon."

"Here comes the real crap. Social media was a huge issue with Amanda. I used it for promotion and marketing, mostly. She wasn't too savvy with social media and was convinced that I used it for staying in touch with old girlfriends."

"May I ask, Jon, did you?"

"You know I'm being brutally honest with you?"

"I do."

"I did not. I never used social media to communicate with old flames … but I did create new friends on those platforms that she felt threatened by."

"Thanks for sharing that."

I paused before the next revelation. "I also used porn a lot."

"Jon, let's save that issue for another time."

"Good," I replied, somewhat embarrassed.

"*Thank goodness,*" Sam thought, relieved.

"We have a few minutes on your side of the session … anything else?"

"I did look onto sites that featured MILF's that brought recollections of my old flame Mimi. But that was just some innocent fantasy stuff."

"Looks like you have another disclosure, given your facial expression, Jon."

"Yeah."

"Please, go ahead."

"Mimi introduced me to BDSM and at first I wasn't comfortable with that desire of hers."

"Jon, you know that BDSM isn't necessarily a bad thing, if two consenting adults both embrace the trust and respect aspects of bondage. And, the submissive actually has the control."

"Yeah, but …"

"Yeah, but what, Jon?"

"My interest and changing perspective of bondage hit home for me soon after Mimi and I got it going regularly."

"There was a foundational reason, do you think?"

"Yes."

"Go ahead, Jon."

"My mother was a domineering, authoritative, insensitive person, who had 'command and control' down to an art form. I had lost my respect for her, and her crappy behavior."

Samantha had to hold her words back, given the very negative description. This was very unsettling for the good doctor.

"What conclusion, if any, can you draw from that relationship, given our session topics today, Jon?"

"My desire to take the lead with women likely grew from my relationship with a dominating mother and my need to control female relationships."

41

SAMANTHA

A fter I left, Sam's occasional uninhibited side surfaced, as the dialogue was difficult and unexpected for both of us. I had some issues ... some serious issues, and Samantha was thinking how to help me. But first, she had her own needs ...

Samantha decided, impulsively, to hit a couple bars looking to unwind and maybe engage in some mindless sex to release her pent-up sexual tension.

"Gotta admit," Sam said to herself, *"that discussion with Jon and the issues he raised got me sidetracked, and solo just isn't gonna do it tonight."*

She put her vibrator for-the-day aside and changed in her office into a black-power, wet-look leather minidress with long sleeves and corset across the waist-line that screamed *I want your sex!*

With the office now vacant, Sam walked downstairs to a waiting Uber and instructed the driver to head to *The Artful Bachelorette,* a unique adult entertainment club that she had frequented often, and always in different outfits to remain unrecognized by the usual men who favored this risqué atmosphere.

What made this place unique was the fact that it was not a typical bar, but a combination art and male nude drawing party for bachelorette parties and special guests, which Sam had become.

Upon arriving, Sam was escorted to a VIP lounge where drinks, provocative music, and a bevy of male heavenliness awaited selected women figures drawing nude representations with their very own handsome naked male muse at their beck and call. Sam could see why this venue was a top destination for bachelorette parties in the city.

Most figure drawing sessions lasted about two hours, and Sam had her eye on one of the nude models, Brandon, with whom Sam had shared drinks before.

She was sure to make eye contact with Brandon and opened her legs slightly in a not-so-subtle attempt that said, "Take me home tonight, big boy."

Brandon concluded his obligatory drawing session, gave his young "artist" an innocent kiss, and walked purposely in Sam's direction.

Extending his, he took Sam's hand and placed a long and warm kiss on her outstretched hand. She had seen him there before and observed his previous behavior and no *red flags* seemed to appear. He had an infectious smile and one of the sexiest bodies Sam had ever seen.

"I am Brandon, and you are by far the loveliest and sexiest woman in this club ... and likely anywhere in San Francisco."

"Why, thank you. My name is Samantha and I must say you have quite a gorgeous body – very athletic and very attractive."

Taking Sam's hand, Brandon replied, "Thanks," and suggested, "Let's grab some champagne and talk, shall we?"

"Sure, Brandon, that would be fine."

As the couple turned to walk toward the bar, Sam thought excitedly, "*I could have sex with this hunk, for sure.*"

Brandon was thinking, "*I would sure like to see what's on the other side of all that black leather and wonder if her panties are a little wet right now.*"

They engaged in some small talk, and then Brandon invited her over to his place for drinks and to get better acquainted. Sam was happy to comply.

They left the club and waited curbside for the valet to bring Brandon's Guards Red Porsche 911 Cabriolet to them. They drove off to his condo building only about fifteen minutes away.

Once inside the upper-floor condo, Sam sees a masculine furnished residence that was actually quite impressive. The lingering smell of old cigar smoke was a bit of a turnoff.

After a few drinks and some straightforward foreplay, they headed to Brandon's bedroom and wasted little time getting undressed and aroused. Sam was mentally sizing up the situation and had no reservations whatsoever.

"I saw the way you looked at me, Sam, and when we first made eye contact, it got me aroused."

"Well, that's no surprise. You are an attractive man, and I didn't come to this event to observe."

"That's why we're here. You're straight, right? Any favorite position? Do you like it rough?"

Gritting her teeth, she responded, "I just want real, sex ... that both people enjoy."

She had been turned off by the cigar smoke, and the detailed dialogue didn't help. "*Oh well*," she thought warily. But then, he put himself into a higher gear.

His heated gaze focused on her ample breasts, taut nipples, and his firm grip on her hips was on the rough side. With his hands on her knees, he spread her warm thighs to an eye-popping wide O. Then, moving up to her chest, took one tight nipple into his mouth, sucking and licking, nibbling with his teeth until she became exceedingly sensitive, almost begging him to stop.

"Hey, slow down, Brandon. What's the hurry?"

He looked up briefly and then gave the other breast the same attention, with pressure on her areola and swiping her nipple tip with his tongue. With a slight jolt of nipple discomfort, Sam's hands roved impatiently for his erection. As she gave his growing penis a tight squeeze, he jerked from her unexpected action.

"Me slow down?"

He ran his hand down her chest and abdomen and then placed his palm on her warm and wet core, pushing against that warmth. He teased her with his fingers while forcing her knees farther apart, widening her thighs so she was open to him. Panting with physical need, and struggling with his rapid pace, Jacqui's skin was tingling and she cried out for him to slow the swipe of his fingers, now probing her hot, wet center.

"Easy, Brandon. I'm feeling really close right now." He slowed his busy fingers slightly, circling, then parting her folds, pinching her clit until she squirmed feebly with each sharp stroke.

"Oh," she cried, as her orgasm was building and she tried to hold back her release until she could better relax.

His thumb and forefinger closed tightly around her bud, increasing the pressure as the fingers slid inside her channel. Brandon was determined to set up a rambling and random rhythm, meant to drive her close to losing her control and dependent on his.

"You are so sexy," he whispered. "Let go. I want to watch you come."

He thrust harder and slammed fully into her channel, shooting pleasurable pains throughout her body. She was reduced to a whimpering, panting mess, coming hard and full, her hot juices spraying her, and her hips helplessly writhing next to him. It was bittersweet.

Moments later, he lifted her legs and thighs uncomfortably high for Sam, his eyes blazing with a male selfishness that annoyed her, as if she was nothing more than a conquest. He was now poised at her wet core with his huge and throbbing erection.

"I'm ready for you. Are you ready for me?" She was momentarily silent.

"Go ahead. I want to feel you inside me right now."

He eased in inch by inch, then thrust hard into Jacqui, squeezing her hips hard, producing a slight scream from a physically spent woman … he was buried deep. She gasped at the shock of her body being overwhelmed so suddenly, the feeling of a man ravishing her with no restraint, and as her muscles slowly relaxed … she cried at his brazen control.

His last thrust, rubbing against her clit with heavy friction, brought him to a moderate climax, not what she would have expected. She heard a slight groan from him as his body relaxed, but she was lost in her own sexual haze, trying to make sense of this underwhelming experience.

The entire extent of foreplay and their less-than-stellar climaxes, lasted about fifteen minutes, ending with him lighting up a Romeo y Julieta, crafted by AJ Fernandez Robusto Cigars.

"Was that good for you, Samantha?"

Pausing and carefully choosing her words, "Well, Brandon, it was shades of a *slam-bam, thank you ma'am* behavior and your selfish, one-sided orgasm mentality and insensitivity, left me a little empty."

"I'm sorry you feel that way … I guess, maybe, I was a little carried away by getting off with such a drop-dead gorgeous beauty. I apologize."

"Apology accepted."

"I assure you that I will be more considerate next time."

Sam said, "Sure," but thinking instantly, "*No way I'm wasting my sex time with this loser.*"

She left but thought about not taking her own advice in that brief and unfortunate encounter.

She thought circumspectly, **"I probably went a little overboard with Brandon. We'll see."**

42

LINA

Finally, our Lina has something good happen, and it comes from Ramon's follow-up to Nikki's request. The timing couldn't be better, as Lina is trying to find some time in her busy life for herself and her happiness.

"Hi, Lina, it's Ramon. Nikki said it was okay to call you."

"Oh yes, Ramon. Hi. Yes, I was expecting your call."

"Is now a good time to talk?"

"Yes, Ramon, now is fine. I'm in the kitchen. Let me walk over to my sofa."

Lina walks into the living room, fixing her hair and thinking, *"WTF. It's a phone call!"*

She sits down and utters, "You still there?"

"Sure. You comfortable? Still good to talk?"

"Yes. Thank you for calling. This is a bit awkward for me."

"Nonsense. I am the one who needs to put your mind at ease, so please … take a deep breath, relax, and tell me what's on your mind, sexually."

"Damn, that's right in-your-face," Lina thought contentedly.

"Lina, tell me about yourself and what issues you have with intimacy or even some discussion concerning boyfriends, okay?"

"Sure. I'm a very conservative lady who has had some seriously bad experiences with men, but I don't feel comfortable discussing this with you."

"I'm sorry. That's not what I meant. Clearly, I am not a therapist or psychologist, but I am a guy who understands women, and someone with relationship experience."

"I'm just nervous, Ramon. Didn't mean to offend you."

"Not offended. Your question is a good one, and needs some explanation."

Lina sighed, as Ramon continued. "Now, tell me the issues that you have, irrespective of any particular guy."

Lina thought for a moment before responding. "Ramon, I'm basically a shy girl and not very experienced with sex, and the guys I've dated don't seem to be very sensitive to me, or maybe women in general."

"Examples?"

"There is a guy I like, Gabe, and we have a lot in common, but when it comes to sex, I really think he wants me to take the lead, and I can't. So, the intimacy suffers and even after sex, neither of us seems satisfied."

"Hey, I get it. Thanks."

"There is another guy, Carl, a nice person I recently met who works as a security cop, and we may even set up a date soon. I just don't want to get too many work projects and different guys going right now."

"I understand. Nikki told me about all the work you are doing, not only in journalism but the many volunteering activities that you are engaged in. Quite impressive."

"Thanks." Lina is starting to feel very relaxed speaking to Ramon.

"Tell ya what, Lina. Look at your schedule. You have my number. Let's schedule a date fairly soon, before you go out on that with Carl, and see what we can do with some quality time together."

"I'd like that. Thank you."

"Do you have any other questions for me right now?"

"That was thoughtful," Lina concluded. "No, Ramon, nothing more now."

"Fine. Thank you for your time and for sharing some info with me, Lina. We will meet soon. Have a good evening."

"Same to you, Ramon. Thanks."

She feels much better after speaking to him and then plans to meet with the girls to go over her book and discuss Ramon.

A warm feeling took over her body, fantasizing about a dream date with Ramon to come.

43

SARA

I had scheduled a movie-in-the-making meeting at Sara's office with her and Troy, to discuss the adaptation of my book series to film. They knew that I had already made a short Amazon Prime Video trailer that I was pushing on YouTube, et al.

"Guys, my objective is to get a preliminary agreement with an LA-based production studio so the dialogue and negotiations could begin soon."

Troy pointed out that it was still a bit premature, and Sara agreed.

"So, what am I still needing before we can get this process moving? You guys know I'm not much for patience."

Troy chimed in immediately. "Jon, we still need to get several legal docs developed, signed, and sent out. There are some conflict-of-interest issues, legal use of a couple book titles, and funding needs that are still being worked on."

"I thought we had those issues well underway."

Sara quipped, "Jon, you are right, but these things take time. You know how slow the publishing business works; the movie biz is even worse."

"Very well. Sorry. What else?"

Sara smiled at Troy and gave an impatient sigh. "Jon, remember when your publisher told you to put more humor in your sexy romance novels?"

"Why yes, I do ... and I did."

Troy flicked a gaze over to Sara and advised, "We think that you need more sex in your science fiction books. Instances of steamy, but tasteful sex in these books. That is what the movie producers are looking for."

Jon grimaced but didn't object.

Troy continued, "Jonathan, even some of the names of your benevolent alien characters, Pulse, Vibe, Vigor, are names meant for sex."

"Can't argue with that. This is the kind of constructive criticism that I need. Will go to work on this ASAP."

Sara took an incoming text and excused herself.

> "Hi Sara, it's Ryan.
> R U my OTP?"

Ryan was an actor friend who Sara dated a couple times, more recently last weekend when they attended a concert, and not her exclusive "one true pairing."

> "Hi Ryan. One of many, I guess.
> What's up?"
> "Gotta new agent. Will text you his contact info."
> "Great. Will put it in our system."
> "Enjoyed the concert."
> "Me too."
> "Later, Sara."
> "K."

♥ ♥ ♥

Sara then headed back to her condo and the evening with Ryan still lingering in her mind. She slipped off her clothes, checked her email and fed Eja. Tired and ready for bed, she poured herself a glass of wine and sat and thought restlessly, *"Ryan is really a nice guy, but he can't be trusted. You never know if you are getting the real Ryan or a damn good acting job!"*

Sara finished her wine, went into the bedroom, and collapsed from exhaustion.

Walking over to the bedroom door to answer a soft knocking, Sara was surprised to see the semi-naked body of Ryan, clutching his manhood and tilting his head in an admiring and teasing way. Sara smiled, gave Ryan a warm embrace, and pulled his lean and athletic body into her bedroom and onto her waiting bed, complete with dreamy, lavender silk sheets.

"I have missed you, my delicious lady, my Princess." Sara placed her arms around his neck and gave him a warm and wet kiss, her tongue exploring his. As they both became more eager to feel the magnetism from their loving hugs and long kisses, the two naked bodies quivered on each other, and Ryan caught Sara in his long arms and spread-eagled her warm and supple body onto the bed. Sara moaned with delight and wild anticipation.

She caught her breath as Ryan placed another deep kiss on Sara, bringing out a rising hunger in their sexual chemistry, and purely lustful thoughts.

Sara was charmed by his passion and got even more excited as his weight pressed softly against her pale breasts and super-sensitive nipples, with hardening tips. His skin was so warm and his musk smell was dizzying. With an easy-going whisper, she said excitedly, "I missed you, Ryan."

"Well, Sara, I'm here now and I'm here just for you."

Sara responded to his sincere and loving voice by wrapping her arms and legs around his torso. She moaned slightly, and he answered by nibbling gently on her ear lobe.

He firmly clasped her legs around his body, faced her, and leaned into yet another wet kiss, with his hands playfully circling her breasts. Sara could see that his manhood was fully engorged, and he was needing her to simply signal her willingness, readiness, and craving.

Sara parted her legs as he guided his tongue from the deep kiss, to her breasts and abdomen. He stroked and sucked her sex jewels thirstily, as the orgasmic pulsations began to roll through her.

Pulling on his buttocks, Sara voiced a not-so-subtle command, "Yes, Ryan. Yes, now!"

Fingering her waiting core, and then sharing her sex juices with those two fingers in her widely opened mouth, Sara was now ready for bigger penetration ... wanting to completely fill her aching vagina.

"Make me come alive with your sex, Ryan. Do it now," she cried.

With his ladies' command, he didn't need any help getting deep and long penetration, as her canal was already wet and puffy. He rocked against her, rolled his hips to give her the pulsating sensations she enjoyed, as arousal spiked her entire body.

Sara was ready to explode as she could feel her partner's coming climax in her inner channel.

Then, suddenly, the alarm on her phone went off and Sara sat up in her bed in a state of utter confusion and with perspiration dripping down her body and sheets wet with the passion of the night.

Moments later a sullen and dejected Sara muttered as she walked toward her bathroom.

"It was a dream ... a damn dream! I had the best sex ever and it was just another damn fantasy!"

44

JACQUI

Remember when I mentioned that some of that Shark DNA showed up in the ladies as well ... here goes.

Our friend, Ross, who got played by Jacqui; got played again. Corrine and Denise set up Ross at the fitness club with some help from Jacqui, who treated Ross to that masturbation treat at the club earlier.

Denise was opening a nail salon soon, so she and Corrine headed over to the nearly completed business suite in a building close to the club. They lured Ross there under the premise of a pre-opening party. It was easy.

They were texting Jacqui, who was with Ross's wife Julie, while the preliminary plan was underway.

"Hey, ya got Julie?"
"Yep. In route."
"Good. Give us about 30 minutes."
"Ross there?"
"Yep, with a buzz. The prick!"
"K. See ya soon."

For about 30 minutes, the three were having a good time. Corrine and Denise had stripped down to their undies, having bought something really sexy for the male shit.

Corrine had a double strap Brazilian panty exposing both butt cheeks in all their glory, and a skimpy tube top leaving nothing to the imagination. Her long legs and tight derriere were no match for horny Ross.

Denise was wearing a lace and ring hardware Brazilian panty, with barely enough fabric to meet her hips. Her neckline push-up bra had tiny rhinestones that matched her panty. Corrine had the butt, and Denise had the boobs!

The two sexy women made sure that Ross was getting a good buzz with the alcohol flowing, and the large and comfy salon chairs were the perfect props for the soon-to-begin orgy. With windows drawn and nobody in the salon, the trap was set.

Corrine opened one of the recliners so it became flat. A soft, smooth leather all-business lounge chair was now converted to an all-sex table. Corrine climbed aboard, dropped her shorts, revealing her hot undies, turned to lay face down and pointed to the spot of pending rear entry into her welcoming backside, and then turned back to face a sweating and partially aroused Ross.

Denise simply sat in a beauty chair, spread her legs, and teased Ross by fingering herself while her scant panty was getting noticeably wet. She motioned for Ross to come close, when she unzipped his fly and grabbed his already growing penis.

"Feels so good, Ross," Denise uttered loudly.

The two culprits had to stall their tease of Ross a bit, as Jacqui was driving a clueless Julie to the same location of this alleged party, under the assumption that Julie would be seeing Denise's new business.

On cue, seeing Jacqui pull up with Julie, Corrine and Denise began kissing and groping Ross, and guiding his eager hands into their *hot spots* for a *ménage à trois* appetizer and the ultimate embarrassment for Ross. The ladies were happy to get mutually aroused, as their climax had nothing to do with any orgasm.

At the last minute, Jacqui got cold feet. She reconsidered her role in this farce, knowing how much it would hurt Julie, and she backed her car out of the parking lot, making up an excuse to Julie, and the two went for coffee instead. She could be seen pulling away.

Meanwhile, Ross with his fly unzipped and all his male glory showing, is stroking his penis and nearly at full erection. But now, Jacqui and Julie are long gone.

"Shit," snapped a totally pissed-off Corrine, watching Jacqui leave.

"Damn it, the fricking party is over," blurted Denise.

Ross looks up at Corrine and Denise with a scowl, "What the hell is going on?"

Denise thought angrily, *"He's a shit … we'll get him later."*

As Ross realized the sex orgy had all been staged, he stormed out of the building, understanding that he had been played, again. Corrine asked Denise what she had in mind for Ross later, given that this trap failed.

"Well, Corrine, we can take a screen shot of him from his Facebook page, and Photoshop it with some naked ladies in a local strip bar and send the incriminating photo to Julie. That'll piss her off, big time."

"That sounds complicated, Denise."

"Not really. But there's more."

"More?"

"Yep," Denise says excitedly, "you use an app that will have the pic disintegrate in about thirty seconds, so it is untraceable."

"You can do that?"

"Hell, I'm the pro at it."

"You're a classic bitch, Denise."

On cue, with her resting bitch face, she taunts …

"Yeah. I feel I have a responsibility to the women of this world!"

45

NIKKI

Nikki headed back to the *Power Pit*, texting Logan and thanking him for a nice night, but still not forgiving him and the affair with Song. Her female intuition screamed to her that the affair with Song was still ongoing. But she had no proof; at least not yet.

Seventeen's tight ass was on her mind as she arrived and immediately looked for the section that 17 was working. Not seeing her at her usual station, Nikki kind of freaked out.

"I am determined to get to know that sexy young thing, and it's going to be tonight, damn it," Nikki thought restlessly as she took a seat and waited for service.

In less than ten minutes, Nikki's female obsession, the young and attractive waitress known only as 17, came over to get Nikki's drink order.

"Good evening. What can I get you?"

"Good evening. Let me think."

Moments later, the waitress asked, "Do I know you? Seems like you and a couple other ladies were at this table recently."

Nikki was thrilled that she remembered their first meeting. "Yes, that's right. I was with a couple BFF's. My name is Nikki and yours will remain anonymous, right?"

"My name is Brandi, and we really need to protect our identity, ya know?"

"I do, Brandi. I'm a lawyer and truly understand what you're saying."

Nikki extended her hand to Brandi and they softly shook hands, as Nikki could see a slow smile appearing on Brandi's face, which gave Nikki a warm feeling.

"So, Nikki, the lawyer from San Francisco, what's your pleasure?"

"Getting into bed with you," was Nikki's first thought.

"I'm not sure. Got any suggestions, Brandi? What do you drink?"

175

"Well, we have a glorified rum and coke drink here called the Lounge Lizard, and when made with 80-proof rum, it packs a punch."

"Describe it."

"Sure. It's slightly bitter and has a cherry-flavored kick to it."

"I'm interested, Brandi. What's in it?"

"It has the basic dark rum and amaretto liquor and Coke. We use a lemon or lime slice as garnish. Stirred together with ice and you've got a drink that echoes that it's five o'clock somewhere."

Nikki was amused with the touch of humor and could see that a slight rapport was building.

"Great. I'll take one. Thanks."

As Brandi left to get Nikki's drink, Nikki's eyes were glued to the delightful derriere that was fading from view. "Yep, gotta make a move now," she whispered softly. "Will find out soon, if she likes women; no need to waste any time."

Returning about ten minutes later, Brandi placed a coaster and the drink on the table and smiled at Nikki. Nikki took Brandi's hand, held it firmly, and said, "You're sweet." Brandi squeezed Nikki's hand a bit harder and said, "You're warm."

"Would you like to meet for a nightcap after work, Brandi?"

Not hesitating a moment, "Yes, I would. I can probably leave in about an hour and a half, if that works for you."

"I'll be waiting here. Can you bring me another Lounge Lizard in about forty-five minutes?"

"Sure can." Brandi briskly moved away with a much more vibrant step than before, turned her head back toward Nikki and smiled as she exited.

True to form, Nikki scanned a fingerprint from the glass that Brandi handed her and sends it off to her lab for analysis. *Can never be too sure,* she thought.

♥　♥　♥

They headed to Brandi's apartment, only a couple blocks away, and split an open bottle of red wine. Nikki took the lead and pulled Brandi down on the couch and gave her a strong kiss. Brandi responded by embracing Nikki and moving her hands around Nikki's neck.

"I can't stop thinking about you," Nikki declared, feeling a heat starting to fill her body as she sees Brandi's breath is coming quicker. The chemistry in the air was thick with mystery and anticipation, as Nikki moved closer to Brandi and simply said, "I want to get to know you, Brandi. I want to know all about you."

"I want to know you too," Brandi said so quietly, she could barely be heard. "I can't remember ever feeling so strongly about a woman that I hardly know."

Nikki reached out her hand, and ran her thumb over Brandi's warm cheek. This mere contact was electric and Nikki sucked a breath as Brandi sighed. As Nikki continued to gently rub her cheek, Brandi responded with a soft smile, and as she leaned into Nikki's gentle touch, Nikki kissed her cheek softly. Feeling Nikki's growing passionate desire, Brandi turned her face inward, and their lips met in a firm kiss.

"I love the taste of your mouth and lips, Brandi."

"It's good to taste you, too," Brandi answered as she sensually sucked Nikki's lips.

Nikki pushed hard against Brandi, grasping her hips and pulling her harder against her body. Brandi moaned and ran her hands up Nikki's arms to take hold of her shoulders and continue the long kiss.

Nikki was now feeling a basic sexual want inside her quickly growing, and Brandi was providing a pleasing sexual anticipation, which was unlike anything Nikki remembered feeling before with a new lover, male or female.

"I need you and it makes me tremble," Nikki uttered as she swirled in Brandi's mouth with her tongue. "I want you, now."

Suddenly, Brandi's hands were in Nikki's hair pulling Nikki toward her, opening her mouth for Nikki to kiss her deeper. "Oh my God, I want you too."

As Nikki's lips were firmly against hers, she lowered a hand from her hip to slide down to the bottom of Brandi's skirt, and as Nikki slipped her hand under, her palm grazed Brandi's bare thigh. Brandi gasped, her leg jerking, breaking the steamy hot kiss.

Now knowing that Brandi was as turned on as she was, Nikki let her hand continue, traveling over the young girl's burning flesh, feeling her tremble, until Nikki touched her lace panties with her fingertips, moving to rim her folds with one finger.

"Oh, God, Nikki. Your touch is so soft and so warm."

Moving her thumb in a slow circle, searching for the firm bud, Nikki brushed the mound of her pubis, at the center of her burning legs. She was wet through the fabric, and Nikki delighted at the audible cry of surprise by Brandi as her excitement flashed. "Please, Nikki. I want to feel you deep inside me. I want you to make me come, now."

Her words were a request, but they almost sounded like an order ... a need for Nikki to quickly be inside her. Nikki paused to watch her beautiful mouth bite her lip in controlled anxiety. Nikki's hand, still between her legs, was now wet with her sweet juices, and with fingers about to probe her treasures, sought the nugget that would release her sexual essence.

"Yes," she says hurriedly. "Yes, right there. Roll it ... roll it."

Nikki did so tenderly, and fondled her with a finger, much better for sexual friction. In response, Brandi put her head back and both could feel her hips move in tandem with Nikki's stroking fingers. Brandi was reaching a point that was clearly an apex for her, and Nikki felt blessed to be the giver of such pleasure, as it was pleasurable for her as well.

"You make me feel so right and so alive," Brandi uttered, as if reassuring Nikki of her loving attention. Nikki continued slowly stroking her, using her other hand to strip her wet panties from her, and momentarily tasting the sweet juices from the warm panties. Nikki moved with her, sensing that it would take almost nothing to send Brandi off in orgasmic bliss.

Nikki slowly kissed her neck and could feel Brandi's heart pulsing through her skin. She moaned at Nikki's passionate caress. Between nips with Nikki's teeth on her skin, Nikki simply expressed her sexual sensation to her new lover.

"I can feel what you are feeling. One more gentle squeeze on your nugget and I want to feel you come."

Within seconds, Brandi erupted in a wonderful array of her pulsing body, ribbons of juices flowing and a piercing shriek of the ultimate climax.

"Oh yes. Oh yes. Oh, God ... yes."

46

SARA

S ara was relentlessly involved in the city's vast and exciting angel investor and *venture capital communities. An entrepreneurial friend of Sara invited her to a fund-raiser cookout at the home of the CEO of* Level 99 Ventures *and it was a VIP list unlike any other.*

Sara seemed to always be on the outside looking in, and to search for seed money for any number of book-to-movie deals that she and Troy were working on, this was the place to be.

Sara was nearly ready for the event, putting the final touches on her silver ruche sequined bodycon dress, with a plunging neckline that was very, very short. Sexy, vibrant, and the perfect appearance for *"look at me; I'm smart and beautiful!"*

Jason, her friend with the invitation, texted Sara to say that he was in the Uber downstairs and waiting for her. She gave Eja some last-minute goodies and headed down to the Uber, convinced that she had the festive look she needed to make a good first impression.

As she climbed into the car, she couldn't believe her eyes. "Hi gorgeous."

"Well, hi Jason. What's with the casual look? We still going to the VC cookout?"

Jason was wearing a tank top and sandals, looking poorly dressed for a trip to the hardware store.

"We sure are. Just don't want any of these money bags to think that I'm sucking up to them and need their GD money."

"That look says it all, my friend."

"Once inside, I'm gonna ditch this SOB before anyone thinks we are there together," Sara sighed.

Soon after they arrived at the event, as Sara tried to keep some distance between Jason and herself, she was able to spot a guy she knew, and excused herself and headed to make small talk with him and anyone else she could find.

Sara spent the next two hours roaming the grounds, to make as many business contacts as she could at this remarkable outing.

As the cookout was winding down, she was drawn into a conversation with six semi-intoxicated young women with plenty of axes to grind.

The red-headed leader of this "brat pack" was the daughter of Rod O'Malley, one of the founders of *Level 99 Ventures* and armed with theories on men that were obviously formed with some general consensus regarding a recurring theme.

"There are three kinds of men, girls, and you have met them all. We have the playboy or male whore, which we all have had to deal with."

"Absolutely," another young woman offered.

The red-head continued. "Then you have the sorry-ass pouter who always gives off the vibe of being a victim, so we can feel bad for him."

"Amen," another lady chimes in.

"My least fav is the pussy, or momma's boy. Just want to smack 'em in the mouth."

"*Gotta admit,*" Sara thought comically, "*there is some truth here, for sure.*"

As she started to move in the direction of an Uber valet stand, she got a text from Patrick, an on-again-off-again boyfriend she dated before she met Brad, wanting to hook up. "*Later, shit head,*" she thought, nastily.

For now, with tonight's yuk-fest in the rearview mirror, she shrugged her shoulders and blurted out her first impression.

"Just got some talking points for my friends the next time we are bar-hopping and bar-talking."

47

SAMANTHA

Based on several personal episodes with men having a huge effect on Dr. Vandenberg, she began a time in her career that was truly a mission to reach the pinnacle of her profession. Following two years of research and graduate-level education, she set a strategy in motion to be what her parents told her she could be – the Best!

She wrote a New York Times best seller, **You and Her**, which laid out in detail how to treat a woman and why old relationship solutions don't work in 2021. It launched her into a series of podcasts reinforcing her status in the community and in her field.

Samantha had tens of thousands of followers on the main social media sites, and created a dazzling website with a full-on male focus titled:

Unleash your Male Mystery ... Regain your Male Mastery

The man who had the market "cornered" on how to treat a woman, our very own Ramon, picked up on all this celebrity vibe regarding Dr. Vandenberg, and contacted Samantha out of both a curiosity and some possible info-sharing.

"Hello, Doctor Vandenberg, this is Ramon Gilbert, a newly minted 'fan' of yours."

"Hello Ramon. Thank you for calling and for becoming a fan. I certainly appreciate the effort and the affirmation. What can I help you with?"

"I admire and respect your tact and determination to help guys rouse their hidden potential, and hone their masculine skills, to passionately reconnect and reestablish their female relationships."

Samantha smiled as Ramon continued. "And, like me, you are passionate about what you are doing, and in helping people make their relationships the best they can be."

"Well, Ramon, you sound like a guy with many of the same interests and desires to help the male/female relationship as I do."

"Thank you. The main difference, of course, is that I'm a guy, dealing with the ladies often, and almost never surprised about what I don't know."

"Great for you to admit that, and I think I'm talking to a very special man."

"Thanks again."

"So, Ramon, what was the nature of the call and can I help in any way?"

"Getting straight to the point. I'd really like to meet and share each other's experiences and perspective. It seems like the categories of men and sex, and how women react to same, are shared by both of us."

Getting her attention with a core remark that hit home, some of Samantha's sexual juices began to flow as she opened her appointment book. She found Ramon's voice to be charming and captivating. *"No wonder he meets his ladies' expectations,"* she thought.

"I'd love to do that. Let's talk this time tomorrow," after looking at her availability, "and set a date to meet."

"That would be fine. Thank you very much, Doctor Vandenberg, and we will chat later."

"I think I'd like to get into his pants," Samantha thought sexually.

"I'd really like to get into her head," Ramon thought curiously.

The magnificent stage was set.

48

SAMANTHA

*S*amantha *and Ramon had a great talk and she was very interested in getting together with him. But, the sex talk with Ramon got Sam's juices flowing, again. This sexual mindset got her thinking about Christian, a fairly well-known sex therapist friend of hers, and a guy with a special skill, similar to Ramon Gilbert. She called Christian and they set up a sex date.*

*A little background on Christian Windsor, if that is his real name. Many of us believe that he changed his name once he got his mojo going. He is straight out of central casting. If the **Young and the Restless** were looking for a blend of Mister Dreamy and Mister Steamy, believe me Y&R would need to look no further than CW.*

He had a gorgeous build, strong shoulders, muscular arms and legs, and a neatly trimmed beard that had every appearance of a guy in a shaver commercial. You get the picture!

With a strong mutual hobby interest, Sam met Christian at the San Francisco Museum of Modern Art, a museum holding an internationally recognized collection of modern and contemporary art, and was the first museum on the West Coast devoted solely to 20th Century renderings.

After touring the museum for a couple of hours, Christian asked Sam, "What is your favorite piece here?"

"Well, it's tough to decide, but I truly love the 1905 oil-on-canvas painting by Henri Matisse, titled *Femme au Chapeau*, or *Woman with a Hat*. It depicted his wife, Amelie, and is so colorful and so fluid. Plus, it was also one of the works owned by the incredible movie star, Greta Garbo, who is one of my idols."

"Wow, Sam, you really know your stuff."

"Yeah, I keep up. Have a couple copies of modern art at my office and studio … can't afford the real thing."

Christian smiled at his lovely and intelligent companion.

"What's your fav, Christian?"

"Easy here. I just love anything by Jackson Pollack."

"Yes, he is a major figure in the abstract impressionist movement."

They stopped at a kiosk for a cappuccino, and then Christian dove right into the main event.

"So, my Dear, still interested in my sex, tonight."

"As much as ever, Christian."

"There is nothing better than having sex with the lovely and intelligent, Doctor Samantha Vandenberg. We're on."

They finished their drinks, and then headed to the valet stand to change the mood. Tonight, they would realize a powerful, sexual energy dynamic; enjoyed by the precious few.

♥   ♥   ♥

Back at Christian's meticulously furnished penthouse suite, Sam couldn't help but wonder why this extremely eligible bachelor was still available. In a couple hours, she would see why.

While Sam was in the bathroom freshening up, Christian prepared and poured them both a soothing blood orange sidecar cocktail. He had many specialties, and bar master was just one.

"Oh great," Sam uttered enthusiastically, entering the kitchen, a *Midnight Ride.*"

"Yep, they are called that, as well."

"What's in yours, Christian?"

"Cognac and Grand Marnier, but the orange bitters and blood oranges are definitely the highlight … seasonal, you know."

Clinking and toasting, most women would be absolutely delighted if their date ended here and now. For the good doctor, her real date was just beginning.

They spent the next half hour talking, and Sam was getting excited at the thought of what was to come. With a heavy sigh, Christian simply got Plan B going.

"Let's head into the bedroom."

"Yes, Christian. Sounds good."

As Christian turned down the bedroom lighting to a romantic ebb, Sam began to undress. Seeing her in a heightened state of anxiety, he simply spoke from the heart, "Let me, my Dear."

Christian would engage in a novel take on strip poker ... one garment at a time; first her blouse, then his shirt, then her skirt, then his pants, etcetera.

When it was down to his blue diamond mesh boxer shorts, and her bra and panties, his magic began. He gently removed her lace bra, with a touch so slight she could barely feel it. He placed her on the edge of the bed, lifted her legs, and slowly removed her thong.

"You are wet. Wet and warm."

Sam said nothing as he dropped his boxers on the floor. He positioned Sam on her back, placed a pillow under her head, and from a small bottle of oil, spread some lightly over Sam's front, neck to knees, and gently turned her over to lightly oil her back, from neck to her butt cheeks.

"What is that wonderful aroma?"

"It's a special blend of saffron, rose oil, and turmeric. I have a lady friend who prepares just the right amount of this beauty elixir, each application distinctive to a particular warm body under stress, and accentuates her growing arousal."

"Oh my God," was all that Sam could think of. *"I'm in heaven and he hasn't even started."*

Something inside her chest relaxed, as if feeling that he understood her and her current lustful needs. He was very comfortable in his skin, an image of ease and self-control. Christian made Sam feel safe and innocent, exploring all the ways he could wrestle the fantasy demons out of her head and replace them with his acronym, IRL, or *in real life.*

"Yes, I am horny, Christian." She reached down and saw him watching her feel herself and her heat. She was wet from his presence, his thoughtful words, and the aroma of his marvelous oil.

"I should be embarrassed as I stroke myself under his watchful and intense eyes," she whispered to herself.

"You always make my sex come alive, Christian. You can arouse my fantasies with barely a touch. Go ahead, turn me on good."

The words just burst from the essence of her being, as if she sensed his growing desire. She moaned slightly, pulling her hand free from its warm and soft place. He watched her move her hand from between her legs to her mouth, smiling cunningly with his next steps in mind.

She touched his lips until he parted them and she pressed two fingers inside his mouth, feeling his moist, warm, and sensitive tongue. She wanted to touch every inch of his body, from his face, to his mouth, to his chest, hips and thighs. He knew she enjoyed caressing him, as he appreciated feeling her lovely body as well.

Once he reached her core, he placed two fingers of one hand in her moist love nest, and two fingers from his other hand in her wide-open mouth, rotating in sync and teasing Sam until her entire body ached with lustful desire. His M.O. had always been attention to his lady's every whim and movement. He was repeating a sexual theme that turned her on … *big time!*

"I can remember the last time we made love … wonderful love … and it began like this," she thought affectionately.

But this time Sam wanted his sex so much more. More rough and more physical. She really wanted him to make her body shake with an orgasmic rush that she hadn't experienced in quite a while.

As she found herself becoming even more soaked, he guided her fingers back and forth in her vagina in a slow, methodical manner, long enough that she could feel her orgasm building. He knew how much her body wanted to let go.

"Stop, for a moment. Let's get in another position" he said caringly, slowly pulling her hand out from her core.

He lifted Sam so her butt was on the edge of the bed and with her sitting in front of him, his thighs were now on both sides of hers.

"Lie back."

She does, exhaling a slight moan as his warm hands ran up her oiled legs and back down again. He rested her feet on his thighs and leaned forward, kissing the inside of her knee.

"Touch me everywhere," Sam invited as she squirmed on the bed.

"Be still, dear Samantha" he replied as he kissed the delicate skin on both sides of her inner thigh.

"Touch me," she begs. "I want your mouth on me. Please."

Christian opened his mouth and soon he was gently sucking her warm and wet core. Sam was sexually pleased, but now her expectations were soaring. Getting her signal to step it up, he sucked her thirstily as she moaned pleasurably.

As her pulse quickened and he sensed her keen state of arousal, he grasped her waist and lifted her up to where she was now standing on the floor, on very shaky legs. As he dropped to catch her wobbly body, she could not miss seeing his massive boner.

He turned them to the wall as he chose stand-up sex, which Sam found pretty fricking hot, with insane orgasms from good technique.

"Rest your back against the wall," he said coolly, "and wrap your legs around my waist."

As their position was complete, his kisses and caresses put Sam into a sexual eagerness that she hadn't felt in a long, long time. This is what she wanted to feel. As he widened his stance, he grabbed her thighs and buttocks to get her into the proper position for insertion.

"Are you good, my lovely lady?"

"Good and ready. Please. Now."

Sam could feel him slowly penetrating her throbbing channel, and her climax was near. She could feel that he was not as close to climax as she was, so Sam tried to focus on holding back. Seconds seemed like minutes, but it was all worthwhile, as they both enjoyed a simultaneous orgasm. Sam was literally having a stand-up orgasm being felt from her head to her now throbbing bottom. Sweat … oily sweat … and big smiles!

She cried, "Oh yes, oh yes … yes, yes, yes!"

He gave out a deep and throaty gasp, allowing both his physical and emotional juices to erupt.

Pausing, and placing her butt softly back on the bed, he uttered, "That was beautiful, my Dear."

She thought appreciably, ***"This is so damn hot, and it takes a real master to get standing sex right. He is special!"***

49

LINA

I was told that Lina had met with the girls to obtain material for her book. At that time, she described a trip to a local marina, where she was told by a close friend a young mother named Elena would be waiting. Elena was an abused wife and sources told Lina that she was not comfortable going to the police.

With notepad and a strategy in hand, Lina headed to the Marina where Elena was located on a bright, sunny Saturday morning, working with her family on their 35-foot-long Trojan Cruiser.

As Lina approached the boat, named *Bon Appétit*, she observed Elena in the cabin and the two boys and one girl in the water, cleaning the algae stain from the boats' water marks. Her husband, Derek, was hosing down the walkway leading to the boat.

Elena was a short, athletic-type woman with voluptuous breasts, which were large for her frame. When Lina saw her, Elena seemed to force a smile. Derek was average height, a well-built man, smoking a large cigar, and yelling out orders to his kids.

Elena saw Lina arriving, knew who she was, and the reason she had come, but turned away to finish cooking the burgers for lunch.

"Hello, I'm Lina Chang, a reporter from the Sentinel, doing a story on life aboard the many ships that are here in this marina and others. Your boat is beautiful."

Derek extended his hand and introduced himself.

"I'm Derek, the owner of this awesome boat. I've always been a big fan of anything called a Trojan!"

The innuendo was not lost on Lina, and Elena, hearing her husband's boasts, shook her head, mildly, in embarrassment.

"Hi Derek. Yes, it is an incredible boat. I have a short survey. Could I possibly get some info from you and your family for my story?"

"Sure. I'm kind of busy doing important things, but my wife, Elena, and the kids, once they get out of the water, will be glad to help you."

"That would be great. Thank you."

"Why don't you go aboard and meet my wife and stay for lunch, okay?"

"I'd love to, if it's alright with the misses."

"It's all right. Take off your shoes first."

"Oh yes, of course."

A somewhat unsettled Lina then asked a question she wished she hadn't asked.

"The name of your boat is the *Bon Appétit*. That's a really cool name. Are one of you a chef?"

"Nope, young lady. It simply means my wife is good enough to eat. HAHA!"

♥   ♥   ♥

From that somewhat productive, but otherwise wasted exercise in demeaning male behavior, Lina thought about all the examples of misogyny she had accumulated, realizing that the upside was tons of material for *Charade in the City*.

From the marina, Lina headed to another volunteering event in the poorer area of San Francisco. She had been there about two hours when Security Guard Carl Blake saw Lina and walked over to talk to her.

"Hi Carl, how goes it?"

"You know, the usual. Just waiting for something to happen."

"Carl, I have a break due in about 20 minutes. Would you like to grab a coffee and get caught up?"

"Sure. See you then over at refreshments."

A half hour later, Lina met Carl. "Sorry. A little late."

"No problem. Not going anywhere. Got you a coffee. The condiments are in the bag."

"Thank you."

"Long day, eh Lina?"

"For sure, Carl. I just wish the wealthier people in this town would step up and help."

"Don't hold your breath, young lady."

"Got it, Carl. What's new in your world?"

"Same old, same old. Taking classes at CCSF and hoping to test out of this mundane security guard shit. Oh, sorry!"

"Don't be. I understand. And, City College of San Francisco plays an important role in the community, enrolling about one in every nine city residents in their classes."

Carl smiled as Lina continued. "How far along are you?"

"Ah, about a year and a half of classes … so not too bad."

"Well, my friend, I wish you the best."

They chatted for about 15 minutes when Lina said, "Gotta get back to work, Carl."

"Hey, before you go, I was wondering if you'd be interested in dinner or a movie."

Lina was not thinking of a date, but didn't want to hurt his feelings. "Sure. Fisherman's Wharf has a couple good bands lined up on Saturday night. How 'bout we meet there?" She wondered pensively, *"He really seems like a nice guy. Why not?"*

Carl had something more romantic in mind, but agreed to start the ball rolling with this idea. "Sounds good to me. Let's meet up around seven. Can text whereabouts."

"Deal, Carl. See you then."

Carl thought, eagerly, *"I'd really prefer to meet at her place … better potential."*

Lina thought, happily, *"This should be a safe first date."*

♥ ♥ ♥

Carl met Lina at Fisherman's Wharf and the entire evening seemed pleasant. There were no warning flags up, so when she invited him over, he quickly agreed and they took an Uber to her apartment.

Once inside, Lina offered him a choice of drinks. Since he preferred beer, she poured him a Molson and fixed herself a Black and Tan. He removed his backpack carrying his phone, laptop, and assorted items, "I actually have a small gift for you that I will give her later."

"Wow, that's nice. You really didn't need to do that, Carl."

"It's not much."

"Can I see it now?" Lina wondered, *"This is strange. Should I be excited or nervous?"*

"Let's just enjoy our drinks and get caught up, Lina. I'm very much interested in your writing and journalism activities."

About an hour later, having gone through two beers each, Carl reached into his backpack and picked up a small, flat bag and handed it to Lina.

The gift was racy lingerie, but to Lina, it appeared as bondage apparel, bringing back ugly memories of her abuse by the rich uncle in LA, which forced her to move to San Francisco.

"Pathetic costumes like these are nothing more than a visual turn-on for any horny man," Lina thought disgustedly, and was petrified.

"What is this? Why did you bring this?"

"Lina, it is a pretty outfit that you will look great in."

"I am in no way interested in wearing this or whatever you have in mind, Carl. I think you should leave."

In an instant, Carl lunged for Lina and hugged her in a very restraining manner.

"Stop!"

"Damn it, Lina, most women would love to tease their man with this beautiful and sexy nightie. What's the problem?"

Lina's heart was racing as a million things went through her foggy mind. She needed a plan. "Stop it, Carl."

There was no mistaking his sexual intent from the gleam in his eyes as he looked Lina over, head to toe. From his broad, leaning shoulders to the sinuousness of his stride, he was ready and Lina definitely was not ... not at all. She was worried, as his size and manner were way more than Lina could handle.

She moved to the corner of the kitchen, which gave herself some room to move, and an idea, if things got any worse.

"I'm on my period," she exclaimed in hopes that he would be dissuaded.

"That doesn't matter to me. Messy, but okay for me."

As Lina tried to move away, Carl lunged at her and before she could react, he had grabbed her waist and was pulling her close enough to him that she could feel his throbbing pelvis.

"I'm not your possession, Carl. Now get away from me!"

As she gasped, he forced his mouth harshly on hers, causing pain on her mouth and teeth as she tried to turn away. His thumbs dug into her cheekbones.

"Stop!"

When he refused to stop, she reached for the long knife on the corner of her kitchen counter that she had moved so closely to, only a few minutes ago.

Lina was able to grab a kitchen knife and point it directly at his face, thinking back to her physical torture brought on by her Uncle Chin. He jumped back in utter surprise with her ferociousness.

"What the hell are you doing?"

"Get away from me Carl. Now!"

His attempt to seduce her failed.

"Get the hell out of my apartment and take this disgusting piece of crap with you."

Flinging the garment in his face, he realized that he seriously underestimated Lina and her defensive prowess.

She went ballistic as the overwhelmed security guard exited the apartment!

50

NIKKI

This is Nikki's chapter, but I'm going to set it up, inasmuch as I am part of this situation with AlienCon in Dallas in 2019. Although I knew who Nikki Wallace was, it was here in Dallas that I met Nikki in a truly remarkable and inspirational encounter.

The annual AlienCon weekend-long exploration of the unknown brings celebrity guests from popular alien-centric TV shows and films, including the ever-popular Ancient Alien series on the History Channel. Southern California hosted the one before this.

This years' event, held at the Kay Bailey Hutchinson Convention Center, was a wildly successful and well-attended conference. Presenters included Giorgio Tsoukalos, David Childress, and Caroline Cory from the Ancient Alien series.

Science fiction writers, like myself, had a fabulous forum to market their books and their future aspirations. It was the Super Bowl for all things weird and wonderful in the alien universe.

It was Day Two and I was signing books from my *Galactic Disruption* series, of which I had three published and two more in process. My own vision board had the movie goals vividly attached, hoping some film producer would wander by, like my books, and sign me to a movie contract.

Well, what happened on this day was dramatic – just not that particular drama. First, let me try to describe a certain number of the attendees. They would dress in costume, befitting a Star Wars, Star Trek, or any number of superheroes or super-heroines. Some looked amazing true to subject … some categorically hilarious.

As I was signing a couple books and making small talk with a fan, a sight approaching my booth took my breath away. Headed in my direction was this tall, stunning, and daunting African American attendee, complete with beige cargo pants, matching Bush Poplin safari shirt, a silver chainmail belt, and high-heel boots.

She had a unique look, compared to the other attendees, given her garb and that long black hair and piercing smile. She appeared to me as an alien phenom-enon researcher, right out of the *Ancient Aliens* series on the History Channel.

Extending her hand to me, she introduced herself. "I am Nikki Wallace. You are author, Jonathan Garrett, and I am pleased to meet you."

"Likewise, Princess Nikki. What brings you to my humble booth?"

Smiling, Nikki responded, "I am an admirer of your work and find myself living in your writings; both as a prisoner and a savior."

"Holy shit. We need to talk, Princess Nikki."

"We do."

"Here, let me sign a couple of my books for you. It sounds like you are aware of my main character, the Warrior Princess."

"Hyperaware."

"Ooh, I like that word, Princess Nikki. I may use it myself."

"Please do, Jonathan."

Pausing, "Nikki, I'm staying at the Marriott on South Houston Street. How about dinner tonight around 8:00?"

"That sounds good, Jonathan. I will meet you in the lobby at eight."

♥ ♥ ♥

As anxious as hell to meet this striking alien goddess, I was in the lobby at 7:30. I had made dinner reservations at the exceptional Five-Sixty by Wolfgang Puck restaurant for 8:15 and was looking forward to this dinner, as much as any in recent memory.

At exactly 8:00, this tall, stunning and sensual beauty walked into the lobby, as men lost sight of their dignity trying to catch a return to their "hi, how are you" lame intros.

She wore this plunging V-neck elegant sweater dress with sexy tunic long sleeves; a perfect winter business dress in a gorgeous shade of wine.

As she approached me, I was delighted to be the focus of her attention and my ego was getting stroked at quite a rapid pace.

I extended my hand to her, kissed her hand, and she responded. "Good evening, Mr. Garrett."

"And a good evening to you, Miss Wallace." We both got a chuckle from that one.

"I have made reservations upstairs at Five-Sixty. It's a revolving restaurant that will give to a birds-eye view of Dallas and the steaks are remarkable."

"That sounds wonderful, Jonathan."

"Let's go, Nikki."

For tonight ... two peas in a pod.

♥   ♥   ♥

Once we were seated, we began a conversation that went until closing time in this wonderful Wolfgang Puck restaurant.

When she told me, her name was Nikki Wallace from San Francisco, I immediately knew who the alien princess was in the real world. Attorney Wallace had a helluva reputation in the city. She was impressive as either the bulldog attorney or the alien princess character, and I was proud to be her escort and felt a little intimidated in her presence.

"I gotta start with the genuine alien interest. I mean I love it. Being my writing genre, I really love it, but what drives this alter-ego persona? Lawyers and aliens just don't cohabitate."

"Jonathan, I really am a believer and always have been. These events allow me to intermingle and participate in all things alien without it screwing up my career and future plans to seek political office."

"Well, I feel like an ass. That makes perfect sense and I should have figured that out. Sorry."

Smiling, Nikki winked at Jon as the waiter brought their dinners.

"Nikki Wallace, you are one hot alien princess, and I am happy to share your tales."

Dinner was an enjoyable evening for both.

Nikki thought about sex later and concluded to herself that there could be a common subject-matter bonding, "*Nope, can't mix business with pleasure.*"

Jonathan was thinking selfishly, "If I can get a movie deal going, this lovely space alien could dress in costume as the main character in my book; posters, photos, retail merchandise, etc.

He thought, reluctantly, "***But likely, no sex, damn it!***"

51

JACQUI

I will need to tee this one up as well. This was the encounter with Jacqui that revealed her hubby's sordid past, and it was not pretty. If it wasn't important to her story, I'd move on without it. I even left out some disgusting details, as the picture is disgusting as is.

"Hey Jon, it's me. How ya doing?"

"I'm good, Jacqui. All good with you?"

"Yeah, sort of. Just got off the phone with the attorneys trying to claim that James and I conspired to molest those girls in Jamaica and here at home. Shit."

"Need some company to blow off some steam?"

"Yep. Could use a dose of sanity. You available?"

"I am, Jacqui. Give me an hour or so. Want me to bring anything?"

"Could use a good scotch."

"Great. It'll come too. See ya soon."

I arrived with a $500 bottle of Glenlivet XXV Scotch, meant to fix what ailed Jacqui, or at least start to.

As I entered the front door, Jacqui gave me a warm and long embrace, totally happy to see her strong "renaissance man." She wasn't wearing anything sexy or suggestive, much to my disappointment.

"You wanna see the docs?"

"Sure, Jacqui. I'm not a lawyer but I have seen my share of similar documents."

"I'll open this fine bottle of scotch and pour us a couple. Neat?"

"Yes, Please."

After a few minutes of review, "This is some complicated shit, Jacqui. Want me to have one of my attorney friends take a look?"

"Wouldn't hurt if you could."

196

"Done. Let's sip on that Glenlivet, shall we?" I gave Jacqui another warm hug.

A smile was returning to Jacqui's face, as I always seemed to make things right for her, whether in bed or helping like today.

She thought realistically, "*I'm just not in the mood for screwing around right now.*"

I could see that Jacqui was preoccupied with the legal crap and just resigned myself to be her friend tonight, not her lover.

♥　　♥　　♥

After some awkward small talk, Jacqui had a suggestion. "Have I ever showed you my shitty husband's sex chamber?"

"No. I would likely have remembered a sex chamber."

"Fine. Let's refresh our drinks and I'll give you a guided tour."

Well, that got my wheels spinning. I remember thinking, "*Maybe sex is still in the cards tonight.*"

As we took the elevator down to LL2, Jacqui's mood shifted from damsel-in-distress to a dominant about to reveal her wishes to a submissive. I could see her batteries getting recharged.

The sex chamber was like something out of a porn movie set. There were machines, chain apparatus, spreader bars and devices that looked like actual torture tables.

"Wow. This is freaky, Jacqui. Did you know about his dark side when you guys got married?"

"Hell no. We dabbled in light bondage and did some role playing, but little did I know that he was setting me up for the big stuff."

"What is that?" I said looking at a device meant to spread a woman's legs and arms apart for penetration.

"That is a replica of a sex table from the 1983 movie *Star 80* that told the story of the murder of a Playboy model by her husband. Don't even say it. I can't get rid of any of this as long as litigation of James is underway."

With a deep sigh, Jacqui pointed to a glass locker filled with video tapes. "Many of these are his victims, all signing legal releases to be part of his 'in crowd' and enabling James to do as he pleased."

I was getting a sick-to-my-stomach feel.

"It wasn't until after his murder, did I realize that I was among those being filmed, both in bed with him, and with multiple partners, and on devices like the

St. Andrews Cross bondage table, where he ran a Wartenberg Pinwheel across my boobs and buttocks."

Setting her drink down, Jacqui walked over to the cross, stripped down to her panties, and proceeded to place her hands and feet in the shackles meant to bind the victim harshly to the arms of the cross.

"Jon, come over here and latch me into these bindings."

"Jacqui?"

"No. I'm serious."

I did what she asked me to do. "In the blue drawer are some Japanese Clover nipple clamps. Find a pair and put them on me with the pendulum weights meant to bear down on my tits."

"I'm really getting uncomfortable, Jacqui."

"Please. I need this right now. Just fricking do it!"

I did what she asked and could see that even the lightest weights were painful to my lady friend.

"Now, pull out one of those open-mouth gags in that red drawer."

One was steel and one was leather. I grabbed the leather.

"Put the gag on me, Jon." I did, but as softly as I could, realizing that I could have attached it with much more force."

Moments later, Jacqui began to cry and I immediately removed the gag and nipple clamps as she was trying to speak.

"There were times when I spent all night here, Jon ... wetting my pants and shivering in the dark."

"Oh my God. I am so sorry, Jacqui."

"Well, there is, as they say ... more to this story?"

"I don't follow, Jacqui."

To this day her remarks give me chills ...

"Jon, he was a deep, dark piece of me that I wished I didn't need ... but sometimes didn't object to."

52

SARA

I'm back with a follow-up episode concerning Sara and her cheating boyfriend, Brad. Remember the "something just came up" episode in Season Whatever? Well, revenge is sweet and you will appreciate the elaborate planning that went into the following. This one is fun!

Via numerous accounts on social media, as well as her own experiences with Brad, Sara felt it was time to turn the tables on her bastard boyfriend, and she had a plan. She would conspire with her friend and a successful B actress, who went by the stage name Cherri Berry. Yep, not making that up.

This would also involve her guy friend and chemist par excellence, Lonnie Strayer, whose background could be described in part by the 2014 film, *Better Living Through Chemistry*, which depicted a trophy wife, sex, drugs, and mayhem.

So here we go. Brad frequents a waterfront sports bar at the Embarcadero. His routine on Friday night is predictable. He goes there with guy friends, who hope to hook up with a lady for Saturday night, if possible. Once his presence is relayed back to Sara, the fun begins.

Cherri, dressed from an actual movie set for a scene in *Walkers of Shadows* has a costume featuring a black and red silk mini-dress, hair tie, arm warmers, lace-up ribbons, and leggings. She also wears a COVID19-inspired black face mask. Quite a sight. She is going to act out the part of a sexy Asian woman looking for sex.

It didn't take long for Brad to catch a gaze of this newbie in the bar. Once eye contact was made, Cherri moved toward Brad with all the warmth and charm of a ninja warrior stalking her prey.

Brad was the kind of guy who thought risky behavior was his entitlement, so it didn't take long for the couple to take their drinks and move away so they could talk and drink by themselves.

"I haven't seen you here before. Are you new to the city?"

"Yes, my name is Alisha. I just arrived from Singapore. What's your name?"

"I'm Brad."

With a slight grabbing of his crotch, she gave Brad a wet, sloppy French kiss, which lit him up.

"Piece of cake," she thought, unquestionably.

The revenge plot with disguise was underway and the next step was intoxication.

"Brad, baby, Alisha needs another drink."

"Be right back ... don't go anywhere."

As Brad left, Cherri brought out a small vial of GHB (gamma hydroxybutyric acid) with street names such as liquid ecstasy and cherry meth; the date-rape drug. As soon as Brad returned with the drinks, Cherri began the process of lightly spiking his drinks to get him high, but not pass out.

At the selected time, Cherri murmured, "I have a friend from Singapore who is meeting me here. Would you mind if she joined us? I think she'd like to meet a handsome American like you."

A somewhat disheveled Brad replied, "No problem."

Cherri texted Sara, who was waiting outside.

> "The shitass is ready."
> "Be right in."

Moments later, in walked Sara, dressed in a similar ninja-inspired casting outfit. This one was a red, long-sleeve matte body suit, with sassy mesh insets, a daring sash and black, mesh stocking riding to mid-calf and black boots. The same black mask created the look of two ninjas out for some fun ... or to create trouble.

Sara moved directly to the corner table where Cherri and Brad were enjoying their third or fourth scotches, albeit Brad's had a little more "juice."

"Ah, say hello to my friend, Anna. She is also from Singapore, but only speaks Mandarin."

"Hello Anna. I'm Brad. Nice to meet you."

He extended his hand to Sara, which she touched softly and nodded her pleasure in meeting him. With the ninja-inspired outfit and the huge mask covering her lower face, Brad was too far gone to recognize Sara.

Working to avoid any interruptions from Brad's friends, Cherri and Sara were able to get Brad to the point where they had to leave the bar. Making sure that he was stable enough for exiting the bar without disruptions or any attention being paid to the three, Cherri nodded to Sara.

"Brad, we are going to leave and take you to our friend's nearby apartment, so the three of us can get naked. My friend Anna and I want to have sex with you. We will please you ... very much."

"Okay, Alis ... Alo. Yeah, okay."

♥　♥　♥

The three moved quickly to a waiting Uber which took them to a sorority house of one of Cherri's friends.

With the help of two sorority sisters, Brad was guided upstairs to a bedroom, which had been set up for the night's festivities.

Brad was somewhat aware of this pending sexcapade, and could only see upside from a threesome with two lovely Asians. Only Alisha spoke.

"Brad, Honey, you, okay?"

"Yeah, I'm fine. Gotta pee."

"Come with me, Brad, and I'll show you where to go."

"Can you help me pee?"

Sara couldn't resist a chuckle, nodding noticeably.

Once inside the bathroom, Cherri unzipped Brad's pants, pulled out his penis and helped her man relieve himself.

"Damn, he is huge," Cherri thought jealously. *"No wonder Sara hangs around."*

As they returned to the bedroom, Sara had already laid out the poster bed with restraints and a couple needed accessories.

"Brad, Honey, we need to strip you down to those shiny black boxers and you need to lay down on the bed."

"Okay."

Cherri mounted the somewhat lethargic Brad cowgirl style and began to kiss his mouth and play with his nipples. Meanwhile, Sara was tying down Brad's feet to the bed posts to spread his legs widely apart.

With one last shot of her concealed drug, Cherri placed a small amount on Brad's tongue and between the booze and the drugs, he was somewhere in la-la land.

The girls then completed the "pose" of macho man Brad. His hands were bound to the headboard posts, his legs had already been bound, his boxers removed and his "junk" was contained in a nasty looking strict leather speed snap enhancement strap. Yes, Brad was truly left in a most embarrassing position. But wait … there's more.

The girls weren't done. They snapped several instant photos of Brad in that compromising pose, with his full name in a placard above his head for the whole world to see. Yep. This could be the social media *Piece de resistance* that would live forever in the annals of history in the City by the Bay.

The next morning, Brad was found by a "surprised" sorority sister, and was freed. As soon as he had gotten his clothes on, he screamed, "I'm gonna sue those bitches!"

The "innocent" sorority sister pointed out to Brad that, apparently, both instant photos, which were laying on a dresser, and noted digital photos were taken for blackmail; so, Brad couldn't press charges. An agitated Brad grabbed the photos and stormed out.

The innocent sorority sister sent out a group text.

Fist bumps all around for the ladies of that particular evening!

53

SARA

Sara had just come back from high-fiving the cast and characters of *Brad's Sad Adventure*, as the girls were calling it. They had brunch at the Benu in the Financial District, and she returned to her condo. It was 2:00 in the afternoon and she decided to head to the gorgeous rooftop pool to cool off and plan her next couple of days.

Once she reached the pool, in her stunning high-leg low-back cutout Brazilian one-piece swimsuit in a sexy snake print, she grabbed a lounge chair in a corner, under a bright California Sun. Glancing in her direction was the pool boy, or pool man, a guy about 6 feet 2 inches, tanned and muscular body, and surfer blond hair. Yep, right out of central casting for *Beach Party Whatever*.

Sara laid on her tummy, with cleavage exposed, giving the young man a double take … or triple take. For the next hour and a half, it was cute and a bit adolescent to see Sara, the pro, working on the young dude with raging testosterone.

Then, sensing an opportunity to meet him, she headed over to where he was skimming the pool. Sara noticed in his bag was a *Sports Illustrated Magazine* with two local baseball stars on the cover.

"Hi there, my name is Sara, and I see you are a baseball fan."

"Hell yeah, big time. I'm Connor. Nice to meet you. Who's your favorite Giant?"

Realizing she had a small problem, not being into baseball at all, she quickly replied, "Well, I'm a girl who prefers the guys making the big bucks."

"Golly, that would be Buddy Gardner and Jacob Watts. You know 'em?"

"No. Sorry, don't know them. Hey, Connor, when you done here?"

"I'm done at 5:00, Sara."

"Great, ya want to come up to my place then? We can grab a couple cold ones and talk baseball."

"Oh gosh, yes. That would be terrific."

"Fine." Jotting down her condo number on his hand, she smiled, walked back over to her lounge chair, gathered her things, and headed back to her condo to get prepared. *"I'm gonna out-do Nikki and her pool boy escapade with Dick,"* Sara whispered to herself.

At 5:05, an enthusiastic Conner rang her bell. Still wearing her swimsuit, she had a couple cold Molson's ready, and they sat down and talked for a while.

"Tell me, Connor, how old are you and what do you do when you're not cleaning pools?"

"Well, I'm 19 and a student at Berkeley."

"What ya studying?"

"Marine Biology."

"Seriously?"

"Yeah, why?"

"Nothing. That's just an awesome major, Connor."

Sara got another cold beer for Connor and decide to go "all in" with this young man.

"Would you excuse me for a minute?"

"Sure."

When Sara returned, she had changed to a white, see-through one shoulder hollow-out cover-up, minus any bra or panties.

In a matter of seconds, Connor slowly rose from the couch, holding his slowly growing manhood, and stared at the imposing beauty in front of him … the thin fabric hiding nothing.

"You look great."

"Why, thank you, Connor."

Sara moved deliberately to get her body up against his groin area and feel his young glory. She wrapped her arms around his neck, and said, "I think, Connor, it's now lady's choice."

"Okay. Whatever you want is fine."

"Then I vote for a wet and wild ride in my rather awesome shower."

"That's a great idea," he quickly replied.

Sara ordered, "Get naked."

After he stripped, and she could see that every inch of this young dude was heavenly, she led him into the fabulously re-done art-deco designed bathroom, decorated in a myriad of repetitive linear and geometric shapes and strong, vibrant colors. It was Sara's signature shower, and it was striking.

The tile floor was awash with rainbow-like patterns and the ceiling light was muted above the center of the bathroom, in more of an ethereal glow. A laser-like revolving ball of light was aimed at the immense shower, large enough to hold a small party.

"Stand there under the center shower head," she said pointing to a large 18-inch circular rain shower, "I'll be back in a minute."

Sara swiftly returned, now wearing nothing, but holding a huge remote device in her hand. As he had gotten into position, she engaged the remote to reveal a series of water jets protruding from the circular walls, and several small shower heads released warm water, including one positioned directly below his groin.

"Oh my God," Connor exclaimed. "This is fricking magic."

Sara joined him, like a mermaid from a mysterious mist, as the room fogged with steam as warm water pulsed from what was now dozens of shower heads, massaging every part of their bodies and giving him a boner that appeared to need immediate attention.

"Close your eyes and turn around, big boy. I'm in charge now."

Connor turned and closed his eyes and simply enjoyed the sensations of the warm, pulsating water and a warm, pulsating woman. Sara moved behind him, her arms around his neck, her damp hair teasing the back of his neck. He could feel her groin snug against his rear end, her legs wrapping his.

"Relax," Sara said, "take a deep breath and relax."

Her breasts were flattened against his back, but not for long. As the shower continued its magic massage, her nipples took the signal and became firm, erect, and pointing deep into his back.

She grabbed his butt cheeks with both hands. He could feel the teasing brush of her firm breasts and the faint prickle of her closely trimmed pubic hair. She moved across him, side-to-side, like an exotic dancer, teasing and brushing her warm wet skin, getting them both all hot and aroused.

"Turn around. I want to see your wet rod."

He did, instantly, wanting to see her naked beauty as well. This marvelous mermaid was magnificent; strong, supple limbs, writhing and maneuvering.

Now she touched him … now she didn't. Sara used every part of her body, playing with him as if she were a cat and he was a powerless mouse, mesmerized by her intoxicating power.

"Grr," she mumbled, while grabbing his junk in one hand. *"Mood two,"* she announced, and the shower took her voice command and lowered the intensity of the jets.

Connor was totally defenseless, which was a new bearing and posture for him. Her other fingertips drummed across his chest, lighter than the water droplets, more elusive, as she shimmied herself down to his massive length.

"I want to feel your breasts … they are so lovely."

She moved away and led his hands to her plump, soft and round breasts, now dangling in front of him like the ripest, most delicious fruit. Sinewy as a cat, she swayed slightly, dragging her nipples from side to side across his face and through his greedy, open mouth.

"Suck 'em," she said. He did. She then made little whimpering noises of pleasure. *"Was a woman ever more designed for sex,"* he thought to himself.

Sara was ready. "I want your sex. Have you ever done the Yab-Yum?"

"I don't think so," Connor responded.

"Okay. Sit on the floor." He did and she straddled his hips, facing him, allowing him to enter her from the front. Since he had to hold himself up and hold her in position, he could not thrust indiscriminately. She dictated the rhythm of the intercourse.

Once his fully erect penis was inside her, she moved from side to side, gently giving him the sensation that his sex needed.

"Good. You're doing very good. If your legs get tired, prop yourself up with your hands and I'll take your stiff rod and work with it."

He felt like he was in a clinical session for sex, as Sara guided his boner into her waiting core. She was getting a good run going on her orgasm, feeling his huge mass filling her up, but he reached his climax much sooner than Sara had hoped.

Connor screamed, as Sara could only muster a smile.

So, her idea of using him today in place of solo sex didn't work. *"Bad timing,"* she thought, sadly.

After a few minutes, he stood up and she gave him a big kiss, and Connor left. Her sexual satisfaction would need to wait until later. It is what it is.

"I'm okay by myself," she thought reminiscent of much of her past sex life.

54

LINA

It was now date night for Lina and Ramon, and Lina was as excited as anything to spend some intimate time with the ladies' choice for all things romantic and sexually hot.

Arriving by BART around 8:30 at Ramon's modest but tasteful condo in the historic Temescal neighborhood of Oakland, Lina was dressed in a navy-blue lightweight blazer with a white V-neck long-sleeve top and faded jeans and white heels, which was dressy for Lina, but perfect for most any casual event.

Greeting Lina at the door, Ramon had already prepared her favorite drink, a Cosmo, but with a slight upgrade. As she walked into his condo, he gave Lina a hug and handed her a drink.

"Welcome to my home. I have prepared a French Cosmo for you. And, you look lovely."

"Thank you very much for having me over." As she smiled at Ramon, she inquired, "So what is in your French Cosmo?"

"It uses Grand Marnier instead of Cointreau as the orange liqueur, and is topped with a small dash of grenadine. It is garnished with an orange to give it a nice hint of citrus oil and an extra bit of color."

Taking her first sip of the drink, she said emphatically, "This is the best Cosmo I have ever had. Thank you, Ramon."

"You're quite welcome. Let me show you around. You can wear your blazer or I can take it from you and hang it up."

Removing her blazer, Lina replied, "Thanks."

They walked into the kitchen and Lina noticed a small café for eating. There was no dining room in his condo.

Pointing, "There is a half-bath if you need to freshen up, and the bedroom is down the hall and we will see it later, if that is still fine with you."

"Sure." Her immediate thought was, *"I'm already in the mood for sex and I've only been here ten minutes."*

"I have prepared a light meal, given your seafood tastes, and not wanting to be eating too late in the evening. Does that make sense?"

"Of course, it does. How thoughtful."

Lina was trembling slightly in anticipation of what was awaiting her. She was already feeling a warmth between her legs. *"Damn,"* she thought. *"This is way beyond anything I expected. Gonna raise the bar, for sure."*

As they moved over to the café table, Ramon brought his dish from the kitchen, made two place settings, and described the appetizer-type offering.

"This is Ceviche. Are you familiar with this Peruvian dish?"

Lina nodded.

"I have some raw, fresh sea bass and shrimp, marinated in lime citrus juices and spiced with aji chili peppers with chopped onions, salt, and coriander."

"It looks lovely."

As they enjoyed the light and delicious meal, Ramon freshened their drinks. Upon finishing the meal, he led her into the living room so they could relax and chat a bit about several issues, but mostly about Lina's needs, desires, and disappointments.

"I wrote this poem especially for you, and for how people think of you."

Lina opened the creased folder and silently read:

LINA

I sing praises to you
As you sit and stare,
And my heart is grateful
That you are really here.
The woman we know that
Is loved through the years,
Often opens her heart
To constant rivers of tears.
Suddenly you smile and
Say nothing has changed.

And I wonder how you are
As I sing to you again.
Then I hold your hand
And ask blessings for you,
Because in this moment of peace,
I don't know what else to do.

Ramon moved closer to Lina, who was shedding a tear, and gave her a hug and said, "I'll leave you for a moment so I can prepare our bedroom."

He then got up and reached for an item behind the sofa. Revealing a black silk robe, he murmured, "I would like you to change into this robe while I'm gone. You can use the small bathroom. Is that acceptable?"

"Yes. It is wonderful."

As Ramon walked towards the bedroom, Lina was still overcome with emotion from that thoughtful and reflective poem. After she changed into the robe, she walked over to the patio and opened the screen door to feel the invigorating breeze and refreshing air.

♥   ♥   ♥

Ramon, clad only in a one-piece, basic wine-colored G-string, met Lina on the patio, and placed his hands on her shoulders. She was glowing and could feel his growing penis.

He gently removed her robe. Once her skin was exposed to the cool air from his patio and the heat of his attention, she opened up to the moment and placed her hands on his hips.

"May I touch you like this?"

"Of course, Lina. Let your body follow your heart."

Her mood had quickened to the point where she wanted her hands on every inch of him at once, but both hands settled on his smooth and sculptured chest.

Everything in the world Lina could find sexy in a man, she easily found here, especially his warm and silky-smooth skin, the heavy drumbeat of his heart, and the sharp spasms of his abdomen as she scratched her short nails over his ribs and abdomen.

Ramon took his lead, replacing her robe over her cool shoulders, lifted her up, carried her into his bedroom, and laid her gently on the bed. The soothing smell and sexy mist of fragrant candles was exhilarating. He gently removed her robe, now warm from her body heat, and spread her legs softly as she began to pant from intoxicating sexual harmony.

Lina expected him to take his long and supple fingers and glide them into her waiting love nest, made warm and wet by his touch. Instead, Ramon's hands slid down her thigh, his eyes watching her face as his fingertips lingered on her parted lips.

"I longed to do this when we would first enjoy each other, my lady … to kiss you from toe to hip to breast to your lips. I recalled you once said that you did not think that sex and love could exist equally in a relationship."

"Oh no, I love this. It's is just something new … something different for me."

"Well, Lina, my Dear, you have earned this attention. I was, and still am, in awe of you."

With that opening, he began to repeat the essence of his total body kiss. "You are perfect," he uttered as he began to suck her toe, her knees, her inner thighs, her abdomen, her stomach, her breasts, and her neck. When his kissing and licking reached her mouth, he eased his fingers into the warm and wet opening between her legs with her knees now raised in anticipation.

"Yes. So good. And oh, so you," she whispered.

He then began to stroke her slightly quivering lower body, his fingers sliding up and down the crease of her sex, as if to offer a slight tease at penetration. But with him it wasn't a game. Every move had meaning. He exuded genuineness.

Lina moaned, and thought, *"This feeling is like nothing I have ever felt."*

He softly licked her neck and cheeks and she turned her head so he could kiss her welcoming lips, his tongue slipping inside and curling over hers. He pushed his middle finger inside her vagina and she cried out softly, as he continued to stroke her with warmth and feeling as if he was enjoying every inch of her love channel.

Releasing her lips for a moment, he asked, "Is this good for you?" To her, the word "good" now seemed so empty, and so bland. With the heat rising up in her trembling body, Lina whispered, "More, please. Ramon. Yes."

He delicately slid his other hand up her body to her mouth, pushing two fingers inside against her tongue and pulling them out, wet and warm. Ramon glided them across her nipples, over her rosy pink areolas, contrasting with her pale breasts.

She quietly sighed, "Oh. Oh."

He could see and feel her nipples peak, and their tautness caused Lina to gasp a bit louder. He then circled his fingers to the same rhythm as his other hand between her now trembling legs. Lina was in awe of his magical manner.

The sexual high from those two points of sensation, the peak of her breast and his fingers probing her feminine domain, simply blended into one intense consciousness. When all she could feel was heart throbbing circles of wet and warm engulfing her body, the vibrations of his words on her skin were electric, "Oh Lina, you are *très bien.*"

Lina felt helpless, but in a very good way, and like nothing she ever felt before. This kind of helplessness was liberating, when every nerve ending rose to drink of this wonderful sensation. Her overpowering thought was, "*This is what it feels like to be touched by someone I trust with my body, trust with my mind, trust with my heart.*"

But now Lina wanted to feel his manliness inside her, before completely falling to pieces, as her sexual release was close to becoming uncontrollable. Ramon sensed the "take-charge" roll reversing, and strongly flipped the two lovers so Lina was on top, cowgirl style.

"Oh God, I am so happy," Lina moaned as tears of joy silhouetted her flushed face.

"Take a pause to enjoy this moment, dear Lina. Take a deep breath and relax."

Lina whimpered, "No one has ever touched me the way that you do."

Ramon tried to slow the pace a bit, but Lina was much too aroused to take his hint. With an impatient sigh, she lifted her hips, took hold of his erection, and lowered herself onto his bulging length as they both let out quivering groans.

"Oh, Ramon …"

They stayed motionless for a few seconds as her body adjusted to his huge size, not yet able to get the angle she needed, but feeling warmth and wetness as never before.

Ramon dropped one hand to her thigh, and then moved it between her legs, his broad fingertips circling … caressing … waiting for the right time. As he grasped his firm organ, his soft, husky, sexy voice quietly expressed his feelings. "Lina, dear Lina, you feel so right for me."

A totally engrossed Lina thought, sincerely, "*I can't stop my body from giving in to this man with all my heart and being … I feel love.*"

In the next instant, there was penetration, and Lina's longing to give in to this man was now sexual reality. Once he guided himself into her, Lina didn't know which sensation to focus on … it was impossible to feel everything at once.

"Fill me deep," she uttered lovingly. "Fill me hard."

The rainbow of his sensual sensations and tantalizing touch was overwhelming. His fingers encircling her hips, the broad length of him now thrusting inside of her, the feel of his delicious mouth on her neck sucking so perfectly, and the utter ecstasy of having his Adonis-like body intertwined with hers. Heaven on earth!

"Harder, Ramon. I can take it harder. Please."

As he drove himself almost brutally into her, he paused to get a head nod from Lina; so considerate! He then gained a perfect rhythm of effort and resolve, to assure her pleasure and utmost satisfaction. He gripped her hips, tilted them, and groaned with additional effort as he pushed even deeper, sliding against her tiny nugget in an arousal summit that she had never experienced.

Lina cried out with an orgasm that shook even Ramon's steady hands … an orgasm so sudden and overwhelming that she lost the use of her arms and fell to her elbows as Ramon held her hips. Ramon thought affectionately, "*La petite mort,*" which was French for one helluva orgasm!

"Lina," his voice coming out in whispering groans, "are you okay?"

Lina now collapsed into Ramon's arms, cradling her head to his chest. With her ear pressed against him, she could hear the heavy, vital pounding of his racing heart.

Ramon slowly rolled Lina onto her side, carefully sliding a pillow under her head, and, as always, watching her face with those clear, warm and rich eyes.

"Lina, it felt good?"

Lina nodded, physically drained.

"I am so happy for you."

"I am so blessed to have you, Ramon. Thank you."

Taking the wilted lady in his arms, "It was, indeed, my pleasure, beautiful Lina."

Lina cried, as tons of emotional memories clutter her mind.

"I can die right now, happy and content. Hell, I feel like I'm in Heaven … maybe I did die!"

55

SAMANTHA AND JONATHAN

The next session with Dr. Vandenberg was difficult. She wanted to continue to have me bare my soul regarding relationships with my ex-wife, several important women in my life, and my domineering mother. I had to shift gears into some dark times, and the memories were as painful as they were vivid.

"Jon, you said you had a poem that you had written out of an intense need to blow off some steam."

"Yes. We had endured several months of what I called, 'complaining and explaining.' She complained and I had to explain."

"And you brought it?"

"Yes, I have it right here."

I reached into his briefcase and gave Sam the poem I wrote to Amanda.

"So, Jon, I can assume the poem is not a romantic poem?"

"Hell no, Sam, I guess I thought it really described some of my relationship frustrations, and gave me a chance to vent. You know, get some things off my chest."

"You say that Amanda took the words literally, and got nothing but anger from reading it."

"Yeah. She blew up and threw the poem at me; later taking the crumbled-up mess back as some sort of sick evidence that I was a monster, I suppose."

Opening the poem, Sam muttered, "Let me see what we have here," and read the poem.

213

THE 12 DAYS OF CHRISTMAS – REAL WORLD VERSION

On the 12th day of Christmas, my instinct said to me:

"I have many friends, all quite smart, but you have 'being right' down to an ART."

On the 11th day of Christmas, my instinct said to me:

"I've told you more than once or twice, I no longer want UNSOLICITED ADVICE."

On the 10th day of Christmas, my instinct said to me:

"This is not an issue for negotiation; I no longer want or need your PERMISSION."

On the 9th day of Christmas, my instinct said to me:

"What gets down to your very soul is your constant worry of things you can't CONTROL."

On the 8th day of Christmas, my instinct said to me:

"Your hearing isn't what is missing; it's the simple fact that you are rarely LISTENING."

On the 7th day of Christmas, my instinct said to me:

"What appears to me to be pretty crappy is that it is my main job to make you HAPPY."

On the 6th day of Christmas, my instinct said to me:

"You create problems when none exist; then overreact, get moody and PISSED."

On the 5th day of Christmas, my instinct said to me:

"To make you smile and laugh is what I try, yet your indifference just makes me CRY."

On the 4h day of Christmas, my instinct said to me:

"Your constant criticism has a frightening pace, leaving me to search for my own time and SPACE."

On the 3rd day of Christmas, my instinct said to me:

"A wise man said 'never complain/never explain,' but your complaining has me always EXPLAINING."

On the 2nd day of Christmas, my instinct said to me:

"You constantly seek out the 'girlfriends' I'd marry, unable to accept that they are all IMAGINARY."

On the 1st day of Christmas, my instinct said to me:

"Taking things for granted causes me great strife, unable to enjoy the good things in our LIFE."

♥　　♥　　♥

Samantha was both puzzled and concerned at how badly Jon assessed the damage from revealing his innermost thoughts.

"Jon, a mentor of mine once said, '*There's a difference between doing things right … and doing the right things right.*' Do you get the drift of that philosophy?"

Thinking for a moment, "Yes, I do."

"Coupled with pure timing, Jon, I can see a crash and burn here."

"I guess. Amanda didn't like it at all, and I told her it was my impression of her, and what was part of our lingering *indifference* to one another."

"Did you consider discussing these critical issues with her before you launched the poem?"

"Yeah, actually I did. It was my belief that there was no 'common ground' at that particular time in our partnership."

"Partnership?"

"Sorry, I meant relationship."

Samantha took down some notes.

Sam asked, "If the shoe was on the other foot, how would you respond?"

"That would never happen because I have always been open and honest with her."

Again, with a noticeable head nod and a slight frown, Samantha took some additional notes.

Without being asked, "My wife had a relentless determination to uncover marital misdeeds."

"Jon, I agree that the people who know you best can hurt you the most." She gave an impatient sigh, "Were you the victim or the perpetrator?"

Looking directly at Sam, "Where there is love there is pain. Déjà vu all over again."

"Jon, men are much better at taking words and making them seem irrelevant, if they don't suit their beliefs and behavior."

"What do you mean?"

"Well, you must flip this around. To a woman, the spoken word of a partner or spouse is extremely relevant, and by that, I mean it will not get an opportunity for clarification. It is what it is, and not a gray area."

I thought about those words, but was still confused.

"The best advice that I can give to a male client who finds himself in such a dilemma is to 'think before you speak.' Take a moment to think about how a woman will respond to your remark, before you make that remark."

"Well, I can't argue with that advice, but guys are more about doing. We react. We just don't think like women."

"Jon, maybe that is the answer to your question."

Sam continued to bring out several more instances in this session, and in past sessions, where that advice should have been followed. I recall sharing some of my encounters with the opposite sex, albeit harmless in my own mind, which could have upset Amanda.

"These women, Jon, who would flirt back at you, were posing a problem that you just could not see clearly."

"Explain."

"Jon, Amanda was a very good person, right?"

"Of course. The finest woman I ever knew."

"And, Jon, the flirtatious types, those you are often attracted to, are often looking for risk, trouble, or just a diversion."

"What is your point?"

"Would Amanda flirt?"

"Hell no."

"You know, Jon, a woman … in your case a woman friend … can't be both a good girl and a girl on the side."

56

NIKKI

I n an irony of ironies, Nikki heads up the investigative team tasked with tying up the legal loose ends and major indictments stemming from the State of California versus James Johnson. Jacqui's husband may be dead, but his trail of sex crimes and both Federal and State criminal behavior had been an overwhelming legal headache for all parties concerned.

Nikki walked into the nearby Starbucks to meet Logan and discuss issues that were critical to the case, yet not of the confidential nature. Nikki had one question in mind that she felt Logan could help her with.

After getting a cafe latte and waiting a few minutes for Logan to show, she texted Sara.

> "Heard about the Brad show"
> "Yep, what ya think?"
> "LMAO."
> "Figured you would."
> "U good with it?"
> "SMH that he didn't know me."
> "Later, Sara."

As Nikki was finishing her text, Logan walked swiftly into the Starbucks with the phone and ear buds typically in place.

"Damn, does that guy ever get off the fricking phone?"

Logan bent over, gave Nikki a kiss, and then, finally, disconnected his "lifeline."

"Hey beautiful, how goes it?"

"Hi Logan. Busy, as usual."

"Let me get a coffee and we'll talk. Need anything?"

"No, thanks. I'm good."

While Nikki waited for Logan to return, she organized her notes and high-lighted the ones that she would discuss with Logan.

As Logan sat down, Nikki spread her document outline on their table as Logan perused the lengthy list of docs.

She sipped her latte as Logan studied the material and looked up a few minutes later. "Easy call."

Nikki smiled and replied crisply, "Shoot."

"The case is solid, even though the defendant is deceased. *The Best Evidence Rule* applies here perfectly, and I don't understand why you didn't see it."

Nikki snapped back, "Listen, that much is obvious. I'm looking for your thoughts on another totally related issue here. Look again."

Logan took a large gulp of his coffee and looked even more attentively at the docs. Nikki was glancing at the time, as she had an appointment in a couple hours, and had to get prepared for a truly exciting commitment.

"Okay. I think I got it." He further flipped a couple sheets of paper and then gave Nikki a direct stare into her serious face and eyes.

"The most likely victim going forward is the wife, Jacqui Johnson. Is that what I'm seeing, Nikki?"

"Bingo."

"Yeah, I can see from your docs where she is being called a co-conspirator with tons of wealth to litigate."

"Nikki, this isn't the opinion that you really want from me, right?"

"Right. Jacqui Johnson is a close friend of mine."

"I knew that. JJ is not a person who you don't see referred to almost daily, with or without the link to her criminal husband."

"This is going to get ugly, Logan. Do you think it would be in our best mutual benefit if I recused myself from the case?"

"Hell, yeah, Nikki. There is a real strong conflict of interest here, and you know that. So why need my opinion?"

"Because I may be her best chance to get a fair shake, even if I am a prosecuting attorney, and I really want to help."

"Sorry, Babe, but you must recuse!"

After that dismal revelation, which Nikki kind of expected, she needed to shift her mind to things more uplifting. She was about to meet with Brandi for a much-anticipated sexual encounter and needed to clear her mind.

"Thanks, Logan, catch you later,"

Giving Nikki a kiss on the cheek, Logan responded, "Sure thing. Good luck with your case."

Back home, Nikki stripped and tossed her business suit in a corner of the bedroom. She drew a bath and added some fragrant salts to the warm water. Her pick today was actually a gift from Jacqui, which prompted her recollection. She grabbed Dr. Teal's Pure Epson Salt soaking solution with soothing Lavender.

She added the delightful salts to the bath and sunk into the bathtub to enjoy her respite from reality. Tying her hair up, she lathered and rinsed herself, gently feeling her feminine core with the middle finger of her left hand as she meticulously sucked the middle finger of her right hand.

In a momentary fantasy, she envisioned herself sucking her lovely partner's entire physical domain in what would be just a matter of hours. She almost got off thinking about it, sensing an explosive climax in the not-to-distant future.

She dried off, went into the kitchen to pour a glass of her favorite red wines, a Silver Oak 2015 Napa Valley Cabernet. Taking a short sip, she moved to the bedroom closet to pull out her stunning evening attire, a vibrant plum cutout slip and garter chemise. She thought, whimsically, "*This matching thong and lace garter set would have made perfect horny attire with a date with Logan.*" Yep, a little bi-sexual confusion, at least for the moment.

♥　　♥　　♥

Upon walking up the steps to Brandi's apartment, Nikki had securely closed her front peacoat pocket, not revealing the naughtiness within, as that sight was for Brandi's eyes only. Nikki took a deep sigh, and knocked on the door.

Brandi answered the door, dressed in a black Anne Klein single-button pantsuit with a notched collar and a classic trouser fit. Black and red high heels made for a stunning sexual expression, and almost an immediate hug by the two lesbian lovers.

As they turned to head into the kitchen, Nikki couldn't help but stare at the firm and tight derriere on the lovely Brandi, but, a smeared white powder was a stark contrast to the black pantsuit.

"What's your pleasure, Nikki?"

"Your fantastic body."

"Thanks. Soon. What to drink?"

"Do you have any scotch? If not, a red wine will work, Brandi."

Brandi poured them both some red wine and they toasted.

With drink in hand, Nikki paused to appreciate the beauty of the gorgeous creature before her. Brandi's longing eyes traveled up and down Nikki's near-naked body, and she remained perfectly still, without a word, in awe.

Nikki's cascading black hair and mocha-rich skin were a perfect visual blend to the vibrant plum cutout slip and garter chemise. The woman was just flat-out sexy.

Nikki slowly let her eyes travel back to Brandi's lovely face. Delicate features and hazel eyes with full red lips under bright red lipstick to contrast with her black pantsuit. As their eyes met, the desire grew in anticipation and heat.

Brandi enjoyed the view of Nikki's subtle curves as she walked toward the bedroom with a regal grace that was immediately tempting to Brandi. "*It's no wonder that women are objects of voyeuristic pleasure by men,*" Brandi thought affectionately.

Nikki turned to smile at Brandi as she entered Brandi's bedroom.

"*I'm sure she feels strongly about her sensuality to any onlooker,*" Brandi assumed.

The women stopped, once in the bedroom and next to her bed, and hugged for a moment. Then Brandi removed her pantsuit and had nothing covering her except pink, lacy panties. Her breasts were smallish, compared to Nikki's, but her nipples were tight.

"I want to taste your nipples in my mouth," Brandi.

Moving toward Nikki, she slowly knelt down, and removed Nikki's slip and garter. Nikki's whole body tightened in anticipation, and a warm feeling began to dampen her nakedness.

"*There is something so erotic about a beautiful woman on her knees in front of me; by choice,*" Nikki whispered to herself. "*It is a sexual want that I can fully appreciate.*"

Brandi sniffed the alluring scent of Nikki's sexy attire before she placed them on a chair behind her. "I love your smell, Nikki. I love to smell it and to taste it. It gets me high."

Anticipation inside Nikki mounted, as she knew later, they would likely flip the roles of Domme and sub, not caring about anything more than what felt right about each other's sexuality. Nikki was longing for the warm contact, and just enjoying the moment.

Sensing her excited state, Brandi fingered her companion's vagina, knowing that she would soon give her mouth access to Nikki's swollen bud, now quite wet and getting hard.

"Yes, I want to feel your tongue on my clit." Brandi took that request and rolled Nikki on her side, lifting one leg, so she could gain entry with her mouth and tongue. Her tongue seemed hot as she licked Nikki in a long, slow caress. She was teasing Nikki a bit, giving off an impression that she liked to get her partner hot.

Brandi pulled Nikki hard against her mouth, sucking her as she let one hand drift over to a sumptuous breast, where Brandi began to stroke and squeeze each nipple with her fingers until the rolling got them both hard.

"Oh, yes," Nikki purred with content. The playful paths of Brandi's mouth and fingers would soon result in a full body arousal for Nikki, and both women understood and anticipated this peak.

She expertly used her tongue to part Nikki's lips further and flick just inside her. She sensed what it would take to get Nikki off ... not much more. The combination of her movements made Nikki buck her hips against her. She wrapped her arms around Nikki's thighs to keep her firmly in place. Brandi sighed, as a groan of pleasure outflowed from Nikki's throat.

"I'm wet for you, Brandi."

"I can feel how wet you are for me."

Nikki clenched her fist in Brandi's hair as Nikki began to come; a slow ebb and then a blast of orgasmic relief, knowing that Brandi could now taste her, and no doubt feel Nikki throb.

The enduring waves of the orgasm still rolled through Nikki's being, as Brandi leaned back and licked her lips. Nikki smiled, as in a moment it would be her turn, and Nikki intended to make her scream with pleasure as she did.

"It's going to be a long and glorious night," Nikki thought hungrily.

57

JACQUI

Following my suggestion that a difficult "reveal" was necessary, Jacqui invited the girls to her Sausalito home, where she planned to describe her hubby's sordid lifestyle and how it impacted her.

Sara, Lina, and Nikki arrived in a sky-high mood, in one of Troy's rented limos, directly from stops at three bars, fitting the group's need. Old habits are hard to break.

They had no idea what Jacqui had in mind, but all three could see from their boisterous arrival, that their mood did not match Jacqui's mood. Yep, Jacqui took on the never-seen-before role of *Debbie Downer*.

A smiling but somewhat contrite Jacqui invited her friends in and hugs were enjoyed all around.

"What can I give the girls that already appear to have the buzz of some seasoned pros?"

Seizing the moment, Sara downshifted warmly to, "How about a nice Chardonnay? I know you have a fine Pahlmeyer Napa that we have had before."

"Sure do, Sara. Have the Pahlmeyer Napa and some fine reds." Jacqui led the girls into the kitchen and had several bottles of wine open, in anticipation.

Nikki began the conversation, after each of them had secured the wine of their choice.

"We should apologize, Jacqui. The fact that you didn't join us earlier was a red flag, and I'm afraid we missed your intent for a get-together at your home entirely."

"No need to apologize, Nikki. I am anxious to do a show-and-tell tonight, for some much-needed venting, and I have been putting it off for some time."

Lina offered, "Please, Jacqui, go ahead. We are your friends and are here for you."

"Thanks, Lina. I couldn't share my grief, embarrassment, and humiliation with anyone but you guys."

Taking a deep breath, Jacqui began. "You have all been to my house before, and we have shared some good times and some laughs. Tonight, will not be one of those nights. Let's take the elevator down to my husband's private chamber, or what he called his playroom."

A gasp or two, then all was quiet as she led them down to LL2, where she had revealed to Jon the horrible secrets that defined this dungeon. Jacqui's plan was to expose all the explicit details of the time spent in her husband's depravation lair.

As the elevator reached LL2, "Oh my God," Lina shrieked.

"This is disgusting," Nikki blurted loudly.

Sara just observed the chains, leather cuffs, bondage tables, crosses, slings, and paraphernalia that she couldn't even begin to understand.

Walking over to a glass cabinet, Jacqui muttered, "This is the library for all things vulgar, smutty, and abhorrent. These are hundreds of my husband's sex and bondage videos that I only discovered after his death."

"Shit, there's a ton of 'em," Sara remarked surprisingly.

"I'm gonna play a couple for you so you can see what I had to deal with."

Nikki answered quickly, "Jacqui, no. You don't need to."

"Yes, Nikki I do."

As the girls talked softly among themselves, Lina thought sympathetically, "*This poor girl has been through a lot.*"

She hadn't seen anything, yet.

Jacqui first showed herself in a gang-bang video where she was only allowed to use the word, "Sir."

At one point in the video her husband, James, with his wife blindfolded, watched as three men had their way with her.

"Apparently," Jacqui said quietly, "my husband thought this was unconditional love … it most definitely was not!"

"Okay, girls, this is the one that you will not believe …"

♥   ♥   ♥

Jacqui was laid out on a bondage table, with an expression of fear on her face. James was the Domme in a position where she was vulnerable, bound tightly, and was likely being punished for some criticized behavior.

He placed a heavy metal choker around her neck, and the clanking of the chains indicated that it would be attached to something or someone. A moment later, a scrap of something soft and silky fell over her face. He adjusted a blind-fold over her eyes and then tied it off harshly at the back of her head.

After an hour of James taking advantage of his bound and frightened wife, he left her there, in the darkened world of his dungeon of horrors, for several hours. As he walked away, he could hear her muffled crying, knowing in his mind that she was properly humiliated and would wait horrifyingly for his return.

Hours later, Jacqui was finally able to hear her husband return. In the time that he had been gone, she tasted many a tear from her crying eyes, dried semen on her leg, and she was now laying in her own urine.

Jacqui recalled thinking to herself determinedly, "*This is not going to happen again ... I'll kill the bastard first!*"

Jacqui's friends were silent ... in shock and saddened by what their good friend had been subjected to.

58

JACQUI

I heard about this baring-of-the-soul and frightening exposé of Jacqui's husband's dungeon, so I gave Jacqui a call. Not revealing that I had been made aware of her emotional terror, she agreed to have dinner with me and to just talk things out. I knew I had to do something for a woman that I truly thought was a special friend. And yes, sex was on my mind, too. Sorry.

I picked her up in my 911 Porsche Cab, and we headed off to Poggio Trattoria, a fine Italian restaurant not far from Jacqui's place, for a nice, relaxing dinner. This was the first time in a while we didn't meet with some kind of an agenda; either business or sex.

I opted for the rigatoni with vodka sauce and Jacqui had one of her favs, tortellini soup and mussels marinara. Following dinner, I took her back to my place, which was the polar opposite of James' awful "playroom." My contemporary home was heavenly, by anyone's standards, and I knew I was blessed in so many ways.

Once inside, I gave Jacqui a warm embrace, and then I prepared a couple Brandy Alexanders. These were the perfect call for a nightcap, a dessert cocktail consisting of cognac and crème de cacao. We toasted to our friendship, and I led Jacqui into my conservatory, a fabulously masculine retreat, within a distinctly masculine home.

Rather unexpectantly, but thoroughly valued, Jacqui came on to me and made every indication that sex was gonna happen, and now. As we finished our drinks, I led her into my large and comfortable bedroom. She sat on the bed, and sheepishly admitted that she needed to pee.

I motioned in the direction on my bathroom, and she slowly made her way into the bathroom and closed the door.

I used this time to light some fragrant candles, as much for my mood as hers, and started my recording of Ravel's "Bolero" in a most quiet tone. I stripped down to my black, silk mesh boxer briefs, in earlier anticipation of sex with Jacqui, and waited for my lady to return.

As Jacqui returned to my bedroom, I hugged her and kissed her neck. I caressed her body, back to front. I reached between her legs for a sign of her arousal.

"I want to touch you, Jacqui. I want to peal your clothes off and feel just how wet I can make your lovely core. I need to show you how much pleasure I can give you."

"Don't." Her voice quivered as her legs moved to feel my pulsing groin.

I paused. "Don't what, touch you? Please you? Want you?"

"No, Jon" she moaned in a shaking breath. "Don't talk and don't stop. I want to enjoy you. You are my rock."

While standing, I ran my hands slowly under her blouse and around to her back, and then back to where my palms could feel her voluptuous breast, momentarily covered by a silky, laced bra. Her head was slightly tilted. I moved my warm hands to her face and then into her hair, while gently pulling her lips to mine.

I gave her a soft and tender kiss, as she spread her legs, so I could press my throbbing penis against her groin.

I lifted her onto my bed, unzipped her skirt, and then rolled her from side to side, gently, to remove her shoes and skirt. I delicately lifted her legs slightly and placed a warm and wet kiss on that part of her panties that clung to her warm core. She groaned as I kissed her groin area softly.

"Oh my, Jon, that is so nice. So good and so soft. I am ready, my love."

I stroked her inner thighs with one hand and seized her waist with the other. I leaned in gently to bring my chest softly onto hers. I then rolled myself directly above her and pressed my hardness against her warm and wet treasure.

"Love me with your tongue, Jon."

Pressing a lingering kiss to her neck made her shiver and catch her breath. I slipped my tongue in and out of her mouth and slowly tasted her warm skin. So soft. I caressed my way across her abdomen, over the curve of her hip, and then down her slightly parted thighs.

Jacqui gasped at the tingles spreading across her skin, as I skimmed across her thigh, planted my palm on the soft skin near her core, and when my middle finger crept just inches away from her wet and warm channel, she began to tremble all over. She moaned as only Jacqui could moan, and I was getting super-aroused.

I seized her lips again, gently taking her waist in my hands and eased her to her side. She turned eagerly for me, and swung her thigh over my hip in a signal for me to take advantage of her. She was warm and ready.

With that gesture, I pushed her back on the bed, removed the buttons on her blouse and with all the precision and sensuality I had, removed her blouse and her lace bra with the gentle touch that only a caring lover would exhibit. I wanted to please her. I wanted her to be happy with me.

My eyes starred at her beautiful breasts, no longer hidden by the white lace of her bra. They were perfect; round, soft, pale, and so real. Appreciating her breasts even more this time, I was in awe and didn't want to move on. I cupped them, grazed her nipples with my fingers, and heard another slight moan. Again, that sensual moan.

As her eyes slowly closed, I began to gently suck her nipples as they began to turn to pink nubs that were firm and upright, suggesting more attention to other waiting areas of her now quivering body.

I took the lead as she moved her thighs wide and welcoming, and pulled my now poised body into hers. She gasped, grabbed the sheets in her fists, and then said, "Now. I want you now!"

Her body briefly tensed as her climax was rising in force. Quickly removing my boxers, I tried to enhance her orgasm by rubbing her G-spot, but she simply wanted my sex and wanted it now.

She guided my throbbing manhood into her shuddering depths and moments later her face flushed brightly and every glorious curve of her body undulated with the force of her bursting climax, completely overshadowing my orgasm and release.

"Oh my God, Jon. I love it. I love you!"

For now, my lady's pleasure was all that mattered.

59

LINA

ina was still gushing with the memories of the wonderful date with Ramon, and was now ready to move on, and Gabe was still the bittersweet partner who she was hoping to get a little closer to. Their last encounter was just short of a disaster, but Ramon had insisted that Lina take control of any stagnant relationships.

Thinking about Ramon's words, wisdom and warmth, she texted Gabe.

"Hey Gabe, you there?"
"Hi Lina. Studying for a civics class."
"I don't want to disturb you."
"Not a prob. What's up?"
"Was wondering if you wanted to go out?"
"Sure. Whatcha got in mind?"
"There is a concert Friday at Stern Grove."

Lina liked this venue for safety and comfort, and it was free, which wouldn't require Gabe to get tickets. She would pack a picnic for them, and they could enjoy the local musicians and talk.

"I'd love to go. Thanks."
"Great. Pick me up at 6."
"Will do."
"Bye, Gabe."
"Bye. And thanks for the invite."

Lina felt that step one was done. Now to plan for Friday night.

♥　　♥　　♥

As Friday night approached, Lina was busy with her evening planning. This was the longest stretch of downtime away from her work, or her writing, that she could recall, but she was convinced the effort was worth it.

She changed into her beige cable knit sweater dress, checked her picnic basket for the umpteenth time, and played with her hair as Gabe buzzed her apartment precisely at 6:00.

"It's so funny," she thought, *"having seen him downstairs a half hour ago waiting for the exact time to buzz me."*

Moments later, Gabe arrived at Lina's front door and appeared a little nervous.

"Hi Gabe, come on in."

"Thanks. Love your dress."

"Thank you. Is that a new bomber jacket?"

"No. I've had it a while. Just wear it for special occasions."

"That was sweet," she whispered to herself as they moved into the kitchen.

"I have some cold drinks packed, Gabe, but would happy to fix you a drink before we go if you'd like."

"No, I'm fine." Glancing at the half-open basket, "Your picnic looks yummy."

With that comment they were off to Stern Grove for a lovely night of music and conversation.

♥　　♥　　♥

Back at Lina's apartment and talking non-stop about the evening, both having enjoyed themselves immensely, Lina recalled Ramon saying, *"Don't force it. Take what is offered. Live for the moment and don't set expectations."*

"Gabe, I had a wonderful time, and enjoyed everything about tonight."

"So did I, Lina." With that comment, she gave a rather tense Gabe a long, yet gentle, hug and kissed him on the lips with a firm and loving feel. Noticing his tension fading, she took his hand and walked him into the living room.

As he was about to speak, she put her extended finger over her lips to suggest, "Shush."

Gabe then settled back onto the sofa as Lina spoke. "Please fix yourself a drink and I will be back in a few minutes, okay?"

"Of course. I'll just get a soft drink."

"Fine. I'll be right back."

When Lina returned to the living room, she was wearing a gray jersey and lace, sleep baby-doll nighty, and motioned for Gabe to join her in the bedroom.

A stunned, but nevertheless eager, Gabe immediately followed Lina into a dimly lit bedroom, with soft music playing and scented candles giving off a romantic glow; an atmosphere that this young man had never experienced.

"Lina …"

"Don't speak. Just listen." Gabe relaxed as he realized that Lina was now in charge, which suited him. Standing as they reached her bed, Lina removed his shirt, unzipped his jeans, and slowly removed his jeans and socks and softly flung them into the corner.

"You have a strong and beautiful body, Gabe, and I want to love it tonight."

She removed her soft and sexy baby doll, placed her hand on Gabe's crotch to feel his manhood emerge, and then gently pushed him onto the bed. Lina then initiated the foreplay as she navigated his warm body with her tongue as she steered her hands into each of his sensitive places.

It was obvious that no woman had ever taken the time or had the experience to give pleasure in the way Gabe was enjoying the voyage. She spent many minutes massaging his erogenous zones with her soft hands and wet tongue.

A few minutes later, taking her lead, he tenderly flipped her over on her back and began to caress her warm and wet feminine core while kissing her breasts and sucking gingerly on her nipples.

"*Oh my God,*" she thought. "*Is this really happening?*"

He straddled her torso, faced her and leaned into a long kiss; and with his hands running through her hair, Lina could see his manhood was full and hard.

"Yes, Gabe. I feel ready for my man."

Lina parted her legs as he swept his tongue from that long and tender kiss, to her breasts and abdomen, reaching her warm and wet core. It was easy for him to penetrate, as her canal was very wet with swollen folds, and she even guided his now trembling hand. Lina was as high as she could be and Gabe even sensed how pleasing the sex felt.

He rocked against her rhythmically, rolled his hips while clutching hers, giving Lina numerous sensations against her channel walls, as arousal quickened her heartbeat.

"Slower."

"Slower, Lina?"

"Yes. Slow the rotating just a bit. I love how you feel inside me, and I just want to feel your wholeness as it fills me up from each angle."

Gabe drew a big sigh and said, "I understand."

"Gabe, let me control our movement. Let me move my body with you inside."

"Of course. You feel so warm and so good. Take a breath and we will go slowly."

They moved as one for several minutes, and then he gently lifted her hips and thighs as he got himself into a better position, feeling some tiredness from the twisting. She responded to the new movement and maintained a heightened level of arousal.

He then changed angles and depth of penetration, getting positive signals from Lina as he expanded his sexual range. His newly developing skills, built upon the moment and Lina's encouragement, were picked up quickly by Lina. As she was quivering with some new sexual feelings laying beneath him, the physical sensations were driving her desire to sense their coming climaxes.

"I could never have dreamed of such pleasure with him," Lina thought reflectively. As her hips pumped upward and her core was burning with a need to come, he twisted one more time with deep penetration.

Lina sensed that they were very close. Grabbing his testicles, she pulled him hard, paused, and then had him thrust one more time with force, and they came together.

"I love this woman," Gabe believed in his heart. **"I don't want tonight to end!"**

60

NIKKI

This chapter highlights the bisexual nature of Nikki's increasingly complicated physical cravings. It's a good problem; but a problem nevertheless. As a
reader, you can draw your own conclusion, but, unfortunately, you have only
a few facts to work with.

As a member of the high IQ and deeply restricted Prometheus Society in college, Nikki was invited to a reunion weekend, made up of the very few California
members, to be held in South Lake Tahoe. Her 155 IQ was considered to be in
the genius category.

She would need some serious balance to go with this onslaught of highly
intellectual people, so Nikki convinced Brandi to be her date for the affair.
Brandi was immediately open to the possibilities, sensing that her regular life
and love life were improving exponentially through her relationship with Nikki.

Nikki borrowed my Porsche Macan for the trip to Tahoe for the three-day
event, running Friday through Sunday, so I got the scoop on their tryst as soon
as they returned. It was mostly good news, but it did open up some thoughts for
Nikki regarding her sexual preferences.

After an exhilarating three-hour drive, the ladies reached the lodge holding
the event, and Nikki got checked in at the Marriott's Timber Lodge, an upscale
mountainside hotel less than a five-minute walk to Harrah's Lake Tahoe Casino.
This would be a fun weekend, she thought.

That night, the ladies, dressed in cool-weather evening attire and trying to
stay out of the radar for any male or female distractions, headed to the casino
for dinner and gambling. Nikki was a bit conservative with the betting stakes,
but Brandi seemed energized by the risk of the games. After a short stint with
minimal losses, they headed back to their hotel rooms.

Nikki prepared a bath for Brandi and went about her prep for her Saturday session.

Upon seeing the naked and dripping wet Brandi emerge from the bath, Nikki immediately shifted her focus. She approached her lady friend, gazed lovingly into her eyes, and they embraced. Placing both hands on Brandi's buttocks, Nikki winked and quipped, "You look good enough to eat, my lovely Brandi."

Raising her head slightly, Nikki continued, "What is that fragrance?"

Taking a deep sigh, Brandi answered, "It's Cartier La *Panthère* perfume. Do you like it?"

"Yes. Yes, I do. I'd like to use a splash later this weekend."

"Of course."

The ladies kissed for a moment, and then Nikki began to undress. Brandi watched with her tongue lightly touching her wet lips. The two naked women stared lovingly at their attractive partners, giving each the impression that the weekend would be memorable.

Brandi slid her hands up Nikki's body, then reached her breasts and stopped for a moment to caress the tightening nipples of her partner. "Oh, yes." Nikki sighed. With one hand squeezing a firm nipple, the other hand moved quickly to Nikki's abdomen. Nikki spread her legs slightly, and Brandi moved with her two fingers probing the already damp core.

"You make me feel like I am the only woman that you want ... that you need, Brandi."

"Yes, sexy lady, and I promise I won't disappoint you. You have a taste that I dream about enjoying, even when you are far away.'

"Then, go down and drink." Nikki spread her legs even wider and with both hands around Nikki's hips, Brandi kneeled in front of her lover and drove her overly excited tongue deeply into Nikki's core. She pulled back, allowing her fingers to probe for Nikki's clit. Upon finding the hard nugget, and rolling it slightly, Brandi moved Nikki to where she could open Nikki wide.

"I want to get deep inside you, Nikki."

Brandi's breath was hot on Nikki's skin, and Nikki shivered with excitement watching her move to enjoy Nikki's love nest with Brandi's wide-open mouth.

"Roll your tongue over my clit ... I'm close."

"Yes, Nikki, I can feel you throbbing."

Sucking even harder, Brandi ran her hands along Nikki's thighs, squeezing gently.

"I love your mouth on my clit, and I am loving your touch on my body."
Brandi pulled Nikki even closer to her.

"This is so good, Brandi. Please don't stop."

Moments later, the unmistakable orgasmic wave began to overwhelm Nikki, as a complete physical release consumed both women. Nikki panted wildly with Brandi enjoying the taste of Nikki's overwhelmingly delicious juices.

Moments later, they fell asleep in each other's arms. The perfect closure of a very good day.

♥ ♥ ♥

Saturday was fun for Nikki, but kind of boring for Brandi. While Nikki was involved in a series of mental gymnastics with her high-IQ friends, Brandi got her hiking gear together and spent the afternoon on the trails.

When they both returned to their room at the end of the day, winding down and relaxing in each other's company, thoughts to another wildly romantic evening began. Anticipation was high.

Tonight, it was Nikki's turn to add aroma and magic to the sexual enjoyment. She was wearing an alluring ultramarine green plunging halter garter teddy leaving nothing to the imagination. Adding NARS Deep Throat blush, the flirty sheer peach just glistened and said, "Yes, and now."

The bathroom door opened enough for Nikki to see Brandi in an ice-blue lace baby doll chemise and nothing else. The sight took her breath away, and Nikki licked her lips, knowing that Brandi dressed that way for her. Nikki reached for tonight's sex toy.

Seeing Nikki's hungry look, Brandi tilted her head modestly and asked, "Is this, okay? Do you like the way I look, for you?" her tone now becoming sexy and teasing.

"You look incredible," Nikki whispered. "Come here."

As Brandi approached, Nikki could barely contain herself. Only the desire to appreciate the sight of Brandi held Nikki back for a moment, before running her hands up and down Brandi's body. Brandi's nipples tightened and her eyes half closed with pending arousal, driving Nikki past any restraint. Nikki wanted her, and it took some discipline not to hurry.

Nikki moved closer and kissed Brandi passionately, giving up on her pent-up need to observe, as Brandi rolled toward Nikki putting her arms around

Nikki's neck. Nikki thought about moving on top of her, but patience was essential, given tonight's "object" of sexual nirvana.

When Brandi pressed her body against Nikki, Brandi's eyes widened as Nikki guided her hand to the shaft of a large strap-on, and, as her hand explored it, her face got a rosy glow.

"Oh, yes. Oh, hell yes," Brandi uttered in ecstasy.

The initial hint of surprise was quickly replaced with undeniable desire, and Nikki knew that she had correctly chosen the instrument of the night. A sly smile crossed Nikki's face as Brandi arched her back while still holding the strap-on firmly.

"Are you going to do me hard, with that?" Brandi whispers.

Nikki nods, "I am."

Nikki slid her hands along Brandi's legs to widen them before moving between her thighs. Nikki trembled with anticipation as she was about to enter Brandi's waiting vagina.

"Never have I wanted this more," Nikki told Brandi in a soothing tone of voice. Moving slowly, Nikki simply asked her, "Talk to me. Tell me what feels good."

"You on top of me feels good," Brandi murmured, lifting her hips a little to show her need and want. Nikki pushed up on her hands to look down on Brandi. It was such a breathtaking sight, with her hair fanned out on the pillow and her desire making her eyes grow darker.

As Nikki watched the beautiful body beneath her, Brandi bit her lip in anticipation, and Nikki's response was to shift her hips to enter her only in the slightest manner.

"Oh God," Brandi gasped, "you feel so good." Brandi then shifted her hips to help take Nikki in, and Nikki pleased her with a slow thrust. Her hands clenched Nikki's back as she threw her head on the pillows while a small cry of pleasure escaped her. Nikki paused, feeling how tight she was with the girth of the strap-on, letting her grow used to it before moving again. Nikki ran her mouth over Brandi's neck, and she moaned at the mixture of sensations.

"Kiss me," Nikki asked, and she does, her lips open and ready to be ravished with Nikki's tongue. Nikki gave her a deep kiss, thrusted again, harder, and Brandi bucked under Nikki, while moaning deeply. Starting a slow rhythm, Nikki could feel her spreading herself open, and Brandi broke the kiss, throwing back her head again as her pleasure mounted.

Lifting her hips to allow Nikki to slide deeper every time, her hands grabbed Nikki's skin, and she wrapped her legs around Nikki, pulling Nikki to her body and rocking back before each new thrust.

Every time Nikki slid in, Nikki's own pleasure mounted, and breaths became quicker. Nikki shifted her body forward until the pressure of the strap-on deep inside Brandi's wet core pressed back against Nikki's clit and aroused Nikki pleasurably.

"Oh God," Brandi cried. "Please let me come." Nikki thought, "*Loving the sound of her voice begging me, I am on the verge … she knows it.*"

"Wait, Brandi." They moved even faster, Brandi's hips raising and falling in perfect harmony with Nikki's own feverish pushing.

"I want you to explode," Nikki whispered. The sight of Brandi wanting Nikki so badly was too much for Nikki to take, as the onrush of Nikki's incredible climax took over.

Nikki shouted, "Come to me. Come to me now!"

They both screamed with their simultaneous releases, as Nikki's body throbbed with her own orgasm, and Brandi's body shook for a moment, until her fast-beating heart slowed enough for Brandi to gently groan with relief and pleasure.

Nikki lowered herself to Brandi's side, resting her head on Brandi's shoulder. Brandi slowly stroked her lover's hair and sighed.

Nikki is thinking here and now, **"I feel Brandi in my soul, and somehow know she feels the same."**

Brandi is thinking longer term, **"We have something magical between us, and I don't know if I can ever let it go."**

61

NIKKI

As fate might have it, Logan asked Nikki to accompany him on a train ride from Oakland to Seattle on the Coast Starlight train, where Logan could relax while working on his upcoming court requirements.

You may recall, it was on the Vancouver to Toronto Canadian Rockies train where Logan met Song and they enjoyed a sexual encounter that basically kicked Nikki to the curb. What is weird about Logan and the "train thing" is he became terrified of air travel during the horrendous infection rate of COVID-19 in 2020 and 2021, and found work obligations easily met on a relaxing train where he could work and enjoy the scenery.

Spoiler alert. There is even more hot and steamy sex in this chapter!

Once on the train, Logan and Nikki headed to their sleeping car to unpack and relax. Although small, these sleepers have berths to accommodate two people and are great for overnight train travel. Logan was able to book one of only a couple private rooms, which made the excursion much more enjoyable. They were called Superliner Suites and quite impressive.

Meals were the only downside, so we will assume the eating experiences paled greatly compared to the sex. Nikki, fresh from her Tahoe adventure with Brandi, brought all the naughty lingerie she knew would get and keep Logan's attention.

He, as well, made sure that flowers and wine were being delivered to the train before they 'set sail.' Yes, both parties were prepared for frolicking sex, and an unwinding event of paradise found, even for only an overnight trip.

The scenery along the Coast Starlight route was breathtaking. The dramatic snow-covered peaks of the Cascade Range and Mount Shasta, and long stretches of the Pacific Ocean shoreline, provided a stunning backdrop for travelers.

Logan liked his sex in the morning, as most guys apparently do. Nikki, of course, liked her sex in the evening, as most women apparently do. I brought this subject up with Samantha and she didn't disagree. *Sidebar: Sam got much more expressive with me given that subject.*

Back to the set-up, and cutting to the chase. Nikki asked Logan to exit the bedroom so she could prepare for the evening. He did, and when he returned, he found his lovely companion laying on her back, legs slightly spread to arouse his sexual juices, adorned in a black lace see-through robe, cup less bra and garter hip-hugger featuring a crotchless pantie set.

Nikki thought naughtily, *"I'll 'come' for you, big guy."*

She cupped her breast with one hand and slipped her other hand over her skimpy panties and touched herself while giving off a moan letting Logan focus on undressing ASAP.

Nikki's pulse rapidly grew as she saw her near-naked man in an awesome low-rise sexy thong, barely containing his massive manhood. Now close to her and noticing him as he moved, Nikki got aroused at the sight of both of his butt cheeks uncovered on the back of his blazing red jock-type underwear.

He moved next to her, and the delicious scent of him rose in her nostrils. As he leaned toward her, Nikki wrapped her arms around him and enjoyed a warm embrace, her breasts pressed against his chest. Her lips opened under the sweet thrust of his tongue, kissing him deeply, while her fingers pierced the silky blackness of his hair to keep him from pulling away.

He spoke her name softly, "Nikki, you are so beautiful ... so precious." Then he dove his tongue deep, gathering her taste, and his erection notched between her thighs, making her grow wet and wanting.

His hands slid down her back, cupped her shapely butt, and brought her tightly into his warm body. She slid both palms over his chest, his course hair tickling her, his ab muscles jumping under her soft caress.

"I want to touch you all over," he said as he brought one hand to her front and cupped her breast. Her nipple hardened under the ring of the cup less bra and her core was openly wet between the fabric lace of her crotchless panties. "I want to please you, Nikki." A shudder worked through her and she arched her body for more tantalizing action.

"I want you to please me ... and I know you can."

Finding her wet core anxious for his touch, he inserted two fingers inside as Nikki gasped in delight at the sensation of two roaming fingers nesting against her clit. His other hand had found her warm and soft breast, and he rolled his fingers over her nipples, which were much harder than before. As her breasts became swollen with need, a bolt of warmth and pleasure shot through her and she opened her legs even further.

"I want you inside me."

She lifted her hips as the resounding heat between her legs allowed Logan direct access to her wide-open core. She clenched his hips and drew him in fully and firmly. "I need you now."

Catching his breath, he responded, "I know. I can feel you throbbing." At that moment, he thrust his erection into her tight channel, which opened under her growing arousal and he could feel her core walls squeezing around him.

"Oh Nikki. You have me so tight; you are so warm."

She then shuddered around him, her body writhing while he enjoyed every bit of her orgasm. "Come for me, Logan. Come for me now."

With one last deep and hard thrust, Logan's climax brought cries and tears to the shaking Nikki.

The terrific sex with her man was, again, a wonderful event that defined the word "bittersweet." She had enjoyed Brandi, her drug habit notwithstanding, and now was thoroughly enjoying her heterosexual moments with a man who, obviously, had a spot in her mind and body.

♥   ♥   ♥

The next morning, following a light breakfast, on cue and back from a lovely joint shower, Logan proceeded to spend as much time and care as possible to show his lady his softer sexual self. As Nikki dropped her orchid-colored modal super-soft Kimono robe, her dark naked body was a stunning contrast to the bright beams of sunlight flowing into their berth.

Logan approached his beautiful lady, wrapped his muscular arms tenderly around her nakedness, and kissed Nikki with as long a sensuous kiss as he had ever given.

As the kiss ended, Nikki spoke softly. "I love it, Logan."

He then softly cradled her in his arms and gently laid her on the bed. He straddled her and began to navigate her entire body with his warm and inviting lips and tongue.

Nikki knew that she was now in a good place … a very good place. She momentarily had flashback thoughts of bisexual sex, rough sex, submissive sex, and a thousand memories of sex with many men and women, and thought, "*I could do this forever … this is a part of my being that I can't reach alone.*"

As Logan moved up her body from a several-minute tongue-lapping of Nikki's wet and welcoming vagina, he turned her over, gently lifted her arms above her head, slightly spread her lovely, long legs, and began a neck, back, and buttocks massage that was as much therapeutic as it was erotic. Again, Nikki moaned and was totally absorbed in this man giving her a morning sex session bursting with heat, passion, and typical Logan technique.

As she laid on her back, having Logan finishing with his wonderful Shiatsu "finger pressure" stimulation, her anxiety and stress level had vanished, replaced by an innate desire, "*Please, go all the way, dear Logan,*" she whispered to herself, softly.

As she felt his hardening erection pressing against her backside, she rolled slightly onto her side, lifted her leg, and took his throbbing penis and inserted it into her, not requiring any lube, as she was as wet and ready as ever.

"Oh God, this is so good. Go deeper and slower, Logan."

In this spooning position, Logan, of course, was the "big spoon" and Nikki, the "little spoon." After several minutes of gentle pulsing penetration, Logan had Nikki roll onto her back, where he took up the position of the Cross, one of her favs.

In wild anticipation, Nikki exclaimed, "Yes. Yes!"

Her legs were slightly spread and draped over his hips, exposed and ready for thrusting from his pelvis with his hips against the back of her thighs. Not expecting deep penetration from this position, Nikki suggested, "Go doggy on me. I can handle you now. I'm wide and wet."

Logan thought about his partner's invitation to seek his favorite position, doggy style, as most heterosexual men enjoy. But he replied in a way that nearly brought the aroused Nikki to an early climax.

"Doggy is my grand finale, Babe, 'cause with the hard thrusting, I won't last long … especially today."

"*Too much info, dammit. Just do it,*" she thought impatiently.

Logan had Nikki roll to a face-down position with her legs spread so he could get into a position known as lazy dog. This prone rear entry is a twist on doggy style, with both laying down in a missionary position and spooning rotated face down.

Once in position, Nikki said, "I'm very close. Go slow."

With the depth of his thrust now controlled, he patiently waited for a signal from Nikki, as he was placing pressure on his penis to hold back.

Within about three minutes, both highly sexed and sweaty partners reached their climatic pinnacle simultaneously. With as loud a shriek as Logan has ever heard, Nikki's moan went to high-output scream … "Yes. My God Yes! Yes!"

Logan ran his fingers through Nikki's glistening hair and simply said, "Thank you, my love."

♥　　♥　　♥

They both tried to stick to the "work-from-the-train" script all day, but neither could focus on work, given the extremely enjoyable sex. The upside of these situations was easy to describe; the downside required some serious soul-searching for Nikki.

Having lunch in their berth a couple hours before arrival in Seattle, Logan glanced at the cool, calm, and relaxed Nikki and inquired, "Are you still planning to fly back to SFO this afternoon?'

"Yes, I really need to get back … wish I could stay for an encore of this trip."

"Me too. Sure, you can't change your mind?"

"No, Logan. I have several appointments that can't be changed. Sorry."

Thinking for a moment, he smiled and offered an impressive gesture to Nikki. "Let me get those roses wrapped for you so you can take one lovely remembrance of our trip with you." He reached over and kissed Nikki's hand.

"That would be wonderful. Thanks."

Getting up, Logan murmured, "Going to check on the flower thing. Be right back."

Nikki gave him a tender gaze as he left her alone to take in all the good things that she just experienced.

"I need to take advantage of this wonderful man and not take for granted the exceptional lovemaking we have … he is special," Nikki thought lovingly.

Once safely down the hallway, Logan sent a text.

"Hey princess, you there?"

241

Almost immediately a reply came.

> "Yep, big guy. Here for u."
> "I'm in Seattle. Can you fly up later today or tomorrow?"
> "Yes. What's the plan?"
> "I'll text you my hotel here later."
> "And then?"
> "We will do Seattle and then take the train back to Oakland."
> "Damn! Looking forward to that."
> "See you soon."
> "Song says super plan!"

Logan turned to make sure Nikki wasn't anywhere close and had a thought to himself as he put his cell in his pocket.

"What the hell … it's my fricking life."

62

SAMANTHA AND JONATHAN

T his chapter will deal with three very noteworthy sessions with Samantha. Each was distinctive and pulled together so well by the incredible Doctor Vandenberg. Let me set up the first session.

I had made an appointment for a Friday afternoon, but her office cancelled it and I had to reschedule. What I found out later was Sam needed a couple more days to complete "the script." I'll explain …

This first session involved role playing. Arriving at her office the following Tuesday, Sam greeted me with her usual upbeat demeanor and directness.

"Hi Jon, thanks for rescheduling. I needed a couple more days to prepare for this session."

"No problem, Sam. What is on today's agenda?"

"Take a seat next to the corner table, where you will find a thin binder." I walked over to the table and sat in a chair next to it.

"As you can see, I also am holding a small binder."

"Hot damn, I can't wait to see what role I'll be playing." I had an immediate sex thought, *"Hope she has a naughty school girl costume and I get to play the stern teacher."*

Sensing a misplaced sexual perception, Sam grinned, "I will be playing Jonathan Garrett and you will be playing Amanda Garrett. I have a script prepared with dialogue, inflections, and the actual verbiage from several of our conversations."

"So, good Doctor, this was part of your detailed note-taking for the last several weeks?"

"Yes. You okay with that? You talk about reality, Jon. This is as real as you get."

As we go through the well-done screenplay, I can easily see how my comments to Amanda were hurtful and unnecessary. With the intention of putting the shoe on a different foot, her mission was successful. I fought back tears as we concluded. Sam had accomplished her goal; I felt like a complete ass!

♥　　♥　　♥

For the second session, I met Sam in a poor area of the city at one of several shelters treating domestic violence and abuse. I recognized the name of this shelter, as Lina Chang had done work here before and I got a glimpse of the dire situation that many women face today.

"Hi Jon, any trouble finding this place?"

"Nope. Lina Chang had done some work here and I've actually contributed to their cause."

"That's great. I know Lina. She's a keeper."

"Yes, she is, Sam."

"But you have never been to this shelter."

"Nope. What's the plan?"

"I want to introduce you to Sister Marianne, who manages several shelters in a part-time capacity. Follow me."

Sam led me to a rickety folding table with organized messes everywhere.

"Sister Marianne, this is Jonathan Garrett, the gentleman I mentioned to you."

Extending her arthritic hand to me, Sister Marianne nodded, "It is good to meet you, Mister Garrett. What brings you to our shelter today?"

"Not sure, Sister. I believe Doctor Vandenberg saw a need here that she wanted to share with me."

Sam interjected, "Actually, Sister Marianne, I would like someone to give Mister Garrett a quick tour of this shelter while we plan for what is next."

With that comment, Sister Marianne motioned for a volunteer to come over.

"Please show this gentleman around our humble grounds."

The volunteer and I left as Sam and Sister Marianne talked.

"Sister, Mister Garrett is a bit of a lost soul, with a track record of selfishness and egotism."

"I'm confused. Why, then, bring him here?"

"Sorry. I strongly believe that there is a very good man inside that shell of isolation and distance. He lives in his own bubble and needs to either bring people into that bubble or move outside of that bubble. Does that make sense?"

"Yes, I like the bubble metaphor."

"So, Sister, you have a session beginning soon that involves some victims of violence and domestic abuse."

"Yes, it is our *Care about You* program."

"Could we just sit in?"

"Of course. I believe we will be doing some disturbing discoveries today. It is venting day."

"Understand. Thanks."

During my tour of the facility, I noticed that a philanthropic couple, friends of mine, the Foresters, had donated $2.5 million to the many shelters managed by Sister Marianne.

"How was the tour, Jon?"

"I'll admit, Sam, it is kind of depressing to see how many people, women in particular, are treated and seem to have so little to look forward to."

"Yes, it is eye opening. Now let's head over to the next coaching session."

As we walked, I reminded myself that the Foresters had invited me to a yacht party, and I needed to confirm my attendance. Just saying …

Sam and I attended the venting session that Sister Marianne described. In order to even observe this session, Sam had to receive permission from the Mission Director. Sam did have a solid reputation via her work with men in general, so permission was not a problem.

The 90-minute session took whatever air of superiority in my balloon, and zapped it. I left with my head hung low and with a sense that either Sam wanted me to feel bad for the women, or feel good, now knowing I understood their predicament.

♥ ♥ ♥

Returning to her office, and as we were discussing that trip to the shelter, which I admit was uncomfortable for me, it was a worthwhile exercise. I would continue to think about what I saw, and maybe any suggestions that I would come up with. It made me think about someone other than myself; that was Sam's intention.

Getting myself situated in an office becoming all too familiar, Sam began by explaining her plan for our third session, as we hurriedly downed some sandwiches. She had my utmost attention, as I had developed much respect for this lady's technique.

"Jon, I am going to project, on my wall screen, several scenes from a variety of Greta Garbo movies to begin this session. Are you familiar with this classic actress?"

"Well, I do watch Turner Classic Movies occasionally, and she is an old actress who I have seen," I said untruthfully. *"Never watch this stuff,"* I admitted to myself.

"Greta Garbo was never an 'old' actress, as she retired in her thirties suffering from serious disillusionment with Hollywood. Her famous line of *'I want to be alone,'* was spoken in Grand Hotel and it is one that I can relate to."

"I think I remember hearing her quote from a screenwriter friend in LA."

"Fine. The point of this exercise, Jon, is to illustrate restraint and focus, as the two main characters in each movie have a passionate relationship with each other, but cannot have sex on the screen."

"Okay. Got it."

"I need to do two things. I will tee up the edited scenes I mentioned. But first, I have period costumes for us to wear as we roleplay Greta and her lover."

"Geez, this is cool. I'm looking forward to this roleplay. The last session was difficult."

Sam smiled, but did not answer. "Let me get our outfits."

Minutes later, Sam returned with my suit, similar to the one worn by John Barrymore in the 1932 film. "You can put this on right here in my office. It'll seem big, as was the case in the movie. I'll get my 'Garbo' on in the bathroom. Give me about ten minutes."

Before long, Sam emerged in a stunning version of one of Garbo's gowns. "This is a reproduction from Garbo's designer, Adrian, directly from the movie *Grand Hotel*. It's a black crepe de chine evening gown with gorgeous rhinestone and sequins embroidered, as you can see, on both the upper top front of the dress and the front and back of the bottom. Exquisite!"

"Wow! You look like her. And that wig?"

"I had this wig specially made from photographs and museum sketches."

As she looked into the reflection of herself in the office window, she smiled ... then pouted. Yep, she was in character. She glanced at me, and rolled the edited movie scenes.

Once the video was completed, it was "Showtime" for the wannabe thespians. Garbo was the aging Russian ballerina and her lover was the former Baron, now a thief who found the ballerina to be an easy mark.

Following another script, Sam and I recreated several of the scenes in the movie, trying to achieve intimacy with much restraint and little physicality. It brought back memories of my ninth-grade acting, which sure as hell wasn't Oscar stuff.

Upon finishing, I quipped, "These roles were hard to do."

"Which part was hard?"

"I really just wanted to get your clothes off and cop a feel, inasmuch as most of you was covered."

"I appreciate the honesty, Jon, and would like you to think about what you may have learned or what may have changed your thinking about two people seeking love ... seeking sex, okay?"

"Fair enough. Thanks for setting this up. I did enjoy it, actually."

I had already discarded his oversized suit, and Sam remained in character as I left her office. On the drive home, my first thought was, *"Damn, I'd like to get her in bed. Bet she could act her way into just about any mood a guy would like."*

Thinking more seriously, I asked myself what was different regarding the roleplay. It came to me as I pulled past the security gate of my $5,500,000 mansion on Bayhill Court in Half Moon Bay, and stopped short of the garage.

"Two things," I thought. *"First, there was a big difference between touching and feeling. I had to pay very close attention to how and where I touched Sam. I had to be sensual, not sexual."*

The second thought hit hard. *"Crap. I had to communicate ... talk ... listen ... be interested in her. Think of stuff to say. I had to work my mind, not my throbbing pointer. And, if she wasn't interested, sex wasn't gonna happen."*

As I pulled my Benz into the garage, I had to laugh a bit, thinking ...

"Shit, these three sessions were like that old movie, A Christmas Carol. The Ghosts of Christmas Past! Guess I saw the light. Maybe time to reverse course, so to speak!"

63

FANTASIES FULFILLED

*A*s you may recall, I had taken down some info regarding a charitable donation by my friends, the Foresters, when Samantha and I were at Sister Marianne's shelter. The couple, John Paul and Tia Forester, were going to host a huge fund raiser on their mega-yacht, the **Carpe Diem**, which is Latin for "seize the day."

"Hi Jacqui, it's Jon."

"Hey big guy. What's up?"

"Got a minute?"

"Sure. You coming over? I can get into the mood quickly if you are."

"That would be wonderful, but this time I'm throwing out an invitation."

"All ears, Jon."

"Good friends of mine, the Foresters, are having a really cool fund raiser on their yacht a week from Saturday, and I am going and would love to have you join me."

"Oh my gosh, that would be great. I'd love to."

"Super. I will text you details as we get closer."

"I know that couple, Jon, from all the press they get. Good people with tons of money, and they support many charitable causes here in the Bay Area."

"Yep, that's them. I'll be in touch. Thanks, Jacqui."

"My pleasure. Thanks for asking me."

I sent a text to John Paul Forester, confirming that I would attend, with a guest.

"Hey JP, how r u and Tia?"

"Good, thnx, Jon. You?"

"Just keeping busy and trying to stay out of trouble."

"You coming?"

"Yes. Bringing a guest with me, Jacqui Johnson."
"Great. Kno her. She will fit right in."
Gonna take my copter. Your helipad still good?"
"Yep. Give us location 10 minutes out to prepare.
And your friend Sara Sullivan's band will be performing."
"Cool. See you then. Thnx."

♥ ♥ ♥

It was the day of the gala on the *Carpe Diem*. I made plans to pick up Jacqui at the Commodore Center Heliport in Sausalito, very close to Jacqui's sprawling home. At 1:00 p.m., I arrived at the Commodore Center, and a smiling Jacqui with overnight bag in hand waved as we landed.

The tall, lovely Jacqui Johnson had a perfect outfit for the gala, a boat anchor print T-shirt and striped skirt set. She hurried over to hop on board, and we were off to meet John Paul's yacht, about 50 miles off shore from the Bay Area.

"Jon, this is exciting."

"Yep. So happy you could make it. We will be there soon, and I'll immediately introduce you to the Foresters. I see you brought a bag in case we stay over."

"Yep. Always planning ahead."

Jacqui thought impatiently, "*I really need this change of scene right now.*" She gave me a kiss as we flew off to the rendezvous.

In less than 30 minutes, we landed, disembarked the copter, and sought out our hosts.

Hand in hand, John Paul and Tia greeted their latest guests, and introductions were made. John Paul suggested we visit the main deck bar for refreshments, and then he would give us an overview of the yacht and later, a tour.

Tia was dressed in a floral printed dress with braided spaghetti straps and decorative beads. Her figure was lean, and she had a noticeable tan from many days on the water. John Paul, not concerned with anyone's opinion, had on a white V-neck silk shirt, blue blazer, and knee-length beige shorts. His floppy sandals completed the casual look.

Once Jacqui and I had our drinks, John Paul described the *Carpe Diem*. "She is just under 400 feet in length, helipad on the stern and an open fore deck. She carries two tenders for shuttling passengers and has four decks with curved balconies on three levels. The lower level contains the saloon and staterooms to accommodate 28 people, and she carries a crew of 35."

"This is very impressive, John Paul, and we thank you for having us."

"Jon, it's our pleasure, my friend," reassured by a smiling Tia.

"Below us, on the second level, we have set up the silent auction. Jacqui, you must see some of the articles to be auctioned."

"Can't wait, John Paul."

"As you can see, we have our guests now socializing on this primary deck, so please make yourselves at home with the food and drink that is available in several locations. Sara Sullivan's band, *Tempest,* will be playing topside around 8:00 tonight."

As we started to mingle, Jacqui recognized a couple people, and I was right at home as we made our rounds through a bevy of "movers and shakers." It was going to be a great night.

"There is Jack and Elissa Sherman, Jacqui. Jack is a retired commercial pilot and now is in training to command Scott Woods' Galactic Voyager, which is being built in Fremont. This will be the first attempt of commercial space flight for any citizen with money."

I waved as the Sherman's were engaged in conversation with several people.

"Over there are Richard and Natalie Rhodes. Richard was a corporate executive who is now driving the economic recovery in Seattle following the pandemic, and his socialite wife handles most of the fundraising. I'm certain that they are here to observe and recruit. There is money in Seattle, but no match for what, and who, are here on this yacht right now!"

"I think I met Natalie Rhodes at an event in Palo Alto last year," Jacqui noted. "She was definitely a magnet at that event, and I just assumed it was because of her good looks. Obviously, she has the smarts to carry her own weight."

"Absolutely, Jacqui."

"Jim and Janet Burrough are a nice story. Jim is a self-made millionaire, and the couple goes out on church-sponsored missions worldwide." Jacqui glanced over at the couple. "He has a philosophical slant to life in general, and Janet just likes to travel and help people."

"Seems to be a lot of wealthy people here, who have no problem giving back to those less fortunate."

"Yes, Jacqui, that is true. I just love being around these people."

As we made a turn at the main saloon, I spotted a couple who waved at me.

"Great. There are two people who I'd like to talk to." They began to walk in their direction.

"Ken McCall is one of my favs. He and Pauline have had one helluva ride. He is a retired NASCAR driver having spent twelve years racing and won two national championships."

"I have heard of him, Jon."

"Highly superstitious, Jacqui, he quit racing just before he was to start his thirteenth season, and is now owner of a race team. Honestly, I think retirement was just an excuse he used, as Pauline was done traveling and patching him up after each race."

They met, introduced one another, and the four began to make the rounds together.

Afternoon turned to evening, and Sara and her band arrived to set up for their musical entertainment. Apparently, their equipment had already arrived via one of the tenders.

"Hey girl," I said as I hugged Sara.

"Hi Jon. Hi Jacqui."

Jacqui gave Sara a hug as well, not recalling that her friend Sara played in a band.

"I'd say that if there was a Renaissance woman, Sara, you would qualify."

"Thanks, girlfriend. It's nice to be placed in the same conversation as famed Renaissance Men Bono, Brad Pitt, and Hugh Jackman."

I winked at Sara and smiled.

"Gotta go set up. See you guys later."

Tia then came by to say hi. She had changed into an elegant dark navy sheath column off-the-shoulder floor-length chiffon evening dress with sequins.

"Are you guys enjoying yourselves?"

"Yes," Jacqui responded enthusiastically. "Very much so. Thanks."

I added, "Tia, I love your dress. You look marvelous."

"Thank you, Jon. Let us know if you need anything."

Jacqui chimed in, "Tia, I brought an evening dress. Is there somewhere I can change?"

"Absolutely." Tia texted an aide who met Jacqui and JJ was off.

I stayed with Tia for a while to catch up, and get some info regarding John Paul's philanthropic efforts to date.

♥   ♥   ♥

Jacqui quickly left to get changed, and then planned to spend some time at the silent auction and a craps table, which was set up for some gambling addicts and to see if she could get "lucky" with a partner for the evening.

Twenty minutes later, the fashion diva Jacqui had emerged resplendent in a navy-blue skew neck asymmetric hem one-shoulder dress with a single silver strap that framed her bustline.

Jacqui clicked on her "find a hot hunk" mission rather easily. After perusing the single men attending, she introduced herself to a fairly prominent actor, Ryan Hudson, and they became an instant "party couple."

"I love your latest movie but confess, I prefer you without the fangs!"

"Well, Jacqui, that's what makes the movie. Makeup and costuming are key. Let's get a couple drinks and mix."

"Mix, hell," Jacqui thought sexually, *"I wanna mix and match our parts!"*

For the next half-hour, they could feel their strong chemistry rising from an ember to a growing flame. They were trying, unsuccessfully, to stay off of the radar of anyone they knew, as they looked for any little cubbyholes to get some foreplay started.

As if a magic wand got waved, I sought out Jacqui and announced, "Tia has just invited us to stay over if you'd like. She gave me two stateroom keys, and I don't need to get back tonight."

"Oh my gosh, that's great. Jon."

With this tantalizing news, Jacqui then introduced me to Ryan, and all was good … very good.

Jacqui and Ryan excused themselves, and quickly headed to their stateroom. Once inside, Jacqui and Ryan got themselves in a warm embrace that got heated abruptly, as the initial chemistry grew to an intense passion.

Jacqui was getting aroused, and, she could see her man was as well. Ryan turned toward the large and inviting bed, picked his lady up and placed her gently on the soft bed. Jacqui sighed with pleasure as he removed her shoes, then his shirt and shoes.

"My, you are strong," she uttered. Ryan just smiled.

As he bent over her, Jacqui put both of her hands around his neck and pulled his athletic body onto hers. She knew he was going to kiss her, but when his hands surrounded her face with a gentle kiss, his dark, silky hair fell forward, and her temperature sizzled like melting butter.

In tandem, they did a mutual once-over. His eyes traveled down her body and hers down his. Jacqui was looking at a god-like figure, fulfilling a sexual fantasy that has been dormant for a while, six feet of sheer sculpted leanness with big, broad shoulders.

"You have a gorgeous body, Ryan." He placed his hands upon Jacqui's hips, and then a gentle kiss became wet and passionate.

"Jacqui, you are a goddess, and I believe in fate. Relax."

Returning to kiss Jacqui and with his hand slipping fingers through her hair, he said, "I have been fixated on you ever since we met; even though it's been just hours ago. The body-on-body sensual feeling that I have right now is clearly special."

He slowly descended onto her body like a cloud, bracing himself with one hand so as not to place too much weight on her lovely frame.

"I feel your warmth … your manhood. Take me on!"

They embraced, and then rolled over to where she was on top of him. Jacqui let Ryan remove her dress, gently slide the lone strap from her shoulder with his fingers, exposing her bra and leaving her with only the tiniest bikini briefs.

Ryan had already stripped down to his black, micro stretch thong with contoured pouch, which exposed his firm butt cheeks. He had been expecting sex tonight, and he knew that any lady friend he would meet, would be sexually aroused, just looking at his massive jewels in that black, silky pouch.

"Oh, my," Jacqui murmured softly.

Ryan realized that any impromptu physical encounter tonight, would end a week-long sexual drought, and his sexy undie selection would set a captivating erotic mood immediately. He had plenty of practice, a fact of his behavior, about which poor Jacqui would be clueless.

Given that his manhood was briefly covered, Jacqui was drawing her attention to every finely honed muscle, his beautiful smiling face, and those sparkling blue eyes. She was warm, wet, and ready to take on anything this man had in mind.

As she settled over him, her warm body and trembling legs were feeling his big, strong hands on her thighs, positioning his thong in contact with her bikini briefs. She slowly removed both items and firmly used her hand to guide his throbbing manhood into place.

"My God, he is huge," she whispered to herself excitedly.

Her mind, body, and soul opened wide, to soak in his masculinity. Moments later, he was deep inside her wet vagina, and they were both on fire. She was writhing in absolute pleasure and he, with his arms around a sexy goddess, groaned loudly in lustful enjoyment.

Jacqui, clenching the last moments of her sex against his, felt ecstasy and screamed, "Oh God Ryan, you feel wonderful. I love it!"

Ryan looked directly in her eyes, having experienced his own orgasmic peak, offered in a whisper, "I have never had such a strong physical bond with anyone like I just had with you. Thank you, my lovely lady."

Jacqui's body went from a trembling crescendo, to a completely relaxed satisfaction.

Following several minutes of complete physical relaxation, and with Ryan's warm body pressed against hers, Jacqui thoughts were longer term.

"Damn it, girl, this cannot be a one-night stand!"

ACT II
REALITY RESONATES

You and I go hard at each other like we're fighting wars,
You and I get rough, throwing fits and kicking doors.
You and I get so damn dysfunctional, we start keeping rhyming score,
You and I get sick over it; we both know we can't do this anymore.
Really though, you knew the deal; oh well, I guess that's what happens,
Two young fools falling in love mix family pain with personal passion.
There are some days when I pretend, I'm okay,
But that's not what hurts … what gets me down today.
What hurts the most is being so damn close and not able to say,
That loving you is what I've tried to do in so many failed ways.
It is so true that I have chased selfish wants and needs,
To the point where my agenda flies by you with alarming speeds.
Even worse you seek out girlfriends you think I should marry,
Never able to accept my sincere truth that they are imaginary.
I have tried in vain to gather guys to become friends of mine,
Attempts with Tom, Mike and Joe failed; they never seemed to have time.
Mimi, Elle and Linda were ladies who'd come and go.
My intentions were not to have sex; only to stroke my very large ego.
And I know I've said it forever, give me one more time to set it right.
It's getting harder to keep life and soul together,
I'm sick of fighting; the cold is biting.
Now I'm writing in earnest; fulfilling thoughts of childhood dreaming,
It's given me a new reason for living; a deeper meaning.
Truth be known I have a female in my life with enormous appeal;
She's sitting next to me now; her heart to steal.

INTERMISSION

I know there seems to be many loose ends, raising several questions. From this point on, I will attempt to close as many of those open issues as I can. Life can't always be studied from a chronological perspective, and I am bouncing around somewhat, as I try to provide relevant detail with these interesting ladies.

If this was a pure love story, between a man and a woman, I could stick to a continuous script. But we have five very unique women, with many fascinating stories, that just don't lend themselves to simple, continuous behavior.

These lives, although fairly complicated, become a mural of life experiences and lessons learned. As in our real day-to-day world, they are often intertwined and always interesting.

A C T III

THE
RESOLUTION

LIFE'S LESSONS LEARNED

64

NIKKI

Not trusting Logan in the least, Nikki hired a detective, Roger, who was very discreet with his clientele. Roger was a well-known and credible professional.

The detective met the Coast Starlight as it arrived in Oakland from Seattle, three days after Nikki said goodbye to Logan and returned to San Francisco. Although Logan didn't give Nikki any clue of pending unfaithfulness, her women's intuition kicked in, and she just wanted to be sure that Logan was staying trustworthy.

Nikki got an incoming text from Roger and nervously opened the text.

> "Nikki, its Roger.
> Sending you a series of shots.
> Let me know if you need anything else."

Rapidly perusing the photos, she stopped to respond.

> "Nothing more Roger.
> These are fine. Thnx."

Roger had, indeed, snapped many pictures of Logan and Song disembarking, holding hands and embracing in one, long, passionate kiss. From the photos, it would appear that this was a couple in love, if not lust.

In one photo, Nikki was particularly pissed, *That bitch even has her fricking hand grabbing his crotch! WTF."*

From the photos, Nikki noticed that the black-haired, dark-complected "Indian princess" going by the name of Song, looked like a somewhat smaller version of herself! Nikki didn't think she was as attractive as her. "*So, it must be she is better in bed!*"

Nikki sobbed as she looked at the photos for a second time. Her heart wanted them to go away, but in her mind, Logan's behavior was just as consistent as ever.

She began to text her friends, and then stopped. *"This is my problem and I need to deal with it,"* she thought crushingly.

♥　♥　♥

Moving on, Nikki concluded her support of the case against Jacqui Johnson with a stunning witness account from Jonathan Garrett, a witness for the defense called at the last opportunity.

I had Jacqui cautiously earlier record her dead husband's account of keeping her in the dark, when it seemed like useless detail. With my various experiences in dealing with male versus female relationships, I thought it was smart to get some indisputable evidence, just in case.

Nikki had provided the audio tape as Exhibit Y in Jacqui's defense, and once they got a voice recording specialist to verify that the voice recording was authentic, and James Johnson did admit to keeping his wife in the dark, the Jonathan Garrett witness testimony was the icing on the legal cake.

The trail ended with Jacqui's acquittal and Nikki finally got her revenge against the lowlife that demeaned her so thoroughly at the sex orgy, Thomas Shaughnessy. She immediately sent out a group text.

"WE WON!"

While she relaxed, enjoying the results of a significant victory, Nikki was approached by her trial nemesis, and took a deep sigh.

"Hey, Nikki, nice work. I am surprised at your resourcefulness."

Not getting an immediate response from Nikki, Attorney Shaughnessy continued.

"So, no hard feelings from that party, right?"

Nikki turned her head toward her adversary and said, "You are a disgusting, misogynistic bastard, and my only desire is for the next time when I can beat your miserable ass in court!"

"So, I guess a date is out of the question?"

"Go screw yourself!"

Nikki closed her briefcase and left her foe with no "come-back" comment.

She smiled and thought to herself, ***"Damn, I enjoyed that!"***

65

NIKKI

As she left the courthouse, Nikki had received several text messages, and knew she would need some time to follow up. She headed to a nearby Starbucks, one of her favorite places to unwind, to gather her thoughts.

Once she arrived, she ordered a cappuccino; and knowing the barista, Terry, she had a perfect response to Terry's question.

"What name on your cup today?"

"*Badass!*"

"One *Badass*, coming up."

Sitting down with her warm and wonderful drink, Nikki scrolled down her lengthy list of texts. One jumped out. It was from her past life regression therapist, Dr. Dawn Baker.

> "GM Nikki. Hope you win today!
> Just confirming our 10:00 app't tomorrow.
> Best Regards, Dawn."

Nikki has almost forgot her follow-up session with Dawn, given her last-minute preparations for the trial.

> "Hi Dawn. We won! Thnx.
> Planning to be there at 10:00 am.
> See u then."

Nikki looked up at the sea of mindless chatter in the store and thought, "*Damn, I have a lot to do before tomorrow's early flight to Palm Springs!*"

♥   ♥   ♥

Arriving at the Palm Springs airport, Dr. Baker had arranged for a driver to meet Nikki and drive her to her appointment. Nice touch from a very professional lady.

Upon entering the office, Dawn greeted Nikki with a warm hug and a delicious cup of green tea.

"It's great to see you again, and congratulations on your well-deserved win!"

"Thank you, Dawn; we were on the fence until we got that tape ... kind of lucked out."

"Yes, I saw that on CNN. You know what they say about luck, don't you?"

"Sure. We were prepared when this opportunity came. Thanks for your kind words."

As the ladies finished their tea and conversation, Dr. Baker suggested that they move to her quiet room, and begin the second stage of Nikki's hypnosis. For the first 90 minutes, Nikki, with prompts from Dawn, navigated her early life with her father, a strong person with a truly visionary perspective on life in general.

During the last 30 minutes under hypnosis, Nikki had recurring images in her mind along with what is called a progressive-type dream.

"Tell me what you are seeing, Nikki"

Slowly, Nikki responded, "I am in a future life ... a scene I don't recognize. My dad has been replaced by another man, dressed in strange clothes."

"Can you describe the scene?"

Nikki shudders a bit and says, "It is like I am in a planetarium, but the ceiling is real."

"Are you in danger, Nikki?"

"No. Very happy and very relaxed."

Moments later, Nikki is awake and they both try to make some sense of Nikki's glimpse into the future.

"I must admit, Nikki Wallace, that has never happened with any of my clients."

"Is it something bad?"

"Gosh, no, Nikki. If anything, it is your mind's attempt to look into the future. I think it is incredible that you have experienced this vision."

What Nikki didn't reveal to Dawn, was a brief glimpse into the near future. Nikki got goosebumps thinking about a pending confrontation with Logan.

She thought, dejectedly, *"I know he will be coming over, and I know what I must do!"*

66

LOGAN

Arriving back in Oakland from the return train trip with Song, Logan replayed the entire encounter in his mind, where it was vividly etched.

Following the previously scripted sexcapades with Nikki, for some bizarre reason, he got the panting Song on her front with him above her. He then bypassed the gentler lazy dog, and with a noticeable cruel streak, Logan went directly to full doggy style, using his belt as an ass-up strap to pound Song hard.

He thought he was giving Song some unwarranted pain. Instead, the sexually promiscuous Song took his brutal thrusting as "rough sex," which she didn't mind at all. *"Yeah,"* he thought remindful, *"Nikki's sexual expectations aren't to just have hard sex … she has a softer side."*

Now his fully erect thrusting penis was going limp before he could ejaculate. Seeing his powerful missile become a limp biscuit, was unnerving and quite unexpected. It was a physical sign; but still an unwanted one.

Logan excused himself, faking an orgasm, and had to masturbate in the bathroom. He fantasized screwing Nikki in her wonderful sexy bedroom apparel and came in a minute.

Before he got off the train, Logan was determined to make things right with Nikki, but the *sexual baggage* playing out on the train with Song turned out to be a foolish mistake. He had no idea that Nikki had hard evidence of his infidelity.

♥　♥　♥

The past couple of weeks had been busy for Logan. Not only has his court docket been crammed, but the Governor of California had been having extensive

263

conversation with Logan, regarding the state's open attorney general position, which would have been a huge promotion and major career opportunity.

"Hi Logan, how goes it? Were you able to get a lot accomplished on your slow train from Seattle?"

"Hello, Governor, all good and the train ride was just business as usual, you know?"

"Hope you used some of that slow time to unwind and get your priorities in order."

"That I did. What's going on with you at the statehouse?"

"Working on budget stuff right now. The income deficits from COVID-19 are making our commitments for many state services shrink severely, but you knew that."

"Yes. Of course."

"So, Logan, you likely know the reason for the call."

"The AG job?"

"Yep. It's yours if you want it, but I will need an answer soon. As you can probably guess, it's a very attractive position … an absolute springboard to the U.S. Congress."

"Yes, I know it is, and I'm very pleased and humbled by your confidence in me. I will let you know soon. I promise. And thank you."

"That's all I can ask for. Take care."

So, the governor of California had offered Logan a lifetime dream, the California Attorney General job, if he wanted it. This position had been his lifelong dream.

♥   ♥   ♥

As a result of the soul-searching, and telling revelation on the return train trip concerning Nikki being his real love, Logan headed to his favorite jewelry store on Post Street, where he bought a 3.0 carat, heart-cut solitaire pendant with sparkling diamond cut cable chain. He explained to the jeweler that this young lady could "be the one."

"May I wrap this for you?"

"Yes. Can you find a blue box? She likes blue."

"Of course. While we do that, may I show you a truly stunning heart-shaped engagement ring?"

"That's a little premature." He paused. "Ah, what the hell, sure."

Minutes later the jeweler brought out a rare gem. A 5.0 carat classical tiffany style engagement ring that happened to be a one-of-a-kind design by a well-known jewelry designer in California.

"Stunning, yes?"

Logan admired the piece and replied, "It is lovely."

"With only ten per cent down, we can hold it for you."

Logan thought for a moment and said enthusiastically, "Yes, please do."

About ten minutes later, he left the store heading for a scheduled meeting with Nikki at her place. When he called her, she was abrupt and seemed a bit annoyed. "*This will cheer her up,*" he thought reflectively.

Upon arriving at Nikki's place feeling as good about himself as ever, and completely comfortable with his decision to commit to Nikki, she met him at the door dressed in her workout clothes, but they didn't go inside.

"Hi Nikki, good to see you."

Logan's attempt to give Nikki a hug was met with a standoffish "No, hell no."

"What's wrong?"

"Seriously?" You don't know what's wrong?"

"No, I don't." Pulling out a nicely wrapped jewelry box, he advised, "I have a gift for you."

Pulling an envelope from her workout shorts she responded, "I have photos for you!"

She threw the group of pictures at Logan, turned and slammed the door shut.

Looking down at the scattered pictures of Song and himself disembarking the train, Logan knew the relationship was now over. He dejectedly walked to his car, and sat silent for several minutes. He then took out his cell phone and sent a text message to the Governor.

> "Sorry, but I am declining the AG job.
> Suggest you interview Nikki Wallace.
> Thank you for your consideration."

The next day, Nikki got a call from the California Statehouse, setting up an interview for the open attorney general position ... not knowing how she was selected.

67

SARA

Sara had reached a point where she was getting stressed out with a myriad of priorities including her job, her time spent with her music and the band that she performs in, modeling commitments that were huge time constraints and, of course, the partying.

She called Nikki and they set up a Sunday brunch so Sara could use Nikki's experience as a sounding board.

Arriving at the *Early to Rise* restaurant on Jackson Street, they hugged and walked into the restaurant where Nikki had made a reservation.

"Okay, girlfriend, what's on your mind? What do we need to talk about?"

As a waitress brought some water to the table, Sara simply shrugged and said,

"Well first, congrats on the AG interview. That's got to be exciting."

"It's just an interview. We'll see. Tell me what's going on with you."

"I'm just overwhelmed with all the crap I'm dealing with right now, and if there ever was someone who could juggle or multi-task, it's Nikki Wallace."

After about an hour of heated, yet productive conversation, Sara was putting two and two together and made a startling realization. Often, guys would call for a date that was, more or less, a role for her to be play at many corporate functions.

"Oh my God," she uttered disappointedly, "many of my dates viewed me as 'eye candy' and didn't consider for one bit that I was a peer. Shit!"

"Hey, don't be too hard on yourself, Sara, this is Silicon Valley. We have all had to deal with that male crap. It's the damn behavior by so many of these 'entitled' bastards that drives me relentlessly to succeed."

"Then there is the bullshit I deal with on social media, Nikki. I know women in general have to put up with this adolescence crap, but many of the harassing comments or flat out lies are coming from men who I have treated well … at least I'm pretty sure I have."

"Okay, this one is easy. Again, 'I resemble that remark.' Men are intimidated by you, and unless they can gain some control over you, their shattered egos have them spreading lies and false stories on any social media platform that is convenient."

"There was a reason, Nikki, why I wanted to have this discussion with you, someone who has been there before. Feeling kind of foolish that I hadn't figured it out."

"You're a good person who always sees the best in people. And that's what you need in return. A good girl won't be out 'sleeping around,' and that goes for guys, too."

"I feel I need to dump Brad and start anew. A difficult decision, but I think I'm now at that point."

"No comment or advice here, Sara. You need to do what you think is best."

♥   ♥   ♥

Sara decided to take a scuba trip to the Virgin Islands with a "great guy" that she met at a huge networking event in the city, a promotion from one of many local dating apps. Both were PADI-certified divers; he with over 200 dives and Sara with about 75 dives.

They would fly into Tortola, and from there, take a dingy to the anchored, 40-foot-long catamaran, *Ladies' Choice*. It wasn't until sometime later that she discovered this was kind of a floating stalking vessel … more on that soon.

Chris was another one of those guy-types which Sara was attracted to: handsome, professional, and fairly wealthy. He was a successful hedge-fund manager, and had several well-known clients. They had gone on a couple dates, but Sara had resisted his sexual advances both times which left him a bit frustrated, if not pissed.

So, Sara was surprised to get a call and invitation.

"Hey girl, interested in a scuba trip?"

Without hesitation, "Hell yeah, Chris, when?"

"Two weeks from Thursday. I can have my assistant book us on a flight into Tortola and then on to the dive ship for three days of diving, returning on Monday. You game?"

"Damn straight. Just need to clear a couple things and I'll be ready to go."

"Great, Sara. Bring that sport camera you talked about. I'll have some spears and knives shipped there for us to use."

Sara pondered that statement, *"He either has some good diving skills, or his ego is on full display. Either way, I'm hooked."*

"Chris, I'm excited. Send me the details when you get them."

"Will do."

"Later, Chris."

The scuba diving part of the trip was literally fantastic. Their dive at Picasso's Gallery was a photographer's dream, and their night dive of the HMS Rhone was truly incredible. The level of diving expertise was exceptionally high, which made for some incredible day and night dives.

However, the romantic part of the trip didn't meet Sara's expectations. Chris set up the "rules of the game" as soon as the divers got unpacked. Apparently, the *Ladies' Choice* was unique inasmuch as certain clients, including this one, focused on *ménage à* trois as the "sex du jour."

So, for Sara, the trip was all diving and no sex, which she accepted. She departed the catamaran having had fun, and a nice diversion from the stress of her day-to-day stuff. It wasn't until she was back in San Francisco a couple days when my assistant, Amy, called her with some awful news.

"Hi Sara, its Amy, Jonathan's assistant."

"Yes, Amy. Jon talks all the time about you being the 'brains' of his operation. He really trusts and respects you."

"Thank you, Sara, but this isn't a social call."

"Oh gosh, what's wrong?"

"Several pictures are turning up on the internet. They show you by name, totally nude in what appears to be a boats' shower."

"What!"

"I'm afraid so. Jonathan even received a few of those pics and recognized you right away."

"Oh my God!"

"I'm afraid it gets even worse."

"Amy, please go ahead." Sara was getting nervous and quite angry, but it did get worse.

"You were being described as a 'naïve prima donna and an easy piece of tail.' Sorry, Sara, but those were the exact words that labeled the photos."

"And we didn't even have sex. Must have pissed him off. What the hell am I going to do!"

"Well, Jonathan has already taken the first step?"

"What did he do?"

"He has given your contact info to a dedicated young female attorney, specializing in what is called, 'revenge porn.' She even has a terrific investigator working with her on behalf of victims. Jonathan believes that you have a strong case. Just let us know, and we'll kick it off."

"That's so reassuring, Amy. Please tell Jon thanks."

"And, Sara, Jonathan will pick up the cost. He is all over this stuff."

"You'll never know," she thought regretfully. ***"Chris seemed so nice."***

68

BRAD

Meanwhile, Brad had been trying to find out who played him, regarding the embarrassing four-poster bed BDSM scene that he suffered at the hands of two nasty, but determined women. He ruled out Sara, because even though she had a motive, she was much too good to stoop to that level of ridiculing him.

Apparently, Brad turned in some favors to get in touch with the preeminent 'influencer' in town with tons of social media followers. She called herself Mona, which had to be a long way from her real name.

"Mona, its Brad. Any clues yet from the description I gave you?"

"Not yet, Brad. Ya gotta give me some time. Someone will rat the perps out … just be patient."

Spoiler alert: No one did!

"Also, Mona, can you find out if Sara Sullivan ever bounced any of this around?"

"That was my first shot, given what you told me about you screwing with her before. Brad, you sure she didn't have a role here?"

"I am fricking positive!"

"Okay, I'll keep looking and get back to you. My followship now is over 100,000."

Brad wondered amusingly, *"Is followship even a word?"*

He was also scared shitless that Sara had gotten ahold of this sexual fiasco.

♥　♥　♥

Several days later, Brad got a text message sent from a burner phone.

"My name is Sue and I have something you want.
Text me back now."

Brad was in shock by the tone and content of this threatening text message.

"This is Brad. Tell me what it is that I want."
"Pictures of you naked, spread eagled on the four-poster bed.
And a big sign on the headboard with your name on it, asshole."

Brad was in shock.

"What do you want?"
"Money, asshole."

Pausing to catch his breath and figure how to respond …

"What do I do?"
"We are gonna meet. I'll let you know when and where."
"You said money."
"Yes. I will make sure that the pics disappear for $25,000 cash."

Brad knew that the blackmail photos would change his life. He gave this situation a lot of thought, and realized that he needed help in a big way if he was going to get out of this mess.

His best shot was to go to Sara, admit what he'd done, and have her and her contacts, like Nikki Wallace, try to help him.

He weighed the good versus bad, with the Sara option, and came to a shitty conclusion. He could likely solve one problem and then create another problem that could be even worse.

After some digging, Brad was informed that Sara had been told of his comic infidelity.

"I'm screwed!" he assumed dejectedly.

69

SARA

Brad decided to meet with Sara for two reasons. One, he needed some info regarding the blackmail issue and could use her help. Two, he felt he needed to start to rebuild the broken relationship.

He headed over to Sara's condo with a bottle of wine, one of her favs, a 2019 Caymus Cabernet.

She wasn't in her usual festive mood. Wearing her gym warm-ups, she received Brad at the door and invited him in.

"Thanks for letting me come over. I have a few things to get off my chest."

"I'm not surprised."

They head for the kitchen, and Sara began to open the wine.

Jumping right in, he asked, "Did you hear about the four-poster bed incident?"

"Who didn't," Sara responded sarcastically.

"Embarrassing. Can't apologize enough for that one."

"Well, you can try."

Sara poured them both a glass of the Cab, and they sat down on her couch. Eja sat between them.

"On top of that, I have a woman who calls herself Sue, who is blackmailing me, or she will go public with the photos."

"*Shit, I wasn't aware of that,*" Sara thought worriedly. "*This could get bad.*"

"Give me the details, Brad."

He spent the next fifteen minutes explaining the sex show in honest detail, as if Sara was at the embarrassment gig. Then he switched to the arrangement with Sue, and got visibly upset.

Sara felt a twinge of guilt, having planned and executed the entire performance.

"I'll see what I can do regarding the Sue thing. What she is doing to you is, of course, a crime."

Brad leaned over Eja and gave Sara a hug, "Thank you. I really appreciate your help."

Sara refilled both wine glasses as they continued to talk. Brad spent the next hour in a self-deprecating montage of every wrong he had done, periodically apologizing in an awkward and weak manner.

By this time, they were both feeling the effects of finishing off the entire bottle of wine. Sara could see that Brad was in the mood for some make-up sex and thought, *"What the hell."*

She led him to her bedroom and they both started to undress. He was very eager to prove he was the lover she needed, which was the answer to the wrong question, in Sara's mind.

His hands immediately grew busy on her body in a heightened attempt to get her aroused. Maybe it was to sidetrack Sara, or to reassure himself. With her sweat bottoms off, he worked his way down her front, over her thighs, bunching her sweatshirt in his hands as he pulled it up over her head. But when his hand moved back to between her legs and he growled, "I want to get you wet," she easily found the tenacity to push his arm away.

"Brad, you can't just fix this with sex."

"What, Sara? Let's try."

Sara was incredulous, "You think you can make me forgive and forget just by making me come? Hell, I can do that myself!"

Brad looked baffled, almost angry at her words. "Isn't that what two people do ... become intimate even when things are scary or too damn surreal to process?"

"Fine. Distract me. I dare you to see if you can make me forget how mad and disappointed I am." Sara was about to unleash the girl who lets herself feel anger ... who can punish.

Brad was losing his make-up sex argument. She shoved his chest hard, lips parted in surprise, both palms flat to his pectorals, and he stumbled back. She pushed him again and his knees met the edge of the bed and he crumbled backward.

Sara climbed on top of him until her hips were level with his face, and she reached down and grabbed a fistful of his hair. "I'm not okay, you shit," as he tried to kiss, lick or nibble any part of the angry Sara.

"I know. I'm sorry."

Sara reached into his pants and easily found his erection. She slid her crotch over his warm and throbbing manhood and faked a lap dance that got Brad highly aroused. Now that she was controlling everything, she moved in for the kill.

"Tell me what you want, Brad?"

"I want to have sex with my 'cowgirl' right here and right now. What do you want, *sunshine?*"

Sara answers emphatically, and sarcastically, "Oh God, I want you in me so deep I can feel you in my throat."

Before he could respond, Sara then jumped off of Brad, and yelled, "Now get the hell out of my house and my life," as she headed for the bathroom, locking the door.

From inside the bathroom she yelled, **"And don't ever call me sunshine, you ass."**

70

LINA

*A*lthough Lina wasn't the one who usually set up the agenda for the girls Friday night out, this time Lina set up the barhopping night, so she could cover a few important issues, and not have the subject matter become a boring evening for her lady friends.

Lina arrived early at the Westin Saint Francis in Union Square, an area that was chic, exciting, but now with COVID-19, less safe than before. As she waited for her friends, she pulled out notes from her romance novel being written, *Charade in the City.*

Nikki and Jacqui arrived together, apparently sharing an Uber.

Lina put her hand up in a welcoming gesture. "Hi ladies."

"Hi Lina," Nikki spoke with a smile. "Thanks for setting up tonight's 'guy-bashing.' I assume you will work it into the conversation."

"Hey, Lina, don't take Nikki too serious," Jacqui chimed in. "She does have an axe to grind, nevertheless."

"No problem. I've taken the liberty to order some wine. Have both a sweet red and a nice white coming."

Nikki thought, *"So unlike Lina to 'take charge.' This is refreshing."*

The waitress arrived with two carafes, one with a 2016 Frank Family Vineyard Cabernet and one containing a Williams Hill Estate Chardonnay. She poured the ladies each a glass, leaving an extra glass for Sara, who was again running late.

Nikki raises her glass, "Here's to us!"

Lina then opens the conversation. "Jacqui, I contacted Nikki about an abusive date that I recently had."

"Lina, Nikki brought me up to speed in the Uber."

"Good. Nikki, what is your opinion?"

"Well, Lina, since you described it to me as an attempted rape, I have created a warrant, depending on what action you want to take."

"Nikki, attempted rape might be a little strong. Maybe we should hold the warrant for now."

As the girls discussed the incident with Carl, Sara joined the group walking quickly from the lobby hostess's stand with ear buds blasting pop music to her movements.

"Hi guys, sorry I'm late. Or, are y'all just early?"

"No, sweetie, you are fashionably late," Jacqui blurted.

"Okay. What's in the carafes?"

Nikki, picking up some slight annoyance in Sara's facial expression, jumped in with an immediate explanation. "Lina took charge and ordered us some delightful wines." Nikki gave a slight head nod to show Sara the importance of what her shy friend Lina had done.

"Then, I'll have the red. Thank you, Lina. Nice touch!"

Sara filled her glass and asked, "So where are we with the 'true confessions' stuff?"

Lina responded confidently, "Nikki is following up with info that I asked her for regarding the dreadful night with Carl."

"Gotcha. Sorry to interrupt. Please continue."

"Lina gave me the details and I drew up a warrant pending Lina's decision whether or not to press charges. Lina, what do you want me to do?"

"He's a shit and deserves to be held accountable. But a warrant might be too strong."

"I understand, Lina, I really do. But to let this guy walk is not fair to you."

As Lina considered Nikki's remarks, Nikki added another slant to Carl's behavior. "Lina, there is another matter involving Carl that you need to be aware of."

"Another matter? What do you mean?"

"Apparently, Carl has been using social media to spread those lies about your close friend, Gabe."

"Gabe? Are you kidding me?"

Sara jumped in eagerly, "Makes sense, Lina, for Carl to spread lies about Gabe to get rid of Gabe, and have you all to himself."

Lina was livid, "Damn it."

Jacqui then advised, "Listen, you know what I had to endure at the hands of my abusive husband, and I wouldn't hesitate to put that Carl bastard behind bars."

A solemn and silent Lina simply gazed away from the girls and thought pensively, "*This isn't fair. I shouldn't have to tolerate this. I don't deserve this.*"

Nikki and Jacqui looked at each other, both understanding the gravity of the situation, but from two distinctly different perspectives.

Sara sensed an immediate need to change the atmosphere and talking points. "Hey, let's put that issue on the back burner for a moment, and share our stories that Lina asked us to compile for her book, *Charade in the City*. I'm sure we all have some good material to supply, and maybe the Carl story is just one more reason why Lina wrote this book in the first place!"

Jacqui quipped, "Yeah, men behaving badly is the plot of the book, so Carl just got himself moved to the front of the line!"

Lina looked up at Jacqui and scowled, "Yes, he did!"

Glancing at her notes, Lina then grabbed each carafe and filled the ladies' glasses. "Okay, back to topic. I will set up a meeting with you guys when I have the final manuscript finished. For now, I will take the additional stories that you sent me files on, edit according, and then start layering."

"Layering?" Jacqui was puzzled by the term.

"Yes, Jacqui, I usually take my first manuscript, say 90,000 words, and go back to the beginning and layer, or expound, on the chapters to add substance and remove 'noise' from my book. I learned that from conversations with author Jonathan Garrett, who Sara actually had recommended."

Lina had been staring at her phone for the last 45 minutes. She had gotten a text from her literary agent regarding her book and was afraid to open it. Finally, the suspense was too much and she opened the text message.

"Okay, girls, just got a text from my literary agent."

As her three friends looked on,

> "Lina, congrats, girl.
> We have a publisher confirmed.
> Contract coming!"

Lina looked up from her phone and smiled, a tear running down her rosy cheeks.

71

GABE

G abe was reaching the proverbial "fork in the road" regarding several issues that were defining his life and likely, future life choices. He met with one of his superiors, Henry Burns, at one of the newspapers where he did contract reporting, and Henry spent many hours helping Gabe navigate Gabe's troubled waters.

This last meeting was the advice session, and Gabe was all ears and taking notes.

"I want to thank you, again, Henry, for taking so much time to help me."

"Nonsense, no need to thank me, my boy. You are an asset to this paper and others, and your career improvement will only benefit your clients."

Gabe smiled.

"Gabe, I have three 'rocks' for you. I call them 'rocks' to separate these urgent priorities from the day-to-day issues that are still important, and consume most of your time and energy"

"Makes sense, Henry, go ahead."

"I think you should meet with a good financial planner and soon. The economy is coming back from the pandemic, and you even mentioned that you were thinking about marriage in the not-to-distant future."

"Well, Henry, the marriage part might be a little premature, but I do have a young lady in my life, Lina Chang, who is becoming very special."

"Understand." Henry handed Gabe a business card. "This is David Bucher, a very good, conservative financial planner, that I use. You might want to give him a call. He treats my money as if it was his, and I trust him completely. Of course, you can certainly talk to others as well."

"Thank you, Henry. I will start by calling David."

"Now, Henry, issue two is your studies. I am totally on board with your choice of a journalism major and your class curriculum. But your grades need to be improved. What say you?"

"Yeah, I know. I think I can do better. I too, am disappointed in my grades."

"Suggestion time, Gabe."

"Go ahead … please."

"I think you are taking on an entirely too heavy class load. I'm sure you want to graduate as soon as possible, but good grades are important short term and long term, if you pursue an advanced degree."

"That makes absolute sense, Henry. I'll cut back next quarter."

"Lastly, Gabe, does Lina know about your bi-polar disorder?"

"No. No, Henry, she does not."

"Well, my boy, it's time to tell her!"

Gabe immediately took out his cell phone and sent a text message.

"Lina, it's Gabe.
We need to talk."

72

BRANDI

B randi was feeling head over heels in love with the wonderful and highly successful attorney, Nikki Wallace, and realizing that a long-term romantic life with Nikki was unlikely; a short-term romance was, in Brandi's mind, a got-to-have.

As she stared longer and longer into today's reality, Brandi was getting considerably depressed at the thought of losing Nikki. As was the recurring remedy for Brandi, drugs and alcohol were becoming go-to necessities.

She fought the urge to seek drugs as a way out, but never had the strength it took, to face her demons by herself.

Under the heading of bad timing, Brandi got a text from Oliver, her junkie supplier.

> "Hey girl, what's up?'
> "Nada.'
> "What ya doin?"
> "BBB."
> "I can fix that."
> "Yeah?"
> "Party tonite."
> "Where?"
> "I'll pick u up."
> "K. When?"
> "10"

In the drug world, "party" referred to cocaine, heroin, or Ecstasy. Oliver picked her up a little after 10:00 and they headed to a bisexual bar that Brandi had been to before, but only for the bumping and grinding entertainment provided by many of the bisexual women who frequented the place. This time, Oliver took his female companion up to a restricted top floor reserved for users.

"Who's your lady friend, Oliver?"

"This is Brandi, and she needs what Eric gave me last week."

"You paying?"

"Yeah."

"Show the lady into the room that Millie is pointing to."

"Thanks."

♥ ♥ ♥

Brandi got in way over her head, in a room with users and "lines" everywhere, and sadistic observers in abundance. She OD'd and later ended up in the hospital, having been dumped onto the street alley away from the bar. Oliver sent Nikki a text from the alley regarding Brandi's condition and then took off.

When Nikki couldn't respond that night, she called me and I rescued Brandi from a situation that paramedics said would have been fatal, "if not for Mr. Garrett arranging for an ambulance and the best Mobile Care Unit in the city to get Brandi to the hospital."

Brandi was under supervision for two days when she got an unexpected visitor.

"Hi Brandi, how are you feeling?"

Still groggy, Brandi quietly responded, "Tired. Who are you?"

"My name is Lina Chang, and I often do voluntary work at this hospital. I am here today covering a COVID-19 story of those infected who have what is called 'long-haul' illness; people who just can't shake the virus and the effects."

Lina didn't mention to Brandi that Nikki had discovered what had happened to Brandi and asked Lina to stop by and check on her. Nikki knew that she could not be seen with Brandi in her drug-induced state.

Lina spent a few days with Brandi as the drugs seemed to wear off, but detox was apparent.

Nikki made arrangements to pick up the costs for Brandi to check into a drug recovery center in Sacramento, California, and Lina became the go-between. It was determined that Brandi's stay would be based on her desire to get well. Usually, it was a three-to-four-month minimum stay.

Slowly Brandi seemed to be getting better in the drug treatment center, and after a few weeks, she began to meet and spend time with other patients. It was in the third week of treatment when Brandi met another recovering addict.

"Hi, my name is Brandi. I have seen you here before and wondered if we could talk."

"Hey, Brandi, my name is Cherri Berry. Nice to meet you."

73

JACQUI

Jacqui felt like a dog chasing its tail. A recent series of dates with selfish and pathetic guys left her empty and feeling used. She set up a Zoom session with the girls on a Monday night, when most of the ladies were either doing laundry, doing remote work or, as in Jacqui's case, doing themselves with solo sex and a fantasy or two.

"Hi guys, thanks for coming on."

Nikki responded first, "No problem. Kind of need a break from what will likely be a shitty week."

"I have some updates on the book," Lina added, holding up a three-ring binder containing the first draft of *Charade in the City*.

Sara, with her Siamese kitty Eja looking on, flashed a big smile and held up a photo of bad boyfriend Brad tied to a four-post bed, with all his naked manhood on shameful display.

"Oh my God," Nikki blurted. "You badass babes did well ... gotta admit."

Lina shrugged her shoulders and grinned, as Jacqui let out a hoot, "Hot damn! That is some fine girl play. Really impressed."

"Thanks, girls. Couldn't have done it without some awesome help."

"So," Nikki asked, "what's your agenda, Jacqui?"

"Just wanted to clear the air a bit and need to bounce some things off of my girlfriends."

"Why don't we just go around and do some much-needed venting?"

"Sara, that is an excellent idea," Jacqui noted. "I'll go first, okay?"

"I met a guy for drinks at the Marriott a couple weeks ago. He seemed nice and impressed me with his listening skills."

"Say what?"

"Lina, a lot of people hear, but don't listen. He seemed genuinely interested in what I had to say."

"Got it. Thanks, Jacqui."

"Well, there was a strategy behind his listening 'skill.' Once he realized I was married to the sex deviant, his questions got way too personal."

"Bottom line, Jacqui?"

"Bottom line, Sara, was that I invited him back to my place for drinks and sex, and he talked me into showing him hubby's dungeon."

Nikki jumped in, "You gotta be kidding?"

"Yep. Nope. He offered to strap me to a bondage board, certain that I missed it and wanted it."

"Shit, that could have ended badly, Jacqui. What happened?"

"Sara, I had him hooked, once he saw all the sex toys. I tied him to a cross and had my way with him till we both passed out from the wine and sex."

Nikki laughed as Jacqui continued her rundown of bad dates.

"I agreed to a date with the hedge-fund icon, Jeffery Fellows, and thought I had a win-win there. Handsome single guy ... hell, that basically describes a ton of men here. He only wanted me to invest with him in several of his risky IPO's."

Jacqui gives an impatient sigh and said, "At least I do have some upside to talk about."

Waiting to continue, she explained her upside. "A while back I had an incredible night of sex on a yacht with actor Ryan Hudson. We are going out next week."

Sara advised, "Jacqui, take baby steps with him."

"Why?"

"I have it from several women that he gets off acting the role of God's gift to women in bed. Wait a minute. Sorry. Bad choice of words. Let me say that there is a fine line with him, apparently, between real love and playful sex."

"Damn." Jacqui lost some air in her balloon.

Nikki jumped in. "I do have some good news that I shared with Jacqui earlier, concerning the grand jury court case regarding the co-conspirator allegations against Jacqui."

Jacqui responded, "As you know, I was acquitted from the co-conspiracy charges, based on the evidence from the tape recording that Jonathan Garrett suggested I get from James. Following a simple script given to me by Jon, I had

James admit to keeping me in the dark regarding the accusations that their prosecutors believed would convict me."

"Great news," Lina added. "Is there more?"

Nikki added, "Well, the court needed to trace all the paper trails regarding the many illegal banking transactions that could have implicated Jacqui in other areas, and those all just came up clean, so her ordeal is now 'officially' over."

"We couldn't be happier for you, Jacqui," Sara added.

"Thank you," a smiling Jacqui replied.

Following a short pause to enjoy that info, Nikki jumped into the conversation with her news. "Well, the bad news is my on-again, off-again romance with Logan is now off. Caught him with that slut Song returning from a train trip from Seattle. It was the same trip that I actually attended with him, on the way to Seattle."

"Holy crap," Sara lamented. "I really thought you guys were gonna make it."

"Nope. But I did get an interview for the state's AG job. Fingers crossed on that huge opportunity."

"We all wish you the best," Jacqui declared.

As the girls all nodded, Lina brought out her talking points. "I have three issues tonight, two good and one bad."

The floor belonged to Lina. "First, my good friend, Gabe, is really focused on his future and from what he has explained, that future could include me."

"How does that feel?"

"Sara, I like Gabe and I am really proud of both his planning and commitment to improve his life, and bringing me into his vision and expectations. So that is good."

"And the bad?"

"I'll let Nikki explain that, Jacqui."

"Sure. This involves the security guard Carl who, as we are all aware, pushed himself on Lina in a sexually threatening manner. I wanted to charge him with attempted rape, but Lina wanted to go to Plan B."

Sara asked, "What was your Plan B?"

"That was probation, 100 hours of community service, and a cease-and-desist order prohibiting Carl from working in any charitable events. Plus, he would be prohibited from coming within 100 feet of Lina. One slip-up and jail!"

Lina completed her issues list. "Thanks, Nikki. Now, regarding my book. I have the rough manuscript finished and just need a few beta-readers. So, let me know if anyone comes to mind so I can start to get some honest feedback. And, I may need some marketing help for the book."

"I guess it's my turn."

A smiling Nikki replies, "Yep, Sara, you're up."

"I have guy updates and movie updates."

"We need a movie about guys behaving badly, Sara," Nikki muttered, as Jacqui and she chuckled.

"Hey," responded Lina, "that's what my book will do!"

"Amen, Lina," snapped Sara crisply. "My guy update is simple. Brad is slowing disappearing into the sunset, and I hired Roger, Nikki's detective, to find out who took those damn shower pics of me and is slamming me on social media."

"He's good, Sara."

"I know he is, Nikki. I already have some leads due to his snooping around."

As the revolving girl-to-girl banter continued, Jacqui had a thought that seemed to make sense to her.

"I just need to hang out with better guys."

74

SAMANTHA

Following some advice from his good friend, Nikki, Ramon attended one of Sam's podcasts, as a guest and "implementer extraordinaire" for all things male-versus-female relationships required.

This studio where the podcast originated was familiar to Ramon, having used it to promote his developing line of sexual accessories for the bedroom.

"Hello, Ramon. I'm Doctor Samantha Vandenberg, but please call me Sam."

"Hi, Sam, it's nice to meet you and thanks for having me on your podcast."

"The pleasure is all mine. We have a couple mutual friends, Nikki Wallace and Jonathan Garrett, who both speak very highly of you."

"That is good to hear. They are super people. What is the agenda for this podcast, Sam?"

"I'll set it up as a high-level view of dating and relationship issues, and then I'll bring you in to actually discuss real-world experiences and your own personal opinions. Is that okay with you?"

"Of course. I am a big fan of your work, and I am honored to be here with you."

Sam thought pleasingly, *"This guy is everything they said he is … polite, experienced, and somewhat humble … not to mention drop-dead sexy."*

"Ramon, are you ready to begin?"

"Yes, let's get started."

Sam began her interactive podcast, setting up the agenda and introducing Ramon.

"Good afternoon and good love to all of you. Today we are going to discuss *'what women need from a man's perspective.'* Joining me today is Ramon Gilbert, one of the truly enlightened men who understands women, and what drives them both sexually and soulfully in a relationship today. Welcome, Ramon."

"Thank you and thanks for having me."

Question number one involved men always explaining and defending their behavior.

Sam responded first, "Defensiveness in men kills trust and negatively impacts intimacy."

Ramon added, "A man should not attempt to control a woman, per se, but instead, see her and treat her as part of himself."

Sam smiled at Ramon and he continued, "A woman craves to be embodied as a special part of the relationship, and never left alone to deal with her issues if a man has a significant role in her life."

Question number two referred to the man's duties in a relationship.

Sam answered first, "Men look at their duties as having bookends; duties are tangible and you define it, you do it, and you are done. Women see them as fluid and often associated with other dutiful needs."

Ramon followed up, "Men are often so focused on getting things done that they often don't collaborate with her or explain what they are doing and why. Confusion never helps."

Question number three dealt with sexual leadership.

Sam offered her advice. "This is a tough one and I'm looking for input from Ramon here. Most men believe that leadership in the bedroom is what the female wants. They think that the woman prefers that she dictate frequency and determines what experience, position, etcetera, the couple engages in."

Ramon adds, "My experience with women is just the opposite. Although they rightfully believe that their body is a temple and she has the choice to say 'no' when necessary, most women I have been with totally prefer the man to take the leadership role."

"Good point, Ramon. Thanks."

"Doctor Vandenberg, if the woman decides when and where sex will happen, what I have observed is a lukewarm sexual connection without much intensity, excitement, or any experimentation. Also, this is an area where boredom and loss of interest may occur."

"Another good point, Ramon. Let me add my professional opinion to my few male listeners and mostly female listeners. If you want something hotter and deeper, you can't let your female partner become the sexual leader and initiator."

Ramon gave Sam his thumbs up.

"If a man is true to his sexual nature, which is to create momentum and give direction to his sexual partner, he needs to grab the reins to physical leadership, by learning what is important and using that knowledge. Ramon is the perfect man to consult with, ladies and guys."

"Thank you, Doctor Vandenberg."

"Let's move on to the lecture portion of my pod cast. Today I will address the five things that women need to know about me. Ramon is still here and will provide any up or down opinions."

Ramon gave Sam a second thumbs up.

"*Number one* is the unfortunate fact that women often have doubts that they are woman enough for their partner. They are overcome by self-doubt, being the lover, wife, mother, and working wage earner. Men must be empathetic; listen and help where they can. Don't be critical of those roles that don't end up in the bedroom. Accept her multi-tasking, and focus on making her feel like the girl-friend and sexual partner … first and foremost."

Sam paused. "*Number two* is that men often feel that the woman doesn't need them. Isn't that true, right Ramon?"

"Absolutely."

Sam continued, "The female need is for safety and security, and the best way to show that is through warm and genuine intimacy."

Ramon chimed in with a relevant opinion, "Women don't need men for survival; they have that covered on their own. They need men for stability, and a future life built on trust, respect, and some predictability."

"Very well said, Ramon." He smiled.

"*Number three* is that women want the man to understand what motivates her deeply. What are the hopes and dreams that she is holding onto? What is she doing in life? She needs her man to help her become the person she imagined herself to be."

Taking a sip of water, Sam smiled, and continued. *Number four* is very important, given the uninhibited nature of what we see on TV, social media, etcetera. Women want to be seen and appreciated as they really are and truly a woman, and not just curves and a body meant for coupling."

Ramon replied, "Men must enjoy, focus, and acknowledge her full and wonderful womanhood."

"That brings us to *Number five* on my list of what I think women must know about men. Men must act in her best interest. Don't dwell on flaws, as we all have them."

Ramon nods in approval.

"When sex is over in the bedroom, it's the end of that particular sexual encounter. Instead of an ending … there must be a beginning. Men must determine the woman's wants and needs nearly as well as she does herself. It sounds difficult, but it isn't. When she can't act on her best interests, she trusts that you could."

They end the podcast on a very high note and leave for coffee. Over coffee they really connect and decide to continue their talks over dinner that night.

Ramon thought enthusiastically, "*She is very different. She has a special gift.*"

"*I'm really starting to like this guy,*" Sam thought to herself, "*and such a great listener.*"

RAMON

Ramon arrived at the restaurant early, and as he waited for Sam to arrive, he whispered to himself, "*This is a much different woman than I have ever met. So authentic, so smart, and so damn sexy. I didn't see this coming!*"

Among the specific topics they would discuss, were the launch of his line of high-end sex equipment and erotic videos, hoping to get Sam's blessing on the project and maybe even get her on board as a minor investor.

Ramon also thought he could help Sam implement the behavioral change in men that she advised and recommended, on her shows and on her website.

"*This is a good blending of talents and drive,*" he thought unmistakably.

Sam arrived looking radiant. She wore a rusty rose satin asymmetrical wide-leg jumpsuit with an open back that fit snuggly on her gorgeous figure, and her eye-popping cleavage was no match for the young guys working in the restaurant.

As she was being seated, Ramon gave her a warm kiss on the hand, which was a blast from the past in Sam's mind, but nothing that she didn't enjoy.

Dinner was far from a regular date. It seemed to hold a special level of antici-pation for both Ramon and Sam. For the casual observer, they acted like a couple of young people in love with their companion, and in love with the moment.

Following dinner, Ramon quickly advised, "How bout we head somewhere else for a nightcap, or whatever?"

With an impatient sigh, Sam replied, "Yes, please," as she thought amo-rously, "*mostly, the whatever.*"

As Ramon smiled, Sam had a different thought. "Let's go to my place, Ramon. You game?"

"Absolutely, Sam. The night can only get better."

♥   ♥   ♥

Back at her comfy home with Ramon, Sam had reached a state of relaxation and romantic anticipation, which Ramon could easily discern.

"You have a lovely home. The décor reflects the sophistication and exquisite taste of the lovely owner."

"Thank you. It's my castle. You are the first man to see my home. No one I ever dated seemed like the type of person who would say exactly what you just said."

As Ramon grinned and got as comfortable as possible, Sam poured them each a glass of red wine and they engaged in small talk for only a few minutes, when the heat between them had her glowing, and him with eyes focused on her beauty and obvious desires.

She knew he was going to kiss her, and she knew she was going to expect much more. Sam had sworn off fabulously good-looking young men lately, given the many disappointments she had been experiencing, but this one had a much different vibe all over it. She was beginning to love the man on the inside, and it was a thought that terrified her. The physical attraction left nothing in doubt.

"I want his sex … I want to feel him inside me," Sam thought hungrily.

When his steady hands surrounded her face and his dark, silky hair fell forward, her temperature sizzled like butter on a hot, summer day. He could not miss her breathlessness and enticing rounded lips, as arousal shot through him in roaring expectation.

Close as he was, his masculine scent shot up her nostrils, pushing her already lively hormones into overdrive. The sight of his well-developed forearms was sexier than any other man she had been with, and his skin smelled of earth and wood, sending her into a drug-like high.

"Dear Samantha," he said with an uneasy laugh, "I've been dreaming of kissing you ever since we met in your office. I'm here now and almost afraid to do it."

"You better get over that, Ramon, because I swear, if you leave me hanging, I'll never give you another chance. I want to taste you."

His grin took on a striking flash. "I love your decisiveness and your resolve," he whispered. "Most of all, I love you taking charge."

Sam replied quickly, "And we haven't even discussed who will be on top."

"The answer is yes, of course, Samantha."

Sam didn't have a moment to wonder what he meant, as he tipped her head up and lowered his. His mouth met her lips in a gentle manner, aware of warm intimacy. He moaned low in his chest, the loveliest sound she'd ever heard a man make, as his arms slid down her back and gently hugged her as his tongue sunk into her warm and wet mouth.

"You taste good and you smell good," Sam said, briefly breaking their kiss. Ramon responded with a stronger kiss, emitting a sucking sound that bordered on primal. In mere seconds, her head was spinning with an erotic rush – almost dizzying.

"*Oh God,*" she thought eagerly. "*What am I feeling?*"

He savored his gentle manner, knowing Sam was becoming captivated by his heartfelt kissing, then slowing his kisses purposefully, enticing her to respond in return. She groaned with pleasure, a sign to Ramon that he had struck an early chord. In her mind, and in her experiences, nothing was better than a man who loved to kiss, and every indication said that Ramon did. Oh yes, he did.

She couldn't suppress a whimper when he stopped. "Touch me," he said, with light breath against her quivering mouth. "Put your hands on my warm skin." His smoldering gaze burned into her from inches away, mesmerizing, penetrating, trying to convey some message she simply could not read. "Your touch is what I want most. It's what I crave."

Sam thought curiously, "*What sort of man talks this way?*"

"Do it," he said, and then swallowed hard. With shaking hands, she slid her arms around his back, which felt like cool marble in her grasp, incredibly smooth, invitingly firm, and certainly strong. "Yes," he uttered, a sound of physical delight, "I love your heat, Samantha."

He gently lifted her off her feet, and set her on the bed. Silently, he methodically disrobed Sam, with the skill of a loving and caring partner, while peeling his clothes off to the guttural moans of his compliant lady. He touched his finger to his lips, then to hers, and then moving his mouth to her neck, had Sam panting like a runner against her pulse.

"*His hands are quick, but soft,*" she told herself.

Tingles spread from his every fingered touch, and Sam was on a sensual ride unlike anything she had ever felt. The effect he had on her was bewildering. Sam was no slave to her needs, no silly romantic, but she squirmed at the sensations, her body growing hotter with every touch.

She fought a groan as his palms reached her pulsing core, and his warm fingers penetrated her vagina. "Look at you," he spoke softly, "a beautiful woman freeing herself to her inner needs and giving her man the satisfaction of pleasing her."

"*Oh my God,*" Sam wondered, "*what the hell is happening?*"

Now, Ramon had one thumb sweeping arcs across her bare and lovely breasts. Caught at their edges, her nipples swelled and took on an aura of pleasured pink. Her back arched uncontrollably as his mouth found one erect peak. She barely noticed the caresses of his second hand. His tongue was clearly skilled, finding nerves she hadn't known she had. As her muscles relaxed, he paused to allow Sam to catch her breath. "My God, Sam, you are so precious."

Casting inhibitions aside, she guided his hand over her soft breasts and inner thighs and then steered his hand directly and softly into her waiting folds. Without resistance, two of his fingers slipped inside and his thumb rubbed slowly against her nugget, her small jewel of womanhood.

"Go ahead, Sam," he rasped, reading her muscle contractions, "Squeeze your thighs around my wrist, holding me in." She obeyed without hesitation. What he was doing felt better than she could believe, better than any other man had ever done for her, better, she thought with surprise, than she could do for herself.

She saw his intense eyes, shocking her with their fire. His face was strained and the sight of his determination told Sam how selfish she was being, not encouraging him to seek his own satisfaction.

"You don't have to continue this; just for my pleasure," she said sheepishly. He laughed and she realized with awe that he was shaking. "You don't know me very well yet. This is your night, my love."

"But you … "

"I just want to watch you come, and enjoy it with you."

Almost on cue, Sam had an orgasm as he spoke that shook her entire body. It was an intense, unexpected burst that seemed to leap from the husky growl of his voice. When it ended, his tongue curled out to wet his upper lip. "This is a start," he said with a grin. "I'm all yours next time … assuming we will have a next time."

"For fricking sure, we will have a next time, and next time, and …"

76

JONATHAN

I reached a point where I really needed to do some serious soul-searching, realizing that I had been very lucky and was blessed to have lived the life I had always dreamed of. Experiencing the dire life so many women had been living and seeing the harm and stress that selfish men had placed on young women today, had me coming to grips with a new purpose and mission.

I actually began some volunteer work along with Lina, which made her happy and allowed me to get some 'reverse mentoring' from a true champion in community service.

I also created the Lina Chang Foundation in the city for abused and underprivileged women, which gave me great satisfaction and enabled Lina to manage a community business with direct and immediate results.

I also contacted Doctor Samantha Vandenberg on behalf of Logan, knowing that Nikki would like someone to help pull Logan out of his downward spiral, and get him to see the light at the end of the tunnel was actually Nikki Wallace.

Under the adage that 'you reap what you sow,' it wasn't long after these actions were underway that I got a call from an excited Sara Sullivan.

"Hey, Jon, it's Sara."

"Hi Sara, what's up?"

"Jon, I have some wonderful news."

"I'm ready for some good news."

"Well, Jamie at Climax Films just called me and they want to meet with us ASAP to discuss a movie deal."

"No shit! Really?"

"Yes, really. I told them I'd get with you and your agent and we'd set up a time to meet."

"Finally."

"Yep, Jon, it took a while, but now we have some momentum building."

"Thank you and tell Troy thanks as well. I can't believe this is actually happening."

"And Jon, there's more."

"Shoot."

"They have set me up with an audition for a part in the sci-fi series movie from the screenplay based on your books, which you so amazingly submitted, as part of your marketing and promotion."

"Man, I always plan ahead, Sara. This time it's a home run!"

"It's a grand slam this time, Jon."

"I'm super excited and can't wait to meet. Let's get this done as soon as possible, Sara. I have never been so eager to get a project going as I am right now."

"That makes two of us. I always thought of your writings as movie material, but nothing like that is ever guaranteed."

"It's what you have been saying all along, Sara."

"Jon, on another matter. I know how highly your friend and man-coach, Doctor Samantha Vandenberg, is regarded by both you and the community."

"That she is."

"Well, based on your recommendation, she has decided to give the four of us a group session next week. We are all pretty happy and grateful to you for suggesting this."

"Glad I could help."

"So are we! I'll send you details soon on our movie meeting."

"Great, Thanks. Have a great day, Sara."

Jon thought whimsically, ***"I'd like to be a fly on the wall for that group session!"***

77

SAMANTHA SURVEYS
SITUATIONS

Samantha became a regular contributor to both the local newspaper, and the highly-rated San Francisco magazine, *City Heights*. Her column in the newspaper became a must read in each Friday edition, before the female readers headed out for the weekend.

Her subject-matter pieces in the *City Heights* magazine led to guest appearances on a number of television shows such as *Good Morning America*, *The Today Show* and *Entertainment Tonight*. In fact, one network had Samantha doing periodic pieces entitled, "Doctor's Orders."

She also joined a local playhouse to continue her acting hobby, resulting from recommendations from Sara and Jon. She couldn't play any role of her favorite movie star, Greta Garbo, but she did get the opportunity to play the part of similarly beleaguered heroines in a couple productions.

Following Jon's request to intercede on Logan's behalf, she met with Logan twice and two consequential results from their session had an impact on Logan.

First, he finally realized just how serious the trust issues with Nikki had become, and couldn't blow it off as "guys being guys." When Samantha told Logan that "women believe half of what men say, and all of what they do," he took the revelation to heart.

Second, Logan took Samantha's advice and met with a psychologist, Dr. Rose Günter, to do a much deeper dive into their serious relationship issues. The real "aha moments" came from those gut-wrenching sessions with a trained specialist, who Dr. Vandenberg recognized would really put the soul-searching efforts into high gear.

According to Dr. Gunter, "Women are attracted to the men they fall in love with, and men fall in love with the women they are attracted to."

Logan even called Dr. Vandenberg to express his thanks for her help and sent two dozen roses to each of the three ladies: Samantha, Dr. Günter, and Nikki.

♥　♥　♥

Sam took on what she called a "den-mother role" for the four girls since Jon strongly believed the ladies needed some sort of intervention. Given all the info Jon had shared with Sam, and probably shouldn't have shared, Sam already had pre-conceived opinions on the personalities and behavior of the "fab four."

The ladies arrived at Dr. Vandenberg's office together, with Nikki indicating that she would like to be the one to take the lead regarding the scope and detail to be discussed. No one disagreed.

Following introductions, Dr. Vandenberg began with a session overview which made sense to the ladies, who were excited at the possibilities to share and learn.

"I would like you to be as open and honest with me as possible. Although meeting with a man-coach may seem unusual and possibly unnecessary, Jonathan Garrett seemed to think it would be a refreshing change to vent some of your frustrations with a therapist who has built a successful practice by listening to and understanding men. I respect his opinion."

No one objected, so Sam opened a notebook and continued.

"Jonathan suggested I begin with the likely 'leader-of-the-pack,' attorney Nikki Wallace." That remark gave the doctor some instant trustworthiness, and the ladies could see that they were in for a serious and well-conceived session.

"Thank you, Doctor Vandenberg."

"Nikki … ladies, please call me Sam."

"Sam, I have a difficult time balancing my crazy busy career, and still trying to be the best I can be to the other people in my life, male and female."

Sam responded, "I can only imagine, given what I have read regarding your career."

"I have had several frustrating relationships, and it may just be that I have a different view on men, and how they behave. A guy will screw up, and then come to me with an expensive gift and all is good. Well, all is not good!"

"I will be getting into that soon, Nikki."

Nikki then paused and with a slight grimace, continued. "And, I have had a few relationships with women, and those have been extremely good and satisfying for me. They seem as 'normal' for me as with any man, from a purely sexual perspective ... maybe even a spiritual sense."

Samantha was taking notes and smiles.

Sara then interjects, "I know one of my problems is I keep making the same mistake."

"What mistake is that, Sara?"

"Well, Sam, I meet interesting men all the time. It's a combination of my work and my personality."

"Yep, I would totally agree," uttered Jacqui emphatically.

"The problem, Sam, is I try to change what I perceive as flaws in their character with devastating results. Even within a committed relationship, the fact that these guys are unfaithful is a big-time stressor."

"Common trait in most relationships, Sara, but many men today can't put the words 'committed' and 'relationship' into the same sentence."

A smiling Jacqui couldn't wait to get involved in the discussion. "I am the victim of my sordid and dark past. I'm sure you know the story of my deviant criminal husband."

"Yes, Jacqui, unfortunately I do."

"Well, I have been saddled with a trashy-woman reputation, and men get their kicks from humiliating me and attempting to subject me to the very experiences I want to forget! I have had dates where men want to go directly into bondage and see how much I like it!"

"Oh my God, Jacqui, I am so sorry for you. I think those issues are best served by a psychologist or therapist who is so trained, which I am not. Sorry."

"Understand."

Lina jumped in, sensing an opening to change the mood a bit with a different perspective. "I work a lot in the community with disadvantaged people and truly give myself to anyone who needs my help and support."

"I am aware of your contributions, Lina, and I applaud you for your unselfish efforts. I even think I know where you are going here."

"Yes, people ... men in particular, take advantage of me. I try very hard to separate my volunteer work from my journalistic and writing careers, but people just seem to want my unconditional love and the men even pout when I don't respond."

"It's kind of a good problem to have, if there is such a thing, Lina. I will get into that aspect of relationships as well."

Lina was still anxious, and as Sam sensed that in her face, Sam added.

"You know what demure is, right?"

"Of course."

"Well. Lina, that partly describes you. Men today are influenced by women sort of flaunting their sex appeal; from ET to bachelor reality shows to entertainment events … even on the nightly news."

Sara chimed in, "For sure!"

Sam continued. "They have this totally male-biased impression that women, deep down, have sex on their mind and they, the men, are happy to oblige!"

The ladies were feeling a sense of relief after having cleared the air a bit. Yes, the venting that Jonathan suggested was a good idea.

"Ladies, let's take a twenty-minute break. We have refreshments in the lobby, and then we'll reconvene and I'll summarize your issues into as succinct a synopsis as I can."

Whispering to herself, Sam thought enthusiastically, ***"Gosh, this could become another revenue stream if I just put a little framework around this relevant type of dialogue."***

78

SAMANTHA
SUMMARIZES
SUCCINCTLY

Following the break, the ladies reconvened in Doctor Vandenberg's conference room and Samantha explained where she was going with the next session.

"I have listened to four very successful, and likely very stressed-out, young women today, and I feel your pain and I do recognize your frustrations. I also fully understand the male perspective which, like it or not, is quite different."

Nikki chimed in, "Exactly."

"One thing to remember, ladies," Samantha added, "is that men have relationships to gain sex, and women have sex to gain relationships."

"Awesome point," snapped Nikki, annoyingly.

"Thanks, Nikki. Let's get back to our agenda. First, I have a question. Do you ladies use dating apps?"

They looked around at each other and Sara replied, "Why, yes, we do … we all do."

"From my point of view, do you think that, given the dating app culture, you professional and successful women might be a little old for these?"

Sara answered immediately, "Nah."

"Very well. Ladies, I am going to do a bit of a 'data dump' to illustrate the dynamics of what is going on in your lives from my professional perspective. Does that make sense?"

"Absolutely," Sara responded. "I really need someone to explain to me what I'm going through, and I know I speak for the other ladies today."

"Okay, let's begin."

Samantha had everyone's attention.

"Lina, there is a natural dynamic centered around a woman's ability to give to other people. When she feels full of love and positive energy to give to others, her essential nature is stable. But when she gives of herself, but doesn't receive love and affection in return, her essential nature becomes unbalanced and often crashes. Does that make sense?"

"Yes, Sam, it does."

"Then, the woman needs the attention, listening, and understanding of those in her circle, as well as developing self-love. Only when she gets the support that she has been missing from those around her, or from a special man, can the tendency to rebuild her essential nature restore her self-worth and build back her confidence."

Sam paused and then continued, looking directly at a solemn and sad Sara.

"Let's go to Sara and her stress."

"Yes, let's," answered Sara.

"Men, especially older men, carry emotional baggage from long-lived hurts and resentments within their prior relationships. They believed that their partners lacked interest in them, both as a sexual partner and as a mere individual ... resulting in perceived rejection. Men internalized this rejection as proof of their own sexual lacking."

"Oh shit," Nikki thought instinctively, *"I resemble that remark!"*

Sam glanced at Nikki and continued. "Taking on an outside sex partner help the men reframe the dynamics of their primary partnerships. In other words, outside partners functioned as evidence that the problem must not be with them. Men believed that their participation in outside partnerships made them better able to act in healthy ways within their primary partnership."

Sam smiled, as she could see that she struck a nerve or two.

"Thus, the men believed that outsourcing their emotional needs to outside sexual partnerships benefitted both their primary partners as well as themselves. Ladies, this is not the last time I will say this; it is that relevant and that important. Please pay attention."

Pausing, "Let's spend a moment on how men react to stress. When male tolerance for stressful situations is exceeded, they usually withdraw temporarily, into the proverbial man-cave, so to speak. This timeout allows them to distance themselves from the problem at hand and think about how to resolve it with a fresh perspective. By contrast, women want their answers right now!"

By this time, all four women were busy taking notes, and Samantha took the opportunity to chat with Sara one-on-one.

"Sara, I think it is safe to assume that you often meet men at clubs, bars and through dating apps. Is that fair?"

"Yes, Sam, but when you put it that way, it kinda sounds bad. Where are you going?"

"I'm just saying that you consistently meet men in venues where those type of men have self-serving agendas ... mainly sex and one-night-stands."

"And?"

"And, I don't usually give advice ... just suggestions." But I would suggest that you need to try to meet men in the type of venue where good, decent guys hang out."

"Like church groups, charity events," Sara responded sarcastically.

"No. That's not you."

"For sure, Sam."

"So, having all these extracurricular interests and truly cool hobbies, why not try meeting guys at acting schools, theatrical improv events, singing promotions, and even high-end career and subject-matter symposiums?"

Thinking for a moment, Sara replied enthusiastically, "Actually ... I like the idea. Thanks."

"My pleasure. Now, let's get back to the group."

With her focus returning to her eager clients, Sam went to description number three.

"Okay, let's get to Nikki and a segment that I will call 'keeping score,' a mental tallying of individual actions intended as expressions of love. Women use a 'points system' that is much different than men. For her, each individual act of love gets a point, regardless of magnitude. Men, on the other hand, assign small acts or small expenditures, fewer points. Larger blocks of points go to what they consider bigger expenditures."

Nikki was now thinking way ahead of Sam's reveal.

"The man thinks he can do one big thing and get enough points to allow him to partially disconnect from needing additional points. The woman assigns single points to big and small acts of love, with no big gain for big things."

Nikki nodded her head and thought, "*This makes so much sense.*"

"The bottom line is the woman would rather have many little things done for her on a regular basis, because women like to think their men are thinking of them and caring for them constantly."

It seemed like Samantha had struck a nerve with her spot-on analysis. She had one more point to make with Nikki.

"Nikki, I have a question to ask, and I don't need an answer. Just give this some thought."

"Go ahead," Nikki said awkwardly.

"Is it possible that you are one of many bi-sexual women who view their female relationships as a form of 'vacation' from a man?"

That remark got a nervous look from Nikki as Jacqui looked up, realizing she was next into the barrel.

"Jacqui, let's do some word association."

"Okay."

"Would you associate men with these descriptors, 'hunters, trackers, predators, chasers, and stalkers,' to name a few?"

"Yes. Yes, I would."

"And, Jacqui, you would be spot-on regarding the evolution of man's DNA from the early days. Their character today is shaped, to a much lesser degree, by those adjectives."

Jacqui was quiet and thinking.

"Using that same tact, would you describe the evolution of women's DNA as 'subservient, obedient, complaint, submissive, accommodating?'"

"Stop. Please."

"I'm sorry if that rings a bell, Jacqui, but some men today have this subconscious or unnatural predisposition to believe that women have an innate desire to be dominated."

"Wait a minute, Sam, I totally disagree."

"I hear you Nikki, but I used the words 'some men' … not most men. And certainly not most men today."

"All right, then."

"Why do you think that porn is so popular today? Most men who look at porn in general and bondage in particular, would never admit to watching it at all. It's like that old joke about boys reading *Playboy Magazine* for the articles!"

"Funny stuff, Sam," Sara quips.

"The bottom line here ladies, are that men and women are different … very different, and you really need to know what makes them tick. And, if you ever find a man who gives a crap about what makes a woman tick … don't let that guy out of your sight!"

They have a round-robin discussion regarding the points that Sam made, and then Sam wraps with a strategy going forward for all.

"In summary, ladies, this is my advice to each of you."

Sam turns her recorder on to have a baseline for continuing sessions in the future, if needed.

"Lina, focus on open and honest communication with those close to you. If there is a special man in your life, don't hesitate to confide in him regarding your needs for warmth and affection. Use examples of your 'giving nature' to others that need to ricochet back to you."

"That makes sense, Sam. Thank you."

"Sara, I'm going to go out on a limb and say that your M.O. probably has been to become the perceived aggressor with men, and without much capital in your 'patience bucket.' Yes?"

"Yes, Sam, you would be right."

"So, then, back off and let the man or men come to you. And make sure that the link is authentic … something that is important for you. And, if you'll forgive me for saying, don't let sex obscure your vision to find the 'right' guy. Life is the game that we all play, and true love is the ultimate prize!"

"That was beautiful, Sam. Thanks."

"Nikki, you have mentioned Logan as someone that you loved, but his unfaithfulness left you empty and cold. I'm not going to say 'forgive and forget,' as no one should control that part of your emotion, but I would strongly suggest that you talk about these issues in an open and honest manner."

Nikki seemed a bit more pensive as she took notes.

"Nikki, try to determine what, if any, deficiency in either him or you could have led to that infidelity. And, stop with the subconscious 'point system.' Don't trip on what's behind you."

Sara thought gleefully, "*Gosh, I have used that phrase before!*"

"Finally, Jacqui, let's put all the cards on the table. I have coached many men in my practice, so I have covered the character gambit of the good, the bad, and the ugly. Jacqui, do you know what the opposite of love is?"

"Hate?"

"No. The opposite of love is indifference, and that is the one characteristic that seems to aptly describe many of your relationships. Indifference, by definition, is lack of interest, concern, or sympathy. That optic needs to change."

"How do I do that, Sam?"

"That is easy, Jacqui. Begin by finding yourself different partners. Find the 'one' that you can use as a template. For example, 'Bill' is the right guy for me. Describe Bill's persona. That's your template. Make sense?"

"I think so, Sam. Gotta think this one through. Thanks."

With those comments, the session was adjourned and Samantha texted Jonathan.

> "We had a great session.
> Thank you for suggesting it."

Moments later …

> "You're my wonderful muse.
> The source of my inspiration.
> Thank you."

Samantha thought curiously, *"I really enjoyed both the session and those four young and amazing women. Wonder if I could fit in with them?"*

ACT III
REFLECTIONS REVIVED

I'm standing on my mountain, far above the clouds.
The wind blows still; I once again face my doubts.
Weighing the costs of fights' emotional games,
I now reflect on the past while hiding my shame.
So many things were in anger said and done,
I made you unsure if I was still the one.
Do I break away and leave the uneven past behind?
Or stay and chase the awful demons from my mind?
To dry your tears and ease your pain,
Only as your beacon of sunshine will I again be sane.
The rising of the moon, the setting of the sun,
If we are to stay together, our Phoenix story has just begun.
No one has touched me the way that you do;
Wherever I go I know the road will always lead back to you.
I sometimes sensed that one of us had to go,
True to oneself, and not part of any show.
Now I have learned to reap what I sow.
Changed for the better, I need you to know.
I want to stand with you on our mountain;
I want to sit with you by our sea.
I'm counting on a new beginning … a heaven,
Until the brightest stars fall down on me.
Don't say goodbye. Don't turn away.
It doesn't have to end today …

FINALE

THE LAST
WORD

Walking the Talk

For those of you who believe in fate … this finale will suit you. For those of you who believe in hope … you will not be disappointed.

*However, for those of you who don't believe in either and feel that you have been dealt a "bad hand," let's recall the words of **Neil deGrasse Tyson** in the opening:*

"When you look for things in life like love, meaning, and motivation, it implies that they are behind a tree or under a rock. The most successful people in life recognize that they create their own love, manufacture their own meaning, and generate their own motivation."

79

NIKKI AND LOGAN

ikki and Logan had been involved for many years, first as friends and colleagues, and then as lovers, which resulted in many up-and-down incidents. Making matters worse was Nikki's affection for Brandi, giving Nikki two intense ongoing relationships. Nikki and Logan were in similar worlds, but Nikki and Brandi were navigating through different worlds ... a love triangle that caused stress and pain. Let's look at both Nikki and Logan's perspective ...

♥   ♥   ♥

Nikki thought a long time about the words spoken by Dr. Vandenberg, and came to the conclusion that "cheating" is something inherent to most men, and Nikki believed her man Logan was somewhere between greedy and stupid. But rather than villainize him and brand him a "cheater," she thought it best to have an open and honest discussion with him before completely writing off the relationship.

In a follow-up call with Dr. Vandenberg, Nikki sought additional advice.

"Samantha, I really enjoyed our group session, and need to get your thoughts on 'next steps,' if that is what I need to do."

"Of course, Nikki, glad to help."

"Sam, our cultural understanding of cheating quite literally doesn't give women much 'wiggle room' to make sense of how it impacts them."

"You are absolutely right."

"So, what to do?"

"Nikki, it boils down to fundamentals. I once believed I had some 'common sense' understanding of infidelity, but many incidents with clients made me see that common sense and simplicity just don't compute."

"Sam, I can handle complicated. Go ahead."

"Men need praise and validation to bolster their sense of masculinity. Successful men need it even more, as most observers see them as not 'needing' additional validation because they already know that they are successful."

"I never looked at it that way."

"I see three topics to consider. You and Logan need to set a high bar for open and honest communication. Tough-love stuff. Then, open up to each other regarding your perceived strengths and weaknesses. And last but not least, set boundaries with regard to behavior and time lines to test your resolve going forward. Does that make sense?"

"Yes, it does."

"Because if you cannot do that, outside affairs will serve as a space where emotional needs from a third party will become a Band-Aid for hurts, imagined and real."

"Oh gosh, Sam, does that ring of reality and hard truth!"

With that in-depth dialogue complete, Nikki knew what she needed to do regarding Logan.

"Nikki, I have one more nugget to throw out ... and this involves your affairs with Brandi and Kim, which we talked about before."

"Why bring them up if we are focusing on Logan right now?"

"Because typical lesbian sexual behavior may be having an effect on your heterosexual feelings."

"Okay. I'm listening."

"You and those two young women shared roles of Domme and sub, right?"

"Yes."

"In the submissive world, do you know what subspace is?"

"I think do. It's the ultimate goal of a submissive ... to be kind of euphoric or floating in good thoughts."

"Yes, Nikki. It's like an out-of-body experience, where the sub gets a high without too much stimulation. It is their sexual expectation. Often, they lose control, which is fine to them."

"Not sure where you are going here, Sam."

Samantha continued. "Nikki, do you know what the term sub-drop means?"

"Not really."

"It is an emotional or physical low, occurring just after an intense sexual high, as we just discussed. It can last for hours ... it can last for days."

"That make sense, Sam. So, where are you going with this?"

"Nikki, you need to understand and replicate your subspace 'high' feelings when you are with Logan. Think about what it took for Brandi and Kim to take you there, and talk Logan through getting you there, but from the man's perspective and capabilities. Does that make sense?"

"It does, and I will. Thank you,"

♥   ♥   ♥

Logan's session was, of course, protected under doctor/patient privilege, meaning Nikki was not aware of the meeting results between Logan and Dr. Vandenberg. The major difference in perspectives between Nikki and Logan were as stark as they were real.

"So, Logan, your description of the relationship with Nikki takes you from the highest highs to the lowest lows. Is that about, right?"

"Yes, for sure, Samantha. When it was good it was very good, but ..."

"Before you continue, may I add my observation?"

"Of course."

"Women in general, and Nikki in particular, view and describe relationships with words like feeling, sensitivity, and caring. Now don't get me wrong here, because men are aware of these attributes as well, but men look much more strongly into the physical aspects of their partnerships, and sex is usually the one glaring indicator of a healthy relationship. Do you concur?"

"Well, I guess. Chemistry is important ... ask any man."

"I do, Logan. That's my business!"

Logan laughed at the brutally honest remark, and was kind of embarrassed.

Sam smiled and continued. "Men take on an outside partner to help them reframe the dynamics of their primary partnership. In other words, outside partners function as evidence that the problem must not be with them."

Logan grinned as her words rang true to him.

"They justify their behavior in outsourcing their emotional needs in sex outside of their main partner, as benefitting their primary partner as well as themselves. Does that make sense?"

Logan thought for a moment, gazed out the office window, and replied, "No, I'm sorry but I just can't buy into that explanation."

"What, then, do you think is the main issue that prevents commitment and trust for both of you?"

"I really think that she is just too damn busy with her fricking career to want or need a man right now."

"So, very simply put, you think you guys are well matched but a victim of bad timing?"

"I guess so."

With that last statement, Samantha gave Logan the three-part advice she gave to Nikki and hoped that they could resolve their differences. He agreed to spend significant time evaluating his relationship with Nikki, in the context of Dr. Vandenberg's advice.

Adding to Logan's journey into consciousness, I spent some time with Logan, reinforcing what Samantha had said, and adding some reflection points from my own perspective.

After several days of deep, soul-searching, he took Samantha's advice to heart, hopefully strengthened by my two cents, and was prepared to face his issues head-on with Nikki over dinner.

Logan came to an important, and possible, game-changing decision. *"If it is to be … it is up to me. I am the problem… and the solution!"*

♥   ♥   ♥

They had a very nice dinner at Commis, in Oakland, and following dessert and an after-dinner brandy, they headed to Logan's place for much-needed conversation and intimacy that would, hopefully, reflect the new feelings from them both.

Logan tried to create a mood of softness and calm. He had cool jazz and warm lighting defining the subtle ambiance of the evening, and tried to think in terms of what Nikki would expect from the evening, and not necessarily his satisfaction. *"It's what I do, not what I say,"* he thought therapeutically.

"Nikki, take my hand and let me make love to you and show you how much I care and how I have changed. Please."

Nikki smiled as Logan took her hand and pulled her up from his sofa. She always loved any expression of contact involving his warm and large hands, and comforting words.

"Yes, Logan, I want that very much. I think we both need a second chance, and tonight is the night to begin," as they then walked into the bedroom.

"You are so beautiful," he murmured as he took her blouse and pulled it up revealing her ample, perky breasts to his wanting eyes. He beamed as he ran his palms down over the delicate swell of her breasts, before he rolled her tender nipples between his fingers. Nikki arched her back upward with a startled gasp, as he pinched her nipples just hard enough to draw a heated groan from her.

"I am so sensitive to your touch. Love it."

She continued to look up into the fiery eyes staring down at her with such passion a lump formed in her throat. A soft moan could be heard as he pinched her swollen tips harder. Nikki responded by reaching up to grasp his thighs.

After his long tongue had played on hers, he slid down her body. He kneed her thighs apart so he could kneel between them, running light kisses and tiny nips along the inside of her right thigh. His heart raced as she lifted up to allow her remaining clothes to be removed, a clear invitation to get it going. The noticeable scent of her arousal burst over his senses pulling a low, guttural growl from him. His erection was full.

She paused and allowed her thigh muscles to relax as her legs fell apart. She felt wanted and he looked so commanding. As his power swept through her, it heightened her own desire to have him, as moisture pooled between her legs, and she wanted him immersed in it.

He took his fingers from her mouth and slid them deep into her wet and warm core. He could feel her tighten around him as he pushed into her. She moaned with pleasure as he probed her clit. He shared her sweet juices as she sucked his fingers, and he aligned his large and throbbing erection into her hot channel.

"Wrap your beautiful legs around my waist, Nikki." The friction gave both lovers a sense of heightened arousal. She responded by pulling him in even closer with her legs strongly enfolded around his waist. They both shuddered as the movement drove him in even deeper. He fought tingling sensations that indicated his pending climax.

"Faster," she groaned softly. "Deeper and faster." As he rocked harder and faster, he could feel her breathing pick up and her body began to tremble. She tightened her legs even more, as she began to put pressure on him to create more friction within her channel.

"Yes. You are filling me up. Yes. Yes."

Moments later, he felt her explode around him, as she collapsed her legs so tightly that he couldn't pull out of her. Nikki screamed. His growl mixed with her cry as they came together, pulsing in a mind-blowing climax, left them both limp and physically spent.

"You've fulfilled my needs in such a sexy and beautiful way," she murmured after her body stopped shaking. "I think I've died and gone to heaven."

"Give me a minute and I'll bring you back," he chuckled. He pulled back enough to press a heated kiss on her soft lips. "I have never felt this way before," he admitted as he stared down at her. "What you do to me ... it's a sensation that only you can bring out of me."

She reached up and gently laid her hand on his cheek as she saw the vulnerability in his eyes and the uncertainty in his voice. "It will be alright," she whispered. "I've never felt this way before with you either, Logan."

Logan thought reflectively, "*I can never take this woman for granted again.*"

Nikki whispered to herself, "*This man is my future ... I know that now.*"

Has the putrid past been replaced by a fantastic future?

80

SARA AND BRAD

*S*ara viewed Brad as basically a good guy with work to do regarding his behavior. Brad saw Sara as the full package, but way to fussy in her choice of a man to even make longer term plans viable. In other words, Sara was determined to change the things she didn't like in Brad, and Brad believed he was unlikely to replace the pieces in Sara's life, driving that ladies' day-to-day lifestyle. Neither of them thought of what it would take for a second-chance romance.

Following her session with Dr. Vandenberg, Sara recalled a date they had months ago, when Sara was in a good place and Brad seemed more than attentive ... even deeply committed.

They had just finished a dinner celebrating Valentine's Day and Brad had given Sara an inscribed necklace. As she admired the gift, Brad proudly exclaimed, "Sara, I truly believe that to be happy with a man you must understand him a lot and love him a little. To be happy with a woman you must love her a lot and try not to understand her at all."

"Brad, that's so sweet."

Actually, Brad couldn't take credit for that quote, as it came from Helen Rowland, American writer, journalist and humorist. – Jonathan Garrett

But today, Sara was trying to absorb the powerful info coming from that group session, and how it would impact Sara going forward. It was important to Sara to realize how Brad was stuck in several stressful situations with work, his alcoholic father, and his intense drive to fuel his manly ego to the fullest.

She did what the highly organized, analytic Sara would do in times like this. Well, maybe not literally. She created a timeline of three *significant emotional events* involving her and Brad, and his cheating, up to and including the four-poster bed sex game, where he perceived himself to be the victim. On top of that mountain, was the crap he pulled on her as she planned an awesome 40th birthday party for the two of them.

"*Oh crap,*" she whispered to her adoring Siamese Eja, "*this is incredible.*"

What Sara discovered was almost a perfect alignment with Brad's infidelity, and episodes of high stress in his life; almost a perfect correlation. Yes, her problem-solving skills rewarded her nicely with a root cause, but not a solution. She immediately called Dr. Vandenberg.

"Sara, what you described to me is tremendous. Before I give you my opinion, may I use this story as an actual case study in my sessions?"

"Well, sure, thanks. It's a compliment from you that I will surely value."

"So, I think you need to find the right opportunity, likely one that is the right place and time, and put these cards on the table. I think that he will respect you for taking this initiative, and will be much more likely to open up and confront his demons."

"Will do, Sam. Thanks."

"My pleasure, Sara. Keep me posted."

♥ ♥ ♥

Brad was struggling with several issues, and the social media slams were, unfortunately, at the top of his list. He was so obsessed with getting this issue resolved, that his work and social life were taking a beating. He had given up on finding the perp behind the four-poster bed incident, realizing that it was small compared to dealing with the subsequent fallout from the escapade.

He called me, I guess as a rather transparent attempt to get my perspective on the blackmail he was dealing with and, indirectly, what impression I might have regarding Sara Sullivan, who Brad knew was a friend of mine.

"Well, Brad, I may be able to help. Text or email the person who is after you and any paper trail that I could use. I do have a friend, a former F.B.I. agent, who may be able to step in and get you some closure. I can't do anything regarding money that was already paid."

"Understand, Jonathan. Appreciate the help."

"You got it."

Just as that somewhat optimistic call ended, Brad reached for his crutch … a double scotch. He knew he was starting a pattern that he had seen and condemned in his dad, but he didn't have the resolve and discipline to just say no. Sara would be here in less than an hour and he had to focus on her, not on himself.

♥ ♥ ♥

Almost as soon as she arrived, Brad had only one thing on his mind; how to love and please his girl. He gave her every indication that his love for her was going to be on full display in his bedroom, and Sara felt the timing was right to pursue her last-ditch effort to save the relationship, and genuine intimacy could be the litmus test.

"Is that a glass of scotch on the counter, Brad?"

"Yep, it is. I poured it a while ago, but it just sits. I didn't touch a drop."

"Good boy. I'm pleased and impressed."

"Thanks. I want to focus on my lovely lady, Sara. That's my drug right now. And your sexy, steel blue eyes are dreamy."

Sara thought, hopefully, *"This is all a good sign ... a very good sign."*

Following some soothing small talk and light foreplay, Sara and Brad got themselves into the mood and were somewhat anxious to "test the waters."

"Let's go into the bedroom, Sara. I want you, and I want you to want me now."

"Brad, I am as ready as I'll ever be, and I sense a level of kindness and caring that we used to share ... long, long ago."

Brad gently laid her down, eyeing every inch of her beautiful and warm body. With her arms around his neck, she was now in a place that was good and would only get better; so peaceful.

His eyes began to roam over her fervently, as she returned the same glow. He bent over her and gripped the front of her top as his already accelerated pulse surged, and a hot wave of desire sent blood flowing into his throbbing penis. Her breasts glowed in the soft bedroom light, matching the gleam in her eyes.

"I have a good feeling about this," she thought, lovingly.

Brad wanted her naked, so he methodically began to remove her clothing. Sensing the urgency and determination in his actions, Sara didn't resist. She helped to remove her bra and panties, showing them both just how wet she had become so quickly.

"I want you ... I need you," he said eagerly.

He quickly removed his pants and climbed onto the bed next to Sara. What he saw was an inviting figure, with two lovely breasts, waiting for his touch and a wet, open mouth that he quickly filled with a kiss and his long tongue. He pulled her legs apart and settled his torso between them before bending over to capture one of her taut nipples in his mouth.

"Oh God," Sara muttered as she let out a slight moan, placing her hands on his hips. He then sucked her other perky breast, and ran his tongue around her areolas until the tips of her nipples got firm.

"My nipples are quite sensitive."

Brad smiled and sucked deeply, but gently, catching each tip between his teeth and biting down firmly to draw a loving sigh from her soft lips. His body reacted sensually to her motion as she arched in response, seeking more of his hot lips and tongue.

He lowered one of his hands so he could slide his fingers into her vagina, testing to see if she was ready. Pearl juices on the tip of his fingers were forming, in conjunction with pre-climax sensations on his firming penis. He pushed his hardness in as far as he could, while sucking on her taut nipples. He pulled almost all the way out before pressing even deeper than before.

She groaned and said sharply, "I want you inside me." He responded by thrusting his hips forward, penetrating her, stretching her tight channel until they were both feeling the same sensation. As the friction inside her increased, and she neared the edge of her zenith, Sara's moans became cries and she shuddered with sexual anticipation.

He grasped her wrists tightly, his heavy breaths and the sounds of his grunts echoing her moans. She released the grip that she had around his waist, opening her sex further to him to take her as hard and as fast as he could.

Pulling her head to one side, he bit down on her shoulder and she exploded under his assault. Her body erupted in an orgasm built on need, love, and trust. She arched into him as a loud scream ripped from her throat, driving him even deeper. She clenched him even stronger, as his climax wrapped blissfully around hers.

A whimpering Sara simply thought reflectively, "***This is a new beginning … but just a beginning.***"

81

LINA AND GABE

*L*ina and Gabe seemed to enjoy a destiny of sorts; a decent match of two good people who needed each other. The question to me was always the same. Would this virtuous couple become the friends-to-lovers common trope that you read about in romance novels? It did seem that they were earning their points on a regular basis, and just needed something to push them to the top. They seemed to reflect one of the sayings in my sci-fi novels: "When you surround yourself with people who support your dreams, you will achieve success more quickly."

♥　♥　♥

Lina thought a lot about what Dr. Vandenberg had said regarding Lina's tendency to give love and positive energy to those around her, and not be willing to accept support from loved-ones in her inner circle.

Lina also realized that the incident with Carl could have been predicted. He assumed he could have his way with her, inasmuch as she never gave off any vibe that it wasn't the case. Rather than follow up on her session with Dr. Vandenberg, Lina, instead, called Nikki for some advice.

"Hey, girlfriend, got a minute?"

"Sure do, Lina, what's up?"

"The session with Samantha opened my eyes, and I think I have it narrowed down to two things that I need to do, and you seem like the perfect person to advise me."

"Okay. I'm listening. I'll help if I can."

"First, I think I need to work on the self-love thing. It's been said that you cannot give love honestly, if you can't love your own self first, or something similar."

"Yeah, I think it comes from being happy with yourself, before you can make other people happy, Lina."

"Yes. Nikki, you are as confident a person as I know. What advice do you have?"

"Well, all right … here we go. You need to step up and take credit for all of your accomplishments. Literally, don't minimize or blow off all the very fine things you have accomplished. And this next book … holy crap, is it ever gonna stir up some shit and make you famous!"

"Nikki, I hope you're right."

"I know I'm right. Now, what is the second thing you said came out of our session?"

"Samantha said that if a woman doesn't get the adequate love and attention in return for what she gives, that out-of-balance dynamic will haunt her and perpetuate high anxiety."

"Lina, dear, you don't own any exclusive rights to that theory. All of us girls face that specific dynamic."

"So, Nikki, what to do?"

"I'm going to step out of bounds a bit to make a point. Your best friend, Gabe, is a guy with a genuine heart who cares about you to the max."

"Yes. I am happy about that."

"From your own description, when it comes to intimacy, which you crave, Gabe has not taken charge."

"That's right."

"Yet, he never tells you how you should feel, or that anything you are doing is wrong?'

"Yes, that's true."

"So, my dear Lina, when it comes to the bedroom, learning methods and techniques from Ramon, you need to become the aggressor … you need to wear the pants!"

Once again, Lina reflects on her previous self-fulfilling thought. "*I need to live the life I imagined!*"

♥　♥　♥

Gabe had just finished rescheduling his classes, per suggestions from his mentor, and pulled up an email with his financial plan nearly complete. He was happy to be making progress with these two important issues.

Without any suggestions from anyone, Gabe researched books on relationships and read, predominantly, the best-selling female authors and counselors from Dr. Julie Archer to Dr. Samantha Vandenberg. He read and re-read the New York Times best seller, *Seeing Her Side,* and is now armed with a new-found appreciation for his relationship with Lina.

He quotes a passage from the book that inspired his inner thoughts:

"Men and women have a tendency to subconsciously monitor the amount of give and take in a relationship. If the balance shifts, one person feeling they have given more than they have received, resentment can develop. This is a time when only communication can help to bring the relationship back into balance."

As he rifled through that book for the umpteenth time, Gabe began to see a light at the end of the tunnel for one of his life's mysteries …

"Now is the time," Gabe thought enthusiastically, *"to meet these critical issues head-on with Lina. Yes, now!"*

♥   ♥   ♥

Armed with a new-found sense of confidence and awareness, Gabe agreed to spend an evening with Lina, who had prepared a simple Italian dinner for them, with Gabe's favorite beer, Coors's Light, to top off the meal.

Following some rather awkward small talk, aimed to get each of them relaxed, Lina announced that they would head to her bedroom. "Can you stay tonight?" She trembled a bit, awaiting his response, and then took a step forward so they were pressed chest to chest, in full body contact.

"I'd like to." Gabe's gaze darkened and his focus cleared. His thumb traced the line of Lina's lips, feeling the wetness and warmth, until she was wanting to feel his mouth over hers.

"Lina, ever since our last night together, I go to sleep thinking how much I enjoy our kisses." His lips drifted over her cheek. She grasped his shoulders and hung on, and smiled at his words.

"I remember the force of your nails on my back when you come, and Lina, the way your eyes get wide when you're aroused, like right now."

"Yes, Gabe, I feel alive with you. I did enjoy our last night together."

His growing erection notched between her thighs, and he slid his hands down to cup her buttocks, lifting up and grinding against her. Her body trembled. He was moving slowly; not the usual herky-jerky.

"You know how badly I want you, Lina, and if it were only sex, I'd feel very lucky. But I want more than just the sex, and you need to know how I feel. I want to convince you that we can be so much more." His lips grew closer, and then his mouth was on hers.

She moaned as her body felt warm sensations from head to toe. "I love your touch, Gabe."

He kissed her hard and deep, his tongue thrusting inside and taking full control. She clung to him and gave it all back, desperate to be skin-to-skin. He lifted her high, and she wrapped her legs tightly around him. He undressed her slowly. She sensed a somewhat different Gabe; relaxed and purposeful.

"Can you tell me what your body needs me to do," he whispered in her ear, his hands all over her body, caressing her nipples, stroking her belly, pushing his fingers deep inside her vagina. She writhed and whimpered and raised her voice to a guttural moan that answered his question, loud and strong. "Umm, my body wants you. Let me take you."

Now confident in their mutual love and greedy for all of him, she hooked her ankle around his and flipped him, sprawling over his naked body with her satisfaction. "Now, Gabe, you can let it out." He groaned.

She slid down and ran her lips from his mouth to his groin, biting him gently in all the sensitive places. She wanted him to feel vulnerable to her wishes and needs. Tonight, she would be the queen. Grasping his growing penis, she lowered herself slowly over him, inch by inch, and sensing that his erection was full, buried him deep inside her, at the same time her body throbbed and shuddered.

His hands cupped her breasts and his gaze devoured her, ignited with lust. For her, a deeper emotion filled her heart.

"Push up and down on me," he murmured appreciatively, softly tweaking her nipples. "Take all you want."

She did, and when the orgasm hit, he covered her mouth with a fierce kiss, swallowing every throaty cry. His lips jerked, and then he followed her over the edge, never breaking the contact. When they finally fell back in a tangle of sheets and naked limbs, she knew the connection between them was so much more than physical.

"You're right," she said.

"About what?"

"It'll never be just about sex, Gabe. You're too important to me."

He smoothed back her hair and dropped a kiss on her forehead, thinking to himself, **"Maybe one day I'll be able to put into words just how much you mean to me."**

82

JACQUI AND JONATHAN

J
acqui Johnson and Jonathan Garrett were becoming the proverbial life-in-the-
fast-lane couple, actually a perfect match if they ever took the time to analyze
and reflect. It even was established in an astrology session that they once oddly
agreed to attend.

He is a Scorpio and she is a Pisces, and those two signs are a seamless sexual
match. Hell, if it is written in the stars, what choice do you have? What at one time
was a forced proximity, and then later times a logical bonding, these two people
thrived on external tension.

Another way of looking at it, and I apologize in advance, is that this remarkable
couple couldn't see the forest from the proverbial trees. Sorry!

♥   ♥   ♥

Jacqui was taking emotional inventory – first, with respect to the *dungeons*
and dragons in the lower level, and then regarding her own mental state. She
stopped with a glass of wine in hand, and tried to recall the talking points from
the noteworthy session with Samantha. *Indifference ... the opposite of love.*

Indifference was the word from Samantha that stuck in her mind, as if etched.
Indifference was a lack of interest, concern, sympathy, and aptly described a
plethora of relationships in her past. She even found the clinical definition of
indifference and posted it on her wine cabinet. She did!

"Indifference is more truly the opposite of love than hate is, for we can both love
and hate the same person at the same time, but we cannot both love and be indifferent
to the same person at any time."

Jacqui had an "aha" moment. She did, indeed, both love and hate her despicable husband, the lecherous James Johnson. The love at times was so strong that she would do almost anything for him. But the days and nights in the "dungeon" brought out the hate, big time, for being put through those deeply ingrained misogynistic attitudes and horrible behavior.

She thought harshly, *"I think I once told Jonathan that James was the piece of me, I wish I didn't need."*

She whispered to herself, *"James claimed he loved me, but he showed disdain and indifference often, without so much as a thin veil of disguise. And by definition, 'You cannot both love and be indifferent to the same person at any time.' Got it."*

♥　　♥　　♥

Okay, this is the part that is a little bit **catharsis** *and a little bit* **cognitive dissonance***. As the narrator, let me explain. These perspectives are important for our stories.*

Catharsis *is the process of releasing strong or repressed emotions … a purification of bottled-up fears, behaviors, or tensions through certain behaviors; in my case, sex! I just can't get Mimi Rainey out of my head. She is a fantasy of mine today that stemmed from a very real relationship many years ago.*

Cognitive dissonance *is a term in psychology for the state of discomfort felt when two or more modes of thought contradict each other. In my business dealings, it could be easily explained by a CEO who would say he believed in this or that, but when his behavior was in play, he simply did something else. Didn't walk the talk. For me, I would give advice that I didn't follow. As a young man I was a real shit about not "walking the talk." As I have grown and matured, I realize that my words and actions have meaning, and now behave accordingly.*

♥　　♥　　♥

The very next time we met, at my home, the moment to truly show this fine woman how I felt about her was near. We had been dancing around the fact that we had strong feelings for each other. Our relationship was an evolution built on the fact that we were open and honest with one another, and I recalled my advice to many people, many times. *"If you find someone who actually does what they say they will do, don't let them out of your sight!"*

327

"Jacqui, I have reached a point and time in my life, where what is important to me, is to have someone to share and enjoy the goodness of life."

"Jon, I am right there with you, one hundred percent."

"Now don't get too excited. This isn't a marriage proposal."

Jacqui laughed, "I understand the need to share. And, I'm not thinking full-time commitment, so don't worry."

After an hour of discussing the virtues of a deep relationship, we were off to the bedroom to take sexual advantage of our growing passion and understanding of one another.

My hands shook as I laid her gently on the king-size bed. The moment she outstretched her hand, a deep sense of fate rose up inside me, as if all my wonderful teasing moments led up to this. I noticed the tiny shiver that shook through her, the lust shining in those gorgeous hazel eyes.

She was turned on, and I couldn't wait to find out how many ways I could make her come in one night, and what other things brought her pleasure. I was excited and felt that she was as well.

I moved slowly, sitting on the edge of the bed, to look down on her. I pressed kisses over her face, arranging her hair so it neatly covered the pillow. The thrill of a long and strange lover's chase shot through me, as she began to tease me with her teeth nipping at my lower lip and her fingers wrapped around my neck

Ready to give her my best, I fiercely thrust my tongue deep into her mouth, holding her head still as I overwhelmed her with all the raw hunger that has been building for months.

"Oh, Jon." She laid still beneath me, clinging to me reservedly, groaning quietly, while her hips raised up for more. I took that movement as a signal to get my growing penis pointed in the right direction, as my erection was in full compliance.

I pulled off her skimpy top, baring her lace-covered breasts to my eager eyes, and stared excitedly over her half-naked body.

"You are gorgeous." When I kissed her firm, she returned it immediately, opening her mouth to mine and wrapping her legs tight around my hips. She was on board and ready.

I slowly broke the kiss, peeled her skirt up so it bunched around her hips and stared at the tiny fabric that covered her warm feminine core.

"Jacqui, you are so damn beautiful." My finger traced the sensitive crease of her thighs, running a teasing path over her shivering skin. "The things I want to do with you … for you … because of you."

Jacqui wiggled her hips and began unbuttoning my shirt. "You don't need my permission, and I think we have been waiting for this for a while." Her boldness was contrasting with her trembling fingers as she pulled my shirt open and dug her nails into my chest.

"Damn, girl. Rough and ready, eh?"

"Yeah, I'm ready. Now get my damn panties off."

In one swift movement, I dragged her panties down her legs and threw them on the floor. Slowly, I parted her thighs wide, opening her up with my hungry gaze that caught her attention and encouraged her.

"I need to feel you, Jon," Jacqui said insistently.

As I gazed at her beauty, arousal was squeezing my penis as her swollen, pink lips glistened wet. I lowered myself down to her, my shoulders braced between her legs.

"Can't wait to hear you ask me nice," I whispered with a slight grin.

"You shit. You're the one who should be begging to get inside this warm love nest."

I licked her, gathering her spicy essence and exploring every slick, satisfying inch. I was content to take my time, savoring every cry and wiggle as I pleasured my lovely lady. Curving two fingers, I pushed inside her vagina, feeling around until I hit the spot with my thumb, that made her heels arch into the bed and her body tighten.

"That's it, Jon. Oh God, that's it."

Now satisfied with my approach, I kept up the steady rhythm while I continued to tease her clit, pressing light kisses that never seemed to satisfy Jacqui's expectations, until I finally felt her entire body trembling on the edge of climax. At that moment, I closed my lips over the nub and sucked hard.

Jacqui came in a sexual explosion, twisting in my grasp, but I held her down and never let up the pressure, extending her intense orgasm, as I had done many times before. She soon collapsed, panting for breath, her muscles limp and her fists clenching the sheets. "Oh, Jon."

Then I slid back up, cupped her cheeks, and took her mouth in a deep kiss. When I finally released her lips, she stared at me with dazed hazel eyes, "I didn't get a chance to beg, big guy," she uttered somberly.

I had to laugh, as she lay gloriously naked underneath, her body still shaking from the release.

"That was just a warm-up." I hesitated. "Now I'm ready to get serious."

As Jacqui tried to recover from the intense, mind-blowing orgasm, my mouth returned to the scene of the beginning of the last seductive move, and I was revving her back up. Cupping both breasts with my warm hands, I moved my mouth to allow my teeth to scrape against her tight nipple, then swiped it firmly with my tongue, bringing the tips to such sensitivity, a sob caught her throat. Yes, there is a fine line between pleasure and pain.

A few seconds later, she was nearly pleading. She wanted to feel the exquisite sensation of me sucking hard on her nipple. Instinctively, she spread her legs and invited me in, to get us both to our summit.

"Jon, I need to feel you inside me, and soon. Please."

As I bent to kiss her thigh, she took her hand, and lined up my shaft with her welcoming core, and I could see her gaze into my eyes with wild anticipation.

I lifted my hips and pushed inside her. She moaned. When I was buried as deep as I could be, I grabbed her ankles and lifted her slightly higher to maximize my penetration angle, and to thrust as hard as I could. She grimaced and cried out as I slammed back hard into her. "Yes."

Loud moans, rapid pants, and beads of sweat were now defining her sexual essence. Oh, those moans … Her fingers and toes curled as I hit her magic bud and sent waves of pulsing sensation throughout her body. She grimaced as she was being ravaged with my rhythmic thrusting and it was good for her, and for me.

"Oh my God, oh my God. Oh, Oh, Oh. Yes!" Jacqui screamed!

Her incredible climax threw her muscles into mini-convulsions, as the sheer pleasure exploded and burned through her entire body. I nearly matched her orgasm as I ripped open a yell that I never had experienced with Jacqui before.

Sobbing, dazed, and feeling in a half-drunk state, she collapsed in contentment. I wrapped my arms around her and felt relief and satisfaction.

Jacqui whispered to herself, ***I don't want another man inside me … ever again!***

83

SAMANTHA AND RAMON

kay, fair enough. You didn't see this one coming. Or, did you? Samantha and Ramon were simply a textbook match, with so many similarities. The energy and vibes from their banter and productive conversations revealed that they had much in common … very much!

Going from one-time friendly rivals, to hot and steamy lovers, may be a fairytale story, but this uneven, early power balance became a laser-focused passion eruption that raised the sexual performance bar to stratospheric heights!

This was a hot-air balloon at 30,000 feet, snow skiing down a mountain at 100 mph, racing an Indy car at 250 mph, sky-diving from space in sub-orbit … okay, I'm getting ahead of myself. More later …

Dr. Samantha Vandenberg had just finished a session with Ramon, and was so aroused her panties were warm and wet. She had imagined several buckets of all the men she had dated, counseled, slept with, had one-night-stands with, and came up with about ten different buckets, or categories, of sexual satisfaction and emotional comfort from these many affairs.

Yes, all the men she knew could be put into ten buckets which she labeled "bang-ability," from a number one as "never again" to a number ten as "whenever is fine." She thought she had the perfect scoring system that would fly in the face of the tallies that she counseled her female clients to avoid.

Now, all ten buckets were merged together into one sad remembrance bucket with a score of one. The only other bucket was Ramon!

Samantha enjoyed frequent fantasy dreams with Ramon, often waking in a pool of sex sweat. *"I love it … I need it … I dream of it,"* she admitted to herself, never acknowledging a dream before.

♥　　♥　　♥

Ramon was busy minding his own business, giving pleasure to selected ladies on a contractual basis. Life was good. He was even now getting a business started, which had been a dream of his for a long while; accessories for the bedroom to enhance a couple's sex life and make Ramon tons of money. What not to like?

Ramon thought to himself after leaving a counseling session with Sam, "*This is the level of arousal that usually takes me a while to achieve physically, and we didn't even touch!*"

Ramon just couldn't wait any longer, so he invited Samantha over to his place, with every intention of having the greatest sex of his life ... no reason not to set the bar high. Tonight, that bar would be very high.

Arriving at Ramon's small, but fashionably decorated condo, Samantha was in a very excited mood. Dressed in a black sequin mini dress, with a deep V, and exaggerated shoulders, creating a powerful silhouette for the shapely lady, the draped front skirt was as flattering in the front as it was showing off the lady's derriere.

"Welcome to my home." Ramon announced as he gave his guest a big hug.

"Why thank you, Ramon, for the invitation. You have a lovely home."

"Please come inside, and let me pour you a glass of a wine that you said was one of your favs ... a 2017 Duckhorn Napa Valley Cabernet from their Patzimaro Vineyard."

"I love that Cab. How thoughtful."

As Ramon poured their wine, Samantha caught the aroma of his dinner being prepared. "What are we having?"

"I know you love seafood, so I am preparing a roast whitefish with cannellini beans and green olives. Slow roasting provides for a moist super-flaky fish without the need for much tending, allowing us to share a bottle of that wonderful Cab."

For the next hour, they enjoyed a fabulous meal, nearly finished a full bottle of wine, and talked themselves into a state of closeness that had thrilling sexual intimacy, as the final destination.

Samantha was as lovely as ever, and dressed in that sexy mini dress, just made his head spin. Naked lust shot out of his soul, seeing the beauty before him who was there with him ... and only for him. She saw the sincerity in his eyes, and her body sent a reassuring message to her heart.

"Come to me, Samantha." Her breath shook deep inside as she slowly approached Ramon, her body warm with anticipation at the tenderness in his voice, and the growing arousal in his groin. When she stopped close, his body heat and the scent of his masculinity struck her hard. His hands cupped her face, holding her still, and his tense gaze probed deep within her sexual being.

Samantha began feeling vulnerable, but Ramon's genuine spirit and easy-going demeanor relieved her of all anxiety. "You're so damn beautiful," he said softly as his thumbs stroked her cheeks. "I've wanted this since the first time we met. I've needed this since the first time we met."

"Ramon," Samantha replied sincerely, "I want to feel in my body, what I have been experiencing in my mind."

"Talk to me, Sam."

"When I go to sleep, I think of you. I have your taste lingering on my tongue. It's seems so real."

"Tonight, my beautiful Samantha, we will savor the taste of each other."

She wrapped her arms around his shoulders and tilted her head back, giving him full access. "I'll be gentle, Sam."

"I don't want gentle, my love, I want you hard and rough tonight."

Ramon smiled and replied, "That I can give you." His mouth took hers and her entire body sighed. As his hot tongue ravaged her mouth, her nails bit into his shoulders as she pushed closer. Once her warm and soft breasts pressed against his hard chest, her nipples grew taut and sensitive, giving off a slight moan that Ramon enjoyed hearing.

The pace quickened, as all clothing disappeared quickly. They kissed in between removing clothes, kicking off shoes, until finally they were in their underwear, he in his favorite silk boxers, and she in a delightful red thong. He scooped her up and laid her out on the bed.

She shivered under his intense gaze, remaining still as he consumed her with his eyes. "You are a beautiful person inside, Sam, but I can barely control myself when I see such a seducing body. My God, yours is amazing. And your green eyes are so mysterious!"

As she smiled, enjoying his loving and heartfelt description, he tweaked her nipple through the lace, ran his hand over her trembling stomach, and raked his fingers over her matching delicate panties.

"This seductress is in need of being seduced. Show me your stuff."

Her nonchalant remark got him hyper-serious in an instant, as Ramon peeled his briefs over his hips, and she was staring at a chiseled body, every inch solid muscle with sturdy thighs highlighting the hard, swollen length of his thick erection.

"Oh my God," she whimpered and moaned with joy.

Her low moan cut the quiet in the room, and she didn't even realize what she had done until he shook his head amusingly.

"Keep looking at me like that, dear Sam, and we both won't last long."

With his hands on a mission, he lifted her hips and tugged down on her wet, lace thong. Her eyes widened in anticipation as she gasped. This time, he was silent. Gently moving her thighs open, he positioned his shoulders in between them.

"Now, Sam, I want to taste you." Samantha's breathing became heavy. He dropped his head and began consuming her with his tongue. He licked and sucked, holding her open with his thumbs, and groaning pleasurably, in pure satisfaction. She purred with contentment and anticipation.

Her hips rotated in sync with the skillful nurtures of his untiring mouth, until the explosive orgasm shimmering in her body hit with full force.

She writhed on the bed and cried out, "Ramon, yes Ramon," her fingers twisting tensely in the sheets, riding out the maximum release that shook every inch of her warm and shaking body. "I can't get enough of you … I just can't."

He kissed the back of her knees, her hip, her abdomen and then her wet, inner thigh. He slid back up, running his tongue between her breasts, then sucking gently on her firm nipples.

"You taste so sweet, Sam," he murmured, as his tongue curled one swollen peak. As her hands found the back of his head and holding him tight to her, he uttered, "I can't wait much longer. I need to be inside you."

Ramon took a deep breath, and moved into a position to give the lady what she had asked for.

"Yes," she cried, wrapping her legs around his hips, opening herself up and inviting him in. "I want to feel your hot sex … your fullness in me." Her body squeezed him tight as she fought to catch her breath at his complete, thrusting penetration of her wet core.

"Stay with me, Sam," he murmured, as she opened her channel by widening her legs, and adjusting to his girth. She rocked her hips a bit as the tension eased, and her muscles relaxed. He groaned, firmly gripping and squeezing her extremely sensitive breasts. She squealed, and he relaxed his grip and pressed his forehead to hers.

"God, you feel so good. Tight. Perfect." She raised a slight moan from his hand leaving her breasts and said emphatically, "You are so damn big, Ramon. I am consumed."

He took her mouth in a deep, hypnotic kiss, and began to move slowly, ever so slowly, as he pulled himself out. He paused as she caught her breath, and then he slammed himself back in, his fullness in her love channel bringing out a long and deep shriek. She gasped at the fiery sensation, her clit pulsing, ready for the perfect contact pressure to explode.

Sensing her high state of arousal, he kept up the pulsing rhythm, moving a bit faster each time, trapping her within the torment of sensual tension, until she was on the edge of a cosmic orgasm. "Ramon," she pleaded, digging her nails into his back, "please come now."

"Samantha, I don't want this moment to end." His intense voice left nothing to be imagined. "I want it all for both of us." In an instant, squeezing her legs tight around his hips, she lifted up and, using the leverage of her body weight and position, flipped Ramon over, with him still deep inside her cavern. Climbing on top, she sank down fully, bowing back her trembling body.

"That's perfect, my love. Take what you want, Sam." With a deep growl, she moved her body to her own quick pace, found the angle that hit the shimmery spot, her clit scrapping against his enormous manhood, until his name flew from her lips – "Oh, God, Ramon!"

Her intense release rushed over her entire body in waves, enjoying the end-less flashes that stretched into glorious pleasure. He grasped her hips, bucked upward for a few seconds, and then surrendered to his own incredible orgasm.

He pulled her close, wrapped his arms around her, and they relaxed into a full and warm snuggle. They were quiet for a while, enjoying a moment that was bigger than words could describe. He spoke first.

"I have had a wonderful life, and this night is the most wonderful part of that life."

A tear slowly flowed down Samantha's cheek as she asserted her deep-est feelings.

"You are a treasure ... my treasure."

335

84

LOVE WITH LITTLE LIES

This chapter, Love with Little Lies, is about me. Now, before you say, "This is very self-serving, eh Jonathan," let me explain. In this chapter, I will try to capture the fabric of struggles and difficulties that women face in today's dating arena, and offer a simple perspective on how men think, and how they lie.

The lessons learned for me over time with these terrific ladies, and bundling the sage advice from both Dr. Vandenberg and Ramon Gilbert, have given me a new and healthier outlook. So don't shrug … just read and draw your own conclusions.

Let's start with five man-facts that I firmly believe in, and you need to consider going forward.

First, men have relationships to gain sex; women have sex to gain relationships.

Second, don't respond or react to what men say; respond and react to what you see them do.

Third, look hard at a man's relationship with his mother; good is very good and bad is very bad.

Fourth, you can learn all you need to know about a man, from your first two or three meetings.

Fifth, if you find a man actually doing what he said he would do, don't let him out of your sight!

Now, moving to some strategy … romantic planning is not usually on guy's radar screen. Men are not thinkers, for the most part; but doers. And, pride gets in the way of any cause and effect thinking; ego gets in the way of soft and sensitive behavior.

336

If this doesn't make sense, let me put it into a simple Q and A exercise. Keep these *ten questions* in the back of your mind, as you meet and try to figure out a new guy friend. See if you are comfortable discussing any of these remarks with a new guy. These are not "want to know." These are "need to know."

1) Are you and your mom close?
2) Are you married/have you been married?
3) Do you have any kids?
4) Where do you live?
5) What do you do for a living?
6) Have you/could you have sex with a man?
7) Do you have any drug or criminal problems in your background?
8) Are you dating anyone now?
9) When was the last time you went on a date?
10) What do you do to "give back" to the community or family?

Now, I am not suggesting that you bring your 3X5 notecard to your next date, but find a way to weave these questions into your conversations over two or three dates. Remember, men use fewer words to communicate than women do, and you can read a lot from their body language. Good reads for you – nervousness, body posture, fidgeting, mumbling and avoiding eye contact. Keep in mind that most communication between the sexes is now deemed to be, nonverbal.

Lastly, keep in mind a thought from an earlier chapter. The opposite of LOVE isn't HATE. The opposite of LOVE is INDIFFERENCE. If you are in a relationship where your man shows indifference to you and your needs, the relationship is likely unsalvageable.

Back to the *ten questions*. You are intelligent, intuitive, and experienced in these relationship encounters. You should easily determine if the man is lying, bragging or just trying to get away from your legitimate probing. His response or responses, will either set off a red flag or not, regarding his answers.

Armed with this exercise, and following the meeting between Logan and Dr. Vandenberg, I tried this "test" on Logan, with fascinating results. I shared Logan's results with him, and he was blown away with how "spot-on" his answers revealed his lying, and hiding the truth.

"I could see how uncomfortable I was with those questions," Logan said contritely.

I responded, "You would have preferred different questions?"

"Or no questions," he replied remorsefully.

It gave him pause to re-think how he would talk to Nikki, given the fact that she would likely conclude, what we had concluded on this "test." Logan needed to make some character changes.

Ladies, it's worth the effort. Please take some time to consider your tactical plan to reveal the truth, and/or expose the lies in your man's true character.

The simple song lyrics below, should set the tone …

"Tell me something, girl.
Are you happy in this modern world?
Or do you need more?
Is there something else you're searching for?
In the good times I find myself longing for change.
And in the bad times, I fear myself."

Lady Gaga – "Shallow"

85

MIDNIGHT
AT THE OASIS

I was in the foyer, awaiting the arrival of my special guests, for a house party to celebrate their triumphs over the last year or so, and share their feelings after coming so far in this journey of reflection and self-awareness.

I had my bar set up, the caterer was waiting in the spacious dining hall of my exquisite estate, and I had special gifts for these ladies.

First to arrive was Nikki and Lina.

"Hi ladies."

Hi Jon," they both gave me a warm hug.

"The bar is open and there is plenty of food in the dining hall. Make yourselves at home as I await our other guests."

Jacqui arrived next and after hugs and kisses, I said, "Before you join Nikki and Lina, I want to show you what I did with those artifacts you gave me from James' estate."

We walked down a winding staircase to a combination game room and trophy room. As we strode to the back of the brick-walled room, Jacqui could already see the three objects which I had on display.

One of the famous Kabuto helmets, worn by the fierce Japanese warriors in the 16th century, a black ninja warrior battle outfit from the 18th century, and then the featured item … the famous Musashi Masamune Samurai sword.

"I was surprised that you included the Samurai sword, Jacqui. It should be in a museum."

"Well, Jonathan, James was killed with a similar battle sword, and even though I hated him for what he did to me, the thought of that sword in my home gave me the 'creeps.' You okay with me leaving it here ... at least for a while?"

"Of course. Let's go back upstairs to greet our remaining guests. At least the cops won't need to run a DNA swab on this sword," I said laughing.

"No, they shouldn't."

I thought bewilderedly, *"Not the answer I expected."*

Several thoughts went through my mind ... but they could wait.

As we returned to the foyer, Samantha was strolling up the walk, and Sara was running to catch up with her. As they both reached the front door, I opened the door and welcomed them inside.

"Hello, ladies. Let Sara walk in first so we can't accuse her of being last."

That got a chuckle from the two women.

"Hi, Jon, thanks for throwing this bash."

"No problem, Sara. Been looking forward to doing this for a while."

Samantha gave me a hug, which I returned with a little more vigor. "Jon, this is nice. And, it will be great to spend some time with these ladies outside of my office."

"Amen, sister," Sara offers nonchalantly.

"Okay, Jacqui, Nikki and Lina are having drinks and some food in the dining hall. I'm going to check on a few things and then I'll join you."

Lina then caught up with me.

"Jon, great party."

"Glad you're enjoying it."

"Got a minute?"

"Sure," I said as we walked over to the kitchen. "What can I do for you?"

"When you were over a couple weeks back, helping me with a last-minute guy's perspective on my *Charade* novel, we talked until 2:00 am."

"We did and it was great ... and your book will be great."

"You spent the night at my apartment."

"I did. I love your apartment."

"But we didn't have sex."

"No, Lina, we did not."

"Jon, we could have had sex ... I mean it would have been kind of natural. But we didn't."

"Lina, where's this going?'

"Jon, why didn't we?"

Pausing, I replied, "Lina, I like you and respect you, and even though you are an attractive young woman, I value your friendship very much. It was my feeling that a romantic evening and sex, even though it would have been terrific, may have jeopardized that friendship, and I just didn't want that to happen. Does that make sense?"

"So, it had nothing to do with me as an attractive woman?"

"Oh gosh no, and I have no regrets, given how much we respect each other."

Lina gave me a warm hug, kissed me on the cheek, and was off to join the other girls.

With that out of the way, and being relieved at the conversation, I smiled and left to get an idea on the delivery of some special gifts. Samantha and Sara were joining Nikki with the large spread of snacks and drink.

When I joined my guests, they had all downed a few drinks and were ready for a fabulous dinner. I introduced the caterer. "Ladies, this is Chef Sebastian Mora, my friend and one of the finest people you will ever meet, and he has won the city's reputation for being a culinary creator, *par excellence.*"

"Evening, ladies. Please look at the menus, as we have some choices, and I can begin serving very soon."

MENU ONE

First Course –
Prosciutto wrapped shrimp, sage brown butter, balsamic fig glaze

Main Course 1 –
Pan-seared fennel-crusted salmon, cumin-infused lentils, ripe tomato jam

Main Course 2 –
Butter-poached main lobster, braised leeks, crispy potato

Dessert –
Crème Brule with Madagascar vanilla beans & fresh berries

MENU TWO

First Course –
Short rib ravioli with creamy mushroom sauce, mascarpone

Main Course 1 –
Orange-glazed pan-seared duck breast, butternut squash risotto

Main Course 2 –
Herb-crusted rack of lamb with roasted fingerling potatoes

Dessert –
Flambéed bananas foster in butter rum sauce & vanilla bean ice cream

"Of course, you can pick and choose from both."

As the ladies viewed the awesome menus, Jacqui nudged Nikki and said, "This is Jon's romantic dinner for two that just grew to dinner for six!"

Nikki replied, "Hell, works for me."

The ladies helped themselves to their choice of a variety of white, red, and rose wines, all from my extensive wine cellar.

Following dinner, I escorted my guests to my conservatory, where local pianist Dylan Brody was preparing to play several popular pieces for their entertainment.

"Samantha leaned over to me and said, fondly, "Thank you for doing this. It means so much to celebrate these women."

Sam gave me a thumbs up as I replied, "Thanks. This was long-time coming."

The final item on my agenda were the presents for the ladies. I presented each one with identical jewelry gifts, including a 5.0 carat heart-cut solitaire pendant with diamond cut cable chain in 14 carat white gold, and 3.0 carat round-cut stud earrings in 14 carat white gold.

They were lovely, and I was swamped with kisses, hugs, and thank you. It was great!

Then, I thought to myself, "*This evening couldn't have gone any better …*"

But the evening wasn't quite over … yet.

86

MIDNIGHT'S
MAGICAL MYSTERY

I t was a clear and stellar California evening sky, with a plethora of star clusters and astronomical wonders raging in the minds and telescopes of star gazers everywhere in the Bay Area. The twinkling of the San Francisco city lights looked like a reflection of the beautiful night sky above.

Yes, I was blessed to have the life I had, and only now am I learning how to share my wealth with others. *"Better late than never,"* I thought, pensively.

As midnight approached and the girls were finishing their last drinks, conversations, and admiring their beautiful diamond gifts, I looked at the smiling faces and got a little choked up, inasmuch as we had all gotten past trauma and disappointment and were now, hopefully, in a good place.

I firmly believed that I had some small part to play in much of the good things happening in their lives, and they had definitely made me a better person from their interactions.

I had a thought, reflecting both my maturity, and my resolve to better myself and the lives of those around me. *"You are never too old to pivot and claim success on your own terms."*

Samantha gave me a hug, and whispered in my ear, "What you have done for these ladies, and for yourself, Jonathan, is remarkable. You deserve much credit."

"Thank you, Sam. Coming from you, that is a wonderful compliment." I kissed her.

As Sara, Lina and Nikki exchanged 'good-byes,' Jacqui pulled me aside, and gave me a warm and heartfelt embrace. "I can't wait to see you again, my love. Call me tomorrow, so we can resume our magnificent second-coming."

I smiled at the term, 'second-coming.' Only my lovely Jacqui would so express herself. "Will do, Jacqui. Have a peaceful night, and we'll resume our torrid romance soon." She winked.

As Nikki, Sara, Lina, Jacqui, and Samantha left the party in my lovely mansion-by-the-sea, I kissed each one and thanked them for coming. I held the door open as they each begin walking to their cars.

"What a special night," I thought proudly. *"An absolutely perfect evening, with the loveliest and most interesting young women here in San Francisco."*

I watched as the five women got into their cars and drove away. But, one car remained, which was odd. My driveway is private, and secured. I thought to myself, *"How did that car get in, and who is in it?"*

Thinking for a moment, with police a 911 call as a possibility, I grabbed my military-style infrared binoculars to sneak a peek at this stranger. In a few seconds, I made out what appeared to be a Ferrari Roma. *"Definitely not a terrorist vehicle,"* I concluded. *"Those babies go for around $300,000."*

The driver got out of the car, which I could see was white, with lipstick-red interior. It was a woman, but with a dark trench coat and multi-colored scarf. Wearing a broad-brim black hat, like you would see in the Hamptons or at the Kentucky Derby, I didn't recognize the woman, the coat, or even the awesome Italian ride.

She stopped to check her phone, and looked as if she was sending a text. She then began the slow walk up to my front door, with the aura of a runway model on the fashion red carpet. This tall, well-dressed woman, was the essence of elegance and grace.

I could feel my heart racing, having no idea who was approaching my house in the midnight darkness. My mind was also racing, but I was clueless as to who was going to knock on my door.

As she strode up the walk to my house, she slowed, and put her phone back in her purse. I took a deep breath and tried to relax, as I calmly moved toward the door to welcome my surprise guest.

The doorbell rang.

I approached the door, took another deep breath, and opened it.

"Oh My God!"

"Hello Jonathan."

After nearly twenty years of not knowing whatever happened …

"Hello, Mimi!"

CLOSING CURTAIN

Wishing I could stay forever young,
Not afraid to close my eyes,
Life is a game played by everyone,
With true love the ultimate prize.
But now I'm aged in wisdom and grace;
Don't need the knowledge of a gifted seer,
The solution to the problems we face,
Are staring back from our own mirror.
The circle of the smiling moon, the rising of the brilliant sun.
We will be two as one soon; now our stories just begun.
Time will bring us near; I'll never be too far.
I want you to know and hear, I'll always be where you are.
You can gently dry my flowing tears,
As I hold you warmly, calming your fears.
But you can't stop all the pain inside,
That I'm trying so very hard to hide.
I will never want you to pull away.
You know that I will forever stay.
No one has ever touched me the way that you do.
Wherever I go I know the road will lead back to you.
Don't ever say goodbye; don't ever turn away.
Day one of our future life together begins today.
No regrets; only good memories of yours and mine,
Cause I will truly love you till the end of time.
With your every breath and smile, I realize;
Every move you're making, I will memorize.
The way that you feel when your fear subsides,
Wherever I go, I'll keep my memories of you inside.
My father told me I will leave this world one day,
So, strive to live the life you will remember.

It is precious, my son, to plan what you say,
A published author's words will live forever.
Romance and all its strategy,
Had me battling with my pride.
But through each year's maturity,
My tenderness survived.

PEACE AND LOVE ...
Jonathan Garrett

Watch for **"Sharks in the City 2"**

ABOUT THE AUTHOR

Garry J. Peterson is a multi-genre, multi-volume author of several books, both fiction and non-fiction, following a successful career in international corporate management. His most recent non-fiction book is a *how-to* business book, **Who Put Me in CHARGE?** Garry has also completed a companion Implementation Guide for this book, **Getting to the NEXT LEVEL.**

As a former consultant and business coach, Garry now spends his time writing science fiction thrillers, adult romance novels, and conducting both motivational and subject-matter speaking engagements.

Garry has written over 300 trade journal articles, white papers, client presentations, and website content. He has given commencement addresses and public service keynote speeches.

He has a passion for hard science fiction, and weaves personal stories, humor, and visionary spiritual thinking into his writings. His current writing project is a five-book science fiction thriller series, **STARGATE EARTH,** with the first three novels now published.

WARRIORS OF THE GALAXY is book three in this series, following book one, **SHATTERED TRUTH** and book two, **ALIEN DISRUPTION.**

STARGATE EARTH is a visionary series that gives the reader an alarming apocalyptic future; and then, despite evil aliens, Garry creates a unified and holistic transformation of aliens and humans into an alliance to save humanity.

Garry follows a writing principle to guide his creativity via a quote from Tom Clancy, *"The difference between reality and fiction is … fiction needs to make sense."*

Garry's most recent writing project is **SHARKS IN THE CITY,** an erotic romance thriller involving five amazing, professional and highly successful San Francisco women, and how they deal with the *SHARKS,* or men behaving badly.

Garry lives in Florida with his lovely wife, Vaune. He plays in a competitive softball league and is an avid scuba diver, water skier, and kayaker. Their daughter, Sarah, lives in Los Angeles.

Visit his website at www.garryjpeterson.com.

You can also follow Garry J. Peterson on *Facebook, Twitter, LinkedIn* and *@Instagram.com/jonathangarrett24.*